Nancy Bilyeau is a magazine editor who has lived in the United States and Canada. She studied History and English Literature at the University of Michigan. After moving to New York City, she worked on the staffs of *InStyle*, *Good Housekeeping*, and *Rolling Stone*. She is currently the deputy editor of the Center on Media, Crime and Justice at the Research Foundation of John Jay College/CUNY and a regular contributing writer to *Town & Country* and *Mystery Scene Magazine*.

Nancy's mind is always in past centuries, but she currently lives with her husband and two children in Forest Hills in the borough of Queens. *Dreamland* is her first novel set in her adopted hometown of New York City. To her joy, researching *Dreamland* was "a subway trip away."

PRAISE FOR NANCY BILYEAU'S THE BLUE:

'Nancy Bilyeau's passion for history infuses her books.' – *Alison Weir*

'Fascinating' – *Ian Rankin*

'Definitely a winner!' – *Kate Quinn*

PRAISE FOR DREAMLAND:

'Achingly believable' – *Publishers Weekly*

'Fast paced, engrossing' – *Library Journal*

Also By Nancy Bilyeau

The Blue
The Crown
The Chalice
The Tapestry

DREAMLAND

NANCY BILYEAU

ENDEAVOUR QUILL

ENDEAVOUR QUILL

First published by Endeavour Quill in 2020

www.endeavourmedia.co.uk

Endeavour Quill is an imprint of Endeavour Media Ltd
Endeavour Media, 85-87 Borough High Street,
London, SE1 1NH

ISBN 978-1-911445-77-7

Typeset using Atomik ePublisher from Easypress Technologies

Printed and bound in Great Britain by
Clays Ltd, Elcograf S.p.A.

MIX
Paper from
responsible sources
FSC® C018072

For Gotham, my home

PROLOGUE

The phantom city vanished an hour after midnight.

The one million lights of Dreamland darkened as they always did, with a clang as loud as a cannon shot, followed by a long, wheezing gush. The rides, the attractions, the sideshows, the restaurants, the dance hall, the entire fifteen-acre fairground stretching from the Canals of Venice to Lilliput – all of it had been shut down for the night. Once they'd thrown the switch on the light panels, it didn't take long for the heat created by the electric bulbs to dissipate, replaced by the cool, salt-flavored ocean breeze. But the smell of the fairground hung on. Nothing could drive away the scent of stale popcorn, roasted peanuts, taffy and cotton candy, fried crab, boiled corn and beer, mingling with the odor of greasy machinery and rank human sweat. That was the fragrance of Coney Island, and no one ever forgot it.

The customers trudged home, and the exhausted park workers stumbled to the narrow beds in their apartment houses in Brooklyn. It was dark and still on the fairgrounds. This was the time when the night policeman made his rounds. The beach was on his left and Dreamland on his right; the seagulls, his only companions, hopped in the sand.

But then, in the moonlight, past the bathing pavilions, he saw the two human figures halfway down the beach, walking slowly toward the water's edge. It was a silhouette of a man, his arm around the waist of a woman wearing a long, dark dress that, in the moonlight, stood out against the white sand. The policeman smiled to himself as the couple sank into the sand. Hadn't he courted his wife the same way? That was twenty years ago, and he still looked forward to coming home, taking off his uniform, and sliding into bed next to her as she slept, the springs creaking as he kissed her soft shoulder.

The policeman kept walking, headed toward Luna Park, where Shoot-the-Chutes and Helter Skelter were rendered motionless until morning. He didn't hear the woman in the sand: a sharp, startled cry. A few minutes later, there was a different noise; a splash in the water.

No one saw the man walk up the beach and onto the promenade, alone.

CHAPTER ONE

I've heard it over and over, my entire life, and it goes about like this: "You've never had a job, Peggy, so you wouldn't understand." Now while it may be true that I can't fully comprehend the details of a person's circumstances – though I think I sympathize more than I'm given credit for – it simply isn't true that I've never held a job. I have. When I was twenty years old, I went to work every day at Moonrise Bookstore, a cramped two-floor shop on East Thirty-Ninth Street, and I was happy. It didn't last, of course.

My job as assistant clerk at Moonrise Bookstore came to an end after five months. It was not because of any dissatisfaction on my part. I didn't want to leave, and my employer didn't want me to go. Yet the job ended just the same. We were both helpless before, as they say, larger forces.

My last day, 22 June, 1911, passed uneventfully up to four o'clock of this particular afternoon. I worked away at my assigned place: half of a table in the corner of the balcony, going over the orders and the inventory and the publisher catalogs. The main floor was for the customers, as well as the novelists, poets, artists, editors and illustrators who made their way to the shop. Moonrise Bookstore might have been a complete secret to the overwhelming number of people who lived in New York City, but it was a beacon for the select few set afire by new and contrary ideas, many of them bohemian. Of course I longed to be on the main floor, but Mrs. Hamilton-Starke, quite sensibly, kept me upstairs – unless there was a gap among the staff and there was no choice but to make use of me. Which is what happened at four o'clock.

"Peggy, could you handle the front?" called out Sylvie, the assistant most trusted by Mrs. Hamilton-Starke, and the one who ran things when the owner left early for the Friday afternoon train up the Hudson.

It seems unbelievable now, but to descend those narrow stairs and take my place on the main floor of Moonrise Bookstore was as thrilling for me as a sashay across the stage would be for a newly-cast Ziegfeld showgirl. Each click of my heel on those steps sent my heart racing, though it was excitement laced with a bit of dread. I simply wasn't much good at practical tasks. My only formal education had been three years at the Jacobi School, where I dove deep into the rich, lovely, hypnotic world of books and plays – Ibsen, Hardy, Turgenev, Wilde, Tolstoy – but I never learned how to take money or a bank draft from someone's hand, calculate change, wrap a parcel, address a mailing. This is largely why I was confined to the balcony.

There weren't many customers, thank God. The bright warmth of early summer had turned people too sluggardly for reading, perhaps. One stern-faced matron of jutting bosom thumped down a pile of books she wished to purchase and have mailed to her townhouse. I struggled in particular with Henry James' *The Golden Bowl* – the sort of book my mother would display but never, ever read. I looked down at that deep turquoise leather cover with gold letters, enclosing a thick tome, as if it were my enemy. But before her skeptical eyes, it was competently paid for, wrapped, and readied. I was mastering the tasks.

The minute the matron had sailed away, Sylvie materialized before me at the counter. She looked quite altered. What always impressed me most about Sylvie was her neat composure; she didn't rattle. What impressed me second-most was her kindness. When I stumbled before her on my first morning at the bookshop, sleepless with nerves, I wore a long dress interlaced with ribbons – oh, how I shudder to think of it – and slung over it my mink furs. She didn't smirk, or, from what I could tell, share a laugh with others later. In no time, I was dressing like her, in simple buttoned blouses and slim skirts stretching to three inches above the floor, and I even tried to wear my hair as she did, parted and plaited neatly on either side of the head, which was not easy given my own thick, long hair that I didn't have enough nerve to cut.

But this afternoon, Sylvie's eyes were wide, and her cheeks were tinged the palest pink. "G.T. Samuels is here, with his editor from Scribner's," she said. My face must have drawn a blank; the name was only vaguely familiar. "You must know about Samuels, Peggy. He's English, and he wrote a novel about – about physical love." At that last phrase, Sylvie's voice dropped to a whisper, she who lived in Greenwich Village on MacDougal Street with another unmarried woman and entertained male callers her parents never met. "He's caused a scandal."

Editor and author wished to discuss the plans for Samuels' two readings next week at the shop, Sylvie explained in a rushed whisper, and I was to take notes in Mrs. Hamilton-Starke's office while the other assistant, Melanie, covered the store.

Consumed with curiosity, I followed her to the office. The door hung open. A funnel of white smoke emanated from within, announcing their male presence.

"This is Peggy, our new girl," announced Sylvie, guiding me through the door. She didn't introduce the men to me; I didn't warrant it.

Two sets of eyes traveled up, since I stood a full head taller than Sylvie. One man bolted to his feet, clutching a pipe. He was somewhere between thirty and forty, wearing a pinstriped suit, with a wispy mustache and a shiny forehead. He was patently the Scribner's editor, and he proceeded to make noises about how the recruits to the calling of literature get younger every year.

I barely noticed him, for my attention was on the other man, who had not gotten to his feet – an unpardonable social sin in New York, and I would have thought in England, too. He looked to be in his late twenties and was the last person I'd expect to author a novel about anything as strenuous as physical love.

I found the male writers and artists who showed up at the bookshop of interest: Perpetually disheveled and preoccupied, they were mysterious creatures compared to the tediously obvious young men of my circle. But G.T. Samuels was in a class by himself. He slumped in a chair; coarse red hair sprouted from his scalp, and he'd started a beard that didn't manage to cover his pointed chin. Most striking were his pallor and blue eyes. I'd never in my life set foot in a Catholic church, but he struck me as a delicate priest, someone who rarely stepped off hallowed ground.

G.T. Samuels didn't say a word to me but nodded in my direction, very slowly, as if that alone were a gesture requiring tremendous effort.

Although I was required to take notes, I'd walked in empty-handed, so Sylvie hunted around the cluttered office for paper and pencil, as the Scribner's editor carried on with chatter.

"What is your family name – Peggy what?" he asked, smiling in encouragement.

I swallowed and said, "Batternberg."

"Ah! Well." With a little laugh, he puffed at his pipe and then said, "It must be quite trying for you, to have people continually ask you if you're related to the richest man in America and to have to explain otherwise."

"Yes," I said. "Very trying."

Sylvie thrust paper and pencil at me, her eyes widening, but she didn't say anything, and in a moment, all mention of my name was forgotten, and I was writing as fast as possible to record the conversation verbatim. What a losing battle. My handwriting was built for beauty, not speed. The Scribner's editor blathered on about the importance of G.T. Samuels to the world of letters; Sylvie kept trying to return him to the practicalities of the shop. Their words came and went as I valiantly scribbled a captured phrase here and there. I could feel the perspiration gathering at my hairline in the small, smoky room.

The conversation paused; my panicked grip on the pencil loosened. I glanced at the person sitting closest to me, G.T. Samuels, who'd been silent throughout their outlining of plans for his readings.

Samuels wasn't listening to his editor drone on; he was looking at me. He gazed at my face and then down at the chaotic scrawls racing across the paper, and a tiny smile tightened the corner of his lips. His light blue eyes, which had seemed blank, almost glassy, to me before, bore an entirely new expression. Amusement.

I looked away, quickly. As my fingers tightened on the pencil again, preparing to resume, a rich warmth crept up through me. I could feel it reaching my face, and, helpless to prevent it, reddening my cheeks.

The discussion about the upcoming readings stalled after another minute. Scribner's, as I'd come to call him in my brain, declared it the perfect moment for a drink. Sylvie objected, but laughingly, and the next thing I knew the editor was jabbing a finger at the cabinet behind me.

"I'm positive Mrs. Hamilton-Starke wouldn't mind," he declared with the ferocity of someone who really had to have that drink, and he flung open the cabinet doors.

Inside was a jumble of liquor bottles, some recently obtained and some dusty, with torn labels. I was positive that Mrs. Hamilton-Starke *would* mind our exposing her clutter of booze.

"This is bleak," Sylvie murmured. "I see vermouth, bourbon, maybe some gin."

"If you have gin and vermouth, you have a martini," I said. "I see a cocktail mixer. But you need ice."

"I can fetch the ice," Sylvie said. "But who could possibly bartend?"

Without thinking, I said, "Well, I can make a martini."

It was as if a giraffe announced it could fly. They wanted to see this feat. However, this meant Sylvie slipping out in search of ice, and I was left alone with the two men. I prayed they would talk to each other, that I wouldn't be expected to entertain them with the sparkle of my conversation, but God was in the mood to toy with my mortal self that afternoon, for Scribner's next question was, "Miss Batternberg, you're a bright young creature at the most progressive bookstore in New York City – tell us, what is your favorite book of the year?"

I froze. I hadn't read G.T. Samuels' new novel, so even though the polite response would be to cite his, I couldn't risk being asked a second question on what I liked best about it, when absolutely all I knew was that it included "physical love." My mind went blank as I desperately searched for some other book to mention.

I produced a long, clumsy stammering that it was impossible, with so much talent pouring into the store, to single out one writer.

Scribner's nodded, barely listening. I couldn't look at G.T. Samuels, certain of disappointment.

Where was Sylvie? Her quest for ice seemed to be taking an endless amount of time, though probably less than five minutes transpired. I blurted, "I saw an exhibition of paintings last month I quite liked. At the Alfred Stieglitz Gallery."

Scribner's brightened and said, "Ah, yes. Stieglitz is certainly making a name for himself on Fifty-Seventh Street."

For the first time, G.T. Samuels spoke. In his rolling British accent, he said, "Was there a particular painting that interested you?"

"Yes," I said slowly, "it was a new work of a man standing on a busy street in New York."

Of course, when I described it like that, the painting sounded ordinary. But in Manhattan, the serious deep-pocketed collectors were only interested in dead artists. I heard the director of the Metropolitan Museum of Art was nearly fired for purchasing the work of a living painter, Pierre-Auguste Renoir. Even for those who were enlightened enough to admire the Post-Impressionists, it was the portraits, country scenes in Europe, and still-life paintings that ruled. To support the work of someone trying to capture a moment on the streets of New York, it was heresy. Yet for me, that was the only painting that seemed truly alive.

G.T. Samuels pressed it, asking me, "How did you feel when you looked at a painting like that?"

"I suppose," I said, clutching my hands behind my back, "I felt glad to see someone breaking rules."

He nodded, anything but bored now. An infusion of strength had appeared in him, and just what he might do with that strength made my pulse quicken.

Sylvie returned with the ice, closing the door firmly behind her, and I focused on my task, measuring the gin and vermouth, straining the mix. It was a pity we had no orange peels or other bitters, but it couldn't be helped.

Scribner's was the first to try a drink, no surprise there, and declared it "magnificent." The next person to be presented with a drink was G.T. Samuels, looking less and less like a wan priest with every second that ticked by as he sipped his martini, his eyes fixed on me.

I heard a stir outside the office in the main part of the bookstore, which at first I paid little attention to, since Moonrise could be a noisy place. It wasn't until the door swung open and two men stepped inside that I realized what was happening – and that it was happening quite particularly to me.

David Batternberg, my uncle, draped in a long black coat, vest, and trousers, all stitched on Savile Row, set off with a silk burgundy ascot, a bowler hat perched on his graying black hair, inflicted such an imposing presence on the little room that the Scribner's editor stumbled back two steps, spilling his martini on Mrs. Hamilton-Starke's second-rate carpet.

"What are you doing here?" I cried, in equal parts confusion and humiliation.

My uncle didn't turn to face me. Without addressing anyone, he said, "My name is David Batternberg, and it's time for my niece to be leaving."

"No," I said. "It's not."

Sylvie glanced at me, cleared her throat and said, "You are welcome here at Moonrise Bookstore, Mr. Batternberg. But it isn't the close of the business day."

"It isn't?" he retorted, eying the bottles of liquor assembled on Mrs. Hamilton-Starke's desk. He tilted his head in the direction of the second man, bearded and dressed in black too, who then stepped forward, to take his place next to my uncle.

"This is Dr. Mackenzie," said Uncle David. As if on cue, the doctor wordlessly transferred from one hand to another a bulging black bag with a wooden handle. We were left to imagine the potions, syringes and bandages crammed inside.

"What the devil?" whispered Scribner's, glancing at me with new interest.

G.T. Samuels asked, "Are we bearing witness to a kidnapping, then?"

"Yes, you are," I said, my voice shrill. "And I do protest."

My father's favorite brother snorted. I felt his hand clamp my arm, and in an amazingly brief passage of time, I was borne out of Mrs. Hamilton-Starke's office, through the store and out the door leading to East Thirty-Ninth Street. I hadn't been able to catch one last glimpse of G.T. Samuels, of Scribner's, or even of Sylvie. Were they shocked, or merely bemused? One thing was clear: They didn't follow.

On the street idled Uncle David's pride and joy, his enormous new cream-colored automobile, a Franklin Model D Phaeton with a smooth front hood that was larger than the table I toiled at upstairs. His liveried driver, standing at attention, rushed to open the back door for us, but he had to push back someone to do it – a young man standing on the sidewalk, clutching a briefcase as he gaped at the automobile as if it were Zeus's chariot. A crowd was forming, men on their way to Pennsylvania Railroad Station, willing to risk missing their trains as they stood mesmerized at the sight of this vehicle.

The driver managed to open the door. First Dr. Mackenzie leaped onto the deep-red hard leather seat, then my Uncle David, far more awkwardly, eased his way in; I got in last.

As the car rumbled forward on the street, I said, tears of helpless rage gathering, "Why on earth did you do that to me, Uncle?"

"The family needs you, Peggy," he said, handing me a handkerchief. "I'll explain as we head uptown. But I would ask that you refrain from hysterics. Remember who you are, please."

With that, I dabbed my eyes with his thick, snow-white handkerchief, and shifted on the seat of the Franklin Model D Phaeton, uncomfortable as all hell, and girded myself to listen to his explanation.

The car turned right onto Fifth Avenue. Whatever was coming, I'd have to cope with it. I was capable of coping with it. I was, after all, the granddaughter of the richest man in America.

CHAPTER TWO

Except Abraham Batternberg wasn't the richest man. He was one of a handful at the top of the heap. It's important to be truthful about such things. Grandfather, a humbly-born Swiss Jew, came to America as a peddler, changing his name from Bernstein to Batternberg when he reached these shores. Through working brutally hard with scarcely time for sleep, he earned enough money to make investments.

He chose to buy ownership of two mines in Colorado. It was purely speculation. He was no expert on what lay beneath the earth's surface. But those two mines turned out to be the gateway to a fortune, millions and millions and millions of dollars. He became a king ruling over the treasures of the underground.

In the last century, others with names like Rockefeller, Fricke, Carnegie, or Vanderbilt had exchanged plain beginnings for vast wealth too, thanks to an eye for a deal and a talent for ruthlessness. What made Abraham Batternberg special was the number of ambitious sons he had to carry on after him: six of them. My Uncle David was the fifth son, and my father, Jonathan, the youngest. A knot in my stomach told me, sooner or later, this conversation would lead to the doings of my late father.

Uncle David had said my family needed me, and I, unquestionably a bit late, asked, "Is there a crisis – is someone ill?"

"No, no. This evening the family is having dinner at home."

"And for this I am abducted?" I demanded.

"A telephone call was put through to your house earlier this week, and a note sent by messenger, neither of which you responded to." He shifted in his seat. "It's quite an important dinner."

As the automobile waited for the Forty-Second Street streetcar to pass, I thought about it. Yes, there had been messages and notes left for me on the foyer table at Mrs. Thompson's house. I hadn't looked at them. One of the reasons I took up residence with my former teacher off Washington Square and pursued the position at the bookstore was to gain distance from my family.

Still, I apologized to my uncle for my negligence. Perhaps, I offered, this Batternberg intrusion might not leave too much of a stain on my record as assistant. I would apologize to everyone, come Monday morning.

In response, my uncle did the oddest thing: he wordlessly reached up with both hands and removed his bowler hat, placing it on his lap. His hair bore a circular imprint from the hat. A few gleaming patches shone through, where his hair had thinned the most. But strangest of all, he wrapped his forearms around the hat, not as if he were protecting it but more that he wanted the hat to protect him.

"You will not be returning to the Moonrise store," my uncle said. "You shall spend the summer with the family."

"Nonsense," I said.

Once again he jerked his chin at the silent Dr. Mackenzie. Our car idling in the shadow of St. Patrick's Cathedral, the doctor fiddled with the clasp to his black medical bag. I sputtered, "Are you planning to have this man dose me with laudanum? Some other potion?"

My uncle sighed, "He is my internist, Peggy. Because of my heart. My wife has concerns."

Dr. Mackenzie proceeded to loosen my uncle's vest, and, without moving the hat, apply a stethoscope to his chest. I didn't wait for this procedure to be completed before launching into my argument.

"It was Cousin Marshall who arranged for the position at the bookstore, he vouched for everything, and he is One of Us," I said. Marshall, my cousin once removed, who dabbled in poetry and traveled frequently – he was in Paris now – invested a little of his money in Moonrise Bookstore. He had been crucial in quieting all the family objections to my idea. It was the time of the New Woman, wasn't it? Marshall demanded of them. And New Women pursued jobs before marriage.

"Marshall may smooth the path to your return this autumn," said Uncle David. "But you're needed by your family for the next two months."

"You keep saying I am needed. They don't need me. I need to have a purpose. You can't take that away from me."

"Yes, I saw evidence of a certain purpose not too long ago," he said dryly. "You and that girl – a suffragette, I'll wager – drinking alcohol with two men. I only thank God your mother wasn't there to witness it."

"I wasn't drinking the martinis, Uncle. I simply made them."

I fear it was this, more than any other fact or argument, that sealed my fate. "A Batternberg, playing barmaid for bohemian rabble," he moaned, as Dr. Mackenzie sought to calm him. "And though I'm afraid to learn the answer, where did you learn how to make a martini?"

"As a matter of fact, in your house," I retorted, "From Ben."

He winced. "Ben has his… quirks."

This was no time to enlighten Uncle David about the nature of his oldest son's "quirks." Instead, I resumed making a case for my independence.

Holding up his hand with a certain weariness, Uncle David said, "There's a great deal you don't know, Peggy. It has to do with your father."

I'm not right about many things. But I'm usually right about my father.

As the car rumbled north, Uncle David told me, for the first time, the truth about my father's estate at the time of his sudden and notorious death. I was painfully aware that my father, Jonathan Batternberg, was the one brother who failed to seize hold of their father's fortune and increase it. Every investment was misguided, every bold venture a mistake.

But that afternoon I learned that my father had actually accomplished what might seem impossible for a Batternberg. He didn't just fail to increase his inheritance – he lost it, and more. My father died in debt.

I stared out the window as I listened to the crisp sentences. There's no small irony in my learning of the depth of my father's failure as Uncle David's automobile rumbled past what the newspaper writers called, faintly reprovingly, "Millionaire's Row." I'd never cared for the brownstone and marble extravagances crowding both sides of the street, and today they were particularly appalling. Cornelius Vanderbilt II's monstrosity at Fifty-Seventh Street taking up the whole block loomed like a French chateau gingerbread house constructed for Swiftian giants.

Perhaps if he'd lived, my father might have been able to recoup his losses, Uncle David said. But Father died at the age of thirty-eight. After they pored through his accounts, my uncles learned the worst but decided to conceal it from my mother. They quietly paid for her expenses, as well as her children's, for the last five years. However, several weeks ago, he said, my mother, Sarah Batternberg, stumbled upon the truth.. There were scenes. She made known her wishes: No more assistance from her brothers-in-law. She'd sell the family house, and with that windfall, move into a small apartment, dismiss most of the servants, and live within her means.

This didn't sound like my mother one little bit.

However, it wouldn't do any good to voice my skepticism. Everyone always rushed to my long-suffering mother's defense, particularly those who found her the most frustrating. Amid the depressing news about the family's finances, I felt surprised and faintly flattered that the family believed I could play a role in the complicated business of moving the household.

I said, "I'm needed to prepare the house to be sold?"

My uncle ran his thick fingers along the brim of his bowler. "Lord no, we have plenty of people to see to all of that. Your mother and sister and brother will be spending the summer out of town, and you need to be with them during this difficult time."

"Oh, no," I said, gripping the handle on the door as if to leap out. "I'm not going to New Jersey."

"Everyone knows you loathe the compound down the shore," he said. "That's not the plan."

"Newport? Oyster Bay?"

"Arrangements have been made for your family to take up several suites at the Oriental Hotel in Brooklyn, with rooms overlooking the Atlantic."

I was speechless for at least a minute.

"Brooklyn?" I finally stammered. "We're going to Brooklyn?"

"Peggy, the Oriental is one of the finest establishments on the entire East Coast."

"Ten years ago, perhaps."

My uncle insisted that the Oriental Hotel held its reputation, as did the neighboring Manhattan Beach Hotel and Brighton Beach Hotel. This was so strange. No one of our extended family had ever, to my knowledge, taken up rooms in the grand oceanfront hotels of Brooklyn. And now? When the raucous Coney Island Amusement Park, also on the Brooklyn shore, had become world famous as America's Playground, this was when we would spend two whole months there.

"Uncle David," I said, "There is something you're not explaining."

The automobile slowed. On our left rose the graceful trees of Central

Park; on our right, on the corner of Seventy-Second Street, stood the house I'd grown up in. My uncle laid his hand on my arm.

"Please go with your mother and sister and brother to the Oriental Hotel, Peggy," he said. "Your stay will extend for less than two months. I'll be there for the first few weeks to help. Helen and I have made the booking."

"And if I don't go?"

Without removing his hand, he said softly, "We could cut you off, you know. No more money. I doubt that your shop girl wages would cover a flat in Greenwich Village."

By that time, Uncle David's driver had turned off the motor. I leaned toward him and said, just as softly, "Do so. In four months' time I turn twenty-one, and I come into my trust from Grandfather. There's nothing you can do to stop it. After that, I won't need a penny from anyone."

Uncle David half turned to the doctor. "My good man, could you give us a moment alone?"

In the time it took Dr. Mackenzie to shuffle out of the automobile, I realized that I'd broken the cardinal rule of not discussing the details of a Batternberg inheritance in front of someone outside the family.

In a flash I remembered something else, a long-ago remark of my father's, that everyone adored David, but he was the brother most to be feared when he was made angry.

"That's quite true about the trust," my uncle said. "Though you won't be able to touch the capital. Just the interest payments."

"More than adequate to my needs, Uncle."

"So, Peggy, let us be clear," he said, in a voice devoid of all feeling. "You are refusing to go with your family?"

I tapped on the door to let the driver know I wanted out. "No," I said over my shoulder. "I will consider it. But not without understanding the real reason for my family going to the Oriental Hotel."

CHAPTER THREE

As I approached the front entrance of the dark-brick house, my limbs felt heavy. It had been three weeks and six days since I last crossed this threshold.

The sound of water greeted me as always, the spotless fountain in the center of the marble floor, burbling away. My mother would obtain a fortune in this house sale. My working at the bookshop, and making the acquaintance of different sorts of people, had made me keenly aware that to harbor complaints about an upbringing amid comfort was in bad taste. But luxuries had never done much for a lonely, confused young soul.

The women were gathered in the parlor – my mother, my sister Lydia, and my Aunt Helen – and I sensed that they'd been talking about me up to the moment of my arrival.

"Oh dear, what are you wearing, Margaret?" was my mother's greeting after pressing a kiss on my forehead with her cool, dry lips.

"I didn't have time to change for dinner, Mother," I said.

"Of course." She forced a smile.

Mother was dressed beautifully, as always, corseted to the expected silhouette for a lady of her social standing. Her light brown hair was pinned and perfumed, a pearl necklace gleaming at her throat. I was a true Batternberg: tall, black hair, high forehead, blue eyes under darkest brows. I didn't look like her at all. My mother came from a family that arrived from Germany two generations earlier than my father's, and they found ways to work that into many a conversation. The Donifer men were bankers, the women were temperamental beauties. My mother, in her youth, was much celebrated, her debut noted in the better newspapers. Now her face was crisscrossed with lines, like a piece of crumpled tissue paper, though she was barely into her forties. Someone unfamiliar with the situation might say, kindly, that becoming a widow before her time had aged her prematurely. I, who was rarely kind where my mother was concerned, would attribute it to more than that.

"Hullo, Peggy," said my sister. Even at her absolute peak, I don't believe Mother was as lovely as my younger sister, Lydia, just seventeen years old. Though she seemed happier than my mother to see me, she kissed me tentatively, perhaps so as not to disturb her elaborate hair arrangement. Her thick golden hair was curled and beribboned, the masses gathered just so to emphasize her long creamy throat. My sister: the perfect Gibson Girl. Her high-neckline, pale-pink embroidered dress was constructed in filmy layers, but one could still make out her tiny waist and slender arms. Too slender. In that brief embrace, I could feel her delicacy, that even through her gloves, her wrists were bony. Was it possible that since I'd seen her last, she'd lost weight?

"Are you all right?" I asked.

"Of course," she said. "Never better."

My uncle said he had enough time for a sherry before dinner. Dr. Mackenzie sent back the first glass, insisting it was too generous a serving, an act highly approved of by Aunt Helen, my uncle's solicitous second wife.

The parlor conversation centered on me, and it was benign. Too benign. My Aunt Helen wanted to know if I had had an opportunity to read EM Forster's new novel, *Howard's End*. Lydia brought up the news story of the day, the trial of the owners of the terrible Triangle shirtwaist factory. My curiosity about what my family was up to deepened.

Our jowly butler, Arthur, announced dinner, and we made our way to the dining room.

This was the space where my mother's worship of English country house décor found its most fervent expression. The curtains were perpetually drawn to keep out the light – heaven forbid the bright vigor of Seventy-Second Street intruded. And though the house was laid with wires for electricity when I was a child, my mother permitted only lamps and wax candles here. Paintings of the staid English countryside hung on wood-paneled walls; her favorites were thoroughbred horses, trainers holding them by the reins. I particularly hated those horse paintings, their precise lines and cautious, pallid colors such a contrast to the bold new art that intrigued me.

A pink-and-gold set of Sevres porcelain was arranged on the shelves of a walnut cabinet. Surveying it all, one would assume that the room was decorated the same as certain rooms of the upper class of England. My mother worshipped the royal houses of Europe, and most of all, the British monarchy. Her particular heroine was Queen Alexandra, and she was keen to read any books or articles written about the Queen – now the Queen dowager. Whether my mother responded emotionally to Queen Alexandra's life, a faded beauty married to a womanizer, even I dared not ask.

A stomping on the stairs signaled the arrival of my fifteen-year-old brother. Surly and spotty, Lawrence careened into the room, grunted his greetings, indifferent to my presence, and took a seat at the table. "The Schlump" was Cousin Ben's name for Lawrence, with his unerring cruelty.

As we sipped the first course – turtle soup served in Wedgewood bowls – my Aunt Helen took up a matter with Dr. Mackenzie. One of her sisters-in-law wanted to secure a Scottish internist for her husband. Had he progressed in forming a list of recommendations of those others like himself?

This was how the family did things. What one branch took up, the others followed, until all were in alignment. Elderly English tailors. Young French embroiderers. Emotive Italian music teachers. Hearty Irish stable-masters. Strict German nannies – that fad was the worst of all, for I hated each one of the German women my mother hired to raise us. Now it would be Scottish personal physicians that my uncles and aunts would fuss over finding, as word spread of Dr. Mackenzie, discovered by Aunt Helen.

It was stifling hot in the room. My mother, taking out her fan, said apologetically to her brother- and sister-in-law, "I should have told Cook to prepare vichyssoise."

Uncle David said he had read in the Farmers' Almanac that this would be an unusually hot summer in New York.

My Aunt Helen said, "Won't it be so nice and cool, enjoying the ocean breezes at the Oriental Hotel?"

With that, my brother slammed his fist on the table so hard the crystal shuddered. "No. I don't want to go there. I don't!"

Lydia said, "Please, Lawrence. It's for the best."

"The best for you," he said, pushing his chair away from the table. "For Mr. Henry Taul." My brother stomped out of the room, his face twisted in disgust, as I watched every single other person at the table – with the exception of Dr. Mackenzie – peer at me with apprehension.

As well they should.

Now I could begin to make sense of this strange plan to spend the summer at a Brooklyn ocean-side hotel. It wasn't anything that my own family would ordinarily want to do, I was right about that. But it was something that Colorado-born Henry Taul might fancy, and pleasing him was of utmost importance to not only my sister Lydia, who this year became his fiancée, but my mother and my uncle and all of the Batternbergs.

Henry Taul was heir to his own mining fortune. He was also a man of sudden, unmovable enthusiasms. I knew this quite well, because just over two years before proposing to my sister, he had chosen me as the object of one of his enthusiasms. It was a brief romance, and it ended badly. Henry and myself, Lydia, my mother, and absolutely everyone else united in acting as if it never happened.

I opened my mouth, preparing my accusation, when something caught my eye. It was Lydia. I saw her fingers quiver on the spoon handle resting beside the bowl. Her eyes, brimmed with golden eyelashes, sent me a message of pleading.

I closed my mouth. I'd not say anything, or do anything, until we'd spoken, just the two of us.

If only I could have taken Lydia by the hand to the next room and had our talk at that moment. But instead I had to endure the next three courses, complete with chocolate-raspberry cake, all of it too heavy for summer. I took note that Lydia had barely touched her meal.

After another tedious hour of conversation over cards with my aunt and uncle before, mercifully, they departed, Lydia and I headed up the stairs to her room. She shook her head at me while our personal maid, Alice, launched into the lengthy procedure of taking down my sister's hair. It seemed this was too sensitive even for Alice, an efficient and understanding woman nearing thirty who we both liked very much.

Finally, finally, Lydia and I were alone.

"So this is Henry Taul's project for the summer?" I asked. "You go at his insistence?"

She nodded and gnawed on her thumbnail, something that would horrify my mother if she were to see it. "He loves the Oriental Hotel, he made all the arrangements for our suites," she said. "Henry said the sea air will benefit his mother's health."

"But why do I have to be a part of this?" I demanded. "Henry doesn't care about me. I would think that my presence would be a deterrent, if anything."

"It's his mother, Peggy. She knows about you, and I don't think she approves of a young woman having any kind of job – I suppose that they are not as progressive in Colorado or Connecticut, where she has a new house – and, I'm so, so sorry, but Henry told me that his mother insists that you join us this summer. She wants to become better acquainted with us all."

"So Henry and his mother will be at the same hotel as us for the entire time?"

"She's in Brooklyn now. She's taking the sea water cure for her legs. Something to do with circulation. I've met her twice; I believe she weighs close to three hundred pounds."

I buried my face in my hands. "Lord, I can't do this, Lydia. A summer in Brooklyn with Mother – and Henry Taul and his mother? It would be so like hell."

I didn't look at her. I waited for the sound of weeping. And waited. It didn't come.

I opened my eyes to peer at my sister. She wasn't weeping or trembling, but staring into the mirror, at her own reflection. Her chin was thrust forward, in that angry bulldog stance she used to take as a child.

While I watched her watch herself, I thought about the strange reversal that took place between us. I was once the romance-minded young female, lost in a haze of Charlotte Bronte, and she was a vigorous hoyden, pestering our parents for tennis lessons and archery lessons. Everything changed when Father died. I became a different person, as did Lydia. She became, while not exactly demure, a fashionable creature, tremendously popular among friends in a way that I'd never come close to – not that I cared about that. The only time she defied convention was to refuse a coming out party, every debutante's dream.

We had quarreled over her engagement to Henry Taul. Not out of jealousy on my part, but my lingering dislike of the man. Every time I tried to sway her from her attachment, it went poorly. In our last argument, she'd snapped at me to never criticize her choice of husband again if I wished to come to the wedding, and I'd retorted that missing the wedding would be a treat, not a punishment.

But nothing could ever destroy the bond between us. It wasn't built on shared interests or cherished memories. It was a sort of camaraderie; we were like fellow soldiers in the same battalion who'd miraculously managed to survive. I understood her in a way no one else could.

"It's not just my future at stake," she said. "It's the rest of us, too. You know Father died in debt? Uncle David said he'd break the news to you."

This was Mother's true plan – marrying a daughter to Henry Taul, who upon his father's death would come into a fortune that rivaled the Batternbergs'.

"Uncle David told me," I said. "I'm in possession of the facts."

I felt a spasm of guilt. In the last two years, I'd cared only about myself, endeavoring to separate from my family, holding myself aloof and spending time with school friends or family in Paris or any other pursuit away from Seventy-Second Street. I had abandoned her to the demands of our mother, and I now saw she meant everything to Sarah Batternberg – my sister was both tool and savior.

"Come with us, Peggy," Lydia pleaded. "It's just for the summer. Wouldn't you be taking a holiday anyway from that book shop?"

My younger sister had no idea of what it meant to hold a job, that one didn't take a school-length summer holiday. But that was not what bothered me most about all of this.

I said, "You can't mean his marrying you depends on my accompanying you to the Oriental Hotel? That I matter so much in this... equation."

She tore at her thumbnail again. "Everything matters right now. Everything. He hasn't set a date. We've been engaged for months, but we don't have a wedding date."

I didn't know that. I'd assumed the wedding was arranged for some misty future point; long engagements were the custom.

"Well, what does Henry say about it?"

Lydia seized a brush and worked it through her hair, still tightly coiled because of all the pinning.

"Lydia, what does he say when you ask?" I repeated. The tension of our situation was becoming unbearable.

"I don't ask. Ever. How can I?" Lydia tore through her hair with the silver-backed brush. It had to be painful, but she kept at it.

She'd shouted at me and threatened me, but I must try again. I could rescue Lydia; this was the moment. I grabbed her arm to put a stop to the brushing. "And you want to marry Henry and spend your life with him – a man who makes you feel this way?"

"Yes, Peggy. Yes, I want nothing but to marry Henry." Her voice broke into hysteria. "Yes, yes, yes."

She dropped the brush and stood there, staring at me. Her exquisite features, her perfectly shaped eyes and nose and mouth, were stretched to the breaking point by fear, by lack of sleep or food. Just underneath the beauty hovered something else, something pointed and… feral. I felt a chill of real fear.

"I'll go with you to the Oriental Hotel, Lydia," I heard myself say. "I'll do it."

My sister collapsed into my arms. "Thank you, thank you."

It was only then that the sobbing came, like a dam breaking. I held her, patting her narrow back and sharp little shoulder blades, like a bird's wings, until she cried herself out and finally became still.

CHAPTER FOUR

The gratitude my family felt at my acquiescence lasted through the next week of packing and shopping and arranging matters. It seemed the season officially began at these Brooklyn hotels the first week of July. All the frantic preparation for our seven-week stay seemed more fitting for a journey to Malta, not another part of New York City.

It must have required considerable effort, but my mother did not criticize her difficult, perpetually disappointing older daughter beyond insisting that I be fitted for new summer clothes, for sporting as well as formal occasions. Everything needed to be patterned, stitched, and sent to Seventy-Second Street as soon as possible. My figure is a bit tricky for clothes, with my short waist and very long legs. I submitted to all the measuring and pulling without expressing my own preferences over color or fit or pattern, with the exception of two dresses for evening. It didn't much matter to me. I couldn't shake the feeling that these were uniforms for a prisoner, not holiday clothes.

No matter the efforts everyone made, the veneer of goodwill in my family was thin indeed – so thin that twice it cracked before we left town. Monday morning, I woke up and dressed in my work wardrobe. I would need to make my way to the shop, explain the situation to Mrs.

Hamilton-Starke, gather my things from the table, and say goodbye to Sylvie and the others.

To my surprise, my mother and sister stood before the front door, hands clasped before them. They were twenty-five years apart in age, yet it struck me how eerily similar they were at this moment.

"You don't have to go to Moonrise Bookstore," said Lydia. "Everything has been explained."

"Explained?" I repeated. "By whom?"

"Your uncle called the owner, Mrs. Hamilton-Starke," my mother said.

"Uncle David? How dare he?" I stormed toward the door.

"No, it was Uncle Bernard."

That made me stop mid-stride. Bernard was the oldest of the brothers, and his actions could never be questioned. That's how it had worked my entire life. When it came to seniority, we could have been the Plantagenets of the thirteenth century. The oldest brother carried the most weight in the family business and had the most authority over our activities, whether it be tutors or schools chosen, even holiday destinations planned. Bernard's intervention in this matter shocked me, though. I found it difficult to comprehend that my joining my family on a summer stay at the Oriental Hotel could be this important, that it necessitated a phone call from him.

"But there are my things to fetch at the store," I said weakly. "It's not much, but still—"

"A box will be delivered this afternoon with everything packed," my mother said.

Lydia aimed her pleading gaze at me.

Turning to her, I said directly, "I can't just disappear to my coworkers, surely you understand."

"But couldn't you send a nice note?" Lydia asked. "And you will see them all when we get back at the end of summer."

A few gracious sentences, written with a quill on my mother's best cream-colored stationery, sealed and delivered by hand to Moonrise Bookstore? I could only imagine Sylvie's face when presented with something so ridiculous. Again I realized that to my sister, my leaving the store was the equivalent of a school holiday.

My mother said, "I very much feel it's best to leave it with your uncle. We are enjoying having you back in the house, Margaret."

I almost did it: swerve around them to push open the door and make my way to Thirty-Seventh Street. But what would be said when I arrived? Uncle Bernard had made his call. Should there be unpleasantness with the Batternbergs, what would my employer do? Cousin Marshall was an investor in Moonrise. I wasn't hired on my merits, after all.

Defeated, I turned away from the door and retreated to my room. I changed out of my slim skirt and plain blouse. I didn't write Sylvie any kind of note, but I put the clothes in a special bag and secreted it away.

As unsettling as that confrontation was, it paled when compared to a tea party two days before we left Manhattan for the Oriental Hotel. My mother loved her tea parties.

I'd slipped out for a walk in Central Park that afternoon. I needed its solace during those tense days of preparation. Everyone complained about the crowds in Central Park, but I found it soothing to join the park-goers in their anonymity. I liked to walk among the young and old, the couples, the families, the aged, all of us united in enjoyment of the rolling meadows, the ponds and woods. I'd taken to plucking wildflowers from a boulder-spotted corner of the park and bringing them home. I disliked the daily bundles that arrived at Seventy-Second Street from the florist, the roses and lilies arranged with stern symmetry in our thick crystal vases. They were like the trickle of water in the fountain: a labored re-creation of the nature that could easily be found just outside the door in its untamed state.

On my return, I immediately knew Henry Taul was here. A blond man, young, wearing a dark blue, gold-trimmed uniform, sat on a bench by the fountain in our home, studying the marble floor. Henry made all his servants wear uniforms. He glanced up, spotted me, and gave me a long look; he had a nose slightly flattened as if from a long-ago fight. Even Henry's employees were arrogant.

In the downstairs parlor sat my mother, smiling, before her towering silver tea service. Cucumber sandwiches and petit fours were arranged on it, perfectly spaced; the hand-painted china cups brimmed with steaming liquid. Just as exquisite as the high-tea presentation was my sister, perched on a chair to the side of my mother, wearing a blue-and-white dress with a sailor collar, her hair gathered behind by a huge bow. My surly brother Lawrence devoured a cookie, sitting in a chair pushed away from everyone else.

Mother caught sight of me in the doorway and her smile became strained. "Oh, Margaret, how… bedraggled," she said. Whether she was referring to me or to the wildflowers I held in my hand, I couldn't tell.

"Hullo, Peggy, how are you?" said Henry.

Around the time when he proposed to my sister, Henry began wearing spectacles. They made his expression a bit harder to read than before, but the careless, friendly tone he adopted with me was intact.

"I am well, thank you," I said, with a touch more formality, placing the wildflowers carefully on the side table.

Henry stood before my family members, arms outstretched, midstory. He always liked to stand, rather than sit, when acting out a story. It could make for an overwhelming presence, as Henry was more than six feet tall with broad shoulders and legs like tree trunks. He hadn't yet lost that smooth face, though, at thirty years of age. When he smiled, as he often did, his face widened to a baby's roundness.

He was completely comfortable in this room, though its décor was largely feminine. The lingering remnants of my father's time were the round cognac bottles lined up on a silver tray and the brown carpet made out of a real bear, complete with its staring, sharp-toothed head. Most guests steered clear of the bear carpet. Henry stood right on top of it.

My mother said, "Henry was telling us about the highlights of his trip to Europe."

Ah, these travels might explain his failing to set a wedding date with Lydia. I sensed no strain between them, no lack of feeling. My sister looked happier in Henry's presence than at any moment over the last week.

Henry resumed his acting out a story; it seemed that he had spent days at the site in France devoted to Joan of Arc. The Maid of Orleans had made quite an impression, which seemed odd to me, but everyone who encountered Henry Taul found him odd at first. You had to get used to him.

My mind wandered as Henry droned on about Joan of Arc. I summoned up an image of G.T. Samuels and his mysterious smile. My brother Lawrence devoured more cookies as my mother and sister hung on Henry's every word.

I was jolted back into the conversation by Henry who, with a grand flourish, presented Lydia with a small, gift-wrapped box.

"Is it for me?" she breathed.

"Who else?" Henry said, with a chortle.

Who else indeed, I thought, as I watched her delicately pick apart the wrappings, open the box, and, wide-eyed, pull out a gold pendant set with a dazzling crystal.

She thanked him profusely while my mother praised the pendant's design. Henry insisted that he put it on Lydia now, right away, and the sight of this smug, strapping man bent over my diminutive sister, dressed like a child, sent a peculiar shudder through me.

"Do you know what the crystal symbolizes?" Henry said fervently. "It's innocence – and purity."

With the word *purity*, my hand tightened on the handle of the fragile tea cup. I watched Henry closely, but as he fastened the pendant around Lydia's neck and then admired the way it hung, absurdly, atop her wide sailor collar, he never looked my way, never betrayed for a second that this could be a statement about me, an accusation, that he was thinking of that night, three years ago, when I was Lydia's age and he'd pulled away, hissing, "Spoiled, you're spoiled."

Frantically, I pushed that memory away.

In a swerve in topic, Henry announced that he expected the two owners of the Triangle shirtwaist factory to be found guilty in the trial going on. That was the position all of New York City took – the owners of this factory, where 185 young women died in a searing fire, were abhorrent human beings, unlike any other business owners. I wondered about that, if they were really so atypical.

"The women shouldn't have been there," Henry said, shaking his head.

"They couldn't help but be there, since the owners always locked the doors on those two floors of the factory, to keep the union organizers away," I pointed out.

He shook his head more emphatically. "I mean, they should not have been there at all. What kind of family sends their seventeen-year-old daughters to work in a factory fifteen hours a day, six days a week?"

"Families that are starving," I retorted, ignoring my mother's frosty glare.

Henry began, once more, to pace the floor. "Do you know what sort of men show up at Ellis Island now, by the thousands? Beaten men of beaten nations. There are more Italians in New York City than there are in Rome. Imagine that. And the Russians? The Russians! I can't even speak of it. This is madness. They sit in squalor in their tenement houses, sending their women to the garment factories while they cook up their plots of violence against this country, their acts of anarchy."

I'd never heard him speak of social issues before, and while what he said was doubtless what others were thinking up and down Fifth Avenue, I found it contemptible coming from him. Who was Henry Taul, notorious for his Harvard University days of playing poker all night, lighting his cigars with hundred-dollar bills, to sit in judgment of anyone? My heart began to hammer in my chest.

"I suppose you must charge my family with negligence, Henry, for allowing me to work," I said, my voice sounding harsh even to my ears. "But of course, that has been put an end to."

Henry did not rise to provocation but stayed silent as the seconds crawled by. His massive shoulders began to rise as if to execute a shrug but stopped, and eased back down. Behind his spectacles, looking down on me, his gaze was cold but not indifferent. I was beginning to wonder if I detected a certain satisfaction there.

The last person in the world whom I expected to speak on my behalf, my brother Lawrence, said, "I think it's terrific that Peggy took a job. She doesn't want to sit in the house and do nothing."

"Thank you, Lawrence," I said, as my mother and sister turned on him, smarting from implicit criticism.

The next surprise came from Henry himself, who said with a chuckle, "We shouldn't chide the boy for defending his sister. I wish I'd had someone to speak up for me – it wasn't easy being an only child."

And so the conversation moved to happier ground, discussing the childhood of Henry. His mother dominated his life – he sometimes spoke of her with resentment, but she ruled him, without doubt. Just as she now threatened to rule the rest of us, her bad legs notwithstanding, it occurred to me. As for his father, Hezekiah Taul never came East, unlike all the other rich men, from Carnegie to Frick, who, once they'd made their fortune, scrambled to make their mark on New York City. He sent his son East but didn't follow. Taul Senior didn't ache to smoke his cigar in the clubs of the Astors. The face of the mine owner could only be glimpsed in newspaper photographs, and I always found it hard to connect the gaunt, white-bearded man staring at the camera like an angry Old Testament prophet with his baby-faced, luxury-indulging son.

As we finished our tea, Henry turned to immediate, pragmatic matters: traveling to the farthest reaches of Brooklyn. He planned to drive my sister out himself in his favorite automobile, with my mother as chaperone. Lawrence and I would follow in another of his cars; our two maids, Alice and Myrtle, would ride in our own car. The thirty-seven pieces of luggage were being conveyed separately.

"I'd rather take one of those fast trains to the hotel," Lawrence announced. "The tracks were laid for this purpose, to get people to the hotels on the ocean." When my mother said it was out of the question, he responded, with spirit, "My uncles want me to study engineering at college, but you won't allow me to even lay eyes on any sort of new technology. I'm forbidden to go down into the subway stations, I can't take the trains. It's unfair."

An idea jumped into my head. "I could accompany Lawrence," I said. My mother pursed her lips as she thought it over. I knew that it was only by invoking Batternberg pride that we could succeed, so I added, "If he's to study engineering, as the family wants, then he really should see such feats in person."

"I'd say yes to it," Henry said. "They wouldn't be forced to mix with the crowds going to the amusement park – that's a separate train altogether."

"Yes, it wouldn't do to have any mixing," I murmured, my temper rising again. I hated that Henry's approval was required.

Lydia said, "But once we're at the Oriental Hotel, won't we be at all aware of the crowds there, Henry? I read in the paper that there are thousands and thousands of people coming into Coney Island every day."

"Not at all," he said, emphatically. "It's a good distance away along the water, and there are plenty of guards – armed Pinkerton guards – hired to keep the bad element from the hotels. They get the job done, thank God. All the worst people of the city parade out to the amusement park. I'm sure you've heard its nickname? 'Sodom by the Sea'?"

My mother twitched in her chair at the word *Sodom*.

"So do not worry for a second, Sweetheart," Henry said with expansive confidence. "You won't even know Coney is there."

"I'm glad to hear it," Lydia said, and, from what I could detect, with all sincerity. He beamed down at her, and in the glow of his approval, the sharpness I'd seen in my sister's features softened. I tried my best to accept it: Lydia adored him. Was it real love? I would have no way of knowing, since I'd never been in love.

I rose to leave, nearly forgetting my wildflowers. I turned back but, stretching out my hand, I hesitated. Just a half hour or so in the parlor had turned my daisies limp and shriveled.

On the day we left Manhattan, my sister and mother were escorted to Henry Taul's jaunty red motor car with a black canopy top, larger even than Uncle David's, with the rather absurd name of American Eagle. His liveried driver leaped to open the doors for them, my sister and mother sitting in the back. Lawrence and I stood on the sidewalk on Seventy-Second Street, waving politely.

As the American Eagle rumbled down the street, I turned to my brother and he grinned at me. The two of us burst out laughing. What a gift. It would be for just a few hours, but we were free. Free.

CHAPTER FIVE

Lawrence and I made our way to the New York and Manhattan Beach Railway depot on Twenty-Seventh Street.

He was an inch or so taller than me – he'd shot up in height in the last year or so – but Lawrence hesitated on the steps leading to the train platforms, unsure of himself. It was a shame to see how my mother's snobbery and smothering had stymied him, and though I had seized on his train trip as a means of escaping from my mother and Henry Taul – at this point I wasn't sure who I wished to avoid more – my feelings for my brother extended beyond gratitude at the opportunity. I felt more kindly toward Lawrence than at any other time I could remember.

"Well, Mister Future Engineer, let's have a look at some engines," I said. I hadn't been sure how sincere his interest was, but it turned out my brother really did like trains, and we circled a few of them resting in the station as he peered intently at their enormous wheels and intricate gears.

Checking my timepiece, I cried, "We're in danger of missing the noon train!" We had to step smart to pick up our tickets. I feared we'd have the poorest seats so, scrambling quickly, we aimed for the first car after the conductor's engine. I spotted two free seats facing forward, by a window. I darted around a slow-moving gentleman wearing a reverend's collar and two chatting matrons to weave up the aisle and lay claim to them. It took a good three minutes for Lawrence to join me. "I've never seen you move like that, Peggy," he said, laughing. "Can you imagine Mother boarding a train without a porter to lead the way – and no first class?"

"I don't believe in first class," I said, and the train blew a deafening horn as if in agreement.

I'd ridden trains before, but not one moving this fast. Nor, more significantly, one that cut through a certain section of the city. I'd lived in New York all my life, but it was not until that Saturday, the first of July, that I had an eyeful of the Lower East Side. It was through freshly washed windows, and from an elevated track, that I could see it, really see it: the sagging, dejected tenement houses, interlaced with narrow streets seething with thousands of people. More people than I thought could possibly fit on any street. I hated the expression, but I couldn't deny these people did look like insects. I was aware of the slums of New York, everyone was, but to bear witness to the dense, pitiless enormity of this was something else entirely. It was a shallow glimpse into deepest misery.

The shining river beckoned, and we ascended the bridge to Brooklyn.

While our fellow passengers chatted happily around us, filled with anticipation for the hotel and beach, Lawrence and I shared a silence. I don't know if it hit him as hard as it did me, the shame over our unearned lives of comfort in the face of such squalor. I would wait for Lawrence to speak, and at last, after we'd passed the houses and shops of Brooklyn and were moving though farmland, he did so. It wasn't what I expected.

"Do you think about Father?"

Ah. Our handsome, amusing, friendly, careless, dissolute, and dishonest father.

With a sigh, I nodded.

"You were his favorite," he pointed out, but not jealously.

I was Father's favorite, for years. It was true. And I gloried in his warmth, his laughter at my precocious remarks. But it didn't last. And I sometimes think the caressing sun being eclipsed by dark, thunderous clouds is so painful that it would be better to have never felt the sun at all.

I said, "You're too young to remember what happened when I was twelve, the baked salmon dinner, but you must have heard about it."

"A little," said Lawrence. I could tell he wanted to hear it from me.

Outside the window, a dirt road ran parallel to our train track, and we flew by a farmer as he shook the reins on his wagon heaped with vegetables. How I envied him right now.

I began the story. "I don't know where I got the idea, where I heard the word, what made me say it. I've wondered about that a dozen times. It started with Father not being home for dinner – perhaps you remember that? – and then disappearing for weekends while Mother stayed with us. And after that, he was gone for weeks at a time. Finally, it became months. He would say it was for business, but I knew it wasn't true.

"That night all of us sat at the dinner table, Father wearing one of his beautiful suits. We'd just finished our baked salmon, and it was being cleared for dessert. Father pushed back his chair, rose to his feet, and carefully laid down his napkin, saying he had an appointment and would have to miss tonight's treat, sadly. And at that moment it just came out of my mouth: 'Are you going to see your mistress tonight?'"

It was never the same between me and Father after that. He was as offended as only the guilty can be. In some half-understood way, I had said what I said for Mother's sake, abandoned and suffering. But for me to put into words what was never acknowledged in front of the children, it was a devastating humiliation, and years later, she was capable, after a glass of wine, of saying I only did it to hurt her.

Three years after I asked my father if he was going out to see his mistress, he died in a boating accident, the sort of boating accident that newspaper writers jostle to write about. On 18 March, 1906, Jonathan Batternberg was one of twelve passengers aboard a yacht, the captain as staggeringly drunk as everyone else, and when they sailed straight into a fog bank on Long Island Sound, they were rammed into pieces by a shipping vessel registered to the nation of Norway. The largest piece of the boat caught fire. Everyone aboard died, except for a nineteen-year-old model named May Calhoun. She was my father's latest mistress.

"That girl in the water," Lawrence said, "she was one year younger than you are now."

Now that was a thought, and an incredibly unpleasant one.

"I know about how it works with the Batternberg men," my brother said. "It's disgusting." His face turned scarlet, his body twisting up like a ball in his seat. "I could never be like that!"

It seemed an extreme reaction. But then I thought back to when I first ferreted out the truth about our father and uncles. I had felt, well, not disgusted, exactly, but appalled. My grandfather, who had always espoused devotion to family, had certain ideas. Each of his sons was indoctrinated into sex by the age of fifteen with a carefully chosen prostitute. The brothers all married proper ladies, but after getting married they proceeded to chase after, dally with, and purchase secret apartments for, improper ladies. After they tired of a mistress, she'd receive money and several pieces of excellent jewelry that could hold value through any "boom and bust" market; a few received actual pensions.

I've never been able to determine if this strain of Batternberg behavior – acquiring loose women – is particularly virulent in my family, or if most wealthy men in New York City act this way. I do think there might be exceptions.

One night last year, the extended family was celebrating someone's birthday at a long table at Delmonico's. We ate steaks and those marvelous potatoes – mashed, smothered in cheese and breadcrumbs – and polished off frosty bottles of champagne. Suddenly a hush fell over the entire restaurant, and, champagne glass in hand, I looked up to spot a tall, bulky older man making his way through the room. He surveyed our Batternberg table with blazing, scornful eyes, set atop a bulbous reddish nose, and tilted his head in greeting only at my oldest uncle, Bernard. "That's JP Morgan," a cousin whispered. He marched onward, and I saw another long, festive table blanch under his scowl. Could this man ever have stashed a buxom showgirl in a secret apartment? My imagination retreated from it.

But there is one thing I do know. Women of my family, and all others like us, cannot behave the same as the men do. After Father died, in my pain and confusion, I fell under the influence of someone who was supposed to look after me but took advantage of that trust. Spurred on by a furious rebellion, I neared that point of no return – of being "ruined" – but I drew back.

Any Batternberg adolescence was difficult – but to have experienced it in the shadow of lurid screaming headlines was agony. I had come through it, yes, but without flying colors. And now I had no idea what to do with my life, beyond not wanting to wed some smooth-faced young banker who after a few years of marriage would slink off before dessert to a secret apartment downtown. Still, I had to say something to Lawrence.

"You don't have to be like them," I said. "I know the family teases me for being a New Woman. Maybe you can blaze a trail to become a New Man."

It was the right thing to say. He nodded, grateful, his complexion returning to a normal shade.

Just after crossing a thin creek, the train slowed. Everyone was on their feet, impatient to charge out the door. The moment my feet hit the platform of the little depot, I understood why.

As New York City never tires of saying, it's the greatest metropolis in the world. Manhattan is an island of delights. But it is also a crowded island, so much so that in order to expand one must go up, not out. New buildings soar seemingly to the clouds: the "skyscrapers," as the newspapers dubbed them. While here, at the edge of Brooklyn, the city pressed not up but out, its face turned toward the Atlantic Ocean, a body of water so vast it puts even Gotham in its place. I drank in the dazzling, open brightness of this place called Manhattan Beach. The blue of the sky enveloped me; there were no buildings blocking it or the gray haze of factories and automobiles. The sky arched to meet the water that rippled in the sunlight. Boats large and small danced on the horizon.

Near the water stood the Oriental Hotel. I'd been bracing myself for some ghastly Shanghai palace imitation. It was nothing of the sort. The hotel was huge, four stories tall, with what looked to be a hundred windows, and a dozen minarets atop the roof, giving it a Moorish flair. I especially liked the elegant veranda that wrapped around the first floor of the building and the emerald green of the lawn, bordered by pink, yellow, and white geranium beds.

Our beaming Uncle David appeared at the end of the platform, trailed by Dr. Mackenzie. Both wore summer resort clothes, complete with straw hats, and carried long bags over one shoulder. "Right on time, good for you," my uncle crowed, as if we'd driven the train ourselves.

He explained that after they'd conveyed us to our rooms, the two men were booked for a game of golf – "Dr Mackenzie said it's medicinal, for my heart" – and so it was necessary for us to hurry along.

"Oh, must we go inside right away?" I asked, basking in the sun and the ocean breeze.

"Your mother left strict instructions. She and Lydia and Helen are all napping, and if you lie down presently you can catch up and be refreshed for tea, that is how she put it."

Lawrence smacked his forehead with his hand. "A nap? You must be joking. I'm not a baby."

"But what of you, Peggy?"

"Me? Not a bit tired," I said. Spying a couple pedaling by on a bicycle built for two, I said, "I'm for a bicycle ride – Lawrence and I could explore while you play golf."

Seeing that his game was in no jeopardy, my relieved uncle obtained our room keys and organized bicycles for our use with the staff. He also prattled on about our new summer dwelling, telling us that in the last thirty years, three U.S. presidents had stayed at this hotel as well as the cream of the English nobility. The presidents' portraits all hung in the lobby parlor, among the mirrors. Uncle David must be in a good mood to resist singling out with disdain the face of Teddy Roosevelt. In our family, Roosevelt was called "hypocrite," "traitor," and "buffoon" – and those were the nicer names.

I continued to be pleased with the hotel. Its veranda was not as enormous as that of the Grand Union Hotel in Saratoga Springs, which stretched seven hundred feet, but it was spacious and nicely shaded. The Oriental's lobby parlor might have lacked the polished grandeur of the Waldorf Astoria, but who could possibly require a long, carpeted, and mirrored "Peacock Alley" this close to the beach and ocean? It looked to be about fifty feet in length, perfectly designed for its scale and situation. One thing was for certain – people dressed in their best here, as they did in Manhattan and Saratoga Springs.

"Sousa dedicated a special song to Manhattan Beach," Uncle David pointed out.

"Lydia loves Sousa, not me," I said, but lightly. The irritability that had dampened my mood for the last week was lifting.

We each had a room on the same corridor on the top floor corner tower. This would be the Batternbergs' private domain. In the room at the end of the hall that I'd been given, I flung open my main trunk and found my split skirt for bicycling, a long-sleeved blouse, and a floppy hat to tie under my chin. For the first time I was grateful that Mother insisted that I be fitted for every sport. I wasn't a woman who excelled at any of the popular outdoors pursuits, but given the choice of sitting inside a hotel with little to do or develop a love of sports, I chose the latter.

Once on the bicycle, it took me some time to overcome my awkward pedaling, including two near spills, but I improved and, following my brother's lead, we explored. Uncle David had explained that the Oriental was one of three grand hotels in this area. There was also the Manhattan Beach Hotel, and finally the Brighton Hotel, the establishment closest to Coney Island's amusement park, or, as Henry Taul had memorably described it, "Sodom by the Sea."

At our hotel, the farthest away from Coney, we weren't looking at the open ocean. The establishment faced a sort of bay opening up into the Atlantic. A large ferry boat packed with people moved through the water, heading for a pier on our side. Lawrence and I pedaled up the path that extended to the east of the hotel until we reached the farthest point on the bay. All along, we passed bathing pavilions stringing along the beach. I glimpsed people in their best resort clothes step into the houses at one end and come out in bathing costumes at the other. Treading across a strip of white sand to reach it, they waded into the water, laughing and splashing and ducking in the waves.

Stopping for some lemonade, Lawrence and I decided to turn and explore in the other direction. Of course Coney Island lay that way. I was curious about it, but I didn't know if my brother felt the same.

The wind picked up between the Oriental Hotel and the Manhattan Hotel, untying my floppy hat. I watched it sail over the top of one of the bathing houses. Rather than stop bicycling to go in search of it, I kept pedaling. The hat was hideous, and I relished the feel of the sun on my cheeks and the wind in my hair. "Do you see that?" Lawrence shouted over his shoulder. He pedaled off to the side and signaled for me to do so. Our path had jutted out onto a spit of land extending into the bay.

What I saw rising in the distance was fantastical. It was a city on the water, of tall towers and colorful spires and wheels and castle walls – and yes, it might have been a trick of the wind or the sun, but all of it seemed to be slightly moving. The sound of piano and horns and flutes floated toward us and that of a thousand delighted screams. It was as if the lid had been opened on a giant's music box.

"It looks like… Oz," said Lawrence finally. *The Wizard of Oz* was his favorite book.

I started laughing.

"Should we get closer, Peggy?" he asked.

I didn't answer, but simply jumped onto my bicycle. The hell with Henry Taul.

The last of the three big hotels – the Brighton Beach Hotel – loomed on our right, surrounded by brilliant geranium beds, and the bathing houses and beach on our left. I'd detected a change in the crowd wading into the water. They were louder, and their bathing costumes scantier.

Whenever I looked in that direction, I glimpsed a forest of bare, wet limbs. Lawrence's attention, I noted, was fixed on the bathers. Well, that was only natural. He'd never seen men and women standing so close to one another, their flesh so revealed. Come to think of it, neither had I.

We passed a pier with a lemonade booth, and a few minutes later the two of us put the brakes on, for before us stood a man wearing a dark suit on the boardwalk, his arms stretched wide to block a trio of young teenage boys. Beyond the man stretched a long stone pier, a building rising at the end of it. The pavilion was crowded with booths for the rest of the way to Coney Island, which rose ahead, no farther than what would be three city blocks. I heard a ragtime tune and inhaled fried food.

"Is it forbidden to keep going?" I asked the man in the suit.

"Are you guests registered at one of the hotels?" he responded.

"Yes, the Oriental."

"Then it's advised that you remain on the east side of the island," he said severely. "Beyond this point is the west side. You don't want to go there."

"But what if we do?" I persisted.

He said, "You'll find it hard to hold onto those bicycles, for one thing."

I looked over at Lawrence. He had retreated a few feet with his bicycle and looked down. The man intimidated him, I was sorry to see.

"Are you a Pinkerton guard?" I asked.

"I work for the consortium of the hotels, Miss. And your name is...?"

I proceeded to turn my bicycle around and walk briskly, with Lawrence right behind me. "Why didn't you give that man our names?" I shrugged; I didn't feel like giving the Pinkerton guard my name. Why should I?

Lawrence wanted another lemonade, and we walked our bicycles back to the pier.

By the time we reached the lemonade table, I was sure that we made the correct decision to turn back. My arms and legs throbbed from the ride, and the small of my back was beginning to ache.

When I heard the first woman's cry, I thought it was nothing but bathers' frolic. But then a second person shouted. I heard, "No!" and "What happened?"

Lemonade cup still in hand, I made my way to the top of the pier. A group of people stood waist deep in the water in a semi-circle, gathering around what looked like the shape of a woman wearing a long blue or black dress. She was face down, one of her feet caught in the pier piling. An arm floated alongside her; I couldn't see the other. Most of her long dark hair was wrapped tightly around her head.

None of the bathers seemed to know what to do. All of us, in the water or on land, felt the same way: frightened, horrified, but unable to look away.

By that point at least twenty people had gathered. The water swelled with a wave higher than the ones before, and it loosened the woman's foot. The man nearest to her in the water reached out and seized her arm, turning her over. I've no idea why he did that – it was obvious this person was dead – except for an appalling curiosity.

Because of the long black hair wrapped around her head, no one could see her eyes, which I am positive was a blessing. But her mouth hung open, her tongue extended, in a waxy gray face. One of her arms was missing beneath the shoulder.

"Step back, step back!" sounded a new voice on the pier. It was a tall, black-haired man in a policeman's uniform, a second, smaller policeman right behind him.

We jumped apart to make room for them. "A week in the water," he declared and turned to the other man. "Organize the removal."

A woman standing to my left said, "The poor thing must have gone out too far and drowned."

I said, "No, I think that's a dress she's wearing. Not a bathing costume. She wasn't out swimming in the water."

"Oh, then the poor thing killed herself?" said the woman, her eyes bright. She was eager to discuss the tragedy.

"Yes, but there must be a hundred better ways to kill yourself than to jump off a ten-foot-high pier," I said. "Unless she entered the water elsewhere."

"Are you a writer for the newspapers?" said the policeman standing on my right. I looked over, curious myself, to spot the writer in question. I'd never met a newspaper reporter. After a few seconds, I realized he was looking at me. Despite the heat, the policeman wore a long dark blue coat fastened to his throat, with two rows of gold buttons running up and down and a shiny golden badge with the words "Brooklyn Police" engraved, and a number inserted between those two words: "152." His skin was olive, his eyes dark with thick eyebrows.

"Of course not," I answered, feeling quite self-conscious.

"But you sound like you got all the answers," he said.

His rudeness made me step back, still clutching my lemonade. I wasn't used to anyone talking to me like that. My mouth opened, to issue a retort, when two things happened: The policeman turned away, to confer with a third officer of the law who had appeared, and Lawrence tugged on my sleeve.

"Let's go, Peggy, please," my brother said. For the first time since I'd glimpsed the woman's body in the water, I remembered Lawrence's existence.

And just in time – my brother's reaction startled me. He'd lost his color. He was clearly distraught.

"Yes, of course," I said, placing my hand on his shoulder. "Are you all right?"

Lawrence turned away, bent over, coughing. It looked as if he would vomit. He waved me off, and after a moment he straightened without being sick.

"I can ride," he gasped. "Let's get out of here."

We pedaled quickly, without speaking. I don't think either of us had ever seen a dead body before. When Father died, he was rapidly recovered; the burial was quick and dignified, as befitting a Jewish funeral. This was so different: How this woman's life ended, I had no way of knowing, but clearly her body had endured horrible degradations in the water.

"That girl in the water was a year younger than you are now," Lawrence had said about Father's mistress on our train ride here. Of course, that girl survived, the only one on the boat who did. Everyone else died, though not immediately. I used to wonder what Father thought in those last seconds – or, God help him, minutes – after the ships smashed into each other and everything was chaos and fire, and the water was pulling him down. Mercifully, those thoughts had stilled in my mind, but now the old horrors stirred.

It was no wonder the sight of the dead girl today had devastated Lawrence. The question was: Why hadn't it done the same to me?

CHAPTER SIX

Just before we reached the Oriental Hotel, I suggested we say nothing of the poor dead girl in the water, and Lawrence agreed. I feared this was the sort of news that would confirm Mother's first instinct, which was to protect her children from the world. I couldn't bear for either Lawrence or myself to be trapped behind barricades.

As it was, our afternoon of bicycling met with disapproval, even without the rest of the family knowing what we'd witnessed. I'd loved the feel of the sun, but the result was a reddened nose and forehead and cheeks showing a tan. No respectable lady wanted to display a face that was anything but milky white. "Now you look like a shop girl," Lydia teased.

Mother was too aggrieved to joke; she just sighed and said, "I can send to the druggist for a bleaching cream."

It was an odd dinner, and not just because of my physical state: lightheaded from the sunshine, muscles throbbing from the hours of pedaling. We'd dressed carefully for going down. Because my arms were smarting from sunburn, I picked my filmiest chiffon. We were not wearing our absolute best gowns or jewels – this was a hotel dining room, after all – but wanted to make a smashing good impression. Tonight the Batternbergs would be dining with Henry Taul and his mother.

Except that, as it happened, we weren't.

The maître d' led us to a table near the windows. The sun wobbled low on the horizon, casting a beautiful rosy golden light onto the bay. But it was difficult to bask in the calming light outside, for inside the dining room we made up a group dining among a thousand people. There was an inevitable din. The tablecloth, china, and crystal, while very nice, were not of the highest quality. We took our seats without a word, looking at one another uneasily. After a few minutes Henry appeared, bouncing across the dining room. He was alone; perhaps the redoubtable Mrs. Taul had been delayed.

"We're all together at last – fantastic!" Henry crowed, taking in the sight of all of us at the table one by one, ending with me. "Isn't the Oriental dining room posh?"

Mother nodded weakly. It was up to Lydia to say, "It looks quite... stylish, Henry." He snatched her hand, kissing it, having no idea that *stylish* was a word the Batternbergs used to describe something just a little déclassé.

Her fiancé sent waiters scampering for bottles of champagne and then launched into his recommendations for dinner: lobster, of course, but we should be sure to sample the littleneck clams. He beckoned to the waiter, who was hurrying over with champagne, and announced that we were ready to order food.

"But your mother, Henry, we must wait for her to join us before we order," protested Lydia.

"Oh, Mother never dines in the main room, she takes all her meals in her private suite," he said. "This isn't the sort of setting she cares for."

It took all our collective self-control to not take offense. What he'd said was astonishingly rude, but the grinning Henry was oblivious. When the champagne came, I drank it quickly. I could not decide whether I should be angry that the woman who'd commanded my presence at this hotel for the summer hadn't bothered to come down to dinner, or relieved.

While we ate, Henry continued to do most of the talking. He'd stashed three of his favorite racehorses at Sheepshead Bay Racetrack. The track was closed last year, pitched into limbo because of the law New York State passed against gambling, bowing to the rise of the morality lobby. But Henry said he was sure that the law would be lifted soon, and he wanted his horses in good condition. "Brooklyn is the horse-racing capital of the nation – those stables can't stay closed long, it would be a real catastrophe," he said, loud enough for people at neighboring tables to turn around. "I spent a bundle to buy the fastest horses in the world. I mean to race them."

At a certain point, two young men approached the table and Henry leaped to his feet to shake his friends' hands and introduce them to Lydia. "I'm marrying the most beautiful girl in the world, fellas," he boomed. Lydia smiled while trying to assume a dignified pose; my mother and aunt and uncle looked as if they would faint. As for me, I was struck by the similarity between the way Henry Taul talked about Lydia and his racehorses.

One of the men said to the rest of us, "I think it's commendable that you would take rooms here. It's big of you. Forgive and forget."

Who knew what that was supposed to mean?

I heard the same song in a different tune from the owner of the Oriental Hotel, a Mr. Frank Lancet, tall and barrel chested with snow-white hair flowing on his wide shoulders, like the senior lion at the Bronx Zoo. "Your decision to reserve rooms at the Oriental is deeply appreciated," he boomed.

After dinner, Uncle David accompanied Henry to the billiards room for cigars. He was obviously miserable without Dr. Mackenzie, but it was his own fault – he'd been praising the doctor's skills to all of his brothers in a manner dangerously close to bragging, and in the afternoon a telegram arrived from my Uncle Bernard, saying he was in need of a consultation on his gout. With that, Dr. Mackenzie packed his bags for Oyster Bay, and a silver car purred up the drive to whisk him away.

We females played euchre in Mother's large room. Lawrence, who I took note had been subdued throughout dinner, vanished into his own quarters.

Mother's card game steadily deteriorated as she alternated between sipping cognac and chiding Lydia to stop biting her nails. At one point she lit into the furniture in her suite. "The dressers are old, a style not even of the twentieth century," she fretted. "The handles on all the drawers have been replaced, they're smooth and shiny, but the drawers themselves? The wood is close to sagging." Again, she was acting as if something had been imposed on her. But Mother hadn't been reluctantly forced here; this was her project, hers and Lydia's. This stay at the Oriental, which was supposed to bring the two families together ahead of the wedding, was getting off to a shaky start. We simply couldn't be the ones to come out and ask to see Mrs. Taul. Etiquette forbade it. Why wasn't she inviting us to call on her in her suite at least? This wouldn't help in the cause of setting said wedding date, I feared.

David's wife, Helen, prattled on genially about nothing, which I know was her way of trying to ease the situation, but my mother and sister looked miserable. As for me, I kept the card game going. If I concentrated on it, which I didn't often bother to do, I could be a devilishly good card player. My cousin Ben had taught me all he knew, and he was celebrated at private schools from Boston to Baltimore as a top card player.

At one point in the game, my mother did something startling. She reached out and held my right hand in hers, squeezing it so tight that her rings dug into my flesh. "I'm terribly glad you are here, Margaret," she said.

"Yes, of course," I murmured. Mother was not physically demonstrative with her children. I felt embarrassed but also, I have to say, rather touched. I'd never fit into my family, not even before Father died. This could be shifting.

As tense as our after-dinner hour was, Uncle David had it worse. I could tell the minute he came to collect his wife that he'd found Henry Taul a hard sail. I overheard what my uncle said as he helped Helen find her wrap. "The man never stopped talking. And most of it was about his tour of Europe. He said he went to specific places that celebrated female purity and virgin martyrdom. What on earth am I to say to that?"

We all retreated to our rooms. It took me a bit of a search to find my nightgown. I smiled to myself when I fingered the handles of my drawers – they were worn and chipped. The hotel hadn't replaced mine. Not that I cared. But I wondered, how did they make these decisions, who was to have furniture refreshed and who wasn't? Did even the staff of the Oriental Hotel discern my lesser status among the Batternbergs?

I usually relished the first night of a holiday, sorting my clothes in different drawers and shelves, anticipating the adventures to come. But tonight I felt no such satisfaction. And strangely, I wasn't ready for sleep. My limbs felt heavy with exhaustion, but my brain whirred.

I took out my book. I'd started *Wings of the Dove*, selected from my mother's set of untouched Henry James tomes. I liked it more than I expected to, perhaps because I felt a strong kinship with Kate Croy, and not simply because she was brunette and young and determined but because she was the daughter of an unhappy marriage, with a selfish, wastrel father who put on a good show for the world. "His plausibility had been the heaviest of her mother's crosses." That sentence lingered.

After two more chapters, I put the book down. Why couldn't I sleep? I feared I knew what was responsible, or who. It was being in the company again of Henry Taul. He had barely exchanged three words with me at dinner, yet his obsession with female purity seemed like it could only be a direct reproach.

I had met Henry three years ago at a friend's garden party up the Hudson. I was staying for the weekend, and barely noticed the arrival of a new guest. By that time, Henry wanted to live down his reputation. While in college he'd landed in the newspapers for his extravagance, his wild weekend-long parties, and for being kicked out of Harvard. His father reduced his monthly allowance after he was expelled – the entire East Coast knew that. He still enjoyed himself, but he was trying like hell to stay off the front page, and the second and third pages too.

I was vaguely aware of everyone fussing over him at the party that afternoon. Everyone but me. I'd found a bench in the shady corner of the garden and was reading *Tess of the d'Urbervilles* – unfortunately, it turned out to be a significant choice – when I heard a sniffing noise. I looked down, and a little white-and-brown dog with inquisitive, damp eyes was nudging my knee.

"Here you are, Charlotte – and who have you found for me?" said a man's voice.

"Oh, is this your dog?" I asked of the tall man looking down at me. "It would seem the other way around. She's brought you to me."

Henry smiled. "Shall we say that we've found each other?"

"It's too soon for that," I answered tartly, and he burst out laughing. I soon learned that few people put up any resistance to Henry's approaches. I suppose that I piqued his interest better than any female ploy.

It's no use lying about the past when I'm alone with my thoughts in the middle of the night. I did like Henry then. He was brash and loud at times, but I found it refreshing after my escorts of the preceding year:

painfully polite Jewish boys who I'd known most of my life. Henry was a novelty. A Protestant novelty, who never cared about our difference in religion. Nor did I – my branch of the family was not very religious, to say the least. We ate shellfish and pork and rarely set foot in a synagogue.

Henry's bank sheet and level of fame allowed him to shrug off unpleasantness, and that included the reputation that I was so sensitive about: daughter of the bad sheep Batternberg. He never cared about that and didn't see why anyone else should, either.

When I appeared with Henry at the opera or theater and the dinner parties afterward, I admit I relished the newfound respect, if not envy, I saw in the women and the assessing gaze of the men. There had been very few invitations arriving at East Seventy-Second Street since Father died two years earlier. Now they came as an avalanche, not just for me but for my mother and sister too. Even my brother was asked to play with the boys of families who'd seemed to have forgotten his existence. I was just seventeen years old, and this was heady stuff.

It was at Saratoga Springs where our romance ended, after just three months. Horse racing was still legal in New York State, and of course Saratoga was one of the places to be if you owned thoroughbreds of good breeding. Dogs and horses were Henry's chief enthusiasms at the time – and, briefly, me. His horse won as we cheered in the owners' box, the curious crowd looking up at him, and at me.

We celebrated that night at an enormous party a friend of his threw for him at the Grand Union Hotel in Saratoga Springs, the same vast establishment where we'd all taken rooms. Henry was a graceful dancer for a man of more than two hundred pounds, and he spun me around the floor as the orchestra played. I always liked dancing with him – I didn't have to slouch across from a short-statured partner. That night I'd had three glasses of wine, though, and suddenly felt a bit dizzy. We went outside for some air.

"Are you leading me down the garden path?" I said, laughing, as Henry pulled me behind a row of hedges and kissed me.

Henry had kissed me before, but not this way: His lips were not gentle. His hard-muscled arms tightened around me, and while I should have felt trapped and frightened, outside, alone in the dark with an ardent man who'd had quite a few drinks, that wasn't the result. I slipped my arms up under his jacket, feeling his smooth white shirt stretching across his back, and I melted into his broad chest. I can still smell the lilacs in the spring air as I kissed him, as demanding of him as he was of me. I nibbled his ear.

Henry drew back suddenly; I couldn't read his expression in the darkness. "Will you come upstairs?" he said, hoarsely. I kissed him as answer. Now of course, I should have said no, should have calmed him down and steered him back into the party. What was I thinking? I wasn't thinking. The wine, the dancing, my body greedily clamoring for more pleasure…

Fifteen minutes later, we were alone in Henry's suite. A voice started to whisper in my head that this was a big mistake. A minute later, though, the whisper was drowned out by the roar of excitement, my senses avid, as Henry cupped my breast with one hand, and with the other unbuttoned the top of my dress, his fingers expertly handling the eyelets and hooks.

But then he stopped. His fingers froze, and he backed away. Henry began to pace the floor as I stood there, astonished, my dress half hanging off me.

He veered back toward me, his expression rigid.

"You're spoiled – spoiled," he hissed.

Horrified, I could only say he was wrong.

"I want you to tell me who it was," he demanded. "Who was the man before me?"

"No one. There's been no one."

"You're seventeen. The way that you kiss me tonight, you've been with someone. I can tell!"

After a good ten minutes of this, Henry dragged me, struggling and protesting, to a smaller room within his vast suite. He pushed me inside and locked the door. Through it he shouted, "When I come back, you'll tell me the man's name, Peggy!"

I went from disbelief to enraged pounding on the door to frightened weeping, and, finally, ice-cold determination to get the hell out of there. Using a pin from my hair, and a technique my cousin Ben had taught me, I fiddled with the key and unlocked the door. I feared that Henry was on the other side, waiting for me with that same threatening stance, but the dark room was empty. I managed to return to my own room in the hotel, where I wept all night.

The first thing in the morning, I went to the room of a school friend staying in the Grand Union Hotel and asked her and her family to take me with them to Manhattan. I was gone from Saratoga Springs before noon. Henry did not come to see me, nor did he write to me. I was angry with him, and I felt ashamed too. I'd been told countless times that it was up to the female to control a man bent on love making. We were supposed to be cool and aloof – and I failed the crucial test. I wanted absolutely nothing more to do with him. Were it not for Lydia, I'd have diligently avoided him for the rest of my life.

Henry had imprisoned me in the Grand Union Hotel in Saratoga Springs. Three years later, I controlled the door to my room at Brooklyn's Oriental Hotel, and Henry had showed next to no interest in me, but I was fighting this nagging sense that here, now, I'd been jailed again.

Beneath the smooth luxuries of the Oriental Hotel, and the attractions of the beach, the boardwalk, and the place I had yet to see, Coney Island,

I felt the existence of something disturbing, something I couldn't put a name to. I saw it this afternoon, in the battered shape of the poor woman floating under a pier. But she was a stranger. There was something else.

I tossed and turned, the sound of the water lapping at the shoreline drifting up to the window, and I yearned for morning to come.

Our maid, Alice, noticed my pitiful state as soon as she brought in some coffee and breakfast – mercifully we were not expected to take all meals in that enormous dining room – and she suggested a bath with soothing oils, followed by a cucumber treatment for my complexion, and then a nap. "Yes," I said, "and please tell my family I'm fine, no need to check on me, and I'll be down later."

Alice's regimen was of great help. When I finally dressed after a long, dreamless nap, it was early afternoon and I felt reinvigorated. My fancies of the night were just that – fancies. Who knows how many women Henry Taul had bullied over the years? It could be I was one of many. Our history held no special significance for him. I should not let the past hold power over me.

When I checked, my mother, sister, and brother were not in their rooms. It was a pleasant feeling, to be on my own. I remembered how much I'd liked the look of the veranda, and, fetching my handbag, I decided to explore it, perhaps purchase some sweets. I stuffed some money into the bag.

On the long veranda, tables were set out for the guests, with waiters bearing silver tea trays on their shoulders. I really had napped most of the day away. As I strolled along, I caught sight of the back of Lydia's blonde head, the hair piled up in one of her intricate arrangements. She was sitting in a circle of wicker chairs painted white, set up around a table sprouting tall crystal vases of fresh-cut flowers and steaming tea. Two of the other chairs were too high backed for me to see who was sitting there, but I assumed it was the whole family. I reconciled myself to tea.

I was no more than ten feet away when I heard him speak. "No matter what the newspaper writers say, I don't believe the Brooklyn racing tracks will reopen this year, which is a shame."

I darted for a doorway back into the main hotel. Once inside, and praying no one from my family had seen me, I pressed my face against the wood panel of a door to collect myself. I would know that voice anywhere on earth. It was Ben.

It took me a few minutes, but, taking deep breaths, I slowed my racing pulse. I composed my face and rehearsed what I would say, and only then did I return to the veranda.

"Here she is at last," drawled my cousin, Benjamin Batternberg. He was sitting in one of the high-back chairs, hatless, his legs crossed, his jacket flung open. His brown hair was tousled, and his dark eyes gleamed at the sight of me. "My, you are nice and brown. Brooklyn agrees with you."

"To what do we owe the honor?" I asked. "I thought you were a student of the law."

"Yale Law School doesn't hold classes in the summer, Peggy," he drawled. "You don't know that?"

I shrugged.

"I thought you'd have picked up some facts about academia in the little bookstore job Cousin Marshall found for you."

And with that, he'd cut me down to size, or so I would allow him to think.

"Sit down, Margaret," said my mother, and I took the chair opposite Ben. It was always best, whenever he was in the vicinity, to keep watch. The worst strategy was to let him gain advantage from lack of attention to his next move. All that obstructed our view of each other was a vase packed with long yellow roses.

My sister said, "Ben and Paul have been here for ages, it seems."

It was only then I noticed Paul, Ben's younger brother, who was nineteen, nearly my age. Ben was the middle child, between the oldest, Rebecca, and the youngest, Paul. But Ben had always been the one in charge of them.

Paul and I exchanged cool nods. On the face of it, he was the handsomer son, resembling his mother, who had been a dark-eyed beauty, rather than the Batternbergs. Moreover, Paul and I were both drawn to art and books, interests shunned by everyone else except for, interestingly, the head of the family, Uncle Bernard. But I'd never warmed to Paul our entire lives. We were anathema to each other.

"Not ages, Lydia," Ben said. "But Paul and I booked at the Manhattan Beach Hotel for a couple of weeks, yes. Going in and out of the city. We made reservations when I heard about your plan to occupy the Oriental as guests of your intended, Henry Taul."

"We are not Henry's guests," said Lydia tightly. "We are staying at the hotel like anyone else."

"Of course, of course," Ben said, and sipped tea, his little finger extended.

My mother frowned as all of a sudden she seemed to spot something of interest on the hotel lawn, determined not to meet my gaze.

The sweet scent of the roses on the veranda took on the cloying rot of a funeral display. Was Henry Taul paying my family's hotel bill for the entire summer? I nibbled a pastry without tasting it, considering that possibility. We were running out of money. And this was an expensive hotel. But how deeply humiliating for Henry to foot the bill for all of us before he even married Lydia.

Setting down the pastry, I peered over at Ben. His eyes danced with bright malice. God only knows how he wormed out that fact, but it was true. Henry must be paying for everything.

I'd been here five minutes and already learned a painful revelation. Some of the stories would turn out to be true, like this one, others would be partially true. That was my cousin's way.

Ben announced, "It's Lawrence who is the man of the hour. I was hearing about your trip from town yesterday, Peggy, and Lawrence's deep knowledge of the trains. We cede the railroads to the Vanderbilts and the oil fields to the Rockefellers, but your engineering knowledge will come in handy in running our mines, Lawrence. Father's been after me to go to Bolivia to see our newest acquisition. Maybe you can come along."

My brother smiled, as did my mother, grateful that someone was taking up Lawrence as a cause. But my heart skipped a beat. Ben had never shown interest in "the Schlump" before.

Henry Taul and Uncle David showed up at the table, returning from seeing Henry's horses stabled at the Sheepshead Bay Race Track. I felt a curdle of apprehension as Ben rose to his feet and shook Henry's hand – "It's so nice to see you again" – but there wasn't a flicker of suspicion on Henry's face. Why should there be? Family members are supposed to look after each other, especially when they're most vulnerable, as when a girl is fifteen and has just lost her father.

But also Henry was plainly in a bad temper. Despite his assurances to all, the racetrack did not seem to be on the verge of reopening for thoroughbred horses. Even worse, they'd heard rumblings of motor car races taking the place of the horses. Not that Henry and all the rest of the men on this veranda weren't mad for automobiles. But it could never be the sport of kings.

Aunt Helen, always tactful, lightened the mood by sharing some newspapers delivered to the hotel shop that afternoon with photographs of the coronation of the new king and queen of England: George and Mary. No one was genuinely interested in this event but my mother;

however, in a sort of unspoken agreement to show kindness to Sarah Batternberg, everyone at the table took a turn with the newspapers, looked at the photos, and commented. Lydia, being the person closest to my mother, studied the photographs with the most care, pointing out an elaborate gem-studded tiara worn by a duchess following the new Queen. Her fiancé made something of an effort to get into the spirit of it, although Henry sulkily grumbled about the superb horse races at Ascot and the British understanding things better than the Puritanical Americans. My cousin Ben said with a wink at Mother, "She's wearing a crown and a diamond necklace and a six string of pearls? The sun may never set on the British Empire – it certainly won't set on Queen Mary's jewelry!"

When my turn came, I was drawn to the face of the proud, plain Queen: frozen into a mask that transcended arrogance and aspired to that of a deity, like the statue of some stern Egyptian goddess. Since the British Empire ruled over a quarter of the earth's surface, she wasn't wrong. I thought of the shooting in East London earlier this year of two Baltic anarchists, how the police and army swarmed in the thousands over a wretchedly poor neighborhood to trap the revolutionaries in the Siege of Stepney Street. What had been the anarchist cry? "No gods, no masters," I murmured, repeating the motto as I gazed at the photo of the haughty queen.

"What did you say, Peggy?" asked Uncle David with a frown. Of course anarchists were the arch enemy of our family, along with trade unionists.

"Nothing," I responded, passing the newspaper along.

"And now," said my cousin Ben, "who's for a stroll around Coney Island?"

Henry said, "You must be joking. None of us have gone there, none of us *will* be going there. It's the dregs of the city."

Ben said lightly, "Oh, everyone needs to have a look, how could you not, so close at hand? And there really are some architectural marvels, even if you don't care for a thrill ride or the dreadful food."

"Is it safe for us to… just walk around, among all those strangers?" asked Lydia, with a delicate shiver.

Ben laughed. "Do you think I'll be kidnapped? Or just blown to pieces by anarchists?"

"That's not funny," said Uncle David. Now I remembered the meetings that the brothers had last year about the growing anarchist threat, though discussion of hiring special bodyguards ultimately led to nothing.

His oldest son said, "I assure you that none of the sales clerks or secretaries know who I am, or cares, in Coney Island. And even if there were a spot of trouble, I am well able to defend myself. So what do you say, Lawrence? Care to join us? I promise to take good care of him, Aunt Sarah." Lawrence jumped to his feet, and my mother did nothing to stop him.

This was alarming – not their going to Coney Island, but Lawrence being in his company for hours. Whatever Ben had in mind for my brother, I needed to witness it, and, if necessary, countermand it.

"I think I'll come along," I said, also rising.

"Delightful," said Ben.

Henry put out his hand, as if to push me back into my chair. "Out of the question," he said, far too loud.

"Peggy is twenty years old, I think she's capable of coping with an amusement park, particularly if she's with me," Ben said, in the same light, amused tone, refusing to acknowledge Henry's belligerent attitude.

"Let's be going," I said, easing my way out of Henry's grasp just as he took another step toward me as if to block my movements. I had to dart around Lydia's chair to escape him. Just before I reached Lawrence's side, I caught sight of Lydia's expression. She looked frankly horrified, her eyes not on me or Ben but on her fiancé, Henry.

CHAPTER SEVEN

It took a while for my heart to stop racing as we walked across the lawn to the lot for both motor cars and horse-and-buggies. I stayed close to Lawrence, with Ben and Paul leading the way to their very own road-sters. They didn't rely on a car with a driver, like their father or Henry. Each owned a Ford Model T.

"Lawrence can ride with me," Ben announced when we got there, holding open a door to his vehicle.

"No," I said. "Lawrence will ride with Paul. We need to catch up, Ben."

"Oh, I'd love that," he said, with a widening smile.

As Ben slid onto the seat next to me, I demanded, "Why this new interest in Lawrence? You've never cared about him before."

"I could ask you the same question, Peggy. Just hold on a moment, while I find my cigarettes. I fancy a smoke while I drive. Do you want one?"

"No, thank you."

"Still abstaining? I thought the New Women smoked."

It was incredibly complicated to start a car while lighting a cigarette. I took advantage of that span of time to calm myself while he did both with his usual unhurried deliberation. We were on our way, along a road presumably connecting us to Coney Island, when Ben glanced sideways and said, "The black sheep of the black sheep. How I've missed you, Peggy."

"Hmmmm," I said, refusing to rise to whatever he was baiting me with.

Ben made a neat turn around a corner, his hands crossing on the steering wheel while the cigarette dangled from his mouth. He removed it and said, "Did you see Lydia's face? I think she's beginning to wonder which sister Henry Taul wants most to control."

"That's ridiculous. He's just bossy, that's all."

Ben laughed dismissively.

"I've always loved the story of you and Mr. Henry Taul," he said. "How you reeled in the playboy, the prince of mines – second only to the Batternberg mines in all the Americas. You caught him like a prize trout and then, after getting a good sniff of him, just tossed him back in the lake. Wonderful. But we can see he's getting his revenge now."

"That's terribly insulting to Lydia," I said angrily. "I can't believe this, even of you."

"I am not the one insulting Lydia," he said. "So hold your temper, my dear." He took another puff on his cigarette. "I'm surprised to find you so well disposed to your sister and mother. Frankly, I was very surprised that you even agreed to this summer stay."

"Why? Because I'm such a lost cause?"

He shot a look at me. "Oh, the opposite. They're going to need that inheritance of yours from Grandfather to live on if Henry Taul bounces away. He's proving elusive on that date, from all accounts. It may come down to you keeping your branch of the family from sliding into ruin. Everyone's been worried that once you gained access to your trust income, you'd give it away to a bunch of bohemians and anarchists. That's why they eased you out of the bookstore."

How loathsome of Ben to try to stir matters up. Making jabs about my trust fund was low, even for him.

But then I felt my back and neck stiffen and my throat begin to close. Oh, no, I realized, with a rush. This was *true*. My family wanted to pull me in this summer to use me as a sort of reserve play at the card table, not because of new-found love for me.

It all came down to control of the money. Our grandfather had set it up so that every single one of the children on our line in the family would inherit $2.5 million at the age of twenty-one, to earn only the interest on the amount until thirty, when the entirety would be available. My mother couldn't touch any of it directly. She inherited nothing from my father because he died in debt. But between her three children, there was more than $7 million to be had as we each came of age.

Ben said, "I really think I should represent your interests, Peg. I'm still in law school, but I can arrange the best counsel. I've some useful contacts. This is likely to get tricky."

"Oh, shut up, Ben," I snapped. "You're absolutely the last person I could ever trust to look after my interests."

"Why is that?" he asked, as if he honestly didn't know. He always acted so dismissive of what happened between us. How older cousin Ben, bound for law school, had taken charge of poor distraught Peggy, and where his "cheering up" had led. "You make too much of it," he said a year ago.

"Well?" he persisted.

"You're too… mean," I said.

This seemed to catch him so by surprise he burst into laughter, choking on the smoke he'd just inhaled. "Mean – *mean*? I would hope so! How else does anyone make any money? You know, Peggy, I take that as a compliment. Nicest thing you've said to me in ages."

The automobile slowed, and Ben turned into a dirt lot. "I don't know why Henry is making such a fuss over Coney Island," he said. "It's not like he hasn't been there himself. I spotted him here a week ago."

Paul pulled in alongside us. Ben handed over a dollar to the teenager guarding his ground like the choicest real estate in all of New York. They'd clearly been here before.

Acting as guide, Ben led us to a street called Surf Avenue and announced, "Welcome to Coney Island, home of not one or two but three separate parks: Steeplechase, Luna Park, and Dreamland. They all compete with one another for customers – no cooperation, from what I've heard."

I was in the foulest mood possible that Sunday afternoon, when I first entered the sprawling, joyous, noisy tumult. It was like being dropped into a hot cauldron of sickly-sweet smells – saltwater taffy, sugared lemonade, and cotton candy – while surrounded by shrieking laughter. A roller-coaster creaked to the sky as we walked in its shadow. Just ahead a young woman, seized up with giggles, rode a camel being led down the walkway. And beyond her, a man in a bright pinstripe suit stood on a platform. I couldn't focus on the rides or other attractions this afternoon. I was still struggling to take in what my mother and the rest of the family had done in severing me from my job and dragging me out here.

I paid little attention to Ben as he continued to function as tour master, explaining the story behind this attraction and that. It was correct that he, Benjamin Batternberg, heir to a vast fortune, seemed perfectly safe. No one gave him, or Paul or Lawrence or myself, a second look. The thick crowd was too highly entertained by all the sights today.

But even more than that, it was Ben's personal style. His clothes were never obviously costly; he favored dark, plain trousers, jackets, and vests, and liked to roll his shirt sleeves and push them up to his elbows. They were rolled up now, exposing his forearms covered with thick black hair. That and rarely wearing a hat gave him a deceptively proletarian air. The only sure giveaway for Ben were his shoes. He loved Oxfords and only wore the best.

The eager crowd couldn't have been less interested in Ben's shoes, or in any of us. Yes, these people in their weekend clothes could be sales clerks and secretaries. To me, they also looked like the true workers of the city, slaving away in the factories and on the wharfs. Yet instead of being stooped with misery, these men and women enjoyed everything tremendously. As we wove our way through the crowds, encircled by joyful cries and surprised shouts, I felt even worse. It wasn't that I begrudged anyone an entertaining Sunday. It was the realization, yet again, that the family money, which everyone at Coney Island might assume would deliver ecstatic happiness, brought me pain. Hot tears pricked the corners of my eyes as I pretended to look at a man on a platform, wearing a striped suit, shouting his invitation to step this way and see for ourselves a family from the Philippines. After a moment we moved on.

"Look at what we have here," announced Ben, staring upward with a smile. The four of us had left the huge park called Steeplechase, returning to Coney Island's Surf Avenue for more sight-seeing. We came to a stop in front of an enormous semi-circle brick archway leading to a separate park, one with a sign atop it spelling out "Dreamland." Underneath that word stood a statue of a giant woman at least one hundred feet tall, perhaps an angel, for wings sprouted from her back. She looked to the side as if she were beckoning, bare breasted, a sheet clung to her waist, wrapped around part of her legs.

"What do you think, Lawrence?" Ben asked. "Do you like your women with this sort of figure? Will she show up in any of your dreams?"

Paul pealed with laughter as my brother looked down and then up at the statue, turning as red as he did in the train carriage.

"That's enough of that," I said.

No one paid any attention to me. The three of them continued to ogle the statue, Paul elbowing my brother. Fifteen was the age when, a generation ago, the Batternberg men were initiated into sex, in a way that only yesterday my brother called "disgusting." I had no doubt that Ben and Paul began their debauchery at a similar age. Back in the days when we told each other everything, Ben waved a little leather-bound book at me titled *The Gentleman's Directory*, containing the names and addresses of the best brothels in the city, which he claimed to visit as "Mr. Franklin."

Ben said, "She's not quite my type. I prefer a long pair of legs."

"Shut up!" I said. I grabbed my brother's arm. "We're going back to the hotel now, Lawrence."

My brother pulled his arm back. "What's wrong with you?"

"Yes, what's wrong with you, Peggy?" repeated Ben.

I abandoned all caution, all strategy, and said, "I insist that you stay away from Lawrence, Ben."

"You're being such a prude," scorned my cousin Paul.

"Geez, Peggy, you're embarrassing me," said my brother.

Ben took a step toward me. There was chaos all around us – thousands of people talking, laughing, singing, or screaming – but in that moment, he saw me alone.

"And why should I be kept away from Lawrence, Peggy? Too... *mean?*"

He dared me to say it while knowing I never would, that our secret was safe. I turned to my brother, who looked disgusted, not with Ben, but with me.

"Why are you spoiling things?" he asked, angrily.

And with that, I was through with it.

"Fine – then I am going back," I announced. "I'll walk to the hotel."

All I heard was Ben calling my name twice, exasperated, but I turned away, and, my eyes swimming with tears, I plunged into the thick of the crowd, now so dense I was barely able to move. I pushed my way through. The thickness of the crowd didn't bother me. The more people, the better. It would make it harder for my family to find me. I paid a dime of admission and I was inside Dreamland.

On my right side, a brace of clarinets and trombones pounded music; in front of me, a square tower with a triangle top soared incredibly high, as high as one of the skyscrapers in Manhattan. More immediately I faced a mountain of water, with people riding down in little wooden cars that reached the bottom with an enormous splash. No matter which way I twisted and turned, I couldn't see the natural water, the beach, or Surf Avenue. I was deep into Dreamland, away from the ocean and the town. But I didn't want to retrace my steps. I couldn't bear to set eyes on anyone named Batternberg. I kept walking forward – I was just one of the crowd.

"See the midgets of Lilliput! The world's most famous little people! You'll never forget Midget City!" screamed a man in a striped suit, standing on a platform.

I was anonymous here, without a doubt, I thought as I passed the Canals of Venice. Henry's or anyone else's fears about my personal safety were ridiculous. Not that kidnapping members of wealthy families didn't take place. I'd read the stories in the newspapers, or heard the hushed tales at Batternberg gatherings, of heirs and heiresses abducted, stolen in the night, held for ransom. Of course no one could abduct me here. But I did wonder how the pleasure seekers of Coney Island would react to my name. Ben had mentioned the Rockefellers on the veranda. The patriarch of that family was most likely the richest man in America – and the most reviled. When John D. Rockefeller Jr got married in Rhode Island, the family had to hire an army of Pinkerton guards for, as feared, the mob gathered to surround the place of the wedding, longing to tear the owner of Standard Oil to pieces for his crimes against the working man.

No, I reassured myself, looking at their happy, heedless faces, listening to them shriek, they wouldn't care about Peggy Batternberg. And I had never hurt anyone, nor ever could.

"Make way for Little Hip, the prize of Captain Ferrari's animal kingdom!" shouted a man holding a rope. Its other end was tied to the neck of an elephant. When I was a child, I loved stories about elephants, and despite nursing all my earned grievances, I smiled at the sight of this lumbering, wrinkled gray beast with such kind eyes.

Heartened, I turned toward some sedate-looking booths. The first one seemed to be created for people who wanted to be photographed, the images turned into postcards. A long line stretched out in front of it, of couples with their arms around each other. The second booth had a sign atop saying: "Art for Sale!" There was no line there. Coney Island art? With a grim chuckle, I headed for it.

I never turned down a chance to see an art exhibition, in New York or in Europe. When I spent a few months in Paris after leaving school, I went with my Aunt Rachel on her tireless treks to find a new Degas dancer statue to buy. What would she say about Coney Island talent?

Stepping inside to a space much larger than I expected, I was rewarded with a garish portrait of a clown riding a bicycle on the boardwalk. Then came a young couple embracing while a dwarf looked up her dress. This was even worse than I feared. However, there was no one else looking at art inside the booth that I could see, and I was enjoying the reprieve from being pushed and pulled, so I kept walking.

Two stalls down, at the end of this dim little corridor, I saw something different. A rod had been nailed into the wall, jutting out awkwardly, with a blue curtain hiding what was behind. As I drew nearer, I saw a small cream-colored sign fastened to the rod where the curtains met. It was not bright and garish, like everything else I'd seen. In a plain, thick, angular typeface, it said, "The Futurist."

I pushed the blue curtain aside and slipped into the booth. I had to blink a few times, because, in absence of natural light, someone had mounted electrical lights to shine brightly. As my eyesight adjusted, I gasped. As I stood there, and the full impact of this art washed over me, I seized the rickety wooden railing in front of me for balance. I felt so overcome it was as if I were in danger of collapsing.

I was looking at a Coney Island that was not a corny fair but part of a dazzling metropolis, a boldly imagined world, rendered with vivid skill. There were three paintings, carefully mounted on a thin wall, using abstract technique but depicting objects recognizable as giant roller coasters and beautiful Ferris wheels and sleek motor cars. Their speed was celebrated; the machines were vibrantly beautiful. The point of view was revolutionary. It was as if I were being pulled into the painting, to exult personally in the speed and movement.

"Who is the artist?" I said aloud. "Who is he?"

From behind me, a man said, "Why? You want to buy?" in a strong accent. Someone had slipped in behind me without making a sound. I turned around and faced a man of my height, standing back a respectful distance. Like the "Futurist" sign, the workman wore not the striped, garish uniform of a Coney Island employee, but plain clothes, a strangely cut tunic without buttons and simple trousers. In perhaps his late twenties, the man had sandy hair, high cheekbones, and a steady gaze.

"Yes, I want to buy. How much?"

He cocked his head, thinking for a moment. "Three dollars for painting," he said.

"I'll have two," I said.

He smiled and then, most surprisingly, bowed. It was a traditional sweeping bow, not at all what I expected.

"Who is the artist?" I said. "You didn't tell me."

"He signs work with name 'Stefan,'" the worker said in that same harsh but lilting accent. I could not place the country of origin.

"Where else does this Stefan show his art?" I took the dollars out of my purse that I'd meant for hotel sweets, trinkets, or gifts, and handed them to him.

"Here. Only here."

That was strange. "How do I find out more about him, about Stefan?" I asked.

He slipped the dollars into a small leather bag and tightened the strings.

"What is your name?" the workman asked. I realized suddenly that his eyes were an odd color, a dark gold, like cognac in a glass. "I shall tell him of you."

"My name is Peggy."

"He can find you where?"

I hesitated. It didn't seem like a good idea to tell a stranger, a worker in Coney Island, my address or anything about me. He smiled again. "You have husband?" he asked.

"No," I said, surprised at his impudence. What did my being married have to do with anything? But I did badly want to find out more about this artist. A solution occurred to me. "I work at Moonrise Bookstore, on Thirty-Ninth Street in Manhattan."

He looked surprised. "A shop girl? This large amount of money for you."

Now that was impudent too, although there was nothing rude or improper about his manner. He seemed quite concerned. I considered not responding to his point, but said, firmly, "It's worth it. This art is very, very good."

He scratched his arm, looking at me. "Stefan delighted to hear."

Thinking the man got his tenses wrong, I said, "He will be delighted, you mean to say? You'll see him soon?" I looked around the booth, wondering if this wondrous talent were about to materialize.

"He knows now."

I shook my head, not understanding. The workman stuck out his hand to shake. "I am Stefan."

Being deceived is never welcome. But Stefan looked so entirely pleased that after the first shock, I couldn't hold it against him.

"Thank you, thank you," he said. Now that we were close, I could see specks of paint on his tunic, the same deep red as on the first painting. His grip was tight and warm, with calloused ridges on his fingers. "These are first sales in days," he said, not in self-pity but matter of fact.

"Well, that's because you're showing them here. I don't think Coney Island is the proper… environment for your work."

His eyes widened and he said, "Mmmmmm." I realized that we were still holding hands, although the shaking motion had ended. I carefully withdrew my hand.

"Peggy, I have question," he said. He said "Peggy" in a way no one else ever had, something that sounded like "Peyagey."

"Yes?"

"Are you hungry?"

"Hungry? I don't know." But I did know the second I said it. I was ravenous. I hadn't eaten anything but that half pastry at tea on the veranda.

"May I take you to dinner?" Again, he bowed with that distinct formality. "It would be my honor."

It struck me that I had never in my entire life consented to a private conversation or a stroll, much less a meal, with a strange man.

I felt myself smile. "Yes," I said. "You may."

CHAPTER EIGHT

Although I could hardly believe I'd just agreed to have dinner with him, the man himself didn't seem surprised by my consent. "Remain here one minute," he said, holding up a single finger as if my seeing it were needed, to convey the point. He slid out the side of the booth, leaving me alone with my paintings, which he'd taken down in their light frames.

It seemed as if he were gone for longer than one minute, and I began to feel ridiculous, and a little angry, standing inside the "Futurist" booth of The Art of Coney Island. Was this some sort of nasty trick that he'd now disappear?

But I heard a soft footfall and, turning, saw Stefan approach, that same steady smile on his face but wearing new clothes: a white shirt and gray jacket with a wide lapel and three buttons. Where he'd found these garments, I couldn't imagine. The jacket was frayed and a bit too big for him, and I was touched that he'd gone to this effort. An answering smile again spread across my face. It just wasn't possible not to smile.

"After dinner, we come back and I wrap paintings for you," he said, holding out his arm for me to link with his.

And so I was escorted to dinner in Coney Island, the Playground of America, or as Henry had described it, Sodom by the Sea. Associating with an artist and a foreigner gave me deep satisfaction. I was behaving in a way that would, if they knew it, cause the maximum amount of distress to my family and Mr. Henry Taul.

As if he knew what I was thinking, Stefan said, "Are you here with friends today?"

"No."

"You came with family?" We were now in the thick of the crowd. Stefan moved through them slowly, making sure with every step that I wasn't being bumped or jostled. He had a gait like no one else. He was completely calm and relaxed in the eye of this storm, but with ramrod-straight posture.

"I'm here alone," I answered.

He stopped, to look at me in surprise. "You came out on train from city by yourself?"

I realized that I'd have to make a bit of an adjustment to the identity of Peggy the shop girl. "I'm here at Coney Island alone, but I'm staying with my family at a hotel near here. It's in Manhattan Beach, just a short distance along the water."

I waited for realization to dawn, for my dinner partner to perceive that the daughter of a family who stays at one of the ocean-side hotels could not possibly be a typical shop girl. But all he did was nod and say, "I shall escort you to hotel after dinner."

There weren't any other questions along those lines from him, to my relief. I didn't want to have to explain.

The restaurant he chose was an enormous one near the ocean, with tables arranged on a platform not far from where the water rides charged down to their squealing conclusion. It crossed my mind that Ben and company might be able to spot me if they chose to go looking, and so I breathed easier when we were tucked in the corner nearest the building itself, surrounded by other patrons, not out on display at the edge. To find me, someone would have to be looking hard.

"Stefan!" shouted an old waiter with a stiff white moustache, who rushed over to drop tattered menus in our hands. They spoke to each other in a musical rapid-fire language I recognized as Italian, though I couldn't speak it myself. My only other language was French – it was more important to my mother than mathematics. At last Stefan shooed him away.

"I beg pardon – to speak in another language not too nice," he said to me earnestly over the checkered tablecloth.

"That's all right," I said. "So… you're Italian?"

"I live six years in Rome and Milan before coming to America, but no, I'm not Italian," he said. I waited for him to clarify his country of origin. He did not.

"I order oysters, I hope you like them, Peggy."

I let it go; I smiled and said I did, while enjoying yet again the way he pronounced my name, unlike how any other person, male or female, had ever said it. I was so very curious about him, but before I could pose my questions, he queried me. How long had I worked at Moonrise Bookstore? What did I do? He was as curious about me as I was about him. I didn't have to lie about my job, and I answered everything.

When I told him that the novels of Dostoyevsky were much in demand at Moonrise Bookstore, he shook his head decisively. "No, he needs to be read in Russian – no translations can do justice."

I said, "Are you Russian then, Stefan?"

"No." Then, so definitively that I thought it might be a trick of the light were we not sitting outside, Stefan's bearing, his attitude, changed completely. His eyebrows gathered; his smile withdrew as he sat back in his chair. An indefinable expression filled his hazel eyes, as if he could see far beyond me, the table, the restaurant, Coney Island, everything. "I understand Russian well – they are brothers to me," he said softly.

At that moment, the waiter appeared with a tray of oysters strewn across ice. Stefan shook himself out of his reverie. "Very good!" he said. "And our beer."

Now, I'd never drunk beer in my life. Nor had I ever eaten oysters dumped on ice so sloppily, without fresh cut lemon slices adorning them.

"I apologize," Stefan said, his face crinkling with concern. "The oysters, this is too… new?"

"No, no, it's fine," I insisted. My fingers edged toward the large, lumpen gray-and-white oyster shells.

"Peggy, watch me," he said, evidently thinking I needed instruction on how to eat an oyster. He turned his head sideways, tilted back slightly, and put the shell to his lips. I saw him nudge the soft whiteness of the oyster into his mouth, his tongue darting to pull it inside.

It was my turn. I picked up an oyster and tilted it into my mouth. Though I missed the presence of lemon, the oyster tasted so good that I closed my eyes for a few seconds. When I opened them, Stefan was watching me closely. He shook his head a trifle, as he had before to bring himself out of his meditation on Russia, then raised his mug of beer, questioningly. I very much needed a drink right now, and I raised mine in answer. But the taste was terrible: thickly sour and harsh. I couldn't help coughing.

"Never had beer before?" he asked.

"No," I gasped.

"First time – can be difficult," Stefan said. "It gets easier."

We finished our oysters, and I did try another sip of beer, which, he was right, wasn't as noxious. Our plates of fried clams and chopped green beans and brown bread followed. It tasted quite good; Ben had unfairly called the food of Coney Island "terrible." I was surprised by how comfortable this all felt. In my world there were rules about how to respond to a strange man tipping his hat to a girl he hadn't been introduced to. It was unthinkable to agree to go to a public restaurant with such a man.

Stefan did not seem to appreciate this shocking break with propriety. Indeed, he took it upon himself to give me advice on my life.

"You love books – you should be writer," he said.

"No," I said. "I'm not a writer."

"Do you paint?"

"My paintings are worse than my poetry," I said lightly. But Stefan did not laugh in response. He looked puzzled.

"I don't possess a natural talent for writing," I said. "Believe me, I wish it were otherwise. I'm not good enough to make an endeavor such as that my calling."

"What is 'good'?" he asked. "You have something to say, that is the key to it. You should go to university. You're intelligent woman. You have ideas. You have taste."

"Because I like your art?" I asked, laughing.

"Exactly!" he joined me in laughter. "But to be serious, I know it costs much money, Peggy, but you could find way. Use your intelligence. I worked on the streets, in shops, every day so could attend art school in Rome. It can be done. It's not right for you to – how you say? – degrade your mind, your thoughts."

I felt my first serious pang of guilt. It was lousy to mislead Stefan this way. Especially when he was showing more genuine interest in my potential than anyone in my own family. The truth is, I'd wanted to go to college, but my mother, my sister, my female cousins including Ben's older sister – they had all talked me out of it. Batternberg women didn't go to college. It would make us less appealing to husbands, that was the thrust of it. The men all took degrees, of course. Ben took an undergraduate degree at Columbia and was studying law at Yale. But it wasn't a place for any female who was One of Us.

I also felt a wide gulf between Stefan and myself in our attitude toward accomplishment. No one in my family or my circle of friends would dream of admitting to a desire to write or paint or sing – much less to announce a talent for it. That's not to say such aspirations didn't exist. But they were hidden or denied in some attempt at modesty, or perhaps to ward off the possibility of ridicule, always the worst fate imaginable. It didn't make any sense, really. I was weary of my own world and eager to delve into that of the man sitting opposite me, a true artist.

"Why did you leave a city like Rome to come here?" I asked. It baffled me why an artist of Stefan's gifts would leave Europe, where the art world was centered. I knew little about the avant garde movement, except from what I saw in magazines mailed to Moonrise Bookstore and gleaned from my trips to the Stieglitz Gallery. Stefan's work seemed to be part of that. Yet New York City had little to offer devotees of modern art compared to Paris, Rome, or Milan. Or any serious culture, really. The United States was the home of Mark Twain and John Phillip Sousa, both of whom left me cold. It seemed to me that when an American possessed true talent, he or she decamped for Europe, like Henry James pretending to be English or Mary Cassatt refusing to budge from France.

He frowned and hesitated, searching for words. "Many reasons. Hard to explain. But in my work, my life, I think about… future. America is future in all things. That's what I believed."

"Believed – past tense?"

He smiled. "Past tense? Not sure of meaning." Just then, the bill arrived, and he paid it – I feared it totaled half of what I'd paid him for his paintings – before he rose and came around to pull out my chair. "You want to know what bring me here, to Coney Island?" he asked. "I show you." I nodded, rose, and took his arm.

We walked past a building bearing the sign "Infant Incubators." I pointed at it in disbelief, but Stefan said, "It's truth, infants in there. Science amazing." As he was explaining the building for infants, a new sound of screaming bells ripped through the cacophony of Coney Island. Turning toward the source of the screeching, I saw dozens of firemen racing toward a six-story building. Stefan explained that "Fighting the Flames" was a nightly attraction offering disaster. The fire was carefully controlled, just one of the pulse-pounding attractions. Each night the firemen rescued all those in distress.

A few minutes later, we approached a long row of people standing on a platform. A closer look revealed they were all young women except for a man in the middle, wearing a red stovepipe hat, who shouted at the crowd, "The most beautiful girls in all of Coney Island! All of them featured performers at Henderson's. Play the game and win the prize: a photograph taken with you and her!" A line of men ogled the women.

We were almost past the platform when one of the women shouted, "Stefan, oh Stefan! Ha! Yes, I see you!"

The woman looked to be about my age but unlike me in every other way. Fiery red hair cascaded over her shoulders in glorious curls. She had a heart-shaped face, and a voluptuous figure spilling out of her tight bodice. "Not a moment for me today?" she called out, with, I swear, a wink.

Stefan shook his head, laughing. We kept moving; he gave no explanation, and of course, none was owed. All we had shared was a dinner.

Yet I felt a tug of jealousy.

The sun was low in the sky, its golden glow turning orange, when

Stefan guided me to the Dancing Pavilion, a truly massive wooden dance floor also looking out at the ocean. Hundreds of couples swirled across the floor while an orchestra played.

"You came to Coney Island to dance?" I asked in disbelief.

He took a step closer to me to make sure I could hear him over the music. I was quite happy that it was necessary for him to do that.

"On the ship, I was on it many, many weeks, and I had cheapest ticket, bad food. Half boat sick. We reach New York City – we see Statue of Liberty, not well, but we see it with mist. I hear such music. I see… nothing. But I hear it. Like dream. After I go through lines, I stay with friends, try to sell work, nothing. Not a penny. 'Too strange,' everyone says. I tell people I heard music day I came to America, they laugh. Stupid foreigner, must be madman. One day I come out to Coney Island to see what it's like – and I hear same song, same instruments. This was it! I heard it. It was real. I moved to this part of Brooklyn next month, took jobs to live while I painted."

I knew instinctively that this was the truth, that Stefan had opened himself up to me. It was the opposite of how the people in my life communicated with one another; we rarely told the whole story about anything or explained our true feelings, it was far too embarrassing.

"There are so many dancers," I said, like an idiot.

"Workers of New York, dance – you have nothing to lose but your chains," Stefan said.

I recognized his reference, and his joke, after a minute. "Karl Marx?" I asked. He nodded, pleased that I understood.

"Would you like to dance with me?" I blurted.

"Very much."

With a smile, I turned toward the others. "Shall we join them, then?"

He laughed. "We must buy dance tickets first, Peggy, and wait for next set. You haven't been to dance hall?"

"Well. I have danced before," I assured him.

He looked puzzled again, as if with me he were trying to work out a challenging sum in his head. He purchased the tickets, and we joined the next throng. The first song Stefan and I danced to was a sentimental, syrupy waltz – who the composer was I didn't know. It was the kind of music I might have cringed at in other circumstances, but I shall never forget the sound of those violins, the brass, the piccolo, the piano and drum. His fingers grazing the small of my back, his arm extended in perfect correctness, shoulders thrown back, Stefan led me across the floor like an old Victorian gentleman exhibiting the utmost propriety, except for the crinkling smile of his eyes as he looked at me. He is handsome, I realized in a rush, with his high cheekbones and deep-set eyes. I'd said yes to dinner with a foreign workman as a lark, furious at my family, but this man could cut a figure in any room, any setting.

Something is happening to me, I thought, as I swirled across the Coney Island stage, surrounded by the hundreds and hundreds of strangers.

Afterward, struck with a new shyness, I could think of nothing to say except that he was a fine dancer, and I inquired where he learned to waltz.

"Military academy," he said, dryly.

That was not what I expected to hear. There were so many parts to this man, fitting together in ways that puzzled.

We returned to the booth where he sold his art, and Stefan made the paintings into a long package protected by plain wrapping paper, a string handle fashioned atop. Darkness would fall within the hour. He led me out of Dreamland, finally, passing under that giant statue, the winged, bare-breasted female that provoked a quarrel that seemed like a century ago.

I couldn't help peering around, uneasily, but there was no sign of Ben, Paul, or Lawrence. For the first time I wondered what they told my mother when they returned to the hotel without me. There would be quite the uproar over my behavior. I hastily pushed that out of my head.

Stefan asked me which way to the hotel, and I pointed west. "It's quite a walk, I'm afraid."

"Good. That right direction. You heard my favorite sound, I want to show you my favorite sight."

By now my hand wasn't in the crook of his arm. We held hands as I savored the sound of his "Peggy" and thrilled to the feel of the roughened grooves of his palm. The promenade was crowded with other people. We could have talked over the din, but after twenty minutes or so neither of us did. We walked along in a silence, although I couldn't say it was a comfortable one. My mind was racing, my heart was not far behind. Everything about Stefan interested me; he was so new. I'd been lamenting the long summer that stretched before me in Brooklyn. Could Stefan become a way to make the weeks pass far more quickly?

"This is perfect," he announced, coming to a stop.

"Is it?" I asked, looking around, confused.

He led me off the pavilion walk and onto the beach. My shoes kept sinking in the sand as we walked toward the ocean lapping the shore. We walked alongside a long wooden piling snaking across the white sand, drawing closer and closer to the water.

"Sit," he said, guiding me with both hands on my hips, to a wooden piling sticking up as high as a chair.

He sat next to me, and pointed in the direction we came in. "Now look."

His arm around me, we looked back where we had begun. It was a city of fire, a city of lights that danced across the velvet sky, with atop the tall tower the sign, "Dreamland," blinking. A truly astonishing sight. It wasn't just the sign. Thousands of electric lights shimmered atop castles and towers and more modern peaks.

"What are you thinking, Peggy?"

"It's beautiful," I whispered. "Like something from another planet."

"It's future," he said, his arm tightening around me. "Everything I seek. No more thoughts of past."

I peered at his profile and sensed the sadness returning. "You don't like the past," I said softly.

He didn't answer for a long time. Stefan gestured at the dark ocean and said, "I never was near sea growing up, but twice to see grandmother. My father took me when I was child. She lived in village on coast of Dalmatia. The second time we went it was day of sacred holiday. Everyone in village puts on clothes of long ago, walks on path on the sea, but most important, carries weapons used to fight Turks in front of them as they walk. It's – how you say – procession. Every year on that day."

Thanks to my indifferent grades in history and geography, I wasn't sure where Dalmatia was in Europe, and I knew little about the Turks except they weren't supposed to be at all nice. Some response to this seemed necessary, so I offered, "They have a deep respect for the past."

"Respect?" he said, with a ferocity I'd not heard in him. "Yes – they respect!" His laugh was bitter.

I had a sense that I was sitting very close to someone I didn't understand whatsoever. But before my feelings for Stefan had a chance to chill, he cupped my face in his hands. "You Americans don't know of such things," he said, and kissed my forehead with exquisite gentleness. Time on the beach came to a lurching stop. I wanted more than anything else for Stefan to kiss me on the lips. For a few delicious seconds, it seemed he would, but instead he pulled away and helped me to my feet.

We walked for a while, the crowd thinning, but I couldn't see too far ahead on the promenade because of a large group of young women directly in front of us. That is why I didn't see the man in the Pinkerton's uniform until we were almost upon him.

"It's guests of the hotels only, after this point," he said sternly. We were a couple that didn't necessarily look like we belonged at the Oriental.

"I am a guest," I said.

"And you?" said the Pinkerton guard to Stefan.

"Her escort," he said, and with that voice he seemed to arouse suspicion. The guard stared at him, and Stefan glared back.

After a few seconds of this, the Pinkerton guard said, "I'll need your names, and then it will have to be confirmed that you are hotel guests before you can proceed."

Stefan dropped my hand; I could feel his mounting anger. But to me, there seemed no other option but to tell the truth.

I said, "I am a guest at the Oriental Hotel, my name is Peggy Batternberg, and my party includes Mr. David Batternberg, Mrs. Jonathan Batternberg, and others. This man" – I realized with a start I had no idea of his last name – "is my friend, seeing me safely to the door of the hotel." I paused a few seconds and said, "I wouldn't want to have to complain to the owner, Mr. Frank Lancet, that we were treated with any lack of respect."

The Pinkerton guard stepped aside and conferred with another, who'd hurried over when he saw a confrontation brewing. The minutes ticked by, during which Stefan said nothing but stared off toward the ocean, tense. I was filled with nervousness myself, certain that now he knew my last name, Stefan would feel deceived.

The guard returned and said, "Very well, Miss Batternberg. We will send word to the hotel that you and your escort are on your way."

We were waved through, but I waited, in dread, for a reaction. When it came, Stefan said only, "You handled him well. American women so bold."

Was it possible that Stefan had never heard the name Batternberg – or Vanderbilt or Rockefeller or Astor? What a sublime feeling it was, to not be judged because of my name. It was very freeing. But I couldn't fully enjoy it, for Stefan still seemed angry.

"You didn't care for that Pinkerton guard," I said.

"He is police, and no, I am not fond police, with good reason." He took my hand again. "I will put aside for you."

We passed the Brighton Beach Hotel and kept walking as I mulled over the contradictions of this talented, sensitive man. But I had a more immediate problem. We approached the Manhattan Beach Hotel in all its massive grandeur – and the Oriental was more elegant still. How would I explain that Peggy the shop girl was staying there?

Desperate to delay this moment, I tugged on Stefan's hand. "Come, let's find a spot to look at Dreamland one more time," I said. He smiled in agreement.

After we passed a line of bathing pavilions and the Manhattan Hotel itself, there was a stretch of open beach and another of those long snaking pilings. We hopped off the boardwalk and once again found a place to sit near the water.

"It's a little smaller in size now, but not faint at all," I said. This time, I was the one who pointed to Dreamland, shimmering in the distance.

Tentatively, hopefully, I lay my head on his shoulder.

I wanted Stefan to kiss me, and when he did, his lips searching for mine, I felt as if my heart were hammering so loudly he'd have to hear it, have to know it. I had never been kissed like this. His fingers were caressing the side of my face, running through my hair, and I was holding him tightly, certain that in our fumbling, ecstatic excitement, we were in danger of collapsing into the sand.

Suddenly his arms dropped; he rose and took a few steps back toward the boardwalk.

"What is it?" I asked, starting to follow.

"A man – watching," Stefan said. "He may have been following us."

I turned to see what Stefan saw, but I couldn't make out any man at all. I did see a couple walking past us, higher up the beach. Coming from the boardwalk, I heard the sounds of a group of people talking, of laughter.

"He is gone," Stefan said, peering across the sand. "But for moment, he was there."

CHAPTER NINE

"It's my fault," said Stefan, shaking his head as he turned back to me.

"What is?"

"To behave so in public place—" He reached out and took both my hands in his and swung them back and forth. "You are too beautiful." He pulled me toward him, but his kiss was for my cheek, and I knew that our dizzying embrace was over for the night.

I said, "Well, thank you, but … I'm not beautiful."

Stefan laughed. "Again, you degrade! I sit near booth, nothing. No one stops for hours. And then – I cannot believe, but an angel appears, you, a gorgeous angel, so young but understands everything."

He put his arm around my waist and guided me up the beach as I tried, and failed, to think of something to say in response. We reached the top of the wood pilings, and he looked around one more time and, following his lead, I did too, but I didn't see any man spying on us. There were people about, not a great many, but some, for it wasn't all that late. No one seemed focused on Stefan and me, and I said as much to him.

"I thought I saw someone before, too," Stefan said. "But yes, gone now."

We found the steps that led to the boardwalk, a few grains of sand in my shoes. The irritation was the least of my problems. I felt a sickening dread, for there, rising on our left, was the colossal Oriental Hotel. The first two establishments had been set back farther from the pathway; of the trio, the Oriental stood nearest to the ocean. It seemed as if every light was on inside the hotel, and at least fifty glowing lamp posts surrounded it. There was some sort of musical performance inside; the sound of violins rolled across the dark, fragrant lawn. With the music, the lights, the exotic Moorish spires up top, the sheer size, it looked like a magical palace. This was where Shahrazad spun her tales for the King; or where Henry VIII wooed Anne Boleyn.

Stefan had accepted without question my explanation of staying with my family at a hotel in Brooklyn. I had no idea what he was expecting – some clapboard three-story house with a "Rooms for Rent" sign in the window? – but it couldn't be this. I had taken such joy in being nothing but a shop girl for a few hours, of escaping from my life as "the black sheep of the black sheep," as Ben so memorably put it. A heavy burden had floated off my shoulders. I hadn't looked ahead even a couple of hours, and now there could be a price to pay.

I snuck a sideways glance at Stefan. I drank in his high cheekbones, the tousle of hair hanging over his forehead. He smiled and squeezed my hand.

"You must tell me where you stay," he said. "Are we close?"

Wildly, I thought of picking a different building and pretending to go inside, but of course that wouldn't work.

I stopped walking and pointed up the lawn at the Oriental Hotel. "That's the place."

Stefan glanced up, and started laughing, appreciatively, at my joke. I felt sick to my stomach as his laughter died down and he looked at me, sharply, and then the hotel.

"You not worker at hotel?" he asked.

"No, I'm staying there with my family."

He paused, and said, "What was name you gave that police?"

"Batternberg." I took a deep breath. "I've been working at the bookstore for five months, but not for the salary. I didn't have a salary. My family didn't even want me to take a job at all. It wasn't... necessary."

He was silent for what seemed like a good minute. I felt him withdrawing from me, as he stood tall on the boardwalk, no doubt thinking over our conversation throughout the purchase of the art and our dinner and our walking through Coney Island, all my evasions, the things I should have known how to do and didn't. At last he said, "Your family, what they do to make living – not my business, Peggy."

My God, I should have left it at that. But to rectify my earlier dishonesty with complete openness, I stammered, "I want you to know, Stefan, because meeting you – our dinner – everything, it's meant a great deal to me. My family, we, I, we... I don't get on well with them. I'm here in Brooklyn because they pretty much forced me to. Not forced, but they said they had to have me with them." The words were tumbling out in a pathetic rush. "I don't want to say why – it's too complicated. But here I am, all summer."

He shook his head, mystified. "All summer here?" he repeated.

"My father's family, the Batternbergs, we're in mining."

"In mining?" he repeated my phrase again.

If only this were just a matter of the language. My mouth dry, I said, "We own mines."

Stefan took a step back, then another. He said something, but it was not in English, nor Italian, but in a tongue of short, muffled vowels and consonants as sharp as knives. After a few sentences he returned to English. "There is name for this," he said. "There is name. You are slumming with me, yes?"

97

"No," I said, horrified, coming toward him, my hands outstretched. "That's not the case. Not at all. Not in the least."

He continued to retreat. It was night, but by the light of the lamps that surrounded the Oriental, I could see his eyes glittering strangely.

"Let me explain," I said, while realizing it was futile, for hadn't I just tried to explain? I kept making things worse.

He took a deep breath and said, "Peggy, I will say goodbye here, not take you inside. I think that best for you. I wish to say, thank you for pleasant evening. Good night."

With that, he turned and began walking, quickly, back toward Coney Island.

"Stefan?" I called out.

He did not turn around or stop.

"Stefan!" It flew out, a loud, desperate cry. And still his pace did not falter. I was vaguely aware of a group of people standing between us, and that my shouting of his name had made their own conversation cease. I twirled around, my face hot, and hurried to find the pathway leading to the hotel entrance. Once I found it I stood there, the violin music in front of me and the soft lapping of water behind me, stunned. I had gambled that, in the end, being completely honest with Stefan was the best course to take, and I lost.

I muttered, "Oh, pull yourself together, Peggy." In a little while, I told myself, I wouldn't think about Stefan any longer. After all, I didn't even know his last name.

Still holding the stringed package of his paintings, I moved through the lobby, past a few dozen couples dancing in a small ballroom to an orchestra. The men all wore dark suits and the women long, flowing dresses, jewels sparkling at their bosoms and feathers in their hair – yes, feathers. The heels of the men's shoes clicked on the polished floor, and I thought about Stefan, and how it felt to waltz on that wooden platform, his fingers on the small of my back, guiding me with his own form of gallantry. Something inside me stirred, a sense of genuine grief, and I feared that what happened today was not something I'd forget about in a short while.

Up on my floor, walking the silent, carpeted passageway, I braced myself for the confrontations with family, the demands to know where I'd been and how I could be so selfish and oblivious. I was in no mood for this. I certainly wouldn't seek anyone out on the way to my room, but if they came to me, wagging their fingers, I'd react in a way not soon forgotten.

I set down Stefan's paintings next to the dresser; I' d look at them tomorrow. Just now it felt like too much to cope with. Alice had thoughtfully left me a pitcher of cool water on the table. I poured a glass and gulped it quickly. I hadn't had anything to drink since the beer with dinner; I could almost taste the salt in the air during our long walk. I poured another glass and glanced at the clock. It was ten thirty. How incredible that so much had happened to me in just a few hours.

A gentle thump on the door made me slam the glass down on the maple-wood table. Whoever this was, he or she would be sorry.

When I opened the door, though, it was to the last person I expected: Helen, my Uncle David's wife.

"So you came back alone," she said.

I reluctantly gestured for her to come in and then answered, "Yes. Yes, I did. And what does everyone else say about that?"

"Nothing," she said mildly. "How could they? Absolutely no one else is here in the hotel – just myself."

"They didn't send you down to question me?"

"No." Aunt Helen took the chair by the open window, smoothing her brown hair gathered up in a tight bun. Evidently, she was in the mood to have a talk.

"Where's Uncle David?" I asked.

"Oh, he left at eight o'clock, to find all of you in Coney Island. He was concerned."

I poured my aunt a glass of water. "About what?"

"Not what, who. The same person he is always most concerned about – and who I think concerns you too, Peggy. It's Ben." She drank her water delicately.

Aunt Helen was a second wife, coming from a family that, though of course respectable, was not anywhere as wealthy as the Batternbergs or as grand as my mother's clan. Helen hadn't given birth to any children, and her three stepchildren were not easy people. My uncle himself had his difficult moments, and there were those whispers I'd heard when I was a little girl about the unpleasant scandal Uncle David caused once upon a time. It probably didn't matter, since it was long ago. Helen always spoke and behaved with a smiling blandness, so as not to risk giving anyone even a second of offense. I had thought of her as deeply boring. And yet now she seemed willing to dive into a discussion of the most dangerous Batternberg of all.

Curious about where this would lead, I said, "I had a bit of a falling out with Ben tonight; that's why I parted ways from him and Paul and Lawrence and saw Coney Island on my own."

She studied me for a minute. "Hmmmm. You look different to me."

"Oh?"

"You're rarely in a good mood, Peggy. I'm not saying that, all things considered, I blame you for being of a sullen disposition, and I hope you don't mind my being so forthright?"

"I don't mind at all," I said, dryly.

"But you're quite altered tonight, and it's not just that your hair is everywhere. The look in your eye, your entire expression."

Was this change in me due to meeting Stefan? I wondered. But I didn't want to tell my aunt about him. Stefan was a precious secret to me.

"Why is Uncle David so concerned about Ben?" I asked. "He's a grown man. Twenty-five years old."

"Oh, come now, Peggy. He's worried about what Ben is doing, what he's planning next. He is the one who knows what Ben is really capable of – though I have always suspected that if there were anyone else besides David and myself who knew something about that, it'd be you."

I looked away. This was no longer diverting – Aunt Helen was entering tricky territory.

I said, "Whatever Ben's character flaws, Coney Island is vast, I don't know how Uncle David expects to find them. But I'm sure they'll all return in one piece."

She nodded as if my deflecting her were no different than what she'd expected. "You know that tomorrow we're planning a croquet game first thing in the morning?" she said. "Then there will be a picnic and other family activities before the Independence Day fireworks."

"Good God, how tedious."

"If you're as worried about Ben pulling Lawrence into his camp as I believe you are, I suggest you be part of things tomorrow," she said.

Now I was impressed.

I didn't want to confide in my aunt by marriage – God, look how being forthright had mucked everything up just now on the boardwalk – but I was heartened to find this ally in the family. We were, in different ways, outsiders.

"Very well. If I've much to do, then I'd better get to bed," I said, and, obligingly, Helen rose to leave. "But where are Mother and Lydia? You said they're not in the hotel either?"

"No, after dinner Henry said he'd be spending the evening with his mother, so your mother and Lydia decided to go over to the Manhattan Beach Hotel, to hear a musical program."

That gave me something more to think about after Helen left. So Henry had chosen to spend the evening with his mother and hadn't brought Lydia along. Things definitely weren't going well. What had Ben said? "They're going to need that inheritance of yours from Grandfather to live on, if Henry Taul bounces away."

As I changed into my silk nightgown and washed my face and brushed out my hair, I reflected on my feelings about money. If it came to it, of course I would help my mother, and Lydia and Lawrence, by diverting my inheritance income after I turned twenty-one. I wasn't a selfish monster. It had never occurred to me to shower money on the people at Moonrise Bookstore. No one there had ever hinted at wanting it either, even those few who knew full well about my background, like Sylvie. To suspect the people at Moonrise of fattening me up for the kill was not only offensive – it showed how little they understood the world of books.

It was my family's behavior, the way they schemed behind my back, which was the problem. It would be best for everyone, me most of all, if Henry Taul married Lydia. Although I'd said I was coming along this summer to help in her quest to marry him, there had quivered a stubborn doubt inside. I just didn't like the man.

Well, I needed to banish that qualm. If they wed, Mother would have all the money she'd ever need, and I'd be left in peace. I could get my job back at Moonrise Bookstore and hopefully live with my former teacher again, or someone else deemed suitable.

Whatever could be done to nudge the couple in the right direction, I should do it, no matter my personal distaste for Henry Taul.

CHAPTER TEN

It was while getting ready for bed, my fingers full of cream massaged into my elbows, that I had an idea. I could try to see Stefan again after I returned to my job at Moonrise at the end of the summer. Hopefully he would have gotten over his surprise and anger at my pretense. Then I'd be a shop girl again – no ploy. Of course, I'd be a shop girl with a sizable bank account, but that could be dealt with. I'd find a way to meet him again, perhaps a café would do.

In no time my imagination was going wild. I could picture Stefan coming into the store at closing time and whisking me off to dinner. And more than that. As I lay in bed, drifting to sleep, I relived our kiss on the beach.

To think of Stefan at night was one thing, but his face was the first thing I pictured when I woke up, and his words echoed in my head as I ate my breakfast of fresh strawberries and buttered toast Alice brought me with tea. It was unsettling. As pleasant as it was to occupy myself with thoughts of Stefan, we hadn't parted on the best of terms. In the light of day, I wasn't that certain I would be a welcome sight to him. I remembered the buxom girl with the red curls on the Coney Island platform, and jealousy curdled.

I joined Mother, Lydia, and Aunt Helen to walk to the croquet grounds reserved for our Independence Day morning. We all wore our croquet skirts, light and full and a good five inches above the ground to accommodate play. I'd found another hat.

We could all see the field as we drew closer. It was marked off at the top of a low hill with a line of trees on one side and a row of shrubbery at the back end, I suppose to give us a sense of privacy while we played. As if a croquet game could be that important.

Lydia asked politely about my evening at Coney Island; I gave her a vague reply. When I reciprocated with a question about her musical evening at the Manhattan Hotel, she said, brightly, "It was lovely. Wonderful pianist. And we met some very nice people. A brother and sister who live on Fifty-Second Street. Mother and I both liked them."

I had to admire her spirit. Her engagement to Henry Taul was a fraught one, with frustrations of which everyone in the family was all too aware, but she had no intention of letting on how hard this was to cope with, even if it was while walking on the grounds of the hotel in the company of Mother, myself, and Aunt Helen.

Uncle David awaited us, along with the two teenage hotel employees who must have been assigned to our game. When we reached my uncle he smiled, although I spotted dark shadows under his eyes and fresh lines along his cheeks. I wondered what happened last night, how long it had taken him to find his sons and nephew, if indeed he ever had. I expected him to say something about my behavior last night, but he didn't.

We went about choosing our balls and mallets, gravitating toward our favorite colors. I picked green, as always, and it came back to me then, how this was the game our two families had played all the summers of my childhood. The two brothers, David and Jonathan Batternberg, took a mock-serious competitive attitude toward croquet, while making sure the children had their moments of glory. It was nice to bask in a pleasant memory of Father for a change.

I heard male voices behind me. Turning, I saw my cousin Ben appear, followed by Paul. My heart sank at the sight of Lawrence also walking deferentially behind Ben.

"Someone will have to sit out," announced Lydia. "Six is the maximum."

My mother immediately withdrew – since my father had liked croquet, she of course abhorred playing – and we had our six. Mother made herself comfortable in a chair beneath a tree, to watch.

"You first, Lawrence, you're the youngest," Uncle David said.

My brother always hated that distinction – of being singled out as the youngest of the grandchildren – and I expected him to scowl, but he didn't seem to mind today. I glanced at Ben, only to catch him watching me. At the moment, everyone was acting as if they didn't know I'd broken away from the family in a fury yesterday, and perhaps some of them didn't know, but there were sure to be words between Ben and myself before Independence Day was over.

Lawrence smacked his mallet against the stick to send his blue ball flying wildly, followed by Lydia, with a much more controlled stroke propelling her yellow ball just where she wanted it to go. Before the next person could launch onto the course, we were joined by Henry Taul.

If my uncle moved slowly, Henry was acting like something plugged into an electrical current. He leaped up the hill to join us, a joke on his lips, his eyes flashing behind his spectacles.

Ben drawled, "I think you need to play next, Henry. There's no holding you back. Now we can't have more than six playing, so—"

"I'll sit out," offered my Aunt Helen.

"Oh, we can't have that," Ben said. "Paul will sit out. The world couldn't be deprived of seeing your ankles on the croquet field."

It was a flash of a few seconds, a look exchanged, but what I saw was unmistakable. Helen and her stepson Ben hated each other. Why didn't my Uncle David do something about this? Without being too obvious, I looked at my uncle. He was fidgeting with his croquet mallet. I wondered if he were deliberately trying to avoid confrontation with his oldest son.

"Be with you in a minute, darling," Henry shouted to Lydia, who bobbed a little curtsey. Only my sister could curtsey in a croquet skirt and not look ridiculous.

Henry took a mallet but, before hitting his first stroke, he took three deep breaths, as if he were trying to calm down. I wondered what could have excited Henry so, on a summer morning well before ten, to warrant needing to subdue himself enough to hit the black croquet ball. When he did hit the stick, his ball was much like the man: full of force, heading in a direction only he understood.

"And now is the moment for our precious Peggy," announced Ben.

With that, a rebellion stirred. "Who designated you the boss of the order?" I asked.

"Just trying to be of help," he said. I took a closer look and noticed Ben had purple shadows under his eyes. It had been a late night for him as well.

"Margaret, please don't pick a fight with Ben – we're trying to have a nice day," my mother said from her shady retreat.

Pick a fight?

I peered over at Uncle David and his wife, hoping they'd say something, do something to back me. But they were both silent, each of them staring at the grass. Were they actually afraid of Ben?

"Come on, Peggy," shouted my brother impatiently. "Let's go!"

It wasn't my brother, or Ben, or my mother, or my aunt and uncle who forced me back into line, but the sight of my sister, out on the croquet field, not far – but far enough – from Henry. I'd made a decision last night, to do all I could to push these two closer together. My creating a scene this morning wouldn't serve that goal.

The hotel boy handed me my green ball, I placed it on the other side of the wooden stick driven deep into the soil, took a step back, aimed, and hit it. Mine was the worst stroke yet today, worse than Lawrence's. It sputtered in a direction nowhere near the first wicket.

Soon enough we were all on the field, taking our turns, accruing advantages, under the July sun. The perspiration gathering on my brow, for it was already a hot day. If not for my hat, tied under my chin, and my long sleeves, I'd probably have turned browner before the game was through. From my spot way out on the field, I could see the staff rolling a cart to our party, with pitchers of iced lemonade and rows of crystal glasses. Heaven forbid the Batternbergs drank anything out of less than perfect glasses. I thought of my beer last night, drunk from an old, chipped mug – that seemed like a different world.

As I once more dissolved into thoughts of Stefan, my ball careened into another's with a crack. It was Henry Taul's; the collision gave him a chance for points at my expense if he chose. He stalked toward me, and without saying a word, put his spats-covered foot over my ball, to hold it still while he made his penalty shot. When his mallet swung, it hit my green ball with such power that it sailed across the entire croquet ground, disappearing somewhere past the farthest boundary.

Everyone laughed, though I couldn't join in as my gaze tracked the direction of my ball. It had vanished. No one else had witnessed up close the intensity with which Henry slammed his mallet.

I couldn't find my green ball in the grass; I searched and searched. After a minute Henry appeared to join in the hunt, his upper lip damp with perspiration. "You're a lousy croquet player," he said.

"Oh, I know," I answered, not caring one bit. Looking back at the field, I took note of Lydia watching us, her mallet in both her hands. "Lydia's a fine player."

"Yes." His eyes fixed on my sister, he said, "She is superior to you in every way."

I took a sharp breath. I didn't want Henry for myself – I hadn't wanted him in years – but this was so staggeringly rude. And he didn't even seem to have said it with intent to hurt me. His tone was thoughtful, as if he were reminding himself of something.

"Well, if she is so perfect, then why don't you set a wedding date with her, Henry?" I said, before I could stop myself. "What on earth are you waiting for?"

He whipped to face me, taking a step closer. His eyes behind those spectacles were dark and malevolent, like a poisonous reptile's. It was all I could do to suppress a shudder. I found Henry repellent, and it was getting more and more difficult to conceal that.

He turned on his heel and strode back into the thick of the game.

"Don't wait for Peggy to find her ball – continue playing," he said.

Not wishing to return to croquet just now, I was glad enough to search for my ball underneath the shrubs. But there was no sign of it. In his athletic frenzy, Henry must have smashed the ball clear off the grounds for play. I felt embarrassed, although why on earth should I? He was the one responsible. I stepped through an opening in the shrubbery to continue the search.

The hill did not extend too much farther past the bushes. From its neat lines of decline, I perceived now that the hill was man made. But there was nothing artificial about the seashore I now faced. I drank in the bracing sting of the salt on the breeze, the smell of sea creatures whose names I didn't know.

Peering down to the boardwalk, I realized with a rush of pleasure that I wasn't far from the spot on the beach where I sat with Stefan and drank in the dazzling lights of Dreamland and kissed him. Looking closer, I spotted a group of people gathered around the same wood pilings we'd sat on. Quite a tight little group they were, not far from the water. I watched as a man ran from the boardwalk to join them. I tensed as I took note of the fact that the running man wore a uniform, the dark blue uniform of a New York City policeman. And there was another man in blue, one bending down on his knees in the sand in front of something. He looked distinctly familiar. My heart began a queer, jerky thump.

"Miss, I've found your ball," said a timid voice behind me.

I turned; it was one of the hotel boys assigned to our game. He held my green croquet ball in his right hand.

"Take it to them," I said, handing him my mallet. "This, too. And tell them I will be back in a moment."

"Who should I tell?" he asked nervously. My behavior must have struck him as bizarre, and he was unhappy at being the one to have to explain it.

"David Batternberg, Sarah Batternberg, Benjamin Batternberg, it doesn't matter. Any of them will do."

With that, I started down the hill, walking on none of the pathways but on the thick green grass, past the geranium beds, breaking into a trot as I headed toward that spot near the water where the people gathered.

CHAPTER ELEVEN

More and more people were gathering on the boardwalk, watching the two policemen confer on the sand, to the left of a smaller group in a tight circle. It was not unlike the crowd that Lawrence and I joined when they found the dead girl under the pier. There must be something extraordinary that they'd found in the sand to warrant summoning the police, but it couldn't be another corpse. My mind swiftly rejected that possibility. I pushed my way to the front of the group, a few inches from the steps leading to the sand.

What were they looking at? The object of interest, whatever it might be, wasn't in the water but on the sand, quite near the pilings where I sat with Stefan just about twelve hours ago. I couldn't see through that knot of people. For a frantic moment, I wondered if we'd left something behind that would draw spectators. But that was ludicrous; the police would not hurry to inspect one of my dropped handkerchiefs, even if I'd lost it. And, the knot in my stomach growing, it would have to be much longer than a handkerchief, based on the circumference of the crowd. At least five feet long.

"Pardon me," said a man's voice from behind.

I didn't move; I had no intention of yielding my place.

A hand tapped my shoulder. "Miss?"

I stiffened and slowly, warily, turned around. The white-haired owner of the hotel, Frank Lancet, stood behind me. "I do need to make my way down there," he said, apologetically. His eyes traveled down to my croquet skirt. "Were you interrupted by this disturbance? I am terribly sorry."

I wondered if he knew who I was, or if he just assumed, based on my sporting clothes, I was a guest.

"I'm fine, thank you," I said. "No need for concern."

He bowed his head and then shuffled past me, lowering himself – with some difficulty, considering his age and girth – onto the beach. He trudged toward the police.

"You know they found a dead woman down there," said a man behind me.

"Oh, no," said a woman's voice, shocked.

"I've been here since the first policeman came," the man replied. "They thought it was a woman sleeping rough, but when they looked closer, she was dead. And she's young."

Clearly this was the truth. I'd known it on some level when, from the back of the croquet field, I saw the people gather in a circle in the sand. But I found it terribly hard to accept, not only because this was the second dead woman found on the same stretch of Brooklyn beach, but also it was inches away from the spot where Stefan kissed me. There certainly hadn't been any dead women in the sand then.

There was a selfish part of me churning with resentment over the fact that the place we'd kissed had become the site of a horrible death and therefore spoiled. But beyond that, I was deeply unnerved.

Mr. Lancet trudged to the knot of people surrounding what I now knew was a corpse. One of the blue-uniformed police broke away to talk to him – I recognized him by his height and his black moustache. He was the officer who'd attended when the dead girl was pulled from the water.

I had to know what was happening.

Using not the stairs but jumping into the sand on the other side of the pilings, I hurried toward the water. *This is a bad idea*, a voice whispered in my head. But there were a few other people milling about the perimeter; with any luck, I wouldn't stand out.

By the time I was within earshot, the two men's voices were raised in anger.

"I won't have you bothering my guests," Mr. Lancet wagged his finger at the taller man. "This business has nothing to do with the Oriental."

"A serious police investigation is not 'bothering,'" retorted the officer. "And this is an inquiry into a homicide, not 'business.' The marks on the body indicate the woman was strangled, and it happened here. No one could move a body to this location out in the open, even in the middle of the night. It's possible someone saw something – an argument, a person acting suspiciously. We need to canvass the guests at both the Manhattan Beach Hotel and the Oriental Hotel."

"You're talking about thousands of people," sputtered Mr. Lancet. "Isn't it bad enough that you haven't moved that body off the beach yet? I've got heiresses coming down off the croquet field to see this!"

Ah, so Mr. Lancet had remembered me from the dining room, knew exactly who I was. I took a step back, realizing it might be best to hide behind another gawker on the scene. But there was no one within a few feet of me right now. If I darted behind someone else, the rush of movement might draw the attention of that policeman.

For the moment, thank God, the officer of the law was focused exclusively on the hotel owner, shaking his head, one of his hands hooked in his belt. "Mr. Lancet, what's happened here is a little more important than some heiress."

"You think so, Lieutenant Pellegrino? Well, that's where you're wrong. If I were you, I'd check with the precinct captain before setting foot in my hotel."

With that, Mr. Lancet turned and stalked back to the boardwalk. Fortunately, he didn't glance in my direction to observe the heiress in question half-crouched on the other side of the pilings. And the police officer, who I now knew was named Lieutenant Pellegrino, marched back toward his colleague, kicking the sand as he went. It seemed to be a standoff.

From my position, I could see something just past a man kneeling in the sand. The man wore what appeared to be a white doctor's coat. I saw a woman's leg, ending in a brown heeled shoe pointed to the side.

Standing there, bathed in the hot sun, an ice-cold prickling of fear ran up my arms.

All the way back up the hill to the croquet field, I thought of what Lieutenant Pellegrino said about wanting to find anyone who might have seen a suspicious man down at the beach last night. Wasn't that exactly what Stefan said – that someone was watching us, and that the same man might have followed us earlier? Did that man remain on the beach, hidden somewhere after we left, to kill this poor woman?

The police would want to know about this person, I was certain of it. But how could I inform the intimidating lieutenant that last night I was kissing a man by the water, whom I met a few hours earlier – a man whose last name I don't even know – while someone else watched? Even in my most defiant state, I recoiled from the prospect of my family being privy to this, and wouldn't the police feel duty bound to inform them?

The real sticking point was that I hadn't seen anyone suspicious with my own eyes. Only Stefan had. My knowledge was second-hand.

No, there wasn't anything helpful I could tell the police.

At the top of the hill, I pushed past the line of shrubbery to rejoin my family's croquet game. Not a single Batternberg remained, nor was there any sign of Henry Taul. Had I been gone that long? It didn't seem so. I waved down the only person still around, the hotel boy, the one who found my green ball, as he tidied the course.

"Where is everyone?" I was a bit out of breath.

"I don't know where they went, Miss. But something happened, and they stopped playing. They gathered in a group. Then they all left together."

"Was it something bad?"

Looking miserable, he said, "I'm sorry – I just don't know. I don't know anything."

"Very well," I said, turning to go, but he stretched out his hand.

"Please, Miss, don't tell anyone I wasn't helpful to you," he pleaded.

"Oh, why would I do that?" I snapped, and then, seeing the terror leap into his eyes, I reassured him that he wouldn't be mentioned. I always hated seeing such fear spring up in the people who served the Batternbergs, it was a grim reminder of how little they had and how much we had. With a word, we could destroy anyone's livelihood. I so relished working at the bookstore, where no one feared displeasing me. I never wanted to feel like Marie Antoinette.

Just a few steps up the path I spotted another variety of servant standing just off the path. It was Henry Taul's driver, the young man I'd seen for the first time in my family's Manhattan home. He was studying his fingernails and didn't seem to see me. Well, wherever Henry's entourage was, he'd be close by.

I retraced my walk to the main hotel, continuing to puzzle over their sudden departure. It didn't seem possible that my family's vanishing had something to do with the dead woman on the beach – or my being on that same bit of beach last night. However, if I'd learned one thing at Coney Island and Manhattan Beach, it was to be prepared for surprises, and not at all nice ones.

Passing through the lobby, I heard, "Peggy! Over here!"

In a corner of the lobby of the Oriental Hotel yawned a doorway that led to a dark bar. I approached it warily. Although the sun shone outside, and the lobby was bright, this bar only had a few lamps lit. Lounging inside it, standing at the gleaming wooden counter, were four males, acting jovial, whom I knew all too well: my cousin Benjamin, who'd called to me, and his brother Paul, my brother Lawrence, and Henry Taul.

"Isn't it a bit early?" I asked, pointing at the mug of foaming brown beer in Benjamin's hand. Lawrence, I took note of with a frown, was drinking too.

"Not when there's a celebration," Ben answered. "Just where did you disappear to?"

"I felt like a walk," I said.

"Spot anything of interest?" he asked.

Did Ben know about the woman in the sand? I studied his expression but there was only the usual sardonic amusement.

"I just felt like taking a break," I said. "I'm a terrible croquet player, haven't you heard?" I glanced over at Henry Taul, who was focused on drinking his beer. "What are we celebrating?"

"Oh, I think Henry should be the one to do the honors," said Ben.

Henry drained his beer to the last drop, set it down on the wooden counter with a thud – a good two inches from the elegant printed coaster – and wiped his mouth of suds with the back of his hand. I suppressed a shudder at this boorish display, so different from Stefan's old world manners last night.

"Lydia and I have set the date for our wedding," he said. "It will be 23 October, just after her eighteenth birthday."

"When did this happen?" I asked, very much confused.

"Henry and Lydia agreed to it right next to the third wicket on the croquet field," said Paul, who was trying, and failing, to conceal his smirk. He didn't possess his brother Ben's control.

"I'm happy to hear it," I said, forcing a smile. "Congratulations." Should I shake hands with Henry? How ghastly. I couldn't bring myself to stick out my hand, nor did he extend his.

"Thank you," he said shortly.

I was at a loss on what to say next. A silence settled over the group, which had been chatting happily up to the time I joined them. The only sound was made by the bartender, placing a row of little shot glasses on the empty shelf below the counter. He kept his head down while hurrying to set up his glasses with a series of soft thuds. One of the glasses collided with another, making a louder *clink*. His hand shot out to right the glass and still it before continuing to set up all the different glasses, the shakers, the miniature buckets of sliced lemons and limes. I suspected the hotel bar had not been open when the Batternbergs sauntered in, asking for beer, but of course this man had rushed in to serve. He was probably as afraid of displeasing the four careless young men as the croquet-field worker had been at earning my displeasure.

A thought stirred. I looked at the four of them, all well-educated presumably, and asked, "Does anyone know where Dalmatia is?"

Ben, who'd been drinking beer when I spoke, began coughing, and had to put down his drink. "What on earth?" he croaked, laughing. "You want to know the location of Dalmatia? Are you planning to tour the Balkans before lunch?"

"I was just wondering," I murmured. This was of limited help. The Balkans – now where was *that?* I realized Henry Taul stared at me with as much bafflement as Ben. I'd had enough of this bar. Turning to my brother, I said, "Lawrence, may I borrow you?"

"Now?" he groaned, looking at Benjamin as if for a rescue.

"Yes, go ahead," Ben said, slapping him on the back.

Now he needed Ben's permission. I could barely suppress my irritation as the two of us walked across the crowded lobby for the elevators. But I sensed that to criticize Lawrence for his slavish devotion to Ben would not bring about a desired result. I'd have to employ some strategy. Once we found an elevator and stepped inside, though, it was Lawrence who had words of criticism for *me*.

"We were worried about what happened to you last night, Peggy – why did you storm off like that?"

"'We'?" I responded.

In the disapproving tone of a man far older than his years, Lawrence said, "Ben thought you'd come back after you cooled down, so we waited and waited by the Dreamland entrance. Then we split up, me and Paul searching in a team and Ben on his own. When Uncle David showed up, he helped us for a while, but it's so big there! We never found you, and when Uncle David used a phone box to call Aunt Helen, she said you'd gone back to the hotel on your own."

This dressing down, coming from my spotty younger brother, was just too much.

"What a fuss!" I scoffed. "I am a grown woman, Lawrence, and perfectly capable of taking care of myself."

"It wasn't very considerate of you, Peggy," he scolded. "Ben told me the truth, that you've always been like that with him. When Father died, he dropped everything and spent all his time with you. Once you recovered from your grieving, you dropped *him*. You've hardly given him the time of day since."

At that I could do nothing but burst out laughing, which made the several other people sharing our elevator car, even the elevator operator, turn and stare at me, while my brother shook his head.

When we'd reached our floor, out in the hallway, I grabbed Lawrence by the arm. "That's not the way it was," I insisted. "Ben twists things, Lawrence. You have to listen to me. Don't spend a lot of time with him while we're here. You can't trust him – you just can't."

"Yes, that's just what Ben predicted you'd say, that he is the one who can't be trusted," Lawrence said, disgusted.

Speechless, I watched Lawrence make his way to his room, key in, and slam the door behind him. What a bungle.

I decided that I might as well find out what the rest of my family felt about me. I went to my mother's room, where I encountered a far different mood. Activity was at a fever pitch. Lydia and my aunt and uncle were trying to come up with a list of preliminary wedding guests. My mother had the telephone receiver in one hand and a pad of paper in the other. From what I could make out, she was trying to ascertain what places would be available for the wedding reception on the appointed day. The Waldorf Astoria led the pack, naturally.

Mother hung up, exasperated. "Why shouldn't anyone have answers for me?"

Uncle David said wryly, "Well, Sarah, it is a national holiday."

She didn't smile, much less laugh. "They'll be sorry when they've missed the wedding of the season." Turning to my sister, she said, "Go on with your list, Lydia. I need that number in order to narrow our choices to the leading five." She glanced at her timepiece. "We have twenty minutes before we should stop and switch to dressing for the picnic."

"Is that still on?" I asked.

No one answered me. It was as if I hadn't spoken.

"Are we holding the picnic?" I said, louder.

"Well, the menu has been altered," answered Uncle David with a grin. "Lobster, caviar, salads, cake, and champagne. I have to say, I hope the Oriental has a great many ice carts."

I announced I'd be going to my room to get changed. No one responded; I was entirely superfluous, after playing the most important part of anyone in this sorry drama. I was the one who provoked the groom to set the date, though no one but Henry and me knew it.

It was difficult for me to bathe and change for the picnic. I'd found my family more tolerable since Uncle David virtually kidnapped me from Moonrise, but that was finished. I should have felt disgust, the same sort that Lawrence exhibited toward me in the hallway. But what washed over me was weariness, as if I were seventy years old rather than twenty. Alice drew a bath for me. It helped cool me, but afterward, all I could do was dry myself, put on my slip, and sit before the dressing table mirror, slowly pulling a comb through my damp black hair. To arrange my hair, to select a dress, it all seemed like too much effort.

Last night Aunt Helen said I looked different. Had it by now retreated, that change in me due to several hours spent with Stefan? The more pleasurable sensations had receded a little in my memory – the oysters sliding down my throat as he watched, the feel of his fingers on the small of my back as we danced – and I was left with the look on his face as he said, "There is name for this, I will remember, yes. There is name. You are slumming with me, yes?" My God, that hurt.

On some level, though, wasn't Stefan right?

I threw down the brush and announced to the reflection in the mirror, "You are a terrible human being."

A knock sounded on my door, and I jumped in the chair. Had someone heard what I said? But a second later I realized there was no chance of anyone outside the thick door hearing my words, and I called out, "Come in." I half expected Aunt Helen, back for some more cryptic comments about Ben.

But it was my sister, exquisitely dressed, bejeweled, creamed, and powdered.

"You had more time than anyone to get ready and here you are," Lydia said, eyebrows raised.

"Here I am," I said and then, realizing she was waiting for some sort of explanation, I said, "It's been quite a day." An unwelcome image flashed before me, of the dead woman on the beach, and that brown shoe turned into the sand.

"It certainly has."

I realized how tactless I'd been, to make a point of the day thus far that didn't acknowledge her news, her triumph, what she'd been obsessed with accomplishing: a date to walk down the aisle. She didn't know about the woman in the sand, about my meeting Stefan last night, about anything. But she seemed to know... something. Lydia looked me over in the mirror, her face set in a cold mask. She was taking in my face, my hair, even my body showing in the slip. I couldn't think of another time she'd looked at me like this, so assessing.

"I think we should have a little talk," my sister said.

CHAPTER TWELVE

"What did you and Henry say to each other?" Lydia asked.

"When?"

"Out in the middle of the croquet field. The two of you exchange words, then you disappear and he heads right for me, looking absolutely furious, only to tell me that he and his mother decided last night on a wedding date and" – her voice dripped sarcasm – "he was going to tell me tonight, but now he just couldn't wait another moment to ask me if I agreed to the date."

"What's wrong with that?" I said.

"He may have spent last night with his mother, but he didn't decide on our date then, Peggy, come now – I'm not a fool. He was acting in response to you. I don't know why, but you have some sort of... hold over Henry."

"Lydia, I don't. Really. We don't even like each other."

She bit her nail and said, "I am well aware you don't like him. But as for what he feels for you..." Her voice trailed away.

I was determined not to tell her what I'd said to Henry that morning about setting the date. It was sure to distress her, to spoil things. I said, "What happened was, while he was searching for my ball, which he'd slammed into the next state practically, he told me I was a lousy croquet player. He got miffed when I made it clear I didn't care what he thought."

Lydia's eyes bored into mine. "Everyone seems to think they have to protect me, but I don't need that. I can take the truth, Peggy. No matter what he said, I can take it."

"That's what people always say," I said. "In my experience, they don't – not at all."

"Then there *is* something else."

I said nothing.

"I promise you that this is the last favor I will ever ask you," Lydia said. "Tell me."

The last favor? Something about that sparked a response in me, made me decide to stop my evasions. I liked the word *last*. If my services were no longer required by my family, perhaps I could leave the Oriental early, return to Manhattan. It wouldn't be necessary to wait until the autumn. That business about Henry's mother insisting I be part of the family this summer was utter nonsense. The woman hadn't deigned to set eyes on me. The wedding date was set; my work was finished.

I could be free.

Looking at her in the mirror, I told Lydia what transpired between Henry and myself, word for word. She took it calmly, but her eyes widened when I told her how Henry said she was superior to me in every way.

"You got what you wanted," I pointed out.

"Did I?"

I couldn't believe what I had just heard – was Lydia now having second thoughts about marrying Henry Taul? In response to what must have been my open-mouthed disbelief, she laughed. It was not a happy sound, more of a mocking; not of me, it seemed, but of others, perhaps even herself. And she wrung her hands as she stood there, laughing, her eyes darkening.

"Lydia," I cried, jumping to my feet and gripping her by the shoulders.

She shook me off and managed to stifle her laughter. "It's nothing – nothing." At the door to my room, she said, calm as could be, "I think we'll have to go on without you, but I'm sure you'll be able to find the picnic place. The concierge can tell you if necessary. It's reserved under our name."

It took me some time to gather myself. As I dressed and pinned my hair, not waiting for Alice to do it, I thought about nothing but Lydia. This was what I most feared, I realized, the real reason I came with the family this summer. I didn't like to talk about it – or even think about it – but there was an unpleasant reality in the family, and it had nothing to do with the Batternbergs.

My mother's family, the Donifers, had a history of mental disorder. We called the women "temperamental," "difficult," or even "hysterical," but it was more serious than that. One of my great-aunts had taken her life.

I didn't fear for my own sanity – if I were going to go mad, surely it would have happened by now. But I had for some years worried about Lydia. Even when she was a little girl, passionate about nothing but sports, there was a germ of something there.

The concierge pointed me in the right direction for our family affair. It didn't take me long to find the picnic, if you could call it that, under a taut white tent to the north of the hotel, near where Lawrence and I had ridden our bicycles that first afternoon. The tent was set back from the boardwalk, with a white rope stretching around the rectangular perimeter. I could see my relatives milling around on the other side of the rope.

Families strolled beneath the Batternberg tent, oblivious, with children waving little American flags. The bathing houses were packed, and the sand covered with people, for it had turned into a blazing hot afternoon. The sounds of splashing and laughter rippled off the beach. A perfect Fourth of July.

From this spot, I couldn't even see the stretch of beach where the police had gathered this morning; the shorefront curved. The celebrating crowds didn't seem aware of any murder. It was as if that had never happened.

Two hotel employees were posted at the entrance to the white tent. As I approached the entrance, where there was a gap in the white roping, one of them stepped toward me, shaking his head.

"Private party."

To my left, seemingly coming from the shrubbery, a low voice said, "She's one of them."

Sitting in a wooden chair off to the side was Henry Taul's flat-nosed driver again, wearing his uniform, as always. Smoking a long cigarette, he gave me a brief look. There was something familiar about his manner. But before I could think more about it, the apologetic hotel staff were ushering me into the family party.

Absolutely no one could have faulted the hotel for any aspect of its service to the Batternbergs that afternoon. There was a veritable train of ice carts, and an army of uniformed hotel employees besides. Uncle David kept pressing crisply folded bills into the hands of the waiters and all the other staff. Perhaps it was his generous tips that kept the food and drink flowing crazily, like a volcano exploding with lava. I confess that caviar is difficult for me to turn down, and I scooped little spoonfuls onto stiff crackers, taking pleasure in its salty richness.

I could feel something new in the air: a change in all the members of my family. Some tension had eased. They were like any other team celebrating the win of the season. If Henry Taul, who'd been finally dragged over the field goal line, sensed the profound relief in the air, he gave no sign of it. He seemed more relaxed, too. His voice was softer, his movements less aggressive than earlier in the day.

As for Lydia, she was the most at ease of all, standing at his side, smiling up at him, laughing at his jokes, sharing chaste kisses. The only thing that gave me pause was that Lydia did not eat a single bite, not at any time that I watched her. And she took only rare sips of champagne.

Getting a great deal of attention was my cousin Paul, who had brought along his prized possession, just delivered to his hotel room: a brand new camera that required no tripod. He carried it around, balanced before him, peering into the top of the black box of a machine before yelling, "Now!" and then snapping the shutter. Everyone submitted to being photographed, except for me. I've never cared for how I look in photographs.

Lawrence was having great fun helping Paul with his camera. Watching my brother, something occurred to me. I suspected the chief reason Benjamin was focused on him, feeding him lies, was that he thought it would upset me. He was using my brother. So I ignored Lawrence at the picnic, not angrily or sulkily, just treating him as if he didn't interest me. If I were honest with myself, this was how I'd felt about him until just a few days ago. The tactic had quite a good chance of working, I thought over my second glass of champagne – or was it my third? Like everyone else, with the exception of Lydia, I was having quite a lot to drink.

Three friends of Henry Taul suddenly appeared at the picnic, evidently at his invitation. I recognized two of the men from that first dinner. They had women with them now – wives or girlfriends hung on their arms.

It was highly unusual for strangers to come to a Batternberg party. We were such a tight-knit clan, and large enough, due to the six brothers and their families, that we didn't need to supplement our ranks. But it

went deeper than that, of course. Batternbergs didn't trust outsiders –
with only certain exceptions. I don't mean the executives who worked
at the family's mining firm. They were highly valued and well compen-
sated, but for whatever reason they never crossed the line and joined
us on social occasions. Only a school friend of a family member might
discreetly receive the go-ahead to join us.

These three brash young fellows and their companions would never
have passed muster, but the fact is, this was not just a Batternberg party.
Henry Taul was half of the equation now. Everyone would need to
adjust, and that afternoon the Batternbergs did just that.

Lydia continued to lead the way. The women who accompanied
Henry's three friends floated toward my sister, who was chatting them
up as any hostess would. They were thrilled. I could tell from the way
they looked at her face, hair, and clothes that these young women were
awed by her. Lydia was beautiful, and not just for a Batternberg. She was
beautiful by any standard. To marry someone right after turning eighteen,
it seemed a waste of a life to me. She could have been the toast of New
York City for years to come, celebrated along the entire East Coast. But
then again, her aim was to marry well, and she'd captured a man who
seemed, on the face of it, to be the supreme catch. Why not just proceed?

I am sure it appeared the smart thing to do, smarter than working
in a bookstore. But thinking of the agitation I'd detected, I suspected
another reason. The uncertainty of the marriage market, where girls had
so little control, could cause anguish. By marrying Henry this autumn,
Lydia was cutting the agony short.

The temperature was inching still higher, and at one point my Uncle
David sat down abruptly in a chair, sending his wife into a tizzy.

"You've had too much to drink and you know it," she said, fanning
his red face.

"Nonsense," he said faintly.

"If Dr. Mackenzie were here, you'd listen to him," she lamented. "You shouldn't have any alcohol in the heat, not when you're so very tired."

After drinking a glass of water, Uncle David insisted he felt better and rose to deal with a matter arising from one of the latest food trays being borne on a waiter's shoulder.

"Why is Uncle David especially tired?" I asked her.

"He didn't come to bed until past one o'clock," she answered.

That surprised me. "Why so late?" I asked. "Lawrence told me that Uncle David called you and you told him that I was back at the hotel. That couldn't have been too long after eleven. Didn't everyone come back then?"

Brushing something off the shoulder of her dress, she said, "Only Paul and Lawrence came back before midnight."

"And Ben?" I asked. "Did he come back to the Oriental the same time as his father?"

"No. He didn't."

Well, why would he have done that? I glanced over at my cousin, who at that moment was nowhere near Paul and Lawrence and their experiments with the new camera. Ben was standing on the periphery of Lydia's group. One of the young women, a brunette, had turned to talk to him. Under guise of having my glass of champagne refilled, I wandered over.

After topping my glass, the waiter approached the brunette and held the bottle, poised to pour. Ben made a gesture with his hand, as if encouraging her to imbibe.

"Oh, I just don't know," she said, with an uncertain smile. She was somewhere in her twenties, petite, with a large bosom. "If I have more to drink, I can't be sure that I'll be able to come up with enough intelligent conversation for a Batternberg."

"Would you be able to accomplish that feat even when you were dead sober?" he asked, tilting his head, smiling.

The brunette put a hand over her mouth, to cover her shocked laugh at his remark. Then her hand dropped and she smiled back, crookedly, her gaze traveling down his tall frame, ending with his prized Oxford shoes, gleaming, freshly polished, in the green grass.

He edged closer to her, bending down a bit to keep talking to her and her alone, and she turned more fully toward him, her back to the other female guests gathered with Lydia, and, beyond them, Henry Taul and whichever man she came to the picnic with.

How did Ben do it? How did he manage to sense which female would find not insulting but stimulating – even erotic – his brand of insulting banter? I had no more desire to occupy a front row to this performance, and, with my full glass of champagne, I moved to the spot closest to the boardwalk and the bay beyond.

I sipped and looked out over the distant rippling waves. There was a time when I laughed at Ben's jokes, cheered on his maneuvering, when I trusted him with my secrets. It was long ago.

The family turned to him to help me after Father died, and he was full of warmth and fun at the start. We had a repertoire of nicknames for each other; he said we would live like pirates, though now I had to wonder at my family thinking that our private games were beneficial. We were too old for pirates – but then, that very much depends on what kinds of pirates. Ben taught me how to ferret out the forbidden: steam open letters, pick locks, ease a phone off its cradle while holding a finger down. In our hideaways we drank cocktails, smoked cigarettes, and played cards as he made me laugh so hard my sides ached. His most cutting jokes were about members of our extended family, and he was utterly merciless. When he took control of our generation of Batternbergs, which he planned to do by the age of thirty, turning our older cousins into his minions, I would be his most trusted deputy, he swore.

A breeze caressed my cheeks as an unwanted memory surfaced. It was a cold, snow-covered day, completely unlike this one. I had fallen asleep with a book one afternoon, in a chair facing the window in Uncle David's brownstone, the third floor study, as a blizzard turned the sky grayish white. I felt the book being gently pulled from my hands, but instead of opening my eyes, I pretended to still be asleep. I don't know why.

Suddenly I was in the air. Ben carried me from the chair to the couch. "You'll get a crick in your neck in that chair," he said.

He laid me down, smoothing my skirts tangled up around me.

"I don't know if I can fall back asleep again," I said.

"Well, then." My cousin sat on the couch next to me, giving me a strange look. After a moment, he said, "Has any boy tried to kiss you?"

"Just one, and it was awful, just terrible," I said, heartbreakingly innocent.

"I think I should help you practice," Ben said. "Prepare you. It's really what any good cousin would do."

I closed my eyes to drive the memory from my mind, our first kiss but not our last. Just at that moment I became aware of someone standing next to me. *Let this not be Ben*, I prayed.

"Here, Peggy, your favorite," said Henry Taul.

I looked down at what was in his hand: a cracker heaped with caviar.

"I've already had plenty – way too much – but thank you."

"But the hotel boys finally brought out the beluga," he said. "You always loved it."

A small part of me feared we were treading on dangerous ground, but a larger part of me was tipsy, and it was hot, and Henry was being nicer than at any other time in the last week, not repellent at the moment. I took his offering. The caviar was supremely delicious.

"You like the finer things in life," he said, "though sometimes you pretend not to."

We really needed to stop talking about me at his engagement celebration to my sister. Still facing the boardwalk and the water, I said, "Do you know where the beluga comes from, Henry? Not the package, but the sturgeon itself?"

He answered, "From a lake that has salt water far away." He swung out his arm toward the Atlantic. "It's the Caspian Sea, bordered by Persia and smaller countries, and Russia. The Russians are the ones who developed the technique for catching the sturgeon and harvesting the eggs."

I seemed to have stumbled onto one of Henry's pet topics. I took another sip of champagne and said, "So you approve of Russians when they are making caviar on the other side of the world, not when they arrive in New York to live among us?"

Henry said, "That about sums it up."

I burst out laughing, and the next thing I knew my cousin Paul had leaped in front of us, cradling his stupid camera. "Smile, you two!" he shouted. "Stand closer together."

"No," I said, putting my hand up in front of my face. "I don't want my picture taken."

"Come on, Peggy," he whined.

"No, Paul. Go away."

He refused to budge. "I need to take your picture."

"Why? Because Ben told you to?"

He scowled. "I'm not leaving until I get your picture."

"No?" I lunged forward and knocked the camera out of his hands and onto the grass.

Shocked, Paul knelt before the camera. He picked it up and said to me, "You might have broken it, damn it. If this weren't grass, it would be in pieces."

"I told you to stop," I said, refusing to back down while realizing that I was creating quite a scene. Everyone at the picnic, including Henry's guests, male and female, stared at me.

I turned to Henry, whose gaze was unreadable behind his spectacles. "You're marrying into a rotten family, hope you realize that," I said. My words, to my mortification, were slurred.

"Margaret!" cried my mother. She was heading for me now, Lydia charging over too, and Uncle David wiping his face, when Henry waved both his arms as if he were at a sports match.

"Stop, everyone, it's fine – it's fine," he announced. "I'm not the least upset or put off." He glanced over at me. "I've known Peggy for a long time, and I'm well aware of how she can be, sometimes."

It was at that moment that Mr. Lancet, the hotel owner, appeared. He was ushered in by his staff, eager to make sure everything was to our satisfaction. He hadn't heard what Henry Taul had just said and didn't pick up on any family strain. The party lurched forward, with everyone ignoring me, the family embarrassment, until my Aunt Helen came over with a glass of water and guided me to a chair.

"Thank you," I murmured. I hated how Henry said, *"I'm well aware of how she can be."* But I was a mess. I wasn't in any position to make a case that I had behaved well a few minutes ago, or in the past.

I didn't want to have anything to do with anyone born Batternberg, and apparently the feeling was mutual.

CHAPTER THIRTEEN

One of the reasons Mr. Lancet came was to make sure we were aware that after sunset, we could watch the Independence Day fireworks from a promenade atop the main tower of the hotel, reserved for us. It was perhaps six o'clock at that point; we had a few hours to go before the pyrotechnics. I couldn't wait to get to my room.

I still felt wobbly on my feet when we left the picnic – my goodness, I really had had too much champagne in the heat. But as I walked, I strove to collect myself. There'd be no stumbling on the boardwalk, I vowed. A cold bath followed by hot tea, and I'd be fine.

I walked a few feet behind my Uncle David and Mr. Lancet. Their conversation drifted back to me, but I paid little attention until I heard the word "Dreamland."

"The fraud, the mismanagement, if I were to tell you even a fraction of what I'd heard these last seven years, ever since the place opened, you wouldn't believe it," said Mr. Lancet somberly. "From the beginning, it's been a sinkhole. I've heard rumors Dreamland might not survive another year, the losses are so serious."

Uncle David answered, "I had a look at that part of Coney Island last night, as a matter of fact, and it didn't look as if it were teetering."

"My good man, they wouldn't let *you* see it. They bury everything that isn't perfect at Dreamland, both the stories and the people whose lives have been shattered," responded the hotelier. "Like the world-famous lion tamer who entertained the crowds – that fellow who went by the name Captain Jack Bonavita. He had quite the setback here. A lion clawed one of his arms to shreds one day, right in front of all the little children. First time he's ever been unlucky like that in his life. The circus people panicked and took him to a quack doctor. Naturally an infection set in and at hospital they had to take off his entire arm. I'm sure you never heard *that* story. They hushed it up."

What an odious person this Mr. Lancet was, to gather up disgusting stories of his neighbor along the shoreline and disseminate them to guests. Who knew if any of it were true? I suppose Coney Island was nothing but an eyesore and source of potential trouble to these cynical moneymen who owned the large hotels. I thought sadly of the idealistic Stefan, holding my hand on the beach as we gazed in awe at the thousands of lights of that Coney Island park.

As we approached the main pathway leading up to the Oriental Hotel, a strange sight unfolded. A group of boys, perhaps twelve years old, ran up and down, waving bundles of newspapers in the air. They fanned out, one of them running right for us.

"Extra! Extra!" he shouted. "New York Herald extra edition – girl murdered in Manhattan Beach!"

Behind the newsboy a frantic hotel employee appeared, trying to chase him down. Other hotel workers were giving chase too. But startled people on the boardwalk were reaching for the extra, the single sheet that the boys had bunched up in their hands, pulling them from packs they had slung over their shoulders.

I pivoted into the path of the newsboy streaking toward us, no easy feat in my still-woozy state. He saw me coming for him and thrust a sheet into my hands and took a penny I quickly fished out for him before scrambling on, a red-faced hotel worker on his heels. I folded it in half and then halved again, to read as soon as I had a moment alone.

Mr. Lancet was creating a scene of his own after he lumbered onto the veranda. "I want them off the property – now!" he bellowed. "This is the work of that Italian police lieutenant. He's at the bottom of this!"

Hurrying past him into the lobby, I clutched the paper, scrunching it into a ball in my hand to hide it until I was up in my room. If Mr. Lancet wanted the newspaper story off the property, that was enough of a reason for me to bring it through the front door. I practically ran for an open elevator, leaving my family far behind.

Once I was alone, I opened my fist, now blackened with ink – this would have to be fresh newsprint. I didn't care. I smoothed out the front-page sheet. Among the other most important news articles of the day was a short boxed off story in the middle, within a thick black border. The headline read: *Darling of Dundas Street Strangled: Police in Search of Witnesses.*

The article itself read: *A girl of twenty-two years of age, Katherine O'Malley, the only child of Mr. and Mrs. Thomas Aloysius O'Malley of Dundas Street, was found on Manhattan Beach this morning, by passersby. Miss O'Malley met her untimely death by misadventure, announced Lieutenant Anthony Pellegrino of the Sixty-First Precinct of the New York Police Department. Marks on the girl's throat indicated strangulation. Miss O'Malley was a waitress at the establishment of Devlin's, on the Bowery Street of Coney Island. Her parents reported her missing at the police precinct early this morning. After Mr. O'Malley identified his only child at the mortuary, he was taken to Kings County Hospital with heart palpitations. Lieutenant Pellegrino asks that anyone who was in the vicinity of the beach south of*

Pier Fifteen, between the Oriental Hotel and the Manhattan Beach Hotel, between sunset and dawn, and observed any person acting suspiciously, to report with all possible speed to the Precinct House at 2575 Coney Island Avenue, Brooklyn, to be interviewed. This is the second young female employed by a Coney Island establishment to be found dead in a public place in three days. Beatrice Stompers, twenty years of age, was recovered from the water off Brighton Beach Pier on 2 July.. Police would not comment if the two victims knew each other or if there was any other connection.

Standing in the middle of the room, my ink-stained hands shook as I read the story twice, then a third time. My stomach, only moderately queasy up to now, seized up and turned over. I was in distinct danger of vomiting – I could taste the beluga caviar, crackers, and alcohol roiling in the back of my throat.

I closed my eyes, willing the nausea to pass, and to my relief, after a moment the worst of it did.

A young woman had been killed, a few feet from the spot where I embraced Stefan, and she was not a nameless corpse, but a real person, a girl cherished by her parents and her neighbors. I couldn't bear to contemplate the ordeal of her father, it was too horrific.

And I had shrugged off any responsibility for knowing anything about this. Instead, I'd gone off with my wretched family and drank champagne and quarreled over nothing, her death gone from my thoughts entirely. It was unconscionable.

As I scrubbed the ink off my hands in the gleaming porcelain sink, I thought about what happened on the beach the night before. I hadn't seen the man who hovered nearby but Stefan had. I remembered all too well how much he disliked legal authorities – *"He is police, and no, I am not fond police, with excellent reason"* – but we needed to help the police. There wasn't a choice.

Tomorrow, I would find my way back to Dreamland, to Stefan. He might not be too glad to see me, but I would find a way to apologize, calmly and with some dignity this time, and to persuade him to accompany me to the precinct.

Now that I had formed a plan, I wanted to pull myself together in every way. First, I craved a bath, but Alice hadn't yet appeared to draw it. I couldn't summon her directly – obviously there were no bells connecting my room to hers – but I could call down to the main desk and be put through to the maids' quarters and leave a message. She might already be off duty and enjoying the Fourth of July celebration, however. I could cope with starting a bath myself.

Squatting to the side of the large tub, I tried to turn the correct levers and handles in coordination, straining to remember how Alice had opened these pipes for the water to come gushing out, but no matter what I did, nothing worked. The pipes wheezed and clicked; no water appeared. Frustrated, perspiring, I pulled on one of the levers with all my strength. It didn't bring water, but I did fall off my heels, hard onto my rear end. For a few wobbly seconds I laughed out loud, all alone, at my ridiculousness. But the laughter caught in my throat, threatening to turn into tears. I was heading toward a sodden scene: sprawled on a washroom floor, sweaty, a little drunk, weeping in self-pity. I grimly resumed my battle with the bath, kneeling this time, and after a few more minutes, I succeeded.

The delicious shock of submerging myself in a bath of cold water knocked the tipsiness out of me. I scrubbed salts into my skin with industriousness, welcoming the pain. It was only then, after my head had fully cleared, that various aspects of the murder of Katherine O'Malley began to nag at me. How did she come to that part of the beach, between the Oriental and Manhattan Beach hotels? Thanks to the Pinkerton guard who'd questioned Stefan and myself, I knew that it wasn't easy to leave Coney Island for these properties. She wasn't a hotel guest – she lived in Brooklyn with her parents – so that meant Katherine must have crossed over in the company of a guest or found her way here some other way. Perhaps she was visiting a staff member at the hotel? But then, how did she end up in the sand late at night with a murderer? My mind went blank on that. And the news of the drowned woman of several days earlier relegated to the last sentences of the story, confused me. Surely that woman's drowning and the strangling of Katherine O'Malley were unrelated, even though both women were close to the same age and lived in the same city. I supposed they might have known each other. But as I'd said myself on that first day on the boardwalk with Lawrence, no one goes swimming wearing all their clothes. The possibility existed that she took her own life. But the water off the Brooklyn shoreline wasn't that turbulent. Someone would really have to put a lot of effort into suicide by walking into the ocean, and fully clothed.

Alice arrived, interrupting my morbid train of thought. It obviously surprised her that I'd drawn my own bath, and she didn't look pleased. I couldn't believe that Alice might think I'd try to take her duties away from her, render her superfluous. But just to be on the safe side, I asked her to fetch a complicated meal of black tea, toast, and, if possible, fresh fruit and steamed vegetables.

"Won't you be joining the others for the fireworks display, Miss?" she asked.

"No, I'm staying in for the night. As soon as you've found my supper, I hope you'll go out and enjoy the show."

Alice returned with a tray in double quick time – motivated, no doubt, by her desire to see the night's colorful display of rockets in the sky. As for me, I felt restored by consuming the tea, toast, and blueberries, in peaceful solitude. It wasn't until I finished the berries that I realized something rather unsettling. This whole regimen of a cold bath followed by black tea and fresh food was something imposed on me and my sister and my brother by our second German nanny, Magda. She'd been a fiercely unaffectionate woman but devoted to principles of good health that she learned in a school of German naturopathy. My parents, distracted, approved of her ideas and gave her a free hand. She was particularly convinced that cold baths and steamed vegetables stabilized moods and prevented disease. Oh, we hated that nanny more than any other. Yet now, when feeling upset and overheated and nauseous, I'd turned not to wisdom of my family but to a childhood cure of Magda's.

The sounds of the fireworks exploding, followed by *ooohs* and *aaahs*, streamed into my window, but I'd set my mind against all that. Nor did I want to contemplate the tragic murders or my meeting with Stefan tomorrow, which was already triggering a nervous quiver in the pit of my stomach. I lit a single candle and opened *The Wings of the Dove*, hoping it would occupy me. Thankfully, James' story succeeded in holding my interest. The main character was deeply in love with a man named Merton Desher, a handsome, intelligent, but penniless journalist, and she was trying to hide that fact from her family while meeting him in secret.

I half-expected some member of my own family to come knocking, but no one did, and I put the latch on the door before reading just one last chapter before bed. However, the heat and the unpleasant excitement of the day – and all the champagne, most likely – caught up with me, and I never made it to bed but fell asleep in the chair, the book in my lap.

I woke with a start, my heart pounding from a nightmare that dissolved before I could try to make sense of it. *The Wings of the Dove* was at my feet – apparently it slid off my lap while I slept. The flickering candle was only an inch high, the wax bubbling in the dish like a tiny volcano. I must have been asleep for quite a while, at least a couple of hours.

I bent down to pick up the novel and, as I did so, something caught my attention across the room, a movement. I rubbed my eyes, still thick-headed, and scanned the room.

The doorknob on the main door turned to the left, very slowly. Someone standing in the corridor, on the other side of the door, was trying to come into my room. I couldn't move or speak. It was as if I were frozen solid in this hot, airless room.

I hadn't locked the door from the inside – I couldn't believe my careless stupidity – but I'd pushed the latch across, of that I was sure. And so even though the knob turned this way and that, the door did not open as the seconds crawled by. The latch held.

Seeing that, I flew across the room to just inches from the door, safely on my side.

"Who is it?" I shouted. "What do you want?"

There was no sound from the other side; the doorknob did not turn.

I was shaking with fear yet, after working up my courage, I unlatched the door and yanked it open. I stepped out into the hall and looked this way and that, my right arm instinctively raised as if preparing to ward off a blow, but there was no one else there. All I saw was the closed doors of all the other members of the Batternberg family.

CHAPTER FOURTEEN

"Tell me," I said to Lydia. "Did anyone seem particularly angry at me last night?"

My younger sister, languidly stretched out on her settee, sipped coffee. It was already uncomfortably warm this morning, yet with her usual indifference to temperature, she chose hot, black, unsweetened coffee to drink. She said, "After a certain point, I don't think anyone mentioned you."

"And *before* that point?"

She shrugged. "Not much was said that I can remember. Nothing surprising, really. I told Paul that he'd been a perfect pest. Everyone knows you don't like to have your photograph taken."

"Thanks for sticking up," I said, relieved she wasn't holding a grudge for my blurting to Henry Taul he was marrying into a rotten family. "I don't look like you do in photographs, you know."

Lydia smiled complacently. Well, I *had* to butter her up before asking my favor. I still intended to follow through with my plan no matter what, but if she'd be my ally, I'd have a lot less to worry about back here in the hotel.

"Why do you care if anyone was mad at you?" she asked, alert with interest. That was one of the challenges of Lydia. Once something caught her curiosity, she could be single-minded about it, a dog with a bone, although my sister seemed more like a silky cat than a canine.

I took a deep breath and said, "At about two in the morning, someone turned the knob on my door as if they were trying to come in, but it was latched. I could see it happening – the knob turning. When I yelled, 'Who is it?' there wasn't any answer. I waited a bit and opened the door and looked out—"

"No, you didn't," Lydia cried, clutching her coffee. "I can't believe you, Peggy! I never would have had the nerve. Who did you see?"

"Nobody."

"So very strange." She thought for a moment. "Why would you assume it was one of us? You know there's a back staircase on the end of the corridor, so it isn't just the elevator and the operator letting us on and off. Someone could have used the stairs to come from another floor. Yes, that must be it." She shivered elaborately. "Just think what might have happened if you hadn't latched. You should tell Uncle David. And Mother."

The last thing I needed right now was closer watch of my movements. "I'll manage that," I said. "Don't say anything to anybody about it."

"Well, if that's what you want," she said.

Taking the plunge, I said, "There's something else I need to ask of you, Lydia. A big favor." I let the word hang in the air, hoping she would reflect on the fact that my being here – and, specifically, my pushing Henry to set a wedding date – was a humongous favor to her.

"I'm all ears," she said. Unfortunately, it was her cool gaze that most concerned me.

"I need to be away from the hotel for a number of hours this afternoon, and I don't want anyone bothering me about it, asking me questions. If you could say we spoke and, because I had a bit too much to drink last night, I was going to take it easy, take a long nap in my room…

That will help tremendously. And you can say you'll check on me, no one else need do so."

A frown line deepened between her eyes. "Are you leaving Brooklyn?"

"Oh no, I won't be far. Just not… here."

Lydia chose that moment to put the coffee cup in a saucer on the side table. She leaned toward me and said, "I will cover for you, Peggy. But only if you tell me what you're about."

I said quickly, "It's better for you not to know."

"And I think it's better that I *do* know," she countered.

I sat back in my chair, frustrated.

"You can trust me, Peggy," she said.

The trouble was, I couldn't. As much as I cared about my only sister – and I probably harbored more feeling for her than anyone else in this world drawing breath – I was incapable of putting my full trust in anyone born Batternberg. However, it seemed I would have to tell her something more to get her to help me today.

"All right. A man," I said. "I am meeting someone. And I don't want Mother or anyone else breathing down my back about it."

With that, Lydia was transformed. She sat upright, her pale skin flushed pink, her eyes sparkled. "A man! Who? When did you meet him? Not since we've come to the Oriental. You couldn't have."

"Do you remember when I went to Coney Island with Ben and the others? I wasn't with them after a certain point – I went off on my own. I met someone then."

She cupped her face in her hands. I could even get a close look at the reddened, bitten cuticles of her fingernails – she was too caught up in what I was telling her to remember to hide her hands. "I haven't set foot there, but Coney Island, Peggy? Really? What sort of man would you possibly meet there who you'd want to see again?"

This was the first time it dawned on me that, not only would my family look askance at my interest in a foreign artist, but such a social connection might reflect poorly on Lydia in the eyes of others, in particular her fiancé and of course the fearsome Mrs. Taul, who had yet to reveal herself. A wedding date might have been set, but until the ring was on her finger, I'd have to be careful.

"He's a journalist," I heard myself say. Thank God for Henry James and the love story I read last night.

"Ah, you *would* swoon over a writer," she said triumphantly. "But why be so secretive? He isn't one of those terrible gossip writers, is he? What do they call them – hacks?"

"Oh, no, no. He's quite… idealistic. But he doesn't have any money, Lydia. Newspapers don't pay too much."

She sighed. "Such a shame," said my practical sister. "But where did he go to school? If it's Princeton, Harvard, or Yale, that'll help."

I managed to hide my wry smile. In America, if a man either made a fortune or attended a ranking university, he was as good as anybody in New York. While across the Atlantic, no one could ever escape their humble beginnings. Or at least not according to *Wings of the Dove*.

"I don't know. I only met him once."

"And yet you managed to arrange another rendezvous – how impressive."

If Lydia knew my goal for this "rendezvous" with Stefan was a trip to the Coney Island police precinct, what would her reaction be then? I put that out of my mind as I thanked her for her help. Tugging playfully on my sleeve, she said, "I only demand one more piece of information, Peggy, and then I promise to play my part to perfection. What's his name?"

Looking her straight in the eye, I said, "Merton Desher."

She flinched. "He'd have to be mighty handsome to overcome a name like that."

And so, my disappearance explained, I slipped out of the Oriental at one o'clock in the afternoon – a time when my family would be lunching together at the neighboring Manhattan Beach Hotel, according to Lydia – to find my way to Coney Island. Mindful of the heat, I wore my coolest summer dress, white cotton with sleeves ending at the elbow, and my plainest hat this time, one with a wide, flat brim, and my hair pinned in a loose bun. I didn't want to call any attention to myself as I walked out the back, the same pathway I'd taken with Ben on the way to his motor car. A tall woman with long black hair tends to stand out, I feared.

I waved to a heavyset, incurious-looking man standing next to his horse and buggy at the stand, offering to convey passengers to Coney Island. With a grunt, he folded up his newspaper and helped me step into the buggy. It didn't seem to surprise him in the least that I was headed there alone. For all I knew, a stream of young women escaped their families every day to seek excitement in Coney Island.

The man delivered me to the gate of the amusement park *too* quickly. I paid him and stepped out of the buggy with a certain reluctance. I still hadn't a clear idea of what to say to Stefan. Disconnected sentences, or just phrases even, bobbed in my brain. I was pretty sure I could come up with a persuasive case for the two of us going to the police to share what we knew. But that shouldn't be the first thing out of my mouth. What should I say when he first laid eyes on me?

There weren't as many people surging through the park as when I first came to Coney Island – after all, that had been a weekend – but their shouts, laughter, and jostling were sufficiently intrusive to prevent more brooding over my reunion with Stefan. Weaving through Luna Park, it took me a while just to locate that enormous statue of the half-naked woman, holding up the word "Dreamland." On my way to finding the Creation Angel, I passed a stone bathing pavilion surging with what looked like thousands of people joyfully splashing in the water. Between the stone pillars I could spot them frolicking as the beads of perspiration trickled down my own back; how wonderful it'd be to feel cool water on my skin. The sun grew stronger by the minute. It had to be the hottest day of the year.

By the time I stepped under the archway to Dreamland and paid my ten cents admission, I felt positively lightheaded. This weakened state was not ideal. In search of relief, I joined the long queue outside a dining pavilion. At first, being there made me feel sicker. The odor of stale food and rank grease curdled my stomach. Once I reached the front of the queue I could manage to order only a large iced tea.

The instant my fingers closed around the tall chilled glass, I felt stronger. There wasn't a free table available, so I sipped my drink standing up, savoring not just its blend of taste, the bitter tea and jolt of sugar, but my square of shade. I looked out across Dreamland from this vantage point, seeing a different place than before. On Saturday, the afternoon's end and the slanting dusk had brought out the park's array of colors. Today, the buildings all radiated white. Under the cloudless blue sky, it was like standing in a valley of pyramids, but instead of the tallest of the ancient tombs taking precedent, it was that soaring white-and-gold Spanish tower at the far end. Across the way, beyond the Shoot the Chute waterway, squatted the exception to this pale parade: A black cavern stared at me with the words "Hell Gate" posted above and what could only be the statue of a winged demon leering at the park-goers. What would the Protestant preachers of New York and all their faithful, those who'd pressured the lawmakers to close race tracks as dens of iniquity, make of this? I had to assume they'd never seen it, never forsaken the pew for the dangerous delights of Dreamland.

Once I'd drained the last drop of cold tea, I stepped out of the shade. I was refreshed and ready – or as ready as I'd ever be. I made my way past "Alps of Switzerland" to the Art of Coney Island building. It occurred to me that, for someone who loved the new world promise of America, Stefan had picked a place that showcased other parts of the globe. I still hadn't made up my mind what to say, but I refused to let that stop me. And now here I was, standing in front of the small art building once more, tingling with excitement. A foursome paused in the doorway, and I held back, impatiently waiting for them to step all the way through before following.

"So you've come back for more of him – what a nerve that takes," a woman said, inches to my left.

I flinched at that; it was so close to what I was poised to do, the coincidence startled me. Or was it a coincidence? I turned toward the person who'd spoken. It took me but a few seconds to place her. The first time I'd laid eyes on this woman, when she called out to Stefan from the platform, she stood out, and now she was even more of a shock to the eyes, among the light, loose summer dresses of other females flitting about. Her emerald-green dress was not just belted but tightly fitted, particularly at the plunging neckline that left little to the imagination. Her long, copper-colored curls cascaded over her shoulders. The feathered silk green hat perched atop her red head was completely absurd for this time of day and this occasion. But as her eyes traveled up and down my figure, a sneer on her rouged lips, the suitability of this woman's hat was the least of my problems.

"I beg your pardon?" I said coldly.

"Oh, isn't she high and mighty," said the red-haired woman, with a mocking titter. "No, I won't be handing over my pardon, Missy. Not after what you did."

She took a step closer to me and said, "You don't belong here."

CHAPTER FIFTEEN

I was dismayed by the knowledge that Stefan must have confided in this person. They had to be close indeed. But I was also deeply offended. To be waylaid like this by someone – insulted in public!

"I've nothing to say to *you*," I snapped, and stepped into the building, the entrance now clear. I walked quickly past the photographic area, toward "The Futurist" sign, without a backward glance.

Now my pulse raced for a myriad of reasons, but when I pushed aside the curtain cordoning off Stefan's work from the rest of the exhibits, I faced a setback. Stefan was nowhere in sight. In front of his paintings, sitting on a stool pulled up to the counter, was another female, this one not much more than a child. She stared down at a newspaper spread out in front of her, her lips moving as she read, and glanced up when she realized someone had stepped into the area. No flicker of recognition – much less hostility – animated her light blue eyes, set close together across the bumpy bridge of a nose in a narrow face. It seemed safe to assume this girl knew nothing of my existence.

"I am looking for Stefan, the artist," I said.

"He not here now," she said in a strong accent, one similar to his, and her eyes returned to her newspaper. I would have guessed her to be thirteen.

"Do you know where he is this afternoon?" I persisted. I'd gone to such trouble to get here, I hated the thought of slinking back to the hotel.

Without looking up, she said, "On pavilion with pushcart. His shift to sell sausages."

"Sausages?" I repeated.

"What – selling sausages not good enough for you?" My nemesis, the redhead clad in green, had followed me to continue her harangue. "No, I bet it isn't. How do you think he pays for room and board, for the dinner he bought you?" She waved dismissively at the wall of paintings hanging behind the counter. "That stuff sure doesn't put a roof over anyone's head!"

Now I was not just irritated but really angry.

"The 'stuff' you refer to is art, and art of incredible talent and vision," I said, my hand on my hip. Observing her more closely, I wasn't surprised by her inability to appreciate Stefan's creations. Her beauty was crude – and somewhat artificial. A layer of cosmetics spread across her face didn't completely conceal roughened skin. Russet lip rouge couldn't compensate for crooked lower teeth, either.

I turned back to the blonde girl. "If you could direct me to where Stefan is on the boardwalk, I'd appreciate it."

"Don't tell her, Marta!" hissed the woman at my side.

The girl looked at me, then at the other woman and back at me, interest sparking in her eyes. She said in her accented voice, surprisingly deep for someone so young and small, "Leave her alone, Louise. I take her to Stefan. Up to him, not you."

To my surprise, Louise turned away, muttering under her breath as she stalked back the way she'd come. This Marta somehow wielded authority. Now the girl resumed her study of the newspaper page.

Looking down, I realized she was reading a strip of the comic "Mutt and Jeff." She nodded as she came to the end, folded the newspaper carefully, and found a place for it in a box on the floor.

Without another word, she left the booth of "The Futurist" and I followed. Once we were out of the building entirely and moving toward the entrance to Dreamland, I quickened my pace to stand next to her. "I wish to thank you for doing this," I said.

Squinting in the bright sun, Marta said, "You like his art."

"Yes, very much."

Nodding, she said, "Art is soul for Stefan."

"Yes, well, this other… individual doesn't seem to grasp that fact. I'm sorry you had to be caught in the middle of such an unpleasant scene, Marta."

For a few seconds she looked up at me warily, as if she weren't completely sure of what I'd said, before shrugging and making a blowing noise with her lips, "Pfffftt."

With that, she led me out of Dreamland. I fell back behind Marta, as she expertly snaked her way through the milling crowd. She was as calm as Stefan in navigating Coney Island. There were two differences: A thin blonde braid bounced on her back as she walked, and she limped slightly. It concerned me to see the drag in her gait, but it definitely did not slow her down. I had to push through a stitch in my side to keep up.

Once we'd departed Dreamland, she turned not toward the long pier holding the restaurant and ballroom or the bathing pavilion, but farther west. We seemed to be headed for another, comparatively smaller pier jutting into the ocean. People streamed to a row of stalls under a long roof stretching down its middle. I expected Stefan to be selling sausages in one of those stalls.

We were still at least 100 feet away from the pier when Marta came to a stop. "What's wrong?" I asked. "Can't you take me to Stefan?"

She didn't answer, just pointed. To our left, standing on the boardwalk, was a cart on wheels, a family crowded around it. Manning the cart was Stefan, wearing a straw hat a bit too small for his head and a striped shirt with the word "Feltman's" on it. He didn't see me, or Marta. He was busy dealing with the children clamoring for sausages. "I'm next!" "No, me!" A heavyset woman, her face red and shiny, struggled to control the children, without success. A fistfight was breaking out.

Stefan, holding a sausage in a long yellow bun, called out, "Hello – hello? You will all get sausages. I have plenty. But please to get in line, the shortest one first, then second shortest. Go on. Yes, you can do this. Show me you can do this. Make Mama happy today, yes?"

The children scrambled to obey, and their Mother said, "Oh thank you, Mister. Thank you."

Stefan threw her a smile. "Ah, good children, yes, they are good." Amazingly, the children quivered with obedience when seconds ago they'd been brawling. Stefan bent down with the sausage and handed it to the youngest child, now first in line, giving him a gentle pat on the arm to nudge him to the side so the next could come forward.

Tufts of dark blond hair stuck out from under Stefan's incongruous hat. But it didn't make him look undignified to me, just different. Like a playful young uncle. Stefan winked at the next child in line, saying, "Ah you like to eat sausages. Good. You grow nice and strong, help your Mama."

"Did you hear that, Jimmy?" A broad smile split the mother's face. "You're going to be my helper."

"Sure, whatever you say, Mister," said the boy. "Just gimme the hot dog." Everyone laughed, including Stefan. As I continued to watch him smile, and laugh, and wink, and pat children on the arm, I couldn't move a fraction of an inch, couldn't tear my eyes away. I realized I was even holding my breath. Tens of thousands of people at Coney Island surrounded us in an overheated sprawl, but for me, there was this one single human being. The redhead, Louise, had scornfully predicted that I'd look down on him for doing this sort of work. Nothing could be further from what I felt at this moment.

After the four children happily stuffed sausages into their mouths, and their mother measured out coins for Stefan, he gripped the handles of his wheeled cart and pushed it a few feet, looking out at the ocean and then swinging back toward Marta and me. As his gaze met mine, he stopped mid-stride. To my dismay, a frown appeared.

"She looking for you, Stefan," said Marta. "I bring her."

"Yes, I can see that, Marta." How wonderful it was to hear that voice again, to enjoy the way his accent curled around "Marta," adding strange half syllables where none existed if anyone else said the word.

My legs turning to jelly, I pushed myself forward. This was it, the moment for my speech, my eloquent, dignified appeal. But all I could do was stand before him, mute, as I breathed in the sight of him. His steady gaze, those angular features, his lean frame.

"Hello," I said. And nothing else.

His lips curved into a smile. "Hello, Peggy," he said. I smiled back at him, my relief so great I nearly staggered from it.

"OK, OK, I go now," said Marta, with a gruff laugh, and she was gone, swallowed up in the crowd.

"I want to say how sorry I am," I said. "I haven't thought of much else but how I want you to know that."

"No, no, Peggy, I am one who must say it," he said, waving his hands passionately. "You did not tell me whole truth – but why should you? We meet, we eat, we dance. A few hours. You were shop girl at bookstore, that much true."

Startled, I asked, "And how do you know that?"

"From a friend's house, I call Moonrise," he said, not at all sheepish.

I found myself laughing. "Well, good for you."

At that moment, a young couple approached his cart, and I stood aside while Stefan supplied them with sausages in those long buns. Now that I stood close by, I realized that the cart itself had some source of heat inside, a few banked coals perhaps, which kept the sausages warm for customers. It was hard to believe, but in this nearly intolerable heat, Stefan bent over a portable stove.

When he was finished serving them, I said, "Apart from apologizing to you, there's something specific I would like to ask of you, Stefan."

"Anything," he said with a smile that sent my insides flip-flopping again. It wasn't easy to set the conversation on the necessary somber path.

"Have you heard of the girl who was killed – murdered on the beach near the Oriental Hotel?"

Stefan stared at me blankly. I told him what I knew, and in the middle of relaying the facts, I took out the newspaper article I'd folded and tucked in my handbag. He held it carefully as he read the article, shaking his head as his eyes scanned the sentences.

"This is bad, very bad," he said.

"Stefan, there's something about this that is especially strange. They found her at the same spot – the very same spot – as where we sat on the beach that night. The wood pilings."

His eyebrows shot up, a ghost of a smile appearing before he resumed his solemn regard.

When I asked Stefan if he remembered seeing a man spying on us, he said, "Ah, yes," and grimaced with distaste. At that moment a seagull chose to swoop down on the cart as if to raid it of food. Stefan waved the bird off. "More trouble with birds than people," he said. Before I could resume our conversation and explain the need for us to make a trip to the police, a fresh crowd of people descended on Stefan, eager for sausages.

He worked hurriedly for this group, glancing over at me every ten seconds or so. Stefan beckoned to me once they'd bought their sausages-in-buns and left. "Sorry – hard to speak here," he said. "What you want to ask, Peggy?"

"It's the police who are asking, they want to speak to anyone who saw something strange the night of the murder. And we did see something strange. Or, rather, you did. The man you said was watching us."

Stefan cocked his head. "We don't know if same man is killer, Peggy. And even if so, I don't know name, where to find him."

"But they are asking for citizens to come forward who can be of help," I said. "I thought too, at first, that we didn't know enough to go to the police, but then when you read how that girl's family is suffering… I just think we need to do it, Stefan. The two of us. We will explain. You may very well have seen the same man who killed her. We could help solve this."

Stefan turned to stare out at the ocean. It was much like that first time he'd appeared lost in thought, seeing some faraway place I couldn't imagine. At last he said, "You request this of me, Peggy? It important to you?"

A part of me wanted to say, "Oh, you're right, of course, we can't help much. Let's do something together instead that has nothing to do with an awful murder." But there was another part of me that felt our meeting, our first kiss, was special. Magical. The death of that poor young woman so close by had darkened it – we needed to seek out the police, not only because it was the correct and moral thing to do but because it would free us of that taint. Allow something more to follow, I hoped.

The way Stefan regarded me, so somber, it was almost as if he dreaded my answer. I said, hesitantly, "I believe it is the right thing to do. And if we didn't come forward, wouldn't we always regret it? Don't you think?"

With that, he took a deep breath, inhaling so vigorously that he whistled as he pursed his lips. After he exhaled, his chest slowly falling, Stefan said, "Then we go to police." He gripped the handles of the sausage cart and pushed, but not to go forward. His muscles bulging under his short-sleeved shirt, he made a quick half-circle in order to go in the opposite direction. Stefan was stronger than I realized.

"Is it – permitted – that you stop what you're doing now?" I asked. "Is that all right?"

"Wiktor owe me favor," Stefan answered. "Is OK."

Just as I made use of a favor from Lydia, Stefan would be calling in a favor from Wiktor, his employer presumably, to make our trip to the police. It was as if a web of favors made possible this destination. Or was that really the case? For the first time that day, I felt a twinge of fear, that this wasn't a web of happy coincidences linking us all, but from the start it was an iron chain, dragging us to something dangerous.

With me walking alongside, Stefan pushed the cart to a booth with the sign "Feltman's." The aforementioned Wiktor, a short, blond man, was unpacking something within. With his slight build and close-set eyes, he looked very much like Marta. I also took note of the yarmulke pinned to his blond hair. He clapped Stefan on the back, with a nod in my direction, agreeing immediately to an early quitting time.

Once we were heading back toward the main part of the park, I mentioned the remarkable resemblance. "Yes, she is little sister to David," he explained.

They all seemed so close to one another, it prompted me to ask, "Are you related to them?"

"Ha, ha, no, David is Polish Jew from Galicia," he said. "He cannot be blood relation to Orthodox Serb from Belgrade. But we have – what is word? – bond, yes bond that is like blood."

"And what is that?"

"Living as subjects of Austro-Hungarian Empire."

Every single syllable – "Austro-Hungarian Empire" – was spat out like bullets. It was another flash of the bitterness that Stefan carried with him, along with his talent and his gentleness. And now I finally knew where he came from: Serbia. Again, I cursed my ignorance, for it might as well be the Moon. As for being Orthodox, it summoned up for me a picture of a dark, incense-choked church and a cavalcade of holy statues. I'd never had a good friend who was Orthodox, much less a man I was interested in.

Before we reached the Creation Angel, Stefan suggested we part ways briefly to allow him to change clothes. He didn't relish meeting with the police wearing his sausage-cart uniform, that was clear. But going on ahead to the Art Building to wait for him there posed a problem. The absolute last thing I desired was another confrontation with Louise, who might still be haunting that part of the park, a particularly unpleasant prospect with Stefan beside me.

"Another meeting place, perhaps?" I suggested.

"Sure. Which place you like?"

"Hmmmmm. How about Hell Gate?"

His eyebrows shot up once more, but he agreed, and, assuring him I knew its location, I made my way alone to the demon-draped attraction of Dreamland.

I had expected that when I stood in front of Hell Gate, it wouldn't disturb me as much as it had when seen across the way. I was mistaken.

Who designed the figure leering on the roof of Hell Gate? That was the question I kept returning to. This artist must be privy to some disquieting visions. The statue, if that's the correct word for this thing, peered over the top of the building, a horned man with blazing eyes, one arm propped on the edge as if to get a better view of who could be snatched from below. The spreading wings attached to his back must have spanned twenty feet in each direction. As for the "attraction" below him, the dark cave I'd spotted from a distance was in fact a grotto. A dozen boats bobbed in murky water, ready for the brave to step into them and be mechanically conveyed farther into the ride, away from what I could see. Screams and shouts emanated from its depths. Within Dreamland, this was a chance to live a nightmare.

I waited outside Hell Gate long enough to see certain couples get into the queue, edge their way forward, jittery with nerves, step into a boat, and slink off into darkness… and then those same couples emerged from the other side of Hell Gate, the ride complete, both laughing and gasping over what they'd seen. One young woman clutched a man's forearm so tight as she staggered away, he cried, "Let go! My God. You can let go now."

As happy and relieved as I was to see Stefan again, and find him not angry with me in the least, I kept turning around to watch the flushed, frightened couples and families entering Hell Gate. There was a silly part of me that didn't feel safe with my back to the dark grotto, as if demons might hurtle out from its depths with me unaware. I don't know where these thoughts came from. I hadn't been raised on fire and brimstone; still, to me, Hell was a pit of roasting flames, not a watery prison. This was more like the River Styx.

"You like Hell Gate?" asked Stefan once he reappeared. He wore the same jacket as when he took me to dinner, I noticed with a tender pang, but he'd fastened a black tie around the neckline.

I shrugged and laughed. "I have no notion of what happens in there."

Stefan assured me that this was like being inside no other attraction at Dreamland.

"That's not all that helpful, since I haven't been inside any of the attractions – or the buildings – except to see your art."

He shook his head. "Peggy, you serious? What? Was day I met you first time you come to Coney?" When I informed him that yes, it was, he said, "Many, many things to do." His gaze strayed over my shoulder. "But you feel pull to Hell Gate. Maybe you should follow."

Impulsively, I reached for his arm. "If you were to go with me, yes," I said.

The amusement died in his expression. "You want me to take you in, sit beside you?"

I hadn't any idea that this would be a serious matter. I said, "Only if you want to."

Stefan said, "If you want this – and want with me – then we must do now."

"Now?" We had made the decision to go to the Coney Island police to discuss his seeing a possible murderer. Jumping onto a boat chugging toward Hell seemed a most unseemly thing to do first.

He repeated, "If you want me with you, it must be now."

It seemed as if Stefan were trying to convey something to me by making this stipulation, but I didn't know what. I was confused – with Stefan everything was new and novel – but also aware that I wanted to be with him, to go with him, however such opportunities presented themselves. I nodded.

And so we joined the queue of other couples waiting for a ride to Hell Gate. I'd noticed that these young men and women clung to each other in the line, or at least held hands. Two days ago, Stefan had not only kissed me but held my hand as we walked in the twilight. I ached to touch him now, to at least feel those roughened fingers, the fingers of an artist, but he maintained his distance, a polite but unmistakable wariness coming off him. This was my chief regret at his learning about my family. I could no longer be Peggy the Shop Girl, someone of his world, but an heiress occupying the wispiest of clouds above. I did *not* want to perch on that cloud.

When it was our turn we stepped into the dimness: a boat bobbing in the dark water. It was a shabby little vessel, and filthy, with an empty candy box on the floor and smears of God knows what on the side where my arm briefly rested. My left shoe settled into something even stickier; I feared for the condition of my leather sole after this journey. But most importantly, I now sat perhaps two inches from Stefan. We were almost touching. I didn't take advantage of this proximity, though. A new shyness paralyzed me as well.

The boat swayed back and forth, but we did not yet move forward. "I wonder what's down there?" I said, peering into the water, first on my side and then on Stefan's. Its surface reflected the electrical lights strung up at the top of the grotto – points of yellow in the inky blackness. But nothing was visible beneath.

I felt Stefan's fingers close, very gently, around my forearm. With his other hand, he took off my hat, and then he pulled me closer to his side so that I leaned across him, brushing against his chest, leaning even closer to the water. I could smell him, neither sausages nor oil paint, both of which I'd expected, but a whiff of Pears soap he must have scrubbed his hands and face with before meeting me.

"Look at your face," he said. "The lights on water, reflecting, what it does to you."

I managed to say, "I can't."

"That's all I see now," he whispered. "Blue eyes and red lips and black, black hair. I think, I think… what shades I choose. Do such shades exist?"

Is he going to paint me? I wondered, dazed.

The boat moved forward with a jerk. He gently put me back in my place on the seat beside him. Some mechanical contraption pulled us forward, from underneath, toward a shredded rubber curtain. The boat in front of ours pushed its way through that curtain and into blackness. We surged forward too.

But we were only in darkness for an instant. Next came a huge room, like an underground stage filled with water, dimly lit. We'd joined a procession of other boats moving in a circle, going faster and faster, as if being dragged into a giant whirlpool. The water swirled toward a center. We had no choice but to be pulled toward that center. I don't know if I took Stefan's hand, or he took mine, but we gripped each other's fingers.

Emboldened, I laid my head on his shoulder and closed my eyes. Seconds later, his mouth pressed on mine, and my lips opened. Kissing him deeply, I threw my arms around his neck, pulling him down as our boat surged and spun. After a short time, it could have been thirty seconds or ten minutes, I've no idea, we stopped spinning and straightened, moving to some other part of Hell Gate. People screamed all around us; frightening scenes of Hell, other demons perhaps, must have been dancing before us, but I never opened my eyes, never stopped kissing him.

My eyes only flew open because of light. We'd left the darkness; our boat eased to a halt. Stefan eased away from me, stroking my cheek with his fingers. I drew a ragged breath, staring up at him.

"Now, Peggy, we go to police," he said.

CHAPTER SIXTEEN

Like those other couples I'd seen emerging from Hell Gate, I clung to Stefan's arm. I felt no lingering fear, only delight and a fierce exultation. I didn't release him even when we'd left the demon's dominion behind. To behave like this in public, in front of strangers, would be unthinkable in my circle. But I wasn't in my circle, I was in the middle of Coney Island, where other couples hugged and flirted and clung to each other, and no one blinked an eye.

As we passed the attraction "Lilliput," the crowd parted but not for us. The most striking of human pairs presented themselves to all. They were wearing rather formal garb. The man in a topcoat stood well over seven feet tall – he would have towered over Henry Taul and over my tallest cousins and uncles. The woman at his side, wearing a deep gray Victorian-style dress with a long train, was barely four feet tall. She was, I assume, one of the "little people." Under her wide forehead sparkled a pair of brown eyes.

"Stefan," said the Giant. Of all the people swarming around him, Stefan was the one he considered worthy of mention.

In response, Stefan tipped his hat, showing as much respect as someone would encountering the mayor of a city.

I smiled to the Giant, and then to the woman who in height did not even reach his enormous belt. She smiled back, but there was a cool assessment to her glance. Perhaps it was suspicion of a newcomer. I remembered the words of Louise: *"You don't belong here."* Is that what they all thought? Was I so obviously an outsider?

I defiantly ran my hand up Stefan's jacket, to grip his arm even more openly as we made our way around the mismatched couple. Stefan didn't seem to mind.

Once out of Dreamland, Stefan told me he had never been inside the police precinct building but had an idea of which one it was. He knew the street and how to get there. "Nothing that far away from you on island," he explained.

What had that man shouted on the promenade when I first came here with Ben? "Four miles long and a half a mile wide – and anything your heart could desire here on Coney Island, America's Playground!" It's true that if you picked an address, any address, it could be reached fairly easily on a spit of land this size. But that didn't mean that it was a simple place to navigate, much less to understand.

The attractions of Luna, Steeplechase, and Dreamland were not the only ones on the west side of the island. As Stefan and I walked to the police precinct that afternoon, I glimpsed some of those other places.

Across the street from the rides and the exhibitions stretched a large restaurant – a cluster of buildings really – with a sign atop: "Feltman's: Deutscher Garten. Clam Bake and Dining Gardens." When I asked Stefan if this place were connected to the stall where he and Wiktor worked, he explained they were all one and the same, that a great many people on the island worked for Feltman's, either in the restaurants or pushing carts on the promenade. As he put it, with a short laugh, "We all work for the German." Ah, so that was the language of Deutscher Garten.

Wiktor had greater ambitions for himself, Stefan said. He planned to open his own establishment, one devoted to sausages, and by doing so, earn the money to not only live more comfortably but also bring over to America members of his family besides a wife and a sister.

"How old is Marta?" I asked.

"Seventeen."

When I told Stefan I assumed she was much younger, he said, "She and Wiktor, they come close to death in Galicia."

"Death?" I stopped walking, appalled. "How?"

"They both starving," Stefan said matter-of-factly. "That the reason why so small. Wiktor, he never ever go to school. Working all the time by nine years old. He works harder than any man who lives. All he thinks about is getting brothers and cousins out of Europe."

"Are they in danger of starving to death too?"

"Maybe. Always possible. But he wants to get them out before war comes, the big war."

That was definitely news to me. A war threatened? While America had known peace for more than two generations, I was vaguely aware of occasional conflicts in Europe. I'd glimpsed headlines in the newspaper or heard my uncles mention Russia or Japan or some other distant country having troubles. But nothing that could be described as "big." Every time I'd visited Paris, Florence, or London with my relations, I'd witnessed peace and prosperity. Certainly the starving were kept out of sight. Once again, I felt the vast gulf between my life and Stefan's.

While we waited for the streetcar to pass, about to put Feltman's behind us, he nudged me to have a last look. From this spot, I got a glimpse of an inner courtyard crowded with small, square, dark green tables, a dozen thick-trunked trees spreading leafy branches, thus shading the patrons. A waitress wearing a frilly red and white apron set a huge pitcher of beer on one table. A ray of sun pierced the canopy of leaves and picked out the white foam bubbling atop the dark gold beer, surrounded by heaping plates of food. I suddenly realized I was rather hungry.

"Could be Berlin, yes?" he said. I nodded, though I had never been to Germany. It did look like a spot of Europe rather than "America's Playground."

After we'd crossed the street, Stefan commented, "Marta does not – how you say it? – go out of her way for many people. She likes you."

I smiled, but I felt uneasy. Stefan didn't know that Louise had confronted me, that Marta was pushed to choose between us. I knew that I should tell him. Being less than honest had very nearly doomed us before we could begin. But I didn't want to bring up Louise – who clearly felt proprietary toward Stefan – in the street. Perhaps after we'd gotten this police interview over with, we'd find a quiet moment, one suited for such a conversation.

We passed a grand theater with the mute and lonely look that all such establishments have during those hours before the next curtain rises. Stretching behind it were at least two blocks of other theaters and dance halls, like a miniature Broadway. I saw a sign for "Henderson's Music Hall" and remembered it was the establishment Louise performed at, according to the man who declared her one of the most beautiful women in the world. For the first time I wondered what she did at Henderson's. Sing? Dance? Act? It wasn't pleasant, having such a rival.

We didn't walk past the theaters, but through a neighborhood of restaurants, hardware stores, grocers, and taverns before Stefan hesitated, pointing at an imposing brown building, one that bore the dreary evidence of being governmental: the faded signs of official type, the wide doors and narrow windows, the forlorn men clustered on the sidewalk, holding briefcases. We drew a few steps closer, and I realized that a courthouse dominated this building, but a side door led to the police precinct.

Stefan stiffened as he stared at the words "Brooklyn Police." I wondered what difficulties in his European past marked him in this way, caused such deep apprehension. I hoped I could help him see the difference. This was America. We headed toward the two steps leading to the police precinct doorway.

To my own surprise, I was the one who hesitated as my determined civic mindedness wobbled. I thought about my mother's vehemence about the importance of a lady staying out of the newspapers. I'd have to make sure that the policemen understood that what we had to contribute must remain a private conversation. That didn't seem too much to ask. There was another area of concern, too. I said, "Stefan, I've been thinking we should say that we were talking when you saw the man. Not kissing. After all, it doesn't matter what *we* were doing, right? My back was to him. You saw him alone."

"If that what you want to say, then that what we say," he answered.

Stefan opened the door for me, so I was the first person over the threshold – and the first to experience the precinct. *This* was like Hell, much more so than Hell Gate in Dreamland. It was hot, the sort of airless, muggy heat that is most oppressive. And *then* there was the noise. A throng of some thirty people filled the small waiting area, talking loudly, some bickering. One woman held a squalling baby. And *then* there was the smell: unwashed people, and worse. Even if I had a perfumed sachet in my handbag, it couldn't obscure the odors of those who should have used the latrine.

Stefan led the way now; I stumbled as I accompanied him to the front desk.

"Complaint?" barked a sweaty police officer manning the desk, his moustache sagging in the heat, his forearms rigidly cradling an open ledger book, covered with rows of meticulous handwriting.

"We're here to help with the murder investigation," I said faintly.

"What?" he said.

I had to repeat myself, speaking loudly to be heard over the din. I added that we were coming forward in response to the newspaper article. "We may have seen something that's helpful."

After emitting an exaggerated sigh, the police officer asked us for our names. I had to spell "Batternberg" twice.

The police officer turned his weary gaze on my companion. "Stefan Chalakoski." He had to spell it three times. If nothing else, this visit to the police meant I now knew his last name.

We were also asked for our addresses. Stefan gave him a house number in Brooklyn. I said my home was on Seventy-Second Street in Manhattan, but for the next six weeks, I'd be staying on the fourth floor north of the Oriental Hotel.

We were told we'd be called once an officer was free to take a statement. I wondered if it would be the Lieutenant Pellegrino who stood up to Mr. Lancet. He had been a bit rude to me when I saw that first girl in the water, but he was clearly keen to catch her murderer. Giving our statement to him might be the most effective route. We returned to the thick of the room. As the people who occupied its three chairs looked fully prepared to fight to the death to retain them, sitting down wasn't an option. Stefan and I made our way to an open space next to one of the grimy windows, a six-inch gap pushed open. It afforded us not the faintest puff of a breeze.

"I don't think anyone is going to call our names at all soon," I said.

His arms folded, Stefan shook his head. He looked no more apprehensive than he had on the street, or back in Dreamland. Being stuck in a hot, foul room wasn't a problem for him. It was the fact that we were here at all.

Perhaps a half hour crawled by. Our names were not called. Nearest us, a man in his middle years who seemed to be drunk kept repeating to an older man by his side, "I've got to get the money back. She tricked me. I've got to get it back."

With a tense Stefan not terribly keen for conversation, my thoughts turned to what I knew about police and their investigations. It was knowledge gained from a distance. I read every article about the Triangle shirtwaist factory tragedy, of course. That case was pursued with laudable police vigor. The ongoing legal affair that most concerned my family, though, was the government's vendetta against John D Rockefeller. Powerful officials accused him of secret deals and price fixing and far worse in creating Standard Oil. He was a "robber baron," the newspaper headlines screamed. He might have been the richest man in the world, but Rockefeller had to go into hiding to avoid subpoenas. And this year, after relentless harassment, the government finally won; the court ruled that Standard Oil was a monopoly and must be broken up.

My uncles greeted this news with tremendous gloom. The American people hated robber barons, though every man dreamed of being one. Spurred on by muckraking journalists, the prosecutors and the police were out to get the rich as never before. My cousin Ben, who though he was still a student acted as if he were the leading lawyer in New York, approved of Rockefeller dodging the police. He recently pronounced, "No one should ever agree to an interview with the police. And if one does, remember that the police cannot detain without arrest, and to arrest they need proof."

And here I was, pushing for an interview at a police station. Yet no one seemed to have the time. I could almost hear Ben mocking me:

"What on earth do you think you're doing, Peggy?" What *was* I doing? I mulled over how much longer we should wait before I suggested leaving the precinct.

"Batternberg! Chalakoski!"

The man standing in a doorway who called our last names was not the desk officer but younger and slimmer with auburn hair, light blue eyes, and a neatly trimmed mustache. Seeing me start toward him, he beckoned with a welcoming smile. Well, at least he didn't possess the bullheaded sourness of Lieutenant Pellegrino. I glanced over at Stefan, but if he was put at ease by the friendliness of the police officer, he showed no sign of it.

"I'm Detective Sean Devlin," he said when we reached him. "There's a room for taking your statements."

He ushered us past the desk. At the end of a short corridor, the detective opened a door. This small room, without a single window, was as hot as the waiting area, but at least it didn't smell. A table stood in the center of the room. Stefan and I took the two chairs that faced the door, and the policeman lowered himself into the chair opposite, placing his notebook down on the table next to a brown folder. He was hardly an intimidating person. Although Detective Devlin must be old enough to serve as a police officer and grow a mustache, there was a smoothness to his skin, more like a boy's than a grown man's. He even had a sprinkle of freckles across his nose. Some women might envy him his delicately arched auburn eyebrows.

"So you read the newspaper and that made you decide to come in?" he asked encouragingly. "You bought the evening newspaper Sunday? Or did you read the stories that came out today?

"Sunday," I said. "It wasn't a full newspaper, though, it was one of those extra editions. The newsboys were selling them outside the Oriental Hotel."

Detective Devlin wrote something in his notebook.

"And you, Sir?" he asked without looking up.

"I brought the newspaper to Stefan to show him today," I said. "He hadn't seen it, and he hadn't heard anything about the young woman's death."

"I'd like to hear it from Mr. Chalakoski," the detective said, tapping his pencil against the notebook. "If he speaks English."

"I speak English."

I snuck a sideways glance at Stefan, sitting erect in the chair, his hands folded in his lap, his jaw set. I couldn't blame him for being annoyed. Stefan's name was foreign, but why assume he couldn't speak English? They should have assigned an older, more seasoned policeman to take our statement.

"You had no knowledge of the murder of Katherine O'Malley that occurred early in the morning of 4 July until Miss Batternberg informed you?" the police officer asked Stefan, abruptly using more formal phrasing than he had before.

"No."

Detective Devlin said, "Tell me what you did see, Mr. Chalakoski."

I waited several seconds, but when Stefan, who I feared was offended, didn't say anything, I launched into the statement. "Stefan and I were sitting on the beach, the same spot on the beach where the girl was found, but it was the night before. It was about ten o'clock. Stefan saw a man acting... suspiciously. I didn't see the man, my back was to him."

"How suspicious?"

Stefan spoke up at last. "He was watching us. Behind another row of wood. He was ..." Stefan struggled for the word, and finally said, "Squatting. Man was squatting. I saw only upper body."

"There was no one else for him to be watching on that part of the beach?"

"No."

"He was alone?" The questions were coming fast now.

"Yes."

"Can you describe him?"

"Not well," Stefan said. "He wore hat. Round hat with brim. But it was too dark to see face." I held my breath, waiting to hear whether Stefan would say he saw the man earlier. He shifted in his chair, and said, "Possible I see same man before, walking behind Miss Batternberg and me on way to her hotel. Same hat. I see jacket, light jacket."

"Did you see the man's face that time?"

"It was almost dark then, he was about twenty feet back, so not too well."

"Was he tall?"

"No."

"Thin? Fat?"

"Not thin, not fat," Stefan said thoughtfully. "Average. But young. The way he walks, young. No beard, no mustache."

The detective wrote some more in his notebook before putting down his pencil.

"Your opinion is that the man followed you?" he asked, but he squinted a little and tilted his head as if he were having a hard time believing it.

"I don't know," said Stefan. "Maybe. I notice him twice behind us, same man, alone. Not too close, but close enough to follow."

"But there were a lot of folks walking near the shore on a Saturday night before ten." The police detective sounded incredulous. "Why would this young man be following the two of you?"

"I don't know," Stefan repeated.

"Did you have words with someone? Was there a fight? Do you know of anybody who's got a grudge against you?"

This conversation was taking a strange turn.

"This isn't about us, Sir," I interjected. "It's about the man we saw who may have killed that poor girl."

"Detective."

"Pardon?"

"Detective Devlin." He leaned back in his chair. His light blue eyes no longer danced with friendliness. "But according to what you just said, Miss Batternberg, it *is* about you. He was following you, then when you left the boardwalk to sit and talk, this man snuck off to watch you. Nothing about this connects to Katherine O'Malley. At least not yet."

The neckline of my dress was damp and my chemise was dripping with perspiration, making it difficult to concentrate, while Detective Devlin didn't appear the least bit discomfited.

"What happened Sunday night after you say you saw this man spying on you?" he asked.

"Stefan and I said good night, and I went up to my room in the hotel," I said faintly.

"You speak to anyone upstairs? Anyone in your family who can vouch for you?"

"Yes, my Aunt Helen." My bafflement over the detective's line of questioning hardened to resentment, and with that, my thoughts sharpened. "What on earth do you mean by *vouch?* What do my activities later that night, or at any time, have to do with anything? You are behaving very strangely toward two people who volunteered to help!"

With that, his smile reappeared. "Yes, we appreciate your help, Miss Batternberg. Because you've helped us answer some questions. Nothing to do with your mystery spy on the beach, the man squatting behind some wood pilings. Let me see here…" He turned toward the brown file, unopened until this moment. I saw that the young detective with the cherub's face and beautifully trimmed mustache possessed hideous hands: his knuckles were thick, and blue veins crisscrossed his freckled skin.

He withdrew a paper, covered with writing. "We asked the Pinkerton guards for observations on Saturday night at the checkpoints leading to the east side, and in one of their logs they wrote this: 'Peggy Batternberg, claimed to be guest at Oriental, admitted at nine thirty. Accompanied by man unknown. Foreign accent. Surly in manner.'" Detective Devlin chuckled. "That sums it all up pretty good, right? OK, but that wasn't much to go on. Nobody followed it up, didn't seem too important. But then we have this other statement…"

As he slowly ruffled the papers in his folder, dread gathered in my throat. I glanced over at Stefan, who sat like a statue, his lips pressed together.

"Yes, here it is. You're not the only ones who came forward, you know. This morning, first thing, some helpful people told us they witnessed a young couple having an argument on the boardwalk, a short distance from the place on the beach where the body was found. The woman shouted the man's name – 'Stefan' – but he walked away from her. Didn't turn around. She seemed upset. We been busy here trying to follow up, searching our arrest records and any other records for a man with first name of Stefan. No breaks. And then lo and behold, the man in question walks right through the door."

Now I was like a statue, motionless. How could this be going so wrong?

"You are mistaken, Sir," Stefan said. They were his first words in a while, and I was proud of his calm dignity.

But the detective acted as if he hadn't spoken at all and returned to his hateful notebook. Pencil in his fingers, he said, "Why don't you tell me where you went after you argued with the young lady that night, Mr. Chalakoski?"

"It wasn't really an argument," I insisted. "As you can see, we aren't angry with each other in the least."

He pointed at Stefan. "Mr. Chalakoski? Your movements?"

"I go home."

"Which way? There's no record from any of the Pinkertons of your leaving the east end before midnight."

"Same way I came. No one ask me questions going west. When I am back at Coney Island, I take streetcar to home."

The detective leaned forward. "Did you speak to anyone at all that night after leaving Miss Batternberg?"

Stefan shifted in his chair and said, "I say goodnight to landlady on way upstairs. She owns rooming house."

"Her name?"

"Mrs. Betty Simon."

"What time was that?"

Stefan said after some consideration, "Around eleven thirty."

"Address?"

Stefan gave one, and the detective leaped to his feet and knocked on the door twice. Another young police officer, this one wiry and blond, opened it five seconds later. Detective Devlin muttered to him for a moment and handed him a piece of paper. The only words I could make out were "alibi" and "before midnight."

Shutting the door behind him, the detective did not sit down again but stood, looking down on us with a tinge of triumph. And with that, I'd had enough.

"When can we leave?" I asked. "We've given you a statement, doing our part to help, and it is not appreciated. You are pursuing an inquiry into our personal lives, which is misguided. It's ridiculous to speculate that Stefan was involved in any way. I see no reason to continue this conversation."

"Just a few more questions, Miss," he said holding up one hand.

He turned to Stefan. "So, I take it you are gainfully employed here on Coney Island, Mr. Chalakoski?"

Stefan folded his arms and said shortly, "Feltman's. I work pushcart out of pier."

"Oh yeah? I love the taste of hot dogs, I really do." He chuckled and turned to me, that smile I knew to be false, lighting up his face. I can only imagine what my face looked like, the loathing he must see there.

"Miss Batternberg, I got a question for you," said Detective Devlin, toying with his pencil. "How do your parents feel about you going to bed with a foreigner who pushes a hotdog cart along the water in Coney Island?"

I was as shocked as if he had slapped me across the face. No one, and I mean *no one*, had ever spoken to me like that in my life.

Stefan leaped to his feet, sending the chair back with a crash. "You will apologize to her, Police Man!" he shouted. "Your filthy words are outrage – *outrage*."

The detective was completely unaffected by Stefan's anger. He did nothing but smile as he stepped back toward the door, reached behind him, and knocked twice. It opened immediately. There was no young blond police officer there this time.

The man standing in the hall, looking straight at me, was Lieutenant Pellegrino.

CHAPTER SEVENTEEN

Everything happened at once.

Detective Devlin walked around the table, saying, "Mr. Chalakoski, come with me please," while Stefan, not moving an inch, repeated, "You will apologize to her for your filth!"

I leaped to my feet, grabbing Stefan's arm and shouting, "He's not going anywhere!"

By now Lieutenant Pellegrino was all the way inside the room and saying something that no one listened to until he thundered, *"We will have calm."*

Everyone shut up, and only then did Lieutenant Pellegrino explain that the police just wanted to interview Stefan and me separately, and that this was standard police practice. "You'll not arrest him," I said, still holding Stefan's arm. "You haven't any reason to suspect him of this murder – it's absurd."

Lieutenant Pellegrino said firmly, "Mr. Chalakoski is not under arrest."

Stefan turned to me, and I saw that his first concern was for me. "I will go with them, Peggy," he said. "Do not upset yourself." Seconds later he was on the move, out of the room, escorted by Detective Devlin who, I noted with a shudder, put his hand on Stefan's shoulder as if he were steering him out. I would have pushed him away. But Stefan submitted to his offensive touch.

"I'll be back in a minute," Lieutenant Pellegrino informed me, closing the door behind him. It seemed he would be the one I'd be talking to after all.

Once more, I sat at the wooden table, a piece of furniture I had begun to hate with all my heart. For the first time I studied its surface, the scratches that were softened but not removed by cheap polish and what looked like cigarette burn marks bordering the edge. How many others had suffered in this room?

Admittedly, my sense of time might not have functioned at its best, but as I sat there fuming, it seemed as if one minute must have passed, then another, and yet another. The lieutenant said we would be interviewed separately, but that, it dawned on me, might very well not happen. Perhaps I'd been told a lie to calm me sufficiently so that Stefan could be removed. And this was how the police treated people who came in of their own free will to help!

I strode to the door and turned the handle, but the knob barely moved a half-inch. I didn't believe it at first and stupidly kept turning the knob. I was locked in.

"*This is an outrage,*" Stefan had cried – and how right he was. I knocked on the door, not two raps as the despicable lieutenant had done, but five, six times. I heard men's voices outside the door – I could almost distinguish words – but no one unlocked it.

"I want out of here immediately," I shouted. "I demand that you unlock the door."

With that, the men on the other side went silent. I resumed knocking, so hard that my knuckles stung. At long last, the doorknob clicked, it swung open, and I was once more face to face with Lieutenant Pellegrino, now holding a glass of water.

"Have a seat," he said.

"Where is Stefan?" I demanded.

"Down the hall. He's doing fine. But you look as if you could use some water."

I drew up to every inch of my height and said, as haughtily as I was capable of, "I don't need water. I do need to leave, and I will leave – with Stefan Chalakoski."

To make my intentions plain, I tried to edge my way past Lieutenant Pellegrino to reach the hallway. He blocked my path, shifting over so smoothly that he didn't spill a drop of water.

"You like to go places where you're not supposed to be, don't you?" he observed.

"We're told in school this is a free country," I said. "Perhaps I should arrange a tour for my school teachers of the Coney Island police precinct. To enlighten them."

The faintest of smiles appeared on his stern bearded face.

"Please have a seat, Miss Batternberg," he said. "I'm tired of holding this water."

"I do not wish to talk to you," I said. "You forcibly removed Mr. Chalakoski, intimating that he is suspected of something, which is ridiculous."

"You're not concerned that we intimate something of you?"

I felt a sickening tug of fear, but that faint smile was still visible. He was having a bit of fun, mocking me.

"No, I am not," I said frostily, before returning to the table. Lieutenant Pellegrino set the glass of water in front of me. I longed to have the courage to knock it off the table with the back of my hand. Instead, I drank the water in a long, greedy gulp. I'd grown incredibly thirsty. While I drank, he righted the fallen chair of Stefan's and then sat in it, next to me. Silently, he pulled a white handkerchief from his police uniform front pocket and handed it to me. What a mess I must be. I used it to mop the perspiration that pooled on my forehead, upper lip, and the back of my neck, saying, "I didn't know policemen carried linen handkerchiefs."

"Only if they're married to my wife," he said.

I folded the handkerchief and handed it to him. "I'm sorry to return it in such condition," I said with stiff politeness.

"Plenty more where it came from. So, Miss Batternberg, you are here today to give a statement. What is it exactly that you wanted us to know?"

"I already told that detective everything!" I protested.

"Now you'll tell me," he said in the tone of someone accustomed to obedience.

Seeing no choice, I repeated all that Stefan and I said earlier, including his suspicion that the man – young, neither fat nor thin, and not very tall – had followed us on the boardwalk earlier that evening. I finished with saying I read in the newspaper that people were urged to come forward with information, and so I sought out Stefan in Coney Island the next day, and he agreed to come.

Lieutenant Pellegrino studied me for an uncomfortably long time. As he was staring at me, I stared back at him. He was a good fifteen years older than Detective Devlin, and while he still exuded severity, I noted the skin softening into jowls below his chin, and the broad chest and shoulders that beneath his uniform might not be completely muscle. The man ate well – presumably the wife who washed and ironed handkerchiefs to tuck in his pocket made sure huge hot meals were on the table the instant he made it home.

"Miss Batternberg, what are you playing at?" he finally asked.

"I'm not playing at anything," I retorted. "I'm telling you the truth. Why is that so hard to believe?"

"Because you're not being truthful. You and Chalakoski, sitting on the beach, on wood pilings, just talking? But by your own explanation, you have your back to someone who is watching the two of you while Chalakoski looks forward, straight at the man. What the hell kind of conversation is that?"

I felt the color rise in my cheeks, but I refused to answer.

"How did you meet this man? You've been at the Oriental Hotel less than a week."

After a minute I said, "Stefan is an artist. I saw his paintings displayed in a building in Dreamland. I bought several. I was quite impressed, and we began a conversation."

I hoped that once the lieutenant understood the truth about Stefan and why he impressed me, his impression of the situation would change. I couldn't have been more wrong.

"Has he asked you for money aside from the cost of the paintings?"

I closed my eyes, desperate for patience. How could I best make myself understood?

"Lieutenant Pellegrino," I began, using his full name and title, which I gathered from the detective was important with the police. "You do not have the correct impression of Stefan Chalakoski. He is a gifted artist and a sensitive human being with a great deal of pride. He would never try to wheedle money out of me, any more than he would have hurt that girl."

Now the lieutenant heaved a sigh, as if he were trying to find patience to deal with *me*.

"Are you aware that he's Serbian?" he asked.

"Yes. From Belgrade."

Lieutenant Pellegrino pursed his lips. "At least he's not hiding that from you," he said thoughtfully.

"Why on earth should he hide it?"

He answered my question with a question. "How old are you, Miss Batternberg?"

"I'll be twenty-one in several months' time."

He drummed his fingers on the table. "I have to assume that you're aware of the damage done all over the world by anarchists?"

I opened my mouth to point out once again how wrong he was about Stefan, but the lieutenant held up a hand to say stop.

"Let me put this to you in a personal manner. I was born in Italy, I came here when I was seven years old. There are Russian anarchists, Spanish anarchists, French anarchists, Polish anarchists. But the Italians, they're something special. The assassinations, the bombs, oh and the conspiracies. An Italian stabbed the Austrian Empress Elisabeth in the heart as she walked across a street. An Italian shot the prime minister of Spain. And the anarchists are over here – more and more of them, all the time. Do you know where the Italian plot to kill King Umberto was hatched? In Paterson, New Jersey. Gaetano Bresci sailed back to Italy to shoot the king. You have no way of knowing this, but I am one of the very few Italian police officers on the New York City police force. I accept that I'm under a shadow of doubt every minute, to those who believe all Italians are born anarchists, bomb throwers, and murderers, even though the truth is that I'm in complete and utter agreement with President Roosevelt, that they commit crimes against the whole human race. When anarchists come to America to attack the ruling class, as they describe it, we hunt them down."

Two things struck me as I listened to Lieutenant Pellegrino. One was that while his words were passionate and his breadth of knowledge impressive, it resembled a presentation – and a practiced one at that – more than any message from the heart. And the second thing was that I hadn't the slightest idea why he was telling me this. He nodded slightly, as if he could read my thoughts.

"Miss Batternberg, I'm not trying to win your sympathy but to make it clear to you that I'm not a man of base prejudices, like many other cops, unfortunately." He grimaced. "I am informed. I know what the hell I'm talking about. As bad as Italy is, the Balkans are worse – and Serbia is the center, the beating heart of the Balkans. Centuries of hatred. I doubt you know the full story about the coup against the king and queen of Serbia several years ago, if you've heard it at all. The newspapers here didn't print details. A group of Serbian army officers decided to overthrow their country's king and queen – they stormed the palace, they found this young couple hiding in a cupboard, and they shot them. Then the officers mutilated the bodies and threw them out the window into a pile of manure."

I recoiled from the details of this horrifying act, but I still managed to say, "Stefan is here to get away from the sort of hatred and horror you're talking about."

"Or does he bring it with him? There aren't many Serbs who come to America, but if they should choose to do so in numbers…" Suddenly he slammed his thick uniformed thigh, his temper close to boiling over. "Do you have any idea how much money you'd be worth to one of these groups, how much they could demand in a kidnap? Half the police on the East Coast would be mobilized. My God, I can't believe your family let you wander off like that!"

"I'm not a child," I said. "And … what are you suggesting? That Stefan is on the verge of kidnapping me? Then why murder Katherine O'Malley on the beach? You've never offered any reason for him to do such a terrible thing, except that he's a foreigner. You yourself, Lieutenant, are proof that someone born outside the United States is not destined to act like a criminal."

It could have been the personal nature of my comment, but Lieutenant Pellegrino tensed in his chair. Now he was definitely having a hard time with his temper. "Motive, eh? You want a motive? We got one. It's not too pretty, but you asked for it. It's my hunch that Chalakoski was planning to spirit you away from the rest of your family, and to do that he tried to seduce you that first night. You resisted on the beach and you argued with him. He was left pretty damn frustrated. So frustrated that I believe he stuck around. He was able to get this girl from a poor family and rape and kill her on the very same spot you turned him down. But he knew you'd both been seen and heard on the boardwalk, and you gave the Pinkertons your name, so that when you found him today, waving that newspaper article, he had to agree to your idea to come here. If he got through it, he'd have your trust forever."

To hear such a depraved scenario assigned to Stefan was nothing less than nauseating. More than ever, the walls of the room were closing in; it was an effort to draw breath. But I could not indulge in vapors now. As mistaken as the police's ideas were, this scenario had a horrible logic to it. The danger to Stefan was real.

"I had no idea that the girl was… violated," I said.

"There are always things we hold back from the newspapers," he said. "We can't tell them everything, to keep the integrity of our inquiry."

Clearing my throat I said, "You are mistaken on several points. We didn't argue because I was unwilling to be seduced, Lieutenant. I had rather misled Stefan that first day. I allowed him to think that I was nothing but a shop girl at Moonrise Bookstore. Once we reached the Oriental Hotel, since I was a guest there, it was obvious that I was more than that. Although I *did* work at the store for several months. In any case, Stefan heard the name Batternberg, and it didn't mean anything to him. It wasn't until I spelled it out for him, that we own mines all over the Americas, that he had any inkling of who I am. He felt as if I'd been slumming with him, which I'm sorry to say I was in the beginning. And yes, we did more than talk on the beach first. He kissed me, and I kissed him. We kissed each other. That's all. You asked for the truth, I've given you the complete truth."

I couldn't read the expression on Lieutenant Pellegrino's face as he absorbed all I had to say. But, temper under control, he changed the direction of our conversation.

"Has Stefan Chalakoski suggested future meetings with you?"

"No."

"Did he mention the name of any friend or associate?"

"No."

Now I had met Marta and Wiktor, and in a manner of speaking I had met Louise, but I felt no compunction about failing to turn over their names to the police. They scarcely fitted anyone's definition of anarchists.

"Where exactly did he take you the first day?"

I told Lieutenant Pellegrino about having dinner on the iron pier, of dancing, of watching the lights shimmer at Dreamland.

"Did he ever mention an establishment named Mabel Morgan's?"

Puzzled, I shook my head.

"The Bowery? Anything on the Bowery?"

"No."

"How about 'The Rot'?"

"No, Lieutenant Pellegrino. We talked about art, music, the lights of Dreamland. Certainly not… Rot."

The lieutenant took a deep breath. I had the feeling that I'd failed him in some specific way; this was not an open-ended conversation.

He had an objective in mind, and I'd thwarted it. "You are confident, aren't you, Miss Batternberg?" he asked. "You stand on the edge of a cliff. I am trying to help you, but you think you know better. At each scene where a girl's body was found, I also found you. Very curious, aren't you, and ready to do whatever you want, go wherever you want."

"So you believe that the woman found dead in the water was murdered too?" I asked.

Regret flashed in his eyes over letting that slip. And his next question proved he had no intention of answering me. "Do your parents know about you becoming acquainted with Stefan Chalakoski?"

"My father is dead, Lieutenant."

Before he could persist in this distinctly unwelcome line of questioning, three sharp raps at the door brought the lieutenant to his feet.

When he opened it, I spotted the same wiry blond police officer who took the name of Stefan's landlady. The lieutenant once more closed the door behind him. But this time I was at the door, my ear pressed to it.

I could hear a man speaking – I assumed it was the blond officer – but, to my frustration, he was pretty soft-spoken. It was otherwise with Lieutenant Pellegrino. "She's absolutely certain she saw him before midnight?" he said, loud enough that every word came through. The other man droned on a bit. "Damn it," responded the lieutenant.

My thoughts raced while I tried to comprehend what these possible developments meant. Someone in the police must have already spoken to Stefan's landlady, and she confirmed that she saw him come in that night, and, most importantly, she saw him before midnight. This must rule him out as the murderer of Katherine O'Malley. I only had a vague idea of what an "alibi" was. Perhaps it was being able to prove one's whereabouts for a certain time and day. Stefan had done that.

This ordeal was at an end.

I turned the doorknob – it was unlocked this time – and stepped out into the hall, coming face to face with Lieutenant Pellegrino, who broke off his conversation with the blond police officer to bark, "Get back in there. We're not finished with our conversation."

"But we are, Lieutenant. We are finished, and I will be going now."

"I decide when you will go, Miss Batternberg."

"Even if I'm not under suspicion? Which you said I wasn't." I heard the voice of my cousin Ben: *No one should ever agree to an interview with the police. And if one does, remember that the police cannot detain without arrest, and to arrest they need proof.*

I swallowed; now was the time to take the plunge. I said, "You cannot detain me without arrest. And if there is anything about that which is unclear, I can have a lawyer here within the hour."

The truth was, there was no way for me to contact one of the Batternberg attorneys without going through my uncle or mother. I prayed that the police wouldn't perceive its impossibility.

The blond officer standing next to Lieutenant Pellegrino stared at me, his eyes round as saucers. I realized that other policemen in the corridor or in nearby offices with open doorways must have heard what I just said too, because the place had gone dead quiet. As for the man whose authority I defied, he looked as if he were holding back his temper once more. And then… he shrugged.

"No need to call in the cavalry," said Lieutenant Pellegrino with sarcasm. "You can go."

"I intend to. With Mr. Chalakoski."

"That's not possible," he said flatly. "We have outstanding questions for him."

I shook my head. "Oh, no. No. No. We came together, and we leave together."

At the opposite end of the corridor, a door opened. It is possible that no one would have heard the strange sounds coming from that room if everyone weren't listening to my defiance of Lieutenant Pellegrino. But in that pregnant silence there was a loud, pained grunt; an "oomph," followed by a snatch of high-pitched laughter. Then the door slammed shut.

There was something about that grunt of pain. Something familiar. At first my mind refused to accept it. No, they wouldn't do that. They *couldn't* do that. I'd have abandoned all thought of its being a possibility, had not the two policemen I stood before behaved the way they did.

"Damn," whispered the blond officer, growing even paler, as his worried gaze flitted in my direction. Lieutenant Pellegrino shook his head at him, forbiddingly, as he refused to meet my eyes.

The next strange sound to be heard during that afternoon at the police precinct of Coney Island was that of my own voice, harsh and strangled, as I demanded, "What are they doing to Stefan?"

CHAPTER EIGHTEEN

Lieutenant Pellegrino shook his head but said not a word. I had felt nothing for him up to now but wary dislike. In his refusal to lie to me, though, he redeemed himself. There must be a kernel of integrity within him to do that.

"Stop it, Lieutenant, you must stop it," I said. "My God, they're hurting him. Stefan hasn't done anything wrong. You know that he was home before midnight – yes, I heard it with my own ears. I did! He has an alibi. So there can't be any basis in law for thinking he's mixed up with this, except that he's a foreigner. Don't do this to him."

Lieutenant Pellegrino looked acutely uncomfortable. I couldn't tell if he was disturbed by the other officers mistreating Stefan or by my forceful plea.

"Stefan must leave with me, Lieutenant Pellegrino," I said. "Take me to him."

My appeal made within earshot of God knows how many others put him in a tough spot. But I was past being tricked into small rooms and there manipulated. This had to happen in the open.

"Take me to Stefan *now*," I cried.

"No," he said finally. "Go outside. He'll be brought out shortly."

"How short?" I pressed. If I'd learned anything, it was that taking a police officer's word for anything was a mistake.

"Within the next fifteen minutes." He pointed at me. "Miss Batternberg, I don't want to see you in this man's company after today, or else I'll have no choice but to talk to your family – to your mother – to advise her of the situation in full."

With that, he turned on his heel and walked in the direction of the door behind which I knew they kept Stefan. A hand slipped around my elbow, guiding me the other way. It was the blond police officer, taking me past the front desk, through the crowded, clamoring waiting area, and the door leading to the street.

If the officer said anything to me, I didn't hear it. All I know is that suddenly I found myself standing outside the police precinct alone, reeling. I felt as if my time inside that building surely stretched over many hours, days even, but the reality was, it was just long enough for the front sidewalk to be bathed in shade instead of direct sunlight. Perhaps five o'clock. Three middle-aged men wearing somber suits shuffled down the steps of the courthouse next door. One of them stopped, cupped his face in one hand, and said, "They bested me. I can't believe it turned against me." Another clapped him on the back. "The Coney crowd are the meanest sharks in the water. I tried to warn you." The third said, "Drinks on me on the Bowery, mates."

The trio walked past the precinct door, glancing my way with mild interest before quickening their pace as they neared the end of the block. Soon enough they'd be sitting in a dark tavern, the sting of their lost court case easing. But it would take me a very long time to recover from what just happened. And what about Stefan? My wounds were of the spirit, his of the body.

Where *was* Stefan?

The muggy heat hadn't loosened its chokehold on the street, but panic churned inside me. If Lieutenant Pellegrino lied and refused to release Stefan from this building, what could I do about it? I was the one who had lied about being able to make Batternberg lawyers come running, and he might have guessed it. Why else would his final threat be to seek out my mother?

The door to the police precinct swung open. A hard-faced woman, dragging a child by the hand, stepped out. I didn't remember seeing them in the waiting area. I felt as if I were losing grip on the situation.

"Peggy."

I whirled around. Stefan stood no more than ten feet away. As I rushed to him, my relief turned to anguish. His left eye was ringed in red, his nose was swollen, and his chin was covered in a bandage.

"My God, what did they do to you?" I burst into tears as I threw my arms around him.

Stefan doubled over in my arms. "No, no, don't," he begged.

I stepped back while he felt his ribs, grimacing. My hugging him had caused greater pain.

"I have to take you to the hospital," I cried.

He shook his head. "My ribs not broken. My jaw not broken. I need rest, not hospital."

"Oh, Stefan, how could they do this?"

"With much skill," he said, and looked over his shoulder. "We must get away from here, Peggy." It was only then that I noticed Detective Sean Devlin standing at the corner of the police building, watching us. He must have been the one to lead Stefan out the side door. To all the world he resembled a friendly young man, fresh out of the school house with his freckled nose, who just put on a police uniform for the first time. I knew better.

I wanted so much to help Stefan down the street, but I could not take his arm, his bruises were too tender. Instead, we walked side by side, slowly because of how much pain he was in, until we made it to the end of the block. By that time, Stefan's face was damp with sweat; beneath the sweat, his skin was gray as chalk.

"You have to get off your feet," I said, alarmed. "And water. You need water."

Turning left, I spotted a hardware store one-third of the way down this block, an empty bench in front of it. Stefan did not argue with me when I urged him to sit.

Now I needed to find him water, not as easy to secure. The hardware store, with its front window crammed with fireworks equipment, was closed. I didn't see any grocers. A busy-looking tavern dominated the far corner, but I was reluctant to leave him alone for however long it took me to talk someone into giving me a glass of water. He might faint right here. How frustrating to know that just a few blocks away stood an amusement park selling every kind of drink imaginable. But how to get him there?

I spotted two boys on the sidewalk, bent over a flat pile of garbage pushed to the side of the street. One of them picked up a shred of something that gleamed like silver in the sun. I called them over. "I'll give you a dollar if you can buy us two tall cups of water from someone and bring it back," I said. "Or iced tea. Or lemonade. Anything like that."

"Sure, lady," said one of the boys, long-faced, about nine years old. He nudged his friend with a delighted glance. The other, with a tangled mop of dark hair, looked even younger, though I saw a clutch of cigarette butts bursting out of his patched shirt pocket.

"Peggy," rasped Stefan warningly.

"Ah. Yes. I'll give you a dollar to buy the drinks and *another* dollar when you bring them back."

"Two dollars?" crowed the boy in disbelief. "Yes, ma'am!" His friend said nothing; instead, he stared at Stefan. Well, he did make for a dreadful sight.

Once they'd scooted off with one of my dollars, I turned my most burning questions on Stefan.

"Which one of the police hit you?"

After a few seconds, he said, "Does it matter?"

"But they can't do this – to pummel someone who's being interviewed. That must be against the law."

"Agree. Who should we make complaint to?" Rubbing his left side with a wince, he said, "They would just say my Slavic temper meant I must be restrained."

To my amazement, Stefan exhibited no rage over being beaten by the police after we went to the precinct to volunteer assistance. It wasn't that they'd frightened him into submission. Nor was he resigned to it, precisely. He didn't seem defeated. If I had to describe his state of mind, I'd say it was a tragic serenity. As much pain as he suffered, he seemed at peace now. And that was more horrible than anything else.

"Did you think that they might do this to you?" I asked.

"I have experience with police, Peggy," he said. "Not here. In Rome, Belgrade. Same everywhere. The surprise was they release so quick. The dark officer comes in, shouts at them all, they stop, put bandage on, push me out door."

"That was Lieutenant Pellegrino," I said. "He kept talking about anarchists, murders, and the ruling class. He had an absurd theory about you, about how you meant to kidnap me. I still can't believe this was their reaction to us coming in. But I made him see that they couldn't detain either of us."

Stefan murmured a sentence in another language.

"Pardon?"

"The English is 'A hundred suspicions don't make a proof.' Dostoevsky wrote in *Crime and Punishment*."

After that, Stefan lapsed into silence. He seemed to be concentrating on bearing his pain. I felt sick with guilt over doing this to him. I was completely at fault. He had *expected* to be mistreated by the police. With a sickening rush, I realized something else.

"Before we went into Hell Gate, you said, 'If you want me to go with you, it has to be today,' you said that because you thought there might *never* be another opportunity."

"It was possible," he said simply.

And did he kiss me like that because he thought we might not ever have another chance? I couldn't bring myself to ask.

Rubbing his swollen jaw, he said, "Anyone looking to prove America has ruling class could see it today."

"What do you mean?"

"Police release me today only because of you, the status of family. No appeal to reason or rule of law would work."

That made me feel worse. I didn't want to be part of a wretched system in which the police – and everyone else – bowed to those with money. It wasn't the first time I'd heard that. But if I were a member of a ruling class, why did I feel lost and powerless most the time?

I said, "Despite all its claims to liberty, America is no better than Europe."

Stefan said, "Is different. In countries ruled by Austria, Russia, man knows he cannot move up ladder, no hope at all. Here, hope lives, but only for few. Man working hard, great effort, is not enough. Some luck necessary. But…" He considered. "Not getting luck can drive man mad."

His insights were like no one else's. And what had I done to him? I blurted, "Oh, Stefan, why did you come with me if you knew it would expose you to their suspicion and their violence?"

"Because you ask me to," he said. Within that bruised face, his expression was brimming with sadness and anger, yes, but also ardor.

I took his left hand and pressed it to my cheek, and he did not shrink in pain. "Stefan," I whispered.

I let go of him, reluctantly, when the long-faced boy appeared on the sidewalk, carrying a crate with no little effort. I spotted a large bottle of water, cups, and two smaller curved bottles shimmering with dark brown liquid.

"Where's your friend?" I asked the boy when I gave him the second dollar. He shrugged as he pulled a small bag from his pocket. As he reverently slipped the dollar in, I spotted strips of tin foil from cigarette wrappings and chewing gum wrappers. Was that what he was picking up before – could this junk actually be worth something? I wondered, with a pang.

Stefan moaned, "Yes, yes, Coca-Cola."

I thought the water much better for him, but when he insisted, I handed Stefan one of the cold bottles with a Coca-Cola label pasted on. To my chagrin, he stuck his hand deep in his pocket, even though it made him curse with pain, to extract a bottle opener. And then to my greater chagrin, he insisted I drink the other one.

"First beer, now this," he said with a shadow of a smile. How could I refuse after that? Once he'd pried the metal cap off the second bottle, I hid my distaste over drinking straight from a bottle and handled the Coca-Cola as Stefan did, held high and tilted to my lips. It tasted both sweet and metallic, exploding with a fizz in my throat like a tiny bomb. I could almost feel Coca-Cola racing through my veins.

I absolutely loved it.

Stefan and I sat on the bench before the hardware store, thirstily drinking our Coca-Colas to the last drop. Afterward, the angry exhaustion of the afternoon subsided. When I told him how the drink transformed me, Stefan nodded but said, "Will take more than Coca-Cola to heal me."

"I will help you get home, Stefan," I said.

"Not good idea," he responded. "Don't look, but across street, two shops down, in doorway… policeman watch us."

Dismayed, I said, "They're *following* us?"

"They will follow me for while," he said matter-of-factly. "I can't have you with me after we rest here. I don't want you in trouble."

"But how will you get back to your home?" I wailed.

The unfairness of this, the violation of privacy, angered me. And then another aspect of it struck me. "How will we be able to see each other again?" I asked. I almost told Stefan how Lieutenant Pellegrino threatened to inform my family if he caught me with him again, but I held back that unpleasant piece of information. Even without the lieutenant's threat, we would have a tense time meeting in Dreamland or anywhere else in Coney Island while being trailed by the police.

Stefan did not answer.

Surging with hurt pride, I said, "I could hardly blame you if you preferred not to see me again."

"Peggy, stop. You know I want to be with you." He reached over, discreetly, and took my hand. "We wait. End of summer not far. I see you, but not in Coney Island. After this all die down."

A part of me wanted to laugh. This was exactly the scenario I'd idly imagined that first night before drifting to sleep. My working at Moonrise Bookstore this autumn, meeting Stefan following a day's work. But after what we'd been through – the passionate kissing in

Hell Gate, followed by the nightmare of accusations and violence in the precinct – I couldn't face waiting nearly two months to see him again. The intensity of our shared experience made enduring long weeks of nothing simply impossible.

"What about if we meet in Manhattan sooner?" I asked. "Could you get away from the police and meet me there?"

He frowned. "How about you, Peggy? How would you do that?"

"Don't worry about me! I can manage it. Let's pick a date. Ten days from today?"

"Peggy, you sure?" he said, hesitantly.

I don't know if it was the Coca-Cola surging in my veins or my anger over the beating, but I said, my voice rising, "Do you want the police to tell us what to do – to run our lives? I know I don't. I absolutely refuse to submit to their bullying, or to anyone's." I peered across the street, to the doorway Stefan spoke of, and spotted a man's silhouette. He was not dressed in a uniform but regular clothes. He stood in the doorway of a closed office, his gaze raking the road with elaborate casualness. It was all I could do to restrain myself from marching across the street to give him a resounding slap.

A smile danced across Stefan's bruised face. "Ah, Peggy, you... magnificent. Like rebel princess."

"I always detest being called a princess, but I'll suffer it on this occasion if you'll agree to meet me in Manhattan."

"I will. Of course I will. Where?"

My first thought was Moonrise Bookstore, but an instant later I had a better idea. "Central Park? The carousel? Can you find it?"

We fixed the date and time, but suddenly his attention was elsewhere. Following his gaze, I spotted a strange trio of people hurrying toward us. In front scrambled the boy with dark tousled hair who'd stared at Stefan and not reappeared. It seemed he went in search of others to share the news of Stefan's condition – did *everyone* in Coney Island know Stefan and feel a proprietary fondness for him? The person charging across the street on the boy's heels was the very one I'd gone out of my way to evade earlier. Yes, Louise, a figure in green, picked up her skirts and ran to Stefan's side, crying, "My God, what have they done to you?" – exactly the words I had used.

"Be calm, Louise," he said. "Nothing is broken."

When she bent over Stefan to get a closer look at the purplish bruise around his eye, her white breasts nearly spilled out of her dress. Averting my eyes, I met the stare of the third person in the trio, giving me a hard, curious appraisal. She was about the same age as Louise, with silky dark curls and a mouth with generously pouting lips and wearing a crimson dress that, while not so low cut in the bosom as Louise's, showed off a perfect figure. I became acutely aware of my own loosely fitting white dress, buttoned to my throat, and my plain hat. Compared to these two, I was the perfect picture of dull, girlish innocence. How mortifying.

"Whatever happened, I'm sure she was at the bottom of it," said Louise, leaving no doubt she meant me.

At that, Stefan pushed away her hand, which had been cradling his chin to get a closer look. "You must not say that," he said. "Peggy did nothing wrong. I will not permit criticism of her."

She didn't persist or argue with him. The two women began to plan how best to get Stefan home – an address Louise obviously knew. But I did not feel quite as jealous now. The way Stefan spoke to her was more of a stern father or brother than an angry lover. Whatever their relationship, I was important to Stefan. He made that clear to all.

When Louise and the other woman, each taking a side, gently pulled Stefan to his feet, he said, anxiously, "Peggy, how will you get back to hotel?" The dark-haired woman's eyebrows shot up at that.

I assured Stefan that it would be easy for me to find my way. I rose to my feet too but hung back awkwardly as they took charge of him. After a few steps, he stopped and turned, moving with stiffness, to say goodbye to me. Louise glanced over her shoulder, eyes narrowed.

"Goodbye," I said. "I'm happy that you have this help."

Louise rolled her eyes; apparently I'd hit the wrong note once again. The woman was impossible.

I stayed put, clutching my handbag in the shadow of a shuttered hardware store as I watched the little party progress toward the heart of Coney Island. Soon enough they'd be among the theaters and the restaurants that bordered the amusement park's massive attractions. It occurred to me that Louise and her companions hadn't demanded to know who laid hands on Stefan. Was violence so common here? As I pondered this, my heart jerked a beat as the man who Stefan pointed out, who watched us from the doorway, moved along the sidewalk across the street. He walked casually, hat pulled low over his face, his hands shoved deep in his pockets. He took no notice of me. Suddenly he craned his neck to see around a woman walking in front of him, as if anxious to keep someone in sight farther up the block. *Was* he the police? Impossible to be certain. Neither fat nor thin and not too tall, he could even be the one who followed us on the boardwalk that first night. I watched, helplessly, as the mysterious man melted into the crowd at the corner, as had Stefan with his trio of helpers less than a minute previously.

How my moods flipped and spun. I was still in the grip of agitation, perhaps fueled by Coca-Cola, when I hailed a buggy driver willing to take money to spirit me to the Oriental Hotel. We passed the large theater, so lonely looking in the middle of the afternoon, now with its doors thrown open and people streaming in like bees returning to the hive. The driver chose a different route than Stefan and I took on foot, and I found myself in the middle of a busy street jammed with theaters and dance halls and taverns. With afternoon slipping to evening, the street was most definitely coming to life. Groups of men sauntered down the sidewalks here. One pair of young men wearing smart suit jackets and bowler hats who stood on the edge of the sidewalk leered at me when my buggy paused a few feet from them. I looked away at once, and they burst out laughing. As the buggy picked up speed again, I thought about Louise and her friend. If I attracted notice in my maiden's dress, imagine what attention they must fend off.

The street sign "Bowery" flashed by. Lieutenant Pellegrino had asked me if Stefan ever mentioned this thoroughfare, along with a specific place called Mabel Morgan's. I didn't see a sign for the latter. I couldn't imagine what he suspected Stefan of when he mentioned this part of Coney Island. Such a milieu didn't seem to have anything to do with anarchists.

Among the many aspects of that bizarre day on Coney Island was the distortion in time. Just as it seemed as if a day had transpired within the walls of the police precinct instead of a couple of hours, when I walked up the pathway to the Oriental Hotel, its minarets soaring and flags flying above, it felt like I hadn't been there for a week. It was half past six, I saw by the large clock mounted on the veranda. Just five hours ago I'd slipped out of the hotel, tingling with excitement about the day before me.

As I made my way across the lobby, I also remembered that that morning I'd arranged it with Lydia that, as far as the rest of the family was concerned, I remained in my room all day. I found it very difficult to care about such things now. Should they see me on their way to dinner, I didn't care. My outrage over what happened to Stefan and me had drained away, replaced by a black pessimism over the state of the human race.

I looked forward to the solitude of my hotel room. I needed to contemplate that and all the strangeness, the painful shocks of the day. I made it all the way to my door and was fishing for the room key in my handbag when the elevator door opened with a clang, and I heard footfall.

"Are you coming down?" called my brother Lawrence.

He was alone, bounding toward me on the corridor. The last time I'd spoken to my brother, just the two of us, he'd been quite critical.

"Not sure I'm up to that," I said cautiously.

"You should, Peggy. They're making a special place for us on the veranda, looking out over the water, because of the heat. We'll be eating late. A sunset supper, Ben says."

Was this Ben's idea, to send Lawrence as envoy to reel me in? It's no fun toying with Peggy if she's not around to be toyed with. Seeing my hesitation, Lawrence said, "Listen, I want you to come. I'm sorry, the things I said yesterday. It isn't right that you sit in a room all day, by yourself, because you think your family dislikes you."

"Is that what Lydia said?"

"No, she kept saying you didn't feel well. But she wouldn't let anyone else check on you but her. So, I thought you must be mad at the rest of us." My brother's features twisted as he strained to express himself on matters he wasn't used to grappling with. "We had a nice time the first day, Peggy, on the trains, and then when we bicycled… I enjoyed that. I don't want us to be sore at each other."

My weary wariness dissolved; his inarticulate appeal touched me. I told Lawrence I'd join the family for dinner. After all, I was completely famished. But I needed time to ready myself.

Alice appeared and a bath was drawn, my hair combed out and

rearranged. She laid out a fresh corset and a high-waisted lilac patterned dress with a square neckline. Another fashionably designed and beautifully stitched and embroidered dress that made me look like a dull ingénue rather than an alluring woman. Alice also put out my jewelry: simple pearl drop earrings and a diamond tiara. That gave me pause.

"You magnificent, Peggy. Like rebel princess." Those were the words Stefan used. With a mirthless smile before the mirror, I watched Alice lower the tiara onto my perfumed black hair.

Lawrence had offered to come back in one hour to escort me to this special supper. Right on time, he reappeared.

"You look pretty," he said. It was amazing what a bath and change of clothes could do; it seemed the terrible experience I'd endured left no visible mark.

"And you are a handsome sight," I said, deciding to make an effort.

Lawrence bowed, and the truth was, wearing an evening tailcoat, his hair parted and combed, Lawrence looked more like Father than he ever had before. I wasn't sure that was a good thing.

Our destination was the veranda that stretched along the ocean side of the Oriental Hotel. I hadn't been there yet. It was more popular in the morning than the afternoon, when the hot sun in the western sky bore down. But it was now somewhere between seven and eight o'clock, and the heat of the day had finally eased. At the end of the veranda stood a forest of potted trees, acting as a barrier to anyone who wanted to continue except through a narrow opening. On either side of the opening stood two men, dressed in hotel uniforms and staring straight ahead, like stone lions in the wild.

Lawrence passed through first, stretching out his hand to bring me in after him. It was quite the dinner setting that the hotel had arranged for us: a long table set with a glowing ivory-white tablecloth, and fringed curtains that hung down halfway from the edge of the veranda roof to shield us from the sun. My family already sat at the table, Henry Taul next to my sister. At the table's head was my Uncle David.

"Peggy... Peggy... Peggy."

Not only did all heads turn at my entrance, but it was all smiles, even a tittering of applause. Ben rose to clap his hands ostentatiously. "I saved a seat for you facing the water," he declared.

One of a half-dozen hovering waiters pulled a chair out invitingly between Ben and my mother. "Feeling better, Margaret?" she asked, while adjusting my tiara.

"Yes, I'm fine," I said to her and to everyone. Lydia, sitting diagonally across, gave me a tiny wink.

A second waiter with a cloth draped over his arm asked if I wanted champagne. I nodded. I heard the gasping suck of a bottle removed from ice, and the cool pinkish liquid tumbled into my fluted glass like a fairy waterfall. As I sipped my drink, a cooling breeze with the faintest hint of salt caressed my face and arms.

"Now that our Peggy is here, let's begin," Uncle David announced. A new gaggle of waiters paraded onto the veranda, holding massive silver trays on their shoulders. When they took off the lids, mounds of sculpted ice were revealed, topped with gleaming shells, lemon slices, and dishes of sauces.

"Cherrystone oysters and littleneck clams," said the head waiter.

A few minutes later came the slices of melon and the asparagus tips, served on the hotel's best china. The silver was polished so rigorously that I could see the diamonds of my tiara reflected in the melon knife.

It seemed that to respond to the heat, everyone ventured into the ocean today, by way of the hotel's private bathing pavilion. After bathing, Lydia and the other females had enjoyed another musical program at the Manhattan Beach Hotel, while the men played pool. I couldn't contribute to any thread of conversation, I was too captivated by the food. It was hard to restrain myself from gobbling it down, savoring every morsel.

But there was something else. I felt strangely aloof from our party, our family, as if I were observing everyone from someplace high above, between the roof of the Oriental Hotel and the first bank of clouds. I didn't feel hostility. I was just… apart.

Leaning over, Ben said, "They suggested chilled salmon for the main entrée. Father told them yes, but I wonder if they'll bungle the mint sauce. There are only three chefs in Manhattan I trust to execute chilled salmon with the proper sauce."

I swallowed my asparagus tip and said quietly, tears burning the corners of my eyes, "They'd better not bungle. After all, we *are* the ruling class."

CHAPTER NINETEEN

Of all the distortions in time, none seemed greater than finding myself in Lydia's hotel suite for the second time. It was exactly twenty-four hours later but felt as if weeks had passed, if not months; more than that, it was as if I, Peggy Batternberg, were a different person. To try to settle my mind, I was the one to sip black coffee this morning.

Lydia stood in the center of her spacious room, wearing her chemise and corset as Alice chose her dress. I assumed our maid's presence was the reason my sister didn't press me for details of my presumed romantic adventure. Or perhaps it was the thick heat, already so oppressive, that accounted for her lassitude. She twirled a strand of blonde hair, staring into space before saying, "I had the strangest dream last night."

"Tell me."

Instead of answering, Lydia lapsed into silence again. Apparently she didn't want to share the details of her dream. As she stood there, waiting for the maid to dress her, I couldn't help but say, "You are positively ethereal, Lydia." It was a polite word for it. The truth was, the girl before me was bony, with frail arms and spindly legs. The corset she chose pushed her breasts toward her collarbone. Otherwise, she'd have no cleavage at all.

Her fine-lashed blue eyes drifted over me. "The fewer clothes I have on, the worse I look. But for you, it's the opposite."

"Lydia!"

An eyebrow arched, she said, "Do you deny you have a good figure?"

"Clothes hang better on you than they ever did on me – or ever will," I pointed out.

Still twirling her hair, Lydia said, "Yes, but there comes a point in time when it's no longer of importance how well the clothes hang, but what happens when they come off."

I suppose it was inevitable that Lydia would contemplate her wedding night with Henry Taul now that the date was set, but there wasn't enough coffee in the world for me to wish to picture that encounter. To my relief, Alice approached at that moment, holding the dress for the day, and there was no more talk along those lines. It was a sailor dress, one of my sister's favorite styles. As Alice fussed with the light blue bow fixed on its neckline, it struck me how much of a beautiful child Lydia looked. Yet by the end of the year she'd be a married woman.

"Peggy, you have to go in the sea after lunch," Lydia said. "It's the only thing to do in this frightful heat."

"I suppose it is."

As she pinned Lydia's hair, Alice said she'd heard that all over the city the parks were filled with people who slept on the ground, afraid that they'd suffocate if they spent the night inside their homes.

"Yes, people are actually dying of the weather," said Lydia, and she yawned.

None of us were sleeping well at night in this heat spell, not even Batternbergs with top-floor hotel suites facing the sea, and ceiling fans. Still, that indifferent yawn was not right. I thought of Stefan, sweltering alone, suffering the pain of his beating in his Brooklyn apartment, of Wiktor and Marta having no choice but to perform labor when, even under the best of conditions, they were not hearty people. I felt a twinge of dislike for my sister. She chose to deny herself food for reasons of nervous strain; Wiktor and Marta had gone without food in Europe and nearly died of it. And people struggled in America too. I thought of the boy who collected bits of gum wrapper and cigarette packet liner from the streets.

"You're looking at me funny – what's wrong?" Lydia was saying.

"Nothing." I began to gather my things. "I think I'll go down to the veranda before it is too hot for it."

She shook her head at me, eyes darting toward Alice. "Stay a bit longer." So, she did want to have a private chat out of the earshot of our maid. I girded myself for the conversation to come. I had no intention of disclosing anything near to the truth about what happened. I prayed my lies would be believable.

As soon as Alice had vanished, Lydia said to me, excitement flushing her wan cheeks, "I helped you yesterday. Now you can help me, later today."

This was *not* what I'd expected.

"Come with me to high tea at the Manhattan Hotel after swimming, Peggy."

I couldn't help but laugh. "This is your idea of illicit activity requiring concealment?"

"We won't be alone. We'll be with Susannah and Jason Campion, the sister and brother I met. I've been attending musical programs with them and having discussions afterward. They're nice people. Very cultured."

"I still don't understand why it would be necessary for me to accompany you."

"Mother's been with me every time up to now, but she thinks I should cool the friendship. You know how snobbish she is!" Lydia's lassitude had vanished; the words now tumbled out. "Even though they're from a perfectly nice and respectable family, Mother says that Susannah is too modern and Jason is too... oh, I don't know. There's not a thing wrong with him, with either of them. Mother just gets her ideas, and now she won't come with me today."

"For heaven's sake, you can't walk over to the neighboring hotel by yourself?"

"That isn't the problem. It's Henry. He doesn't like me to see new people without his being there. If Mother is with me, he's not going to make a fuss. But without her..."

I continued to be baffled by Lydia. "The solution seems to be Henry joining you, not me."

"He's going to that stupid race track after swimming this afternoon. Please, Peggy, just say yes and stop quibbling." Her lower lip pouted angrily. "I didn't hesitate to help you yesterday, and I'm not asking for details this morning. I find it hard to understand why you'd object to this."

"Oh, I have no objection," I said.

"And you won't mention to Mother that we're seeing Susannah and Jason? If she asks, just say you and I are having tea?"

I agreed, finding the subterfuge a little sad. Lydia's movements were so constricted.

Like everyone else in New York City, I wanted to be out of doors, not stuck inside. Even our electric-powered fans seemed to be doing little but blowing warm air from one corner to the other. The shaded hotel veranda seemed a better prospect, and I found a table set for two guests that was not taken. In less than a moment, a hotel waiter appeared before me.

"I'd like an iced tea," I said.

"Very good, Miss. Will anyone else be joining you?"

"No, not today. Would it be possible to receive the morning newspapers as well?"

"Of course, Miss."

I drank not one but two iced teas while I read *The New York Times* and *The New York Tribune*. In the last six days, the heat spell had inflicted nothing less than hell. Even stories of the Triangle shirtwaist factory trial were shoved aside for tales of the city's suffering. *Electric fans and ice are luxuries that very, very few can pay for*, noted one article, making me shift uncomfortably. The largest headline said, *Heat's Scythe Mows Down Fifty-Six on Fifth Day*. And many more seemed to have been driven mad. A man had shouted, "I can't take it anymore," and jumped off a pier into the East River – he couldn't swim, and rescuers had a devil of a time dragging him out of the water because he fought off their help. Another man tried to attack the police with a meat cleaver. It was even worse in Boston and New England, where the temperature had crawled above 100 degrees for two consecutive days.

My eyes wandered to another headline. *Kaiser Wilhelm Addresses Group on German Encirclement* described the German leader's threats over a treaty between France, England, and Russia. I thought again of Stefan saying that a catastrophic war was brewing.

"So you've taken up the newspapers," said Henry Taul as he took the chair across from mine.

"The heat spell is quite the story," I said, scrutinizing Henry. These temperatures were wreaking havoc, even on him. Strands of damp hair clung to his head. He'd missed a button on his white linen shirt.

He waved to the waiter, who immediately pivoted toward us to take Henry's order of lemonade. "I'm worried about my horses," he said. "Over a thousand horses died in New York in the heat spell of '96. I've taken on extra men at the track to keep mine as cool as possible."

His chief concerns were for his animals, not human beings. Words of scorn leaped to my lips, but I forced them down. I'd vowed to not be rude to Henry this summer, for the sake of my family. And there was something else. His eyes were sunken behind those glasses; he had no color. "You look tired, Henry," I heard myself say, and I shifted even more uncomfortably in my chair. My tone was too intimate for a woman speaking to her prospective brother-in-law. It was difficult to find the right degree of familiarity in my dealings with him.

Henry reached impatiently for the lemonade when the waiter tried to put it on the table. He drank it in one voracious gulp, his Adam's apple pulsing in his thick throat. Setting down his glass, he stared down at the little wicker table which was all that stood between us. As the seconds ticked by, I wasn't sure if I should resume my reading the newspaper. There was such a thing as a comfortable silence between two people. We were not experiencing one.

"My mother will be meeting you, all of you," he said abruptly.

"Oh?"

"Why shouldn't you meet her?" he asked belligerently.

"No reason. It's only that Lydia didn't mention it. I just saw her."

He stood up. Apparently, it was time for Henry to move along, and as always, I wasn't sorry to see him go. "You and Lydia are thick as thieves, aren't you? " he said.

"We're sisters, that's all."

"Yes, you are."

He just stood there, seemingly on the verge of saying something that couldn't come out.

Weary of this, I said, dryly, "Well, I shall await further instruction."

That did it. The boards of the veranda creaked under his well-heeled shoes as Henry Taul strode away. The heat definitely brought out the worst in him. With a determined snap, I picked up the newspaper again, but my concentration was broken.

Lydia was right about one thing – in this heat, there was nothing to do but venture into the ocean this afternoon. After our lunch of lobster salad in the hotel dining room, all the Batternberg women gathered for the procession to the bathing pavilion. We would spend a half hour precisely outdoors, to prevent sunburn. To cover the short distance between hotel and pavilion, provisions were made. When each of us stepped away from the shade of the veranda in order to follow the walkway to the beach, a hotel maid walked a step behind, holding a parasol high to shade our skin from the sun. First came Mother, then Aunt Helen, then Lydia, and finally, me. Alice trailed behind me, holding her parasol in one hand and a satchel containing our bathing costumes in the other.

As we made our stately way toward the white strip of sand shimmering at the foot of the pulsing ocean, I felt so ridiculous that I was tempted to apologize to passersby on the boardwalk. How spoiled and shielded we were. What would my dealings with the world be like if every layer of protection were removed? Yesterday I'd gotten a taste of it. In the police precinct, the detective hurled an obscene insult at me while his superior, Lieutenant Pellegrino, pressured and manipulated me. And yet they'd known full well who I was, who my family was, the whole time. What sort of treatment would I have received within those walls if I were from an ordinary family – or from a poor one?

Walking in single file, we reached our destination: the first bathing pavilion, with "Number One" painted discreetly on the door. The maids came in with us, and Alice put them to work, helping us disrobe in curtained stalls. Before disappearing into one, I noticed that the Batternbergs weren't the only females occupying this pavilion. Two women accompanied by their own maid were preparing to step out of the pavilion, already wearing their bathing costumes. The younger one wore something resembling what I'd glimpsed on other women jumping in the surf: a striped belted dress hanging to one inch below her knees.

I'd not paid much attention when fitted for my beach clothing in Manhattan, but when I held in my hands my own bathing costume, I was appalled. It was made of dark blue wool, with long sleeves, a high neckline, and, under its skirt, pants that reached the ankles. Every bit of skin was to be covered except for my face, hands, and feet. This was how I was intended to meet the sea.

"Why is it of such a dark color?" I mused.

The young hotel maid sharing my stall said, "So that no one can see through it when it's wet, Miss. You can't have it be trans... trans..." She frowned, searching for the word.

"Transparent?"

"Yes! You can't be transparent in the water. There could be gentlemen nearby."

I closed my eyes for a moment and then called out, "Alice, did you bring your sewing scissors?"

"Miss, I'll be there in a minute to help," she replied, sounding frazzled with four Batternberg women and four maids on her hands.

"I just need the scissors," I said, and directed the wide-eyed maid assigned to me to fetch them. Once armed with Alice's sharp scissors, I went to work in my curtained stall, humming a little tune.

"There – what do you think?" I asked my maid, holding up the fruits of my labor. I'd cut away the sleeves and snipped the threads attaching the pants. It was now a sleeveless dress that reached, perhaps, my knees.

The maid burst into giggles and said, "It's shocking, Miss."

"Yes," I said, with deep satisfaction.

Lydia called out that the rest of them were ready for the water, and I replied that they should go ahead; I'd follow shortly.

After I'd put on my modified bathing costume, my thick black braids pinned under a bathing cap, I pushed aside the curtain of my stall. None of my family remained, only the maids. I stepped out from the stall to make my way toward the open door.

A gush of female gasps heralded my appearance in the larger part of the pavilion, along with Alice's mournful, "Oh, Miss Peggy. Now you've done it." Quickening my pace, I headed for the wooden doorway hanging open.

As my feet landed in the hot sand and the blazing white sun toasted my face and arms, I could only see one thing ahead of me: the sparkling blue water. I ran toward the ocean, joining the women of my family. They had already ventured in and stood in a cluster, the water not even reaching their knees. My mother, wearing an enormous hat, was the first one to lay eyes on me, and her reaction was predictable. "Margaret, what *have* you done?"

"Don't worry, Mother, nothing is transparent," I sang out as I stepped into the delightfully cool water, the balls of my feet sinking into the firm sand. I provoked other reactions – principally Lydia's, who laughed and said, "Wish I'd had the nerve."

My mother proceeded to scold her for desiring to follow my horrendous example. Not wanting to have my outing spoiled, I pushed my way into deeper water, directly in the path of a white-crested wave. When it crashed against my stomach and thighs I nearly capsized, but righted myself. After being trapped in the inescapable heat, I thrilled to this assault. The cold water carried such a salty, stinging snap.

Soon enough, the water reached my waist. The next wave cost me my bathing cap, and I decided it was time to swim. The last German nanny we'd had insisted on lessons for Lydia and me. It had been quite a while since I practiced my swimming, but it soon came back to me.

I ventured out until my feet no longer touched the ocean floor, and the waves transformed into safer rolling swells. When a slimy, feathery plant of some sort wrapped itself around my leg, I shuddered. But disentangling myself wasn't difficult, and after practicing my breast stroke I shifted to back-stroke. I stared at the wisps of clouds drifting across the sky and two seagulls circling. It reminded me of the seagull Stefan fended off yesterday, and for a moment I lost myself to memories of his strong arms pushing the cart, followed by how it felt to be pressed against him in Hell Gate. Nine days to wait. When I closed my eyes, the sun warmed my eyelids. My arms reached high like two lazy wheels while my feet paddled. The saltwater was buoyant; it was easy to float along.

When a spray of water hit me, I thought for a second I'd aroused the interest of a predatory fish. My eyes flew open – and I saw the slick black haired head of my cousin Ben, just a few feet away. He'd flicked water on me to break my reverie.

"You've discovered the secret," he said, treading water.

"What's that?"

"You have to push out past the waves to swim. Most other girls won't do that. They definitely don't swim out this far."

I looked back toward the shore. I'd gone farther than I realized. I could make out my mother still, thanks to her hat. I also recognized Lydia, covered neckline to ankles in the requisite dark blue wool, while Henry Taul loomed over her, wearing nothing but a scoop-necked T-shirt and swim trunks.

"That's quite a bathing costume," Ben said.

"Have you come to criticize?" I groaned.

"Are you joking? I never criticize a girl for taking off her clothes in public, and I'm sure I'm not the only man here today who votes that ticket."

"I did it for myself, not for *you*," I said, and with that, I side-stroked away from my cousin. Let him find someone else to tease. The sounds of people – both the laughter and chat of those on the Oriental Hotel private stretch, and the faint roar of the thousands of others spread across miles of Coney Island beach – were nicely removed from my own domain of the Atlantic Ocean.

I so enjoyed the swim that it was only after my brother Lawrence ventured out twice to tell me Mother said I must come in, that I made my way back to the bathing pavilion.

CHAPTER TWENTY

My mother's reactions to both what I wore and how far out I swam were predictably acerbic. I nodded, making sounds of contrition. My bout of rigorous exercise had so refreshed me and distracted me from my troubles that I found it easier than usual to cope with her.

After the beach, it was back to our rooms to change once more, this time for tea at the Manhattan Beach Hotel. Lydia, I took note, had abandoned her sailor dress for something more sophisticated: a rose-colored dress with a dropped waistline.

As vast as the Oriental seemed, the Manhattan Beach Hotel was more so. I wondered if it were true that this was the largest such establishment on the east coast. It was like a village rather than a hotel, with its complex of buildings, gardens, piazzas, and verandas. Somewhere within were the rooms of my cousins Ben and Paul. But of far more interest to Lydia were this brother and sister, Jason and Susannah. I was curious about them. For Lydia to make such an arrangement with me, circumnavigating Mother, they'd have to be something special.

The hotel's high-ceilinged, oak-paneled tea room was sprinkled with not only tables sprouting polished silver tea sets, but also a dozen large vases stuffed with red and white roses and gorgeous pink lilies. The floral scents mingled with that of baked, creamed, sugared treats as the maître d' led us to our table, where the celebrated siblings awaited.

My first impression was that they might be twins. They had hair of identical color, a shining chestnut brown, and turned the same wide, welcoming smiles at us. As we took our seats and I was introduced, I realized that Susannah was older, in her late twenties, while Jason looked to be a year or two older than me. She had the rounder face and stronger nose. Jason, with his oval-shaped face and delicate profile, was in truth more attractive.

"I'm so sorry we're late," said Lydia. "Our swim ran over."

I jumped in to say, "It's my fault entirely. I had to be practically dragged out of the water."

Lydia gave way to a meaningful laugh, which Susannah seized on, wanting to know what made the swim so special for me. With a shrug I told of my spontaneous decision to modify my bathing costume and then my intense enjoyment of the salty, waves-tossed ocean.

Susannah said, "Ah, you are quite different from your mother."

Now it was my turn to laugh. "Lydia," I said, "I believe I like your new friends."

Lydia and Jason looked at each other and chuckled. But Susannah leaned toward me, unsmiling. "You are more connected to your id, while your mother, Mrs. Batternberg, exists in a state of complete repression, governed by her super-ego."

"I beg your pardon?"

"Please don't be offended by my sister," said Jason Campion. "She is a disciple of Dr. Sigmund Freud and applies his theories to everyone we meet."

The Interpretation of Dreams was a popular seller at Moonrise Bookstore, and I'd attempted to read it, intrigued by Dr. Freud's theories of a mind that functions beyond what we realize: the unconscious. But for me the book, long and detailed, was too hard to understand. Susannah was pleased that I knew anything of Freud at all and urged me to give *The Interpretation of Dreams* another try. "I can give you a dream journal, it will help enormously. You keep it by your bedside and fill it out the moment you wake up."

"Yes, Lydia, how about you, do you have anything to report on your dreams?" asked Jason.

"Sorry, I don't remember a thing from last night," Lydia said.

At that moment, our waiter arrived with a little cart on wheels bearing the tea tray. He was a man with a fierce gray mustache and a pronounced Scottish accent, dressed in a Victorian topcoat of a previous generation. I had no doubt that many of the patrons of the tea room came specifically to bask in his rolling Rs. As he oversaw a young woman's pouring hot water over the tea-leaves-stuffed brewing baskets, and another woman's offering us cucumber or salmon sandwiches, I wondered why Lydia told Jason and Susannah she didn't remember anything from last night. She had informed me this morning that she was disturbed by a strange dream.

I took tea only, no finger sandwiches. "I prefer to concentrate on scones with clotted cream or cake with icing," I told Susannah. The response could not have made her happier.

"You are an excellent subject for me," she exulted. "Tell me, if there were any food or drink you could have right now, apart from the scones or cake, what would you desire most?"

"Truly?" I asked. When she nodded, I said, "A cold bottle of Coca-Cola."

"Peggy, you must be joking," exclaimed Lydia. "They're not going to have Coca-Cola in a nice hotel."

Susannah Campion dived into a satchel resting at the side of her chair. I spotted a thick book with a dozen markers thrust into pages – that must be Freud's. She withdrew a slender notebook with the words 'Your Dreams' printed on the cover, explained she'd had them custom-made for her prospective subjects. "I anticipate you will have less obscuring of meaning in your dreams," she said, thrusting a notebook into my hand. "You are not as blocked from your unconscious as most young American females."

As we made our way through the first course of our high tea, I learned that the Campions were alone in the world, their parents dying several years ago and, left unsaid but clearly the case, leaving their two children handsomely provided for. Jason had just graduated from Columbia with his undergraduate degree, planning to begin medical studies at Princeton this autumn. They celebrated Jason's degree from Columbia with two weeks in Austria and Germany, followed by a few days home in Manhattan and now several weeks here in Coney Island. While in Europe, they had made a pilgrimage of sorts to Vienna, the home of Sigmund Freud. He had made no public speeches while they were there and would accept no appointments that had not been made months in advance. However, simply breathing the same air as Freud, walking in his footsteps, had transported Susannah. Then it was on to Munich, home of a hundred museums and concert halls and, most important to Jason, the base for composer Richard Strauss.

"Why follow up such heights of culture with a trip to Coney Island?" I asked.

"It's an excellent place to study mankind in extreme emotional conditions," said Susannah earnestly. "Dr. Freud himself traveled to New York City and other American cities two years ago, and I know he specifically spent time in Coney Island, focusing on Dreamland."

"Well, that makes sense," I said, wondering if Freud's visit came before Stefan was exhibiting his art in Dreamland.

"I have tried to obtain every printed interview since that time, and I regret to say that I cannot find even a syllable on what he thought of Coney Island," she said with a sigh.

"What do *you* think Dr. Freud would have made of it?" I asked.

"I'm still composing my opinions, but I think it is a place that exerts a pull that these thousands of people cannot resist because it's the only way they can feel their emotions – through experience of the extreme: fear, contempt, delight, and of course, lust," she said, glancing over at Lydia and Jason as if to be sure they were immersed in their own conversation and not listening to her. Apparently she believed these cerebral creatures were unprepared to hear about such desires. "It's especially the case for the poor factory workers. They labor such long hours, and in such unpleasant conditions of deafening noise and dirt, even risk of continual injury, that ordinary amusements just can't stir them to excitement. They must descend hundreds of feet very rapidly, witness accidents, look upon people with deformities, or make advances of a romantic nature on strangers."

I nodded, trying not to let on that I'd been the enthusiastic object of a stranger's advance.

"Why the fixation on disaster if it were not needed to stimulate the jaded park attendees?" Susannah continued. "There are the buildings set on mock fires, the staged train collisions, the simulated floods and exploding volcanoes."

This was one of the most interesting conversations I'd had since leaving my job at Moonrise Bookstore. Unfortunately, Jason swooped in with a question about Munich for Susannah, and a moment later the talk of the table switched to music – specifically, to Richard Strauss – and my attention wandered.

As the three of them happily debated the music of Strauss versus

Wagner, I became aware of an unusual young woman sitting two tables over, directly in my line of sight. She was an ash blonde, wearing an exquisite lavender dress with filmy sleeves and a matching hat. It was an ensemble perhaps too formal for afternoon tea, especially as she wore ostentatious long earrings set with diamonds that flashed whenever she turned her head. She didn't need such enhancements to impress anyone, for she was astoundingly pretty, with a creamy complexion, an upturned nose and vivid blue eyes. What struck me most was that she was alone but did not seem to want to be alone. When the Scottish head waiter came to her table, she chatted with him until, with an apologetic bow, he was forced to move along. Was she a pampered young wife whose husband was too busy working to join her? That didn't make sense. A couple without children or other family wouldn't come all the way out to the Manhattan Hotel, only to separate during the day. Hadn't she made a single friend at the hotel to share teatime with? I tried to imagine a scenario that explained her.

Our own tea reached the happy stage of scones and cake slices, and I shrugged off the mysteries of the stranger. The raspberry scone made for a heavenly collapse of crumb and cream in my mouth. "I don't need to seek out extreme experiences to enjoy something – I have it right here," I told Susannah, who laughed. I glanced over at Lydia to see if she'd deigned to eat anything and was delighted that she was halfway through a slice of lemon cake. In this company, her appetite returned.

I was sorry to have to say goodbye to the Campion brother and sister. Lydia was right, they made enjoyable companions. Jason seemed quite reluctant to part as well, suggesting they peek inside the music room to see if any orchestra members rehearsed for a later performance. I told them to go on ahead and I'd meet them, for all this tea necessitated a trip to the women's lavatory.

I followed a discreet sign in the lobby to a door leading downstairs. If this were the Oriental Hotel, I'd have had no problem finding my way around, but I got lost in the lower level of the Manhattan Beach Hotel. After locating the lavatory, I took a wrong turn trying to find the stairs, passing the forlorn tailor and shoe-repair shops that I thought I remembered, but after those two establishments, along this narrow hallway, were only closed office doors. The corridor itself was surprisingly filthy, with broken lights. It seemed all effort was being expended on what was visible above.

I came to the end of the hallway and turned left, hoping to reach a more populated area. Exactly the opposite happened. I found myself on an even lonelier and dirtier corridor, this one with a folding chair in a dark alcove jutting to the side. I'd caught something in my shoe and decided to sit and remove the irritant. Then I'd try to properly retrace my steps.

I heard footsteps walking my way. By the lightness of the step and the click of heel I could tell it was a woman. A few seconds later, a blonde in a lavender dress and hat swooshed by. I was amazed by the coincidence. This was the mystery woman who drank tea alone, and she seemed to know her way around this warren of dreary corridors stretching below the Manhattan Beach Hotel.

I began to rise to ask her for directions when two men rounded the corner to head in the same direction. Now I had more people to query, which was a relief.

But the graceless way the taller of them loped along, the cut of the other's black hair – I tensed as I realized I *knew* these two.

What were Lawrence and Paul Batternberg doing down here?

The lavender-clad woman had stopped and turned as if to greet them, her diamond earrings shimmering in the dim light. Peeking out farther from my alcove, I watched my brother Lawrence and my cousin Paul greet her. Except they didn't greet her. The three of them stood together for a few seconds, but no one said a word.

She held out her hand, and Paul put a thick white envelope in it.

"It's ridiculous to do this down here," she said. I had imagined a woman of her elegance would have a low, lilting voice, but hers was high-pitched, even nasal.

"You know that's the way it has to be," said Paul.

"Nobody ever asks me what I think," she complained.

Paul shrugged and said, with sarcasm, "Hope you have a nice week."

The two Batternbergs, instead of turning around, continued down the hallway, while she was the one who doubled back in my direction. I pulled back into the alcove so that she couldn't see me and listened to her footsteps grow fainter until I couldn't hear them at all.

CHAPTER TWENTY-ONE

"We were about to give you up for lost," said Lydia after I finally found the correct route back to the main lobby of the Manhattan Beach Hotel and on to its Music Room.

"I *was* lost for a bit, but here I am," I said, forcing a smile.

Lydia and Jason Campion resumed their appraisal of the violin rehearsal they'd witnessed.

"Strauss would never say too many violins," she teased.

"No, but you would, and I confess, you'd be correct," said Jason. He was not tall, at least an inch shorter than me. Which meant that he was close to Lydia's height. She didn't have to tilt her head back to talk to him as she did with Henry Taul. Even in my present flustered state, it pleased me to see my sister enjoying herself.

But that was to be taken from me after I shifted my gaze to Jason. His hands linked behind his back, he inclined his head toward her as if she held an invisible string. His lips curved into a smile no matter what words she spoke, and his brown eyes gleamed with deep admiration. This young man was falling in love with my sister. No wonder my mother tried to discourage Lydia seeing him again.

What about Lydia? I recognized no symptoms of infatuation. But after we bade our farewells to the Campions, she linked arms with me and said with a sigh of regret, "Back to the Oriental we must go." Is this how a woman should react to returning to the side of her fiancé? Yet a crowded hotel lobby wasn't the place to probe my sister's emotions – if I should do that at all. Lydia hadn't pressed me on what happened during my day with Stefan. Perhaps she should be awarded the same privacy.

As we left the hotel to make our way through its prize rose gardens, my thoughts returned to what I witnessed below. The envelope contained money, I suspected. Why were my cousin and brother paying this pretty young woman? I was fully aware of the reason most men handed cash to women, but I couldn't believe a sexual link existed between her and the two young men of my family. She and Paul didn't seem to even like each other. Then again, most females didn't care for Paul, me included.

As Lydia and I eased around a ridge of yellow rose bushes, it struck me that there was another Batternberg who was fully capable of charming women. And he was the same person who virtually ran Paul's life. Yes, the more I thought about it, the more I was certain that the lavender-clad beauty must be Ben's kept woman. She wasn't a prostitute, but such an arrangement meant she wasn't suitable for being introduced to the family. For convenience's sake, he'd stashed his doxy in the same vast hotel – now I knew why he wanted to be apart from us – and, for whatever reason, sent Paul with some money for her. Perhaps it was her weekly allowance. High tea wasn't cheap, and neither were those diamond earrings.

I hesitated to believe it, though. She didn't seem quite his sort. Ben had three types of females in his life. At society functions, he would be seen with an attractive girl from a nice Jewish family, the proper escort for an ambitious young Batternberg. The women who made his pulse race fastest were the residents of the city's poshest brothels, I remember vividly the attention paid to his little black book. In between were the quick conquests to stave off boredom, like the girl he'd flirted with at our Independence Day picnic. The woman I saw in the tea room and, shortly afterward, the downstairs corridor, didn't fit into any of these groups. Expensively dressed and full of complaints, she seemed like too much bother for Ben. But we'd grown apart; it was possible he'd changed in the last few years. She was pretty enough to be any man's type.

If this were indeed the situation, I hated my brother's being exposed to Ben's sordid private arrangements. This is just what I was afraid of that first evening in Coney Island: the corruption of Lawrence. Should I try to wring the truth out of him? For all I knew, he and Paul could be on their way to the Oriental, walking behind us. I turned around to scan the crowd.

I didn't spot my brother or cousin. But I did see a face I knew: the strangely insolent, flat-nosed driver of Henry Taul's, whom I'd glimpsed twice the day of the picnic. Instead of acknowledging me, he looked away toward a grove of trees.

Was he following us? I shook off the notion. All the talk at the police precinct about Stefan and me being followed by a strange man had made me too suspicious. I knew this driver was one of Henry's favorite employees. But I also knew Henry was supposed to have spent the late afternoon at the race track, supervising the comfort of his horses. Who drove him there and back? There was so little driving to be done on this holiday that it wouldn't make sense for Henry to give this man the afternoon off just when he was needed. It occurred to me that Henry was perfectly capable of driving himself, like Ben and Paul. And perhaps this man was given another important task to perform. *Keep an eye on Lydia.*

Spying on his fiancée. As distasteful as that prospect seemed, it aligned with my memories of being Henry's girlfriend. At first he'd seemed so confident and casual, until one day he was full of questions about who

I saw and spoke to at a party he hadn't attended – and then of course he was locking me in a lavatory when I wouldn't answer the question about who'd "spoiled" me.

Yes, I was discarded spoiled goods, but Lydia was the pure and beautiful young girl he'd decided to marry. How vigilant would he be where she was concerned? I feared no limits existed. If the Taul driver were spying on her, what did he see? Lydia and her sister having high tea with a brother and sister. Harmless. I just had to hope that the driver didn't get close enough to detect the worship for Lydia pouring out of handsome young Jason Campion.

Considering her fiancé's possessive nature, I wondered if I should advise Lydia to break off from the Campions. I didn't want to. In fact, I passionately didn't want to. They were kind, intelligent people. But there a fear nagged me, a growing dread that I couldn't completely define.

It was Lydia who spoke first. As we walked up the steps to the Oriental Hotel, she said, squeezing my arm tighter, "You know, this holiday has brought us together, Peggy. I haven't felt this close to you since – gosh, since we were in the nursery."

A near-painful gush of happiness seized me, and I squeezed her arm back. I had established a feeling of genuine family with my sister – and my brother. I couldn't upset this delicate balance with suspicions or accusations and so decided to say nothing to her about Henry's driver trailing behind us.

As for the other matter, there was no need to embarrass Lawrence with my questions. I knew who was running the show as far as the junior class of male Batternbergs was concerned. Ben's affairs were no concern of mine, but I could at least ensure that my fifteen-year-old brother was no longer privy to his sexual circus.

That night, at another late dinner held on the ocean-side veranda, I sat between my mother and Ben yet again. There would apparently be a seating chart for as long as this heat spell necessitated our special table. By the time the soft-shell crabs arrived, talk had turned to forming a late outing to Coney Island. Tuesday night's fireworks outside Dreamland were not to be missed.

"Will you favor us with your presence, Peggy?" asked Ben.

I felt a distinct aversion to experiencing Coney Island with him. Dreamland belonged to Stefan and me now.

"I think not," I said. "I'm making progress with my book."

"How retiring of you," Ben said, but he did not try to change my mind.

I decided to stir things a bit.

"Are you happy with your rooms at the Manhattan Hotel?" I asked. "I had tea there this afternoon, it was nicely done, but downstairs, the corridors below the lobby, it's quite disordered."

I studied my cousin's face, waiting for him to show uneasiness as he realized I might have run into Lawrence and Paul or his mistress making their rendezvous. No such realization sparked. He said, wryly, "Oh, they never stop talking about how the hotel is the preferred destination of presidents and princes – meanwhile, the rooms are dusty, the staff dim-witted, and the water is hot when you want cold or cold when you want hot. Paul complains so much that I fine him a dime every time he grouses."

"It doesn't bother you?"

He shrugged. "Faded glory interests me."

It was true that Ben was indifferent to the fastidious standards of conduct, hospitality, and dress most members of my family obsessed over. Protocol made him impatient. He was picky about fine cuisine, but I'd also seen him happily devour food bought on the streets. He'd love the sausages Stefan sold on the promenade.

"If you're so curious about the hotel, why don't you personally survey my rooms?" he asked, his eyes dancing.

I could swear that Henry Taul leaned across the table in order to better hear my response. Lydia was oblivious, deep in conversation with Aunt Helen. Henry and Lydia sat next to each other but were not united. For a second, I pictured smiling Jason Campion hanging on her every word.

"How about tomorrow morning?" I asked Ben.

His hand, holding a spoon of consommé l'Adelina, halted on the way to his lips. He gathered himself, sipped the soup, and said, "How enchanting."

"I won't come too early," I said. "If you're planning to sleep in."

"I don't sleep in," he said with a side glance. "Room 505."

When supper concluded, instead of billiards and cigars in the hotel, Ben gathered up his acolytes and headed over to Coney Island for fireworks. I decided to follow through on my announced excuse and return to *Wings of the Dove*. But as my determined reading progressed, I realized the direction the novel was taking with considerable dismay. The character I most liked, Kate Croy, a clever woman with a secret lover, Merton Desher, befriends an extremely wealthy and extremely sick young woman, Milly Theale. The purpose being that if Merton manages to marry Millie and she dies quickly, Kate and Merton can enjoy her fortune. The naivete of Milly disgusted me, and yet how could I of all people rejoice in her exploitation? This novel was ruined.

I tossed Henry James aside, only to endure a shallow, broken sleep. It must be this grueling heat spell. Would I be any more comfortable sleeping on the beach, like the unfortunates who poured into the parks, desperate for relief? It was not a choice I could make. But such a scenario entered my dream. Wearing only my nightgown, I hurried down the carpeted hallway outside my room, seeking to leave the hotel, when the hallway turned into the dark and dirty corridor under the

Manhattan Hotel, and I was not only lost but in fear, with a shapeless shadow gaining ground.

I woke with a start, my forehead damp with perspiration. The morning sun was bright. I staggered to my open window. The day brought no breeze, no drop in temperature. I turned to glare at the dream journal I placed by my bedside, at Susannah's suggestion. I had no intention of reliving my nightmare by recording it.

I was admittedly in a sour mood when I strode through the gardens of the Manhattan Hotel, approaching the entrance. I had not decided how to bring all this up with my cousin, and I was angry with myself for the nerves fluttering in my stomach. When I knocked on the door to Room 505, Ben called out, "Come in" right away. I worried he would be half-dressed, lounging on his bed. "Alone at last," he'd croon.

I couldn't have been more wrong. Ben had a thick rectangular table set up in the center of his suite, and it was covered with papers, both loose and in folders. There were bound books stacked, too. Ben himself sat at the table, wearing a white shirt with the sleeves rolled up, next to his father, who was wearing a summer suit. The men had a pot of coffee on the table, half-filled cups in front of them.

Uncle David and Ben each greeted me, with Ben suggesting I have a look around until he could take a break to entertain me. I had no interest in evaluating the furniture, linens, or water temperature of Ben's suite. What aroused my intense curiosity was what he was up to at this long table. At our many meals and gatherings, no one had given any indication of bringing work with them to the beach holiday. It couldn't be law school business, for my uncle wouldn't be closely scanning those sorts of documents. I edged closer to the table and saw among the papers some highly detailed maps, the sort I had a hunch were used for mines. Some were in English and some in Spanish. One of the English-language maps said "Taul" at the top.

Two things occurred to me as I stood at the edge of that table, looking down on my relatives scrutinizing a Spanish-language map. One was that the consolidation of mines owned by the Batternbergs and the Tauls was more important than I'd realized, than perhaps Lydia realized as well, and after all she was to be the human glue between the families. The second was how shocked they would be if I were to pull out a chair and join them, saying, "Could you use a third head on this? Tell me what the situation is." It had long been assumed that I would have nothing to do whatsoever with the family business. But women were writers, teachers, doctors. I'd read that women were taking law degrees, even though we didn't yet have the right to vote.

Uncle David looked up as if he could hear my rebellious thoughts, and he frowned. He didn't seem pleased that I had gotten close enough to read the maps and papers. I forced myself to stroll around Ben's suite. I peered in his bedroom. His clothes from the night drooped across a chair. Thumb-eared books towered next to the bed. I really could not picture the delectable blonde of yesterday venturing into this domain. Ben must visit her in her rooms.

Back in the main area of the suite, I noticed a line of photographs propped on a table near the window. They were casual pictures of members of our family, myself excluded, I was relieved to see. Most were of Ben, Paul, or Lawrence. One showed Lydia smiling adoringly at Henry Taul, his arm around her.

"I'm the one who needs a break," said Uncle David, standing and stretching. "I'll go down for *The New York Times*." With a nod to me, he was out the door.

Ben joined me at the photograph display. "Paul's taken this up pretty ferociously. He's actually booked a separate room and boxed it up with interior walls to serve as a darkroom."

"It's Paul who I've come to talk about," I said, turning to face my older cousin.

"Oh?"

I could sense his wariness as strongly as if it were a pomade emanating from his thick black hair. Last night I'd thrown him off by suggesting I'd come to him like this. He knew that something significant must be behind it, that I'd never go out of my way to be alone with him again. I felt a flicker of fear over the coming accusation. But it was too late now to halt what I'd set in motion.

I said, "When I was downstairs, in the corridors beneath the lobby, I saw Paul and Lawrence handing an envelope that I think contained money to a young woman, a blonde, a very expensive looking blonde, and one whom I've never been introduced to."

I waited for him to recoil, to bluster. Ben did neither of those things. He said, calmly, "Why come to me?"

"I think she is yours."

"Mine? Do I now own human slaves? If so, I've not been informed."

"Your kept woman," I snapped. "Girlfriend, if you want to be genteel about it. You told Paul to give her an allowance and he was following orders."

Ben held up a hand. "Peggy, I think you were confused about what you saw. Mistaken."

"Am I blind? Dumb? I don't think so."

"For the sake of argument, if this sighted blonde were my doxy, why should you care?" His voice was hard now, like the lash of a whip. "What business is it of yours?"

"I couldn't care less who you keep, except for a certain degree of pity for your latest trophy. But I really do not want my brother exposed to these illicit arrangements. He's fifteen years old."

"Ahhhh, so this is all motivated by sisterly concern," he said, folding his arms.

"You admit that Paul and Lawrence took money to her at your request?"

Ben burst out laughing. "Are you playing lawyer, Peggy? This is now officially the high point of my summer."

Furious, I said, "Maybe I should take this up with your father."

The laughter died. Ben's hand shot out to grip my shoulder, so tight that a spasm of pain shot through me. "Say nothing to my father about this."

"Why?" I cried. "Why should I help you? I *will* speak to Uncle David."

Panic flashed across Ben's face before, with visible effort, he resumed control. "I don't want my father to know that I'm keeping her here in the hotel. He can't learn about Thelma's presence. Your brother won't be anywhere near any more necessary… errands. Does that satisfy you?"

I stared at him, my thoughts spinning. So, her name was Thelma. And he was afraid of his father finding out.

Ben said, "It better satisfy you. Or else—"

At that moment, the door to the hallway clicked open, and Uncle David strolled in, a bundle of newspapers under his arms. "There's talk of suspending the mail service because of the heat spell," he announced. "More dead in New York, and it's even worse in New England."

"That's terrible," I said, moving toward the door.

"Leaving us, Peggy?" my uncle asked.

I paused at the door, glancing back at Ben, standing motionless before that line of propped-up family photographs. "Yes, I have… shopping," I said.

Out in the hallway I intended to walk quickly to the elevator, eager to find myself out of this hotel, but my heart was beating so fast, I had trouble drawing a full breath and had to reach out to the wall. I had expected the conversation to be unpleasant, but not to provoke threats. Ben's reaction didn't just disturb me, it frightened me. I was chagrined to discover he could still intimidate me.

During a holiday the days are supposed to pass quickly. My God, but the next few hours felt interminable. I didn't want to talk to anyone, to go anywhere. My room was an inferno. The only refuge seemed to be the ocean. I simply couldn't wait for the rest of my family to make their way to the bathing pavilion. After lunch, I took my modified bathing costume from Alice and went alone, right after lunch, not waiting the recommended full hour. The sky was half-covered with wispy clouds. But I could feel no rain quivering in the air as I walked down the beach.

The crushing waves and buoyant salty water proved a tonic for me, body and soul. I practiced all my swim strokes, pushing myself harder than the day before. I waved off Lawrence when once again he was sent to retrieve me. Only when I was good and ready did I emerge from the water, my skin and hair soaked along with the bathing costume that clung to me.

I didn't see Mother or Lydia or any of my other family among the people lounging on our part of the hotel's private strip of beach, the one spreading down from "Pavilion One." They must have given up on me, which suited me perfectly.

There was a tight cluster of young people standing together, laughing, that I needed to make my way around. "Excuse me," I said, veering to the left of the group to reach the pavilion. My arms and legs had that pleasurable throbbing from exercise, and my feet sank into the sand as I more or less staggered toward the pavilion, my head down.

It was a shock when I smacked right into someone, head first, and fell back in the sand. Embarrassed, I laughed and made a shade of my hand as I peered up at the tall man looming over me, his back to the sun. It was Henry.

He leaned down and offered me his hand. I took it – warm and damp with grains of sand from his hand or mine, now grinding together into my palm and fingers. He pulled me up as easily as if I'd been a rag doll. His bare shoulders and the top of his chest glowed with a fresh tan.

Now face to face, physically closer than we'd been in years, and with fewer clothes on than during that last fateful fumbling in his Saratoga hotel room, I found myself speechless. So was he.

I decided the only thing to do in the situation was nod and continue to the bathing pavilion. I made it to the doorway when, feeling a pinprick of uneasiness, I looked over my shoulder. Henry wasn't anywhere near; he had returned to the water with a resounding splash and hard athletic kick.

I was fairly unnerved by the encounter with Henry, which followed on the heels of my quarrel with Ben. It was tempting to have dinner brought up and eat alone, for I needed time away from my family. But the air was still so heavy and thick in my room that it was impossible. I had no choice but to go down.

At first it seemed I made the right choice, for it was more comfortable on the dinner veranda than any other place on the island. The occasional ocean breezes felt like merciful balm. The place next to Lydia sat empty. Her fiancé did not join us, and no one remarked on his absence or asked Lydia about him. I wondered if Henry made anyone else as uncomfortable as he did me. I sat next to Ben as always, but we didn't speak to each other. We were at a stalemate – or was the better term "checkmate"? Our mutual antipathy did not go unnoticed. I caught Aunt Helen in a thoughtful stare in our direction, oblivious to conversation.

That conversation, besides comments on the food, centered on the other branches of the family: minutia on various Batternberg relatives not present – their health, improvements made on their homes, university choices, servants needing to be fired, notable purchases of art or furniture. This was what I grew up on, and I long ago learned how to endure the tedium by occasionally voicing agreement or asking an innocuous question so that I seemed attentive, but was in reality occupied by my own thoughts. The charade was helped along by two glasses of chilled champagne.

Most of us had finished our lamb chop and green beans almandine when Henry Taul suddenly appeared. He said, "It's happening now. Come or you'll miss it. Everybody."

Lydia half turned in her chair, frowning. It was Uncle David who spoke from the head of the table: "Henry. We're at dinner. Please have a seat." Beneath his geniality was the chill of disapproval.

"It's the Siege of Alexandria," Henry said, booming with enthusiasm. "The Oriental Hotel puts it on every other Wednesday night. Hundreds of people and real ships. If you sit here through your coffee, you'll miss the battle."

Lydia looked unconvinced. My mother shot a look at my uncle, who seemed more intent on silently gathering the opinion of his oldest son. From where I sat, I could not read Ben's expression. It was Lawrence who swung the tide when he said, "That sounds like fun, Henry."

"Yes," I echoed. "Why not?" The boredom of our table had been in danger of putting me to sleep in my chair.

"Very well," said Uncle David. "Lead the way."

The waiters did not hide their surprise when the Batternberg party stood up to leave abruptly. Lydia silently walked at Henry's side as he hurried us along the veranda and down to the water, in the direction of the Manhattan Beach Hotel. The day was just beginning to fade to twilight.

"Is this in imitation of the amusement park, that the fine hotels feel they must put on such spectacles?" my uncle wondered.

"They've been mounting it for years," Henry insisted. "I saw it the last time, and it was splendid. Everyone from Wall Street should come out and see."

"Why should they do that?" asked Ben, lighting a cigarette.

"Because we are Rome! America is Rome! We are the empire the world should fear, not the British, the French, or the German. Don't you see?" Henry was beside himself.

Hundreds of eager people already waited, held back behind a rope stretched between poles along the beach. On the other side, close to the water, marched two dozen men dressed in ancient garb, gripping swords. I assumed these were to be the Egyptians. Many, many more men stood on the decks of three ships sailing toward us, the soldiers in full Roman gear. On each boat torches blazed, which in this heat seemed ridiculous, although I had to admit that the orange-white flames reaching up to the violet sky added to the spectacle. The breastplates of the men's armor glowed.

We took our place to the side and the back of the crowd. Our view wouldn't be the best for observing the "battle" to come, but I don't think any of us cared too much. We were primarily there to appease Henry Taul. I thought of that table in Ben's room, covered with maps of mines.

Any hope that Henry would calm himself died after the trumpets from a small orchestra blasted across the beach. He leaped over the rope separating spectators from soldiers as if to join them. A horrified hotel employee tugged on his shirt, and the word "safety" floated up the beach, but Henry pushed him away. Pinkerton guards came forward, but the white-maned Mr. Lancet emerged from the front of the crowd and seemed to be directing employees to leave Henry alone. The son of one of the richest men in the country must be allowed to run amok.

"Oh, for God's sake," said Uncle David. Paul began to laugh, and Ben elbowed him to stop, though I saw his shoulders shaking too.

Lawrence just seemed confused. My uncle craned his neck, worriedly scanning the faces of our fellow hotel guests, fearing that Henry was making a spectacle of himself within the spectacle. Fortunately, the crowd seemed wholly captivated by the Roman ships. They looked like clusters of torches gliding magically toward the sand.

My sister stood apart from the rest of us. She never turned away or covered her eyes. She tracked Henry's running up and down the beach, shouting and clapping his hands, with tense concentration.

I moved closer to her, to offer silent support.

We both watched as two young men slipped past the rope to stand with Henry. Both wore the Taul uniform jackets, and even in the dimming light I recognized the driver from earlier today, spotted in the Manhattan Beach Hotel garden. The other man was dark-haired and vaguely familiar. I'd seen him on the periphery of our gatherings as well. The way they flanked Henry, it was as if they were allies more than servants.

Unable to hold back any longer, I said, "Lydia, I think Henry's driver might have been following us earlier, when we left tea."

I waited for her to deny it. Instead she said, "Yes, Henry has them do that."

"Them?"

She raised her finger as if to point but then quickly lowered it. She must have meant the dark-haired one as well as the blond. "They run his errands, and sometimes the errand is to keep track of me."

"That doesn't upset you?"

After a long silence, Lydia responded. "Henry says it's because he loves me dearly, and he doesn't want anything bad to ever happen to me."

And with that, she threw back her little shoulders, put a smile on her face, and waved to her fiancé, who was at that moment plunging his fist into the air as if he held an imaginary sword.

CHAPTER TWENTY-TWO

The heat spell of 1911 was talked and written about for many years, but for those who lived through it in New York and the rest of the Northeast, what is lost in such accounts is what it was like to be in the middle of it, the feeling of alternating panic and enervating despair over whether this would ever end. Each day it seemed as if it simply must be the last. But the next day would dawn, as pitilessly hot as the one before.

The morning after Henry Taul behaved so oddly at the Alexandria battle spectacle, my mother began to talk of leaving the Oriental Hotel. Since we had yet to be introduced to Henry's mother, this was quite an admission of how much she was suffering, that she would forego the all-important meeting. But it was not just her own physical discomfort. Mother said several times, "This heat can cause temporary imbalance of the mind." Yes, the stories of those driven to insanity made for gripping newspaper stories: the poor desperate souls who drowned when they threw themselves into lakes, rivers, or oceans without any ability to swim, the tragic few who shot themselves. But I believe the person my Mother meant was Henry. She had decided that the heat spell unhinged him, and were we to escape its reach, he'd become normal again. It was true that Henry's behavior was increasingly bizarre, but the truth was he'd always been an eccentric of rapidly shifting moods. Mother hadn't spent much time in his company until this holiday. I'd known him longer than anyone else in my family, though of course this was never referred to. Henry's vast fortune and good looks smoothed over the fault lines of his character, like a thickly woven Turkish carpet stretching across a buckling floor. Now that my family, and that included Lydia, had spent more time with him in strained circumstances, they could see the breaks and splinters.

The problem with abandoning the hotel was, where could we go? Saratoga Springs, Oyster Bay, Newport, the resort hotels and weekend houses all sweltered just as much as those of New York City. The bigger obstacle was Henry, who said, "My mother can't be suddenly moved, especially since these salt water treatments are helping her legs." Mother backed down, but she wasn't happy. The next two days she spent in her suite, fans whirring and her personal maid Beatrice pressing her head with cold compresses, as she struggled to plan Lydia's wedding.

It was spotting that bucket of ice in her suite that gave me an idea. With *The Wings of the Dove* abandoned, I longed for something to read to pass the time until my meeting Stefan. I went to the shop in the lobby of the Oriental Hotel and was happy to see a corner shelf devoted to books. But none of the novels appealed to me, for they were ridiculous Western adventures or shallow romances. My own daydreams were dominated by a blissful aching for Stefan, but I didn't want to sully the emotion I felt by equating it with the love affairs depicted in popular novels.

My attention drifted to the table of weekly newspapers and magazines for sale: *Saturday Evening Post, Town Topics, Ladies' Home Journal*, and, to my delight, *Harper's Bazaar* and *Vogue*, along with many more. "Are you interested in any of our publications, Miss Batternberg?" asked the saleswoman anxiously. Her face was flushed red and shiny. The hotel hadn't seen fit to place an electric fan in the windowless shop in which she toiled. Her hair was scraped up into a tight bun, but the brown tendrils that escaped down her neck were wet with perspiration. I felt badly for her.

"I'm interested in all of them," I said. "Can I purchase a copy of each?"

"Of course! How lovely!" she said. "Anything you like, you have only to ask. We can order any book, or for that matter anything you desire. A special treat you'd like to eat or a drink that's not available on a restaurant menu? I hope you'll let me know."

"How about bottles of Coca-Cola?"

She blinked for a few seconds, stunned, but then rallied. "Yes. Certainly. How many bottles?"

"Let's begin with a dozen." I gave her my room number. She didn't ask whom to bill the items to. I admit to some satisfaction over the prospect of either Henry Taul or my mother eventually paying for the Coca-Cola.

And so I fashioned a method for surviving the heat spell: I arranged for my own large bucket of regularly refreshed ice to be stationed in my room, and I submerged the bottles in it. Every morning and many of the late afternoons, I took down a bundle of magazines and cold Coca-Colas and set myself up on the shadiest section of the veranda. I also arranged to drink Coca-Cola at lunch while everyone else stuck to iced tea or lemonade. In the early afternoon I swam. At night I joined whomever else was dining at the hotel.

On Thursday evening the smallest group yet gathered for dinner. Henry had taken Lydia into town in his motor car to dine at Delmonico's, and my mother was eating a light meal in her room, Aunt Helen keeping her company. That left me as the only woman at the family dinner. I noticed with some amusement how different a direction the conversation took. Uncle David and Ben talked over the latest troubling news coming from Mexico and an election that established a leader who claimed to be for the interests of the common man. The winds of revolution were not wholly welcome in a country where the family's mining interests could be affected.

After dinner, wanting to postpone the moment I must go upstairs, I found a place on the veranda yet again. I opened a soda bottle with a loud snap – I was getting quite proficient with the opener I'd obtained – and poured my fizzy Coca-Cola into a tall glass, all the while balancing *Town Topics* on my lap. I glanced up to catch two frumpy, gray-haired matrons observing me. To go by their expression, I was an orangutan on display at the Bronx Zoo.

Relishing their disapproval, I turned the pages of the weekly magazine until I reached the irresistible column "Saunterings." This was a feature like no other magazine's. It revealed salacious stories of New York while naming no names, doubtless to fend off furious protests and lawsuits. They were called "blind items." I was rarely sure of anyone's identity. We Batternbergs were off to the side, not at the pinnacle of Manhattan society. If it were 1875, and Mrs. Astor sent out her invitations to the "Four Hundred," no one from our Jewish family would make it onto her long list. Times had changed since those parties, and on Wall Street, the Batternberg name was often said in the same breath as that of Rockefeller and JP Morgan, but we weren't considered blue bloods. Some of my aunts and uncles minded that. I honestly never did. Ben didn't either.

But reading one "blind" item made me feel an unpleasant tickle of recognition:

What incorrigible playboy is trying to settle down with the

delectable daughter of a deep-pocketed family, hoping the news won't follow him to New York from Paris about an all-night party with twenty of the most ravishing ladies of the night France has to offer, a party costing $25,000. Of course staying up all night is an easy proposition for this gentleman, with the help of his favorite friends. Paris, we hear, will never completely recover.

That couldn't be Henry, could it? I thought, dismayed. Some said that the word "playboy" was invented to describe Henry Taul, with his round, youthful face and outrageous antics. But those days of debauchery were behind him. And he hadn't mentioned that Paris was on his European trip. It had to be someone else. America's army of privileged sons made a playground of Paris, London, and Rome. I put the newspaper aside.

Reports must have been made of my veranda reading, because the next morning, when I poked in my head to see Mother, she had a list of complaints ready. "You must stop drinking Coca-Cola in public and reading tawdry magazines, and you absolutely must stop wearing that bathing costume. Apart from its indecency, you wear it every single day. The same item of clothing." She shuddered.

"Alice scrubs it and lays it out to dry every night," I said. "It's clean."

My mother cleared her throat. This meant something distinctly unpleasant was seconds away.

"In my generation, Margaret, many girls were married by the age of twenty-one," she said, as gently as she was capable of. "I realize that you think you are more advanced in your ideas than the rest of us, that you are a modern woman, but the truth is, in spite of your position at that bookshop, you're very young in your ... shall we say, *experience of life*. You are not aware of doing so, but your actions, the way you dress and so on, they can be provoking."

"Provoking," I echoed. It couldn't have been the gray-haired ladies who fussed over seeing me last night. I wondered just who was running to her with complaints.

Mother said, "It is all very well for the girls who work in factories to act in a certain way, but you are a Batternberg, you absolutely must remember that at all times."

I thought of Stefan's kissing me on the beach and in Hell Gate, of my clinging to his arm afterward, and I said, "I will."

To placate her, I read my magazines in my room before going down to lunch. There was nothing to do today besides swim; for tomorrow, I'd agreed to accompany Lydia for another outing with the Campions. This time we were to hear a botanical lecture in the Rose Garden of the Manhattan Hotel. Horticulture history interested me about as much as orchestral music, but I agreed to go.

I was impatient to swim and, gathered with my family at the restaurant for lunch, I ate but a few forkfuls of lobster salad. I did drain my Coca-Cola with a certain wistfulness. From now on, I'd drink it only in my room, I decided. Ordinarily, I'd resist conforming to Mother's wishes. Still, with the date for my seeing Stefan drawing nearer, I thought it prudent to call as little attention to myself as possible.

As had become normal, I went on ahead to the bathing pavilion sans Alice. I was quite capable of changing clothes myself. I hated to think this was the last day to wear my cherished bathing costume too, but it would have to be retired.

When I stepped out of the pavilion onto the sandy beach, I felt a wave of exhaustion ripple through my entire body, and my head throbbed. There was only one tonic for this: the bracing cold water of the Atlantic.

I crossed the sand with determination, trying to ignore the heaviness weighing down my arms and legs. My body, incredibly, craved a nap. I was certain the ocean would revive me, and thankfully it did. I moved out farther, until the water was almost waist high. Suddenly I was struck with dizziness and felt sick to my stomach.

Is this sun stroke? I wondered. I'd heard of people becoming ill, even feverish, from being in the sun too long.

But if I left the water for the hot beach and airless hotel, wouldn't I feel even worse? I decided to go a little deeper, up to my shoulders, and see if cold water submersion helped. If not, I'd have no choice but to return to dry land.

Over the last several days, I'd become quite skillful at entering deeper water while minimizing the impact of the waves, most of them small but occasionally large and crushing if a ferry boat had just passed. In my present dazed and nauseous state, that ability fled. I watched dully as a large wave bore down on me, and I didn't even have the sense to turn or brace myself, much less dive under the wave. With the force of a powerful slap across the face it stunned me, and then I was sucked underwater. I struggled feebly, my arms and legs flailing, until, gasping, I came up for air. Agonizing stomach cramps hit, and to my shock, I bent over and vomited in the ocean.

That's when I knew I was in serious trouble. I looked at the other people around me for a familiar face, but my eyesight was too blurred, whether it was salt water or illness, I didn't know. They were just distant pale blobs in the dark blue water.

"Help me," I said. It was a hoarse croak after the vomiting.

I staggered back in the direction of the beach but found it excruciatingly difficult to push through the waist-high water. It was as if my brain were disconnected from my legs.

"Look at the wave – it's a big one," squealed a girl. With dread, I turned around to see a white-crested wave, even larger than the last, curling toward us all. A ferry must have just passed. Nothing could stop it. I had ten seconds at the most before it hit. I'd never get close enough to the shoreline to escape being upturned again. Sour clots of vomit burning in my throat, I didn't want to suffer another vicious pummeling.

My only hope was to turn and force myself to swim under the wave right before it crested. I gathered every bit of my strength. At the back of my mind I thought, wildly, *This will be quite the story to tell everyone later.*

In those last few precious seconds, I went forward, into the sea, and as the wave rose and roared before me like an angry god, I lifted my arms and linked my thumbs to dive into the wall of blue, dazedly using the form my German nanny taught me over ten years ago.

I closed my eyes and mouth tight and threw myself under and into the back wall of the wave, knowing from experience that if it curved and then descended into its final crash while I was underwater, the impact would be minimal. Pushing every muscle, kicking my feet with desperation, I did it. I was well under the wave. With a flurry of kicking, I'd be able to pop up above the surface.

Like a fist to my stomach came another cramp, and the convulsing began. *Not underwater,* I thought in a panic and tried to stop the vomit from happening while still kicking my feet to get to the top. It was no use. My head felt as if it were bursting open when the sickness erupted. I was vomiting, choking, flailing, the salt water rushing down my throat. I'd never known pain like this in my life.

When the blackness came, it was an act of divine mercy.

CHAPTER TWENTY-THREE

Everyone thinks that in a life-and-death situation, they'd fight to survive. I'd always assumed I would be a fighter par excellence. But the truth is this: When the black numbness was ripped away, and my lungs were on fire, my head was pounding, and the nausea was turning my stomach inside-out, I craved the darkness. I lay in the wet grainy sand, curled in the fetal position, feeling cold. I coughed up a string of vomit mixed with saltwater. A babble of voices surrounded me.

"Thank God, thank God," said a strange voice nearest my ear. "She's alive."

"Oh, Peggy, Peggy," a girl sobbed. I realized as if from a great distance that it was my sister, Lydia.

I tried to respond to her, but all the voices spun. I was being sucked into the dizzying tunnel again, but this time I resisted. I feared the tunnel. Another flash of sunlight bored into my eyes. Too bright. I clamped my eyes shut. Someone tried to push my body so that I would lie flat on the sand, face up, but another pair of hands grabbed my shoulders, saying, "She should stay on her side." Someone put a blanket over me, which made me feel a little better because I was so strangely cold.

"Where the hell is that doctor?" shouted my cousin Ben.

I reached for the sound of his voice, my hand groping in the sand past the blanket.

"Ben," I said, though it sounded like the thick gargling of a monster. "Don't be mad at me. Don't. Ben... Ben?"

He gripped my hand, and said, "I'm here, Peggy."

A new deep-pitched voice said with authority, "We need to keep her awake. Peggy – Peggy?"

It wasn't a matter of fighting or resisting. In a blink, I lost all hold on consciousness. When next I woke I was lying on smooth sheets, but that same deep voice intoned: "There is little possibility of brain damage because she did gain consciousness on the beach. She was able to speak to her cousin. That means her loss of consciousness underwater did not last long enough to destroy significant brain function. But I'm concerned about her inability to wake up as well as the vomiting on the beach and disorientation. Those are serious after-effects of a near-drowning."

"No," I groaned, opening my eyes to a small white-walled room.

Immediately they swarmed over me, my brother Lawrence and Uncle David and Aunt Helen and Paul. Lydia took my hand and pressed it to her damp cheek. Looming above her, Henry Taul looked at me as if I were a ghost. A man in a long white doctor's coat politely pushed his way through. "Hello, Peggy," said the owner of the deep voice. "I'm Dr. Deitch." He had a pale face, one from a storybook, composed of knobs and corners – a pointed chin and bulbous nose. When he asked for space to be created in which to examine me, my family stepped back.

The doctor examined my pupils with a small light, placed a cool stethoscope on my chest, and took my pulse at my wrist and my throat. He wrote in a notebook, then beckoned for a young nurse who pressed on my abdomen through the paper-thin gown they'd dressed me in, asking me if it hurt. The stomach pain was not as severe as before, and

I tried to convey that with dazed nods or headshakes.

"What hospital is this?" I asked the doctor in the raspy voice that now belonged to me.

"You're not in a hospital, you're in the medical suite of the Oriental Hotel," Dr. Deitch said smoothly. "I am on the staff of the hotel, as are my fine nurses."

That struck me as a little strange, but I pushed myself to tell him what I'd been trying to get out. Speaking slowly because I was so short of breath, I said, "I didn't vomit... afterward. I was sick to my stomach and dizzy and weak before I... went underwater." I couldn't say *drown*. Wasn't that word reserved for those who died?

This revelation led to more examination and many more questions about what I ate for breakfast and lunch and the nurse taking my temperature, which she proclaimed normal. I still felt nauseous, but even worse, when I tried to sit up, I was struck by a crippling dizziness. The doctor frowned and wrote more on his clipboard. The nurse told me to lie still.

"Doctor, is there something we should know?" asked Uncle David impatiently, and the doctor retreated to discuss my condition with Uncle David and Aunt Helen. They spoke in low voices. Lydia slipped onto the chair by my narrow bed. Her eyes were bloodshot and her cheeks puffy. Henry remained on the other side of the room, talking to Paul.

"I'm sorry," I said.

"What should you be sorry for? You didn't do this on purpose. It sounds like you got sick all of a sudden while in the water, and then the waves overwhelmed you, and you passed out."

I nodded but was already feeling guilty about the fact that I had felt sick before I walked into the ocean. I shouldn't have gone in the water at all. It was foolish and reckless.

"If you're up to it, you should talk to Mother," said Lydia.

"Where is she?" I asked.

"She collapsed, Peggy. She took it very badly when we told her you were pulled from the water, unconscious. She's in the next room. They gave her smelling salts and she's resting."

After taking that in, I asked, "Who pulled me out of the water?"

"Ben! Don't you know?"

I shook my head, my eyes darting around the room. Lydia said, "He hurt his arm somehow, so they are seeing to him in yet another little room." She smiled. "Maybe we should have it named the Batternberg Wing."

Not long after that they brought Mother to see me. She had to be helped through the door and across the floor, my brother on one side and my Aunt Helen on the other. Her face looked ghastly: eyes staring and black in a gaunt face. I must have made quite the picture myself, for she recoiled the closer she got. They helped her into the chair.

"Margaret, I was so worried," she said. "I thought we'd lost you." Her lower lip trembled. "And after your father… for you to go the same way as Jonathan…" She shuddered violently and then, to my astonishment, she collapsed on top of me, shaking and sobbing.

Lydia covered her face, Henry Taul enfolding her tightly in his arms. My brother looked away as he fought for control of himself. My aunt was teary, and my uncle ashen; even my least favorite relation, Paul, dropped his head. It was all so deeply upsetting, so painful, that my eyes filled as Mother pressed her head on my sheet-covered chest, everyone falling to pieces around us. It was a scene that did not seem real. Who would have believed it of the Batternbergs, that arrogant and aloof clan capable of leaving the other tough-as-nails New York families quaking? Yet here we were.

Dr. Deitch gently pulled my mother off me. He then suggested that I recover with only the nurse in the room. One didn't need an advanced degree in medicine to perceive that this group breakdown wasn't good for me.

The nurse switched on an electric fan and turned down the light after ushering everyone out. My body badly needed rest. Moreover, they needed to monitor me carefully through the rest of the day and the night, seeing if the dizziness passed and checking for fever and other mysterious complications. I'd be spending the night in the Medical Suite. Where this was located within the Oriental Hotel, I had no idea.

The nurse informed me that Dr. Deitch wanted me to be given a teaspoon of water, to see if I could hold it down. The nurse propped me up and lifted the spoon into my mouth as if I were a helpless baby. The water made my ravished throat ache, but I did not throw up, and after a little while I felt stronger and ready for another teaspoon. This pleased the nurse enormously.

"Would it be permissible for me to see one person from my family?" I asked her after a little more time passed. I had drunk more water, and the nurse's repeated temperature checks showed no fever.

The door opened, and I got my first glimpse of Ben. His arm was in a sling, but other than that he looked the same. A tear-ravaged Ben I simply could not cope with.

"People may think I get up to trouble because I crave the attention, but this is the kind of attention I don't want," I said, attempting a joke.

"I would never think that," he said quietly. His seriousness made it possible for me to say it:

"Thank you for saving me."

He inclined his head and said, "Of course."

"It wasn't easy." I gestured at his sling.

"You know, it wasn't," he said, relaxing into the chair by my side. "Someone should advertise that information – finding an unconscious woman underwater and carrying her out of the Atlantic is very tricky business. But I suppose if it were widely understood, rescue rates would plummet."

"I didn't even know that you were in the water too, that anyone in the family was out with me."

"And miss catching a glimpse of your showgirl legs?"

I couldn't be annoyed at his comment, I felt so grateful. Without Ben I'd be dead, there just wasn't any way around it.

The nurse, who'd been busying herself at a table laid out with ominous medical instruments, told me she'd be back in ten minutes and slipped out to the main hallway.

Ben took a deep breath and said, "I hope that gives me enough time."

"For what?"

"I have something to say to you, Peggy."

Ben looked so somber that it made me bunch up the top of my sheet with my right hand.

"I'm sorry for what happened when we were younger," he said haltingly. "It was wrong of me to lead you into it. I've told you that you make too much of it, that many cousins play such games, but that is my own guilty conscience coming up with excuses. The truth of the matter is I abused your trust. I lost your trust."

I continued to stare at him, wordless. Ben apologizing to me?

"I considered for a while that we should probably get married," he said.

This was a joke, it had to be. "To make an honest woman of me?" I said with as much sarcasm as I could muster.

"Hardly that. I didn't completely seduce you, remember? We drew back." He paused; an eyelid rose. "And you are still a virgin?"

"Ben!"

"I'm sorry, I'm sorry." He waved the hand not in a sling. "Shouldn't have asked that. No, I wanted to marry you because out of all the women in this world, you never bore me."

"Ah, and here I thought you had in mind us forming a dynastic scheme, like Queen Victoria's descendants all marrying one another."

"But that's the problem. The European royals marrying their cousins, it's fading away, or it should be fading. Not a very twentieth century thing to do. That's the Old World. I have to make a New World marriage, choose a wife who will impress the public, hopefully present some qualities that I lack."

"*You* want to impress the public?"

"I have a plan for each decade of my life, Peggy. In my forties, I intend to run for public office. Why do you think I'm taking a law degree?"

"You can't be serious, Ben."

"Now why do you say that? Because no one from the best families in New York fills a public office. It's just not done. While in England, there are families that serve for generations – for centuries – at the pinnacle of power. Prime ministers. In America all a man is supposed to do with his life is make money. Or live an idle existence, spending his father's – his grandfather's – money. It breeds some pretty pathetic specimens."

"Like Henry Taul?"

He winced. "Exactly. When someone from a good family, given the best education, does decide to serve his country, he can shoot right to the top. Look at Teddy Roosevelt."

"All right, now you really must stop. Please. I can't take it any longer. You despise Roosevelt."

"I don't despise him. He's a worthy opponent." Seeing my expression, he laughed and said, "Enough of my plans for the future. Ah, I wonder if I could have a cigarette here. Damn, left them in the other room."

I rearranged my pillow and sat up higher, so we were closer to face to face. I was tired of everyone looming over me. "It's just as well you abandoned your plan for me, Ben. It has a flaw. I'd never marry you."

A slow smile spread across his face. "I could persuade you to marry me, Peggy. It wouldn't be easy. But I could manage it."

I shook my head. "It wouldn't matter what you did or said. Not with the way you are. I don't want your kind of husband. I don't want any Thelmas."

Ben's smile disappeared. And with that, some instinct I'd had all along clicked into place and I knew. "She's not yours, is she?" I demanded. When he didn't answer, I said, "Come on, Ben! I almost died today – and who knows, maybe I came close to taking you with me. You act like you've opened your heart and soul, but this – she – can't be discussed?

"No, she can't."

"Tell me the truth. I won't breathe a word to a living soul, I swear it. Does that make a difference?"

He ran his hand through his thick hair. "I would have to rely on your discretion, and you're not a discreet person."

"About this, I would be."

"Very well then. If I have your word." But he still hesitated, as if it were physically difficult to come out with it. He was a person who, from my earliest memory, had an arsenal of eloquence at his disposal, never fumbling for the right word. It was an ability he wore as easily as other men wear a hat.

"Thelma is my father's mistress," said Ben, watching me carefully. "She has been for four years, ever since she was eighteen and he found her dancing in a show."

I had few happy touchpoints within my family, but one of them was my Uncle David, my father's favorite brother, steadier and kinder than my father ever was. He did not miss birthdays or anniversaries, he had shoulders big enough for everyone to lean on. It hurt, very deeply, to lose this illusion.

"He's always been like this? There's always been a Thelma?" I managed to ask.

"Since before I was born, before he was ever married. This is… a way of life, Peggy. My mother had no choice but to endure it." Ben withdrew into himself, slumped in the chair, no longer the sardonic older cousin but a little boy himself. I realized I'd not heard Ben speak of his mother for many years.

He continued, "I was ten years old when something fairly… dramatic happened. It took a great deal of money and pressure on the politicians to keep it out of the newspapers. I think it's what killed my mother, weakened her heart." Just for a second I could picture that aunt, a dark-eyed beauty, a book of poetry under her arm, forever praising her oldest son's brilliance.

"But how can this be happening now?" I asked bleakly. "He's not in good health, and Thelma – she's so young."

Ben laughed scornfully. "Have you been listening to Helen? Or to her partner in conspiracy, Dr. Mackenzie? My father is forty-eight years old and in excellent health, Peggy. As you may have gathered, one of my duties here is to keep things running smoothly vis-à-vis Thelma. I shouldn't have sent Paul to her with money. That was my mistake. And he has paid dearly for bringing along Lawrence! Who has no idea who Thelma really is, by the way. And will have no further exposure, I promise you that."

"Why did you send Paul?" I asked. "It's not like you to do something careless or stupid."

"Now that's what I call a backhanded compliment." Ben winced as he adjusted his arm in the sling. "I'm having a bit of a problem with Thelma."

"She doesn't like you?"

"I would far prefer that. She likes me too much. I have to be very careful."

"Ah, I see. Well, you don't have to worry about that where Paul is concerned. I could tell from ten feet away that she can't stand him."

"Girls rarely like Paul. The ones who do are as… shall we say, as unusual as he is. And that is as sure a path to scandal as my father experienced fifteen years ago. The police and newspapers aren't as easy to pay off these days. So, another one of my happy holiday duties is to keep Paul on a tight leash."

We were silent together for a moment. I could understand Ben's life better now, and that of the other men in his family. Or could I? There was still a niggling sense I had of other shadows in other corners unexplored.

Ben suddenly gripped the edge of my mattress. "This feels so strange, to be talking about this with anyone. But you're the only person on this planet I could talk to. I don't want you to turn away from me any longer, Peggy. When you were on the sand, looking like you were dying, and you reached out for me, saying, 'Don't be mad at me, Ben'… my God!" He drew a deep, ragged breath. "Your hand, your little hand. If you had died, before I made things right with you…"

With that very hand I touched his face. I tugged on the tuft of black hair sprouting to the left of his part, a stubborn cowlick that never stayed down. I hadn't touched that tuft of hair, hadn't wanted to think about it, since I was fifteen, giggling in his bed, fully dressed under the covers while he shushed me, a candle flickering on the table. It felt strange to me too, to push through the shame and anger quivering between us for years and struggle toward the possibility of a new trust in Ben.

A click and swoosh on the other side of the room made my fingers freeze. The door was open. Lydia stood there, but her head turned to answer someone in the hallway unseen. She was saying, "That's the best news, Nurse."

Standing next to her was Henry Taul, looking right at me, his mouth dropped open as if he had just been dealt something of a shock.

CHAPTER TWENTY-FOUR

Lydia hurried over, looking fresh and lovely, her face repaired from the tears shed several hours ago. I barely heard her solicitous words, for I was watching Henry – and Ben – with mounting fear. I remembered the questions Henry asked me over and over, gripping my arms so tight it was like I could still feel the pinch of his fingers gouging my skin: "Who's the man? Who spoiled you?" Did the look in my eyes, my touching Ben's hair, finally give him the answer that he demanded five years ago?

But Henry did not do or say anything that indicated he was upset. He merely seemed restless, tapping his hand against his thigh as he gazed around the little room. I'd noticed that earlier he was uncomfortable here. Henry asked a perfunctory question about my health and seemed to listen to my answer. I began to think the shock I saw in his face was my imagination. Ben insisted on giving Lydia his chair, and after a few minutes he said he would find the doctor and make inquiry on how long this ridiculous sling was needed. Henry nodded to Ben as he left. There was no seething glare.

But even should he suspect that Ben and I got up to some very questionable behavior years ago, why should it matter to him today? He wasn't marrying me, but Lydia.

The nurse took my temperature – still normal, thankfully – as well as checking my throat and eyes and my heartbeat. A little later the doctor returned, and with only Lydia there, tested me in other ways. I could not seem to control my arms or legs very well; I was quite wobbly.

It was at this point I discovered that I presented something of a mystery.

"Your present condition does not indicate either food poisoning or an infectious or chronic disease," Dr. Deitch said. "But you were significantly ill in the water, weak and vomiting. And you are still weak, although that is attributable to the trauma of losing consciousness."

"What about sunstroke?" I asked.

"That is most likely it. You had not been exposed to the direct sun for more than a few minutes before the first bout of weakness, according to your own account, but it is extremely hot." He paused and then continued. "Sunstroke's symptoms are dizziness and disorientation, even nausea, but not apraxia." At my puzzled expression, he explained that was the word for my lack of coordination.

"But she *is* getting better?" asked Lydia.

"She is," said Dr. Deitch, but not with the enthusiasm I'd have preferred. And indeed, the doctor was insistent on my staying in the Medical Suite throughout the entire next day. I didn't like the thought of being confined, but it was true I didn't have my full strength back.

I ate dinner served in bed, a plain one: chicken soup and brown bread, with sliced cantaloupe. I lacked appetite; still, I pushed myself to eat it all. After dinner every member of my family came to visit me, including Mother, who had, like Lydia, resumed her customary self-control. Henry Taul did not reappear, with Lydia making vague excuses for him. That was fine with me.

I found it difficult to look Uncle David in the eye, now that I knew the truth. Yet he acted the same as ever: seeing to everyone's needs, a relation we could all depend on. I forced myself to act normally toward him. I had made a promise to Ben and I intended to keep it. Still, I was relieved when Uncle David left my room for the night, along with Ben, my mother, Lawrence, and Paul. Only Lydia and Aunt Helen remained.

Putting on the thicker robe Lydia had brought, I felt ready to walk, slowly and tentatively, around this small room. I wanted to peer out its single window and get my bearings. Parting the filmy curtain and looking down, I determined the room's location: second floor and facing east toward the end of Coney Island. Brittle yellow marsh grass quivered slightly, bordering a dark turquoise creek. On the other side of the creek rose a couple of rather ramshackle wooden houses, boats tied to their docks.

"You should rest," said Aunt Helen.

She did not leave but sat by my bed for a while, her hands busy with needlework. I studied her serene profile, wondering what she knew of her husband's mistress. Establishing his kept woman in the neighboring hotel was such a heartless thing for Uncle David to do.

After falling asleep, I suffered a nightmare of thrashing impotently in darkness – a horrible repetition of what happened in the ocean. After I woke, I struggled to make sense of strange surroundings. It took me some time to grasp what happened, to remember that I nearly drowned and was being kept here to recover.

Something else frightened me: I wasn't alone. In the dim light, in the far corner, sat a young red-haired woman. Although she wore a nurse's long white dress and hat, I found her being here unnerving.

"But Miss, it was your aunt who ordered that someone be in the room all night, that you could not be left alone," she said in a light Irish brogue.

I couldn't believe that Aunt Helen would do that – it seemed an overreaction – but it was two o'clock in the morning, and there was no one to appeal to besides this young night nurse. I couldn't relax until

I cast back for a pleasant memory. I seized on sitting with Stefan that first night, looking at the gauzy electric white lights of Dreamland in the distance. That finally returned me to sleep. To my delight, a vision of Dreamland segued into my next dream, a less violent one.

First thing the following morning Dr. Deitch checked me again. "You show no signs whatsoever of pneumonia, which is what we're on the lookout for. And your apraxia has lessened. I think I can clear you to return to your own room at the end of the day. In the meantime, you can have all the visitors you like."

There were indeed visitors, but several did not turn out to be a comfort. And though I didn't know it at the time, the seeds were planted that day for a dreadful harvest.

Lydia breezed into my room near mid-day, her eyes bright with excitement. "The morning lecture on roses was simply fascinating," she said.

"You went over to the Manhattan Hotel by yourself?" I asked, surprised. I didn't care a bit about missing the lecture, but Lydia had explicitly told me she didn't want to see the Campions without my being there as chaperone. She went anyway. I realized that she must have wanted to see them very badly – or was it just one of the siblings she could not bear to miss?

"How could Henry disapprove of my walking in a garden – it's just ridiculous," she said, tossing her head. "Especially since he's at the racetrack today, fussing over his horses, as usual."

"I don't think it's the garden, it's who you walk in the garden *with*," I said gently.

As if she hadn't understood me, Lydia said, "Are you well enough to see Jason and Susannah? They were horrified to hear about your accident, and they would like to pay a call. They're waiting on our veranda now." I agreed, and she darted away to fetch the brother and sister.

Jason Campion stepped shyly into my room, a pale vision. He wore a white seersucker suit and white hat, and he held out to me a bouquet of white roses. They were the first flowers anyone had brought me for the longest time, and I was incredibly touched. I took the bouquet, inhaling the roses' dusty yet sugary fragrance.

"Careful for thorns," Jason said. He smiled, his limpid brown eyes bathing in their warmth, and said, "'But he who dares not grasp the thorn'…"

Lydia chimed in with "'Should never crave the rose.'"

Now they're finishing each other's sentences, I thought. Feeling I should change the subject, I told Susannah, "I had a dream about Dreamland last night, what would Dr. Freud say about that?"

"Did you write down the details in your dream diary?" she asked hopefully.

"Oh, Susannah, you never stop pushing those diaries on us," said Lydia, laughing. "It's as if—"

Lydia stopped; her head turned. Following her gaze, I saw a man standing in the doorway. It wasn't Henry Taul, but the man wore a uniform bearing Henry's initials. He was sallow and sharp featured, with a moustache. He looked like a weasel. I was sure he was the second servant I glimpsed with Henry on the beach during the Alexandria siege.

"What are you doing here?" demanded Lydia.

"I have a message from Mr. Taul," he said, with a slight accent. "He will be back at the hotel for cocktails before dinner."

"I find it hard to believe you needed to seek me out expressly to say that Mr. Taul will be back before dinner," she said with a haughtiness rarely voiced by my sister. The Campions exchanged glances. They too were surprised by the change.

"Pardonnez-moi," he said with a shallow bow, but that only angered her further.

"I don't want you peering into the room of my sister, who is not well," she said, and as if that were not enough, "I don't want you here!"

He disappeared, and Lydia turned back to me, her chest rising and falling with fury. Alarmed, I said, "Are you all right?" With a supreme effort, she smiled and assured me she was fine. But the opposite was true. Once the Campions had left, I pleaded with my sister to confide in me.

"I can't endure him," she admitted. "His name is Francois. I think he came to spy on me, not to deliver a message. And to slither his way into a sick room to do it – it's beneath contempt."

A cold dread of suspicion stirred.

"Francois is a French name, isn't it?" I asked. "Is he – is this man from Paris?"

"He's French, but is he from Paris? Oh, I've never asked. I don't care to know."

Trying my best to keep it casual, I said, "Lydia, when Henry went on his long trip through Europe, was Paris part of the itinerary? I supposed Francois would have been useful if he had."

"Yes, he stayed in Paris at the beginning of his holiday," she said. "Francois goes out of his way to be useful to Henry, he's a horrible sycophant, and I don't doubt he was dancing attendance in Paris."

One of the few advantages to sitting in bed, recovering from an accident, was that being distressed by something was not as noticeable as otherwise. These revelations horrified me, for now I was nearly convinced that the blind item in *Town Topics* described Henry Taul, throwing a party for prostitutes so extravagant that news of it circulated among the gossips of Paris and drifted across the Atlantic. This Francois must be one of the "friends" who aided Henry in his disgusting activities, though how he would keep Henry up all night I didn't know. I'd think the prostitutes would be charged with that task.

How could I let Lydia marry Henry? I shuddered at the thought of her sharing a life, and a bed, with such a man.

Saying I looked tired, Lydia left for lunch with Mother and I didn't stop her. While I was still in an agony of indecision over what to say or do, Aunt Helen appeared. "Did you tell the nurses that someone must be in my room last night at all times?" I asked.

"I did."

"Tell me what you are thinking," I urged.

She said, "You must prepare yourself for a shock, Peggy."

"I've had quite a few shocks of late. I don't see how you could possibly do worse."

Aunt Helen looked around to be sure we were completely alone, the doors tightly shut, before saying, "I think it's possible you were drugged, and that's why you collapsed in the ocean. Someone secretly gave you a drug, and only you."

She was right. This was worse.

"How? When?" I bleated.

Aunt Helen said, "For lunchtime in the hotel restaurant, you had begun giving those bottles of Coca-Cola to the kitchen staff beforehand, so they had them all ready to pour into a glass with added ice. Someone could have had access to your drink then. And no one else at the table – or the hotel – drank Coca-Cola."

"This drug put into the Coca-Cola… what would it be?"

"I believe it was chloral hydrate. That's the strong sedative given to people before they have surgery. I had it before an operation last year, and I read up on it. Between thirty minutes to an hour after swallowed, it takes effect. I remember reading about the side effects, the nausea and vomiting and dizziness. And if given in too large a dose, a person experiences apraxia. I've never forgotten that word. You don't get that from sunstroke or bad food.

If you'd been taken to a hospital, they could have performed tests. The required equipment is in any hospital. But the hotel owner, Mr. Lancet, was insistent that you'd receive better treatment here. This doctor obviously isn't the best. And by now the drug must have passed out of your system."

"So there is no way to prove this happened?"

"No."

"But would anyone do this?" I asked, still reeling. "Was it a waiter I offended? Why would someone in the kitchens want to hurt me?"

She took my hand. "No. Not someone on the hotel staff, Peggy…"

For the second time in two days, my eyes filled with tears. Aunt Helen thought it was someone I knew. "Who?" I whispered.

"I'm not sure. I have suspicions, but… I don't know."

"You must tell me!"

She tightened her grip on my hand and said, "I do know you're not safe here. You need to leave the Oriental Hotel, Peggy. I'll help you. Now that your sister and Henry Taul are officially engaged, it's not necessary you be here to present a united front. You could spend the rest of the summer with one of your other uncles and their families. Perhaps Bernard's family out on Oyster Bay. Or a close friend from school?"

I said, "To take such action, I'd have to be certain. While yes, my relations with the rest of my family have been a bit… strained, I just can't believe someone I've known forever would secretly give me a drug. I came close to *dying*."

"It was very hard for me to tell you this. I wish more than anything I hadn't needed to. But I couldn't live with myself if the person… tried something else."

My throat ached; tears burned. "But why? Why would anyone want to hurt me?"

She was silent as she gathered her thoughts. "It could have been done to punish or to prevent. For four days, you swam after lunch. Perhaps someone wanted to stop you from doing so. It wasn't foreseeable that you would suffer the side effects of a large dose in the water and come close to drowning. Chloral hydrate is supposed to sedate you. Most people, feeling that tired, wouldn't have ventured into the Atlantic Ocean."

What had my mother said? I could be "provoking" without realizing it. But even if the intent were to induce me to fall asleep in my room, not drown me, to engineer a secret drugging was something so perverse. It suggested a mind that was… wicked. And ruthless.

"I suppose," I said, "the only person I can rule out is you."

She smiled.

"And Ben – he was the one who saved me," I said.

The smile faded.

I inhaled sharply. "You *do* think it's Ben. But my God, why would he hurt me? And then risk his own life for me?"

"He was the only member of the family in the water when you went under. You two just had a serious falling out, on top of not getting along very well for the last couple of years. What better way to ensure your loyalty – and to restore the closeness you once had?"

"No, no, no, you're wrong," I said. "He wouldn't do that. Never." My shrill denial of this possibility brought the nurse into the room to check on me. I muttered to her that I needed nothing.

"I realize you're very upset, and that's natural," said Aunt Helen quietly. "I'll give you time to think it over, to decide the best course of action. I only ask that we keep this between us for now."

Another person who wished to swear me to silence. I nodded, and my aunt slipped out, leaving me in a torment. I knew she hated her stepson. I also knew Ben could be cunning and selfish, even cruel, but to commit this terrible act? Unthinkable. And yet he was quite close to me in the water just when I required rescue. I paced the room, realizing with each step that my strength was just about restored in full. No dizziness, no nausea, no wobbly limbs. I'd had enough of this room. I put on the robe and cracked open the door, searching for the nurses or the doctor.

My room was on a short corridor that branched off from a much longer one, like the bottom part of the letter "L." You'd have to know the medical suite was here to find it; the rooms were discreetly situated in the hotel. I could hear people talking in the main part of the hall, doors shutting, the hum of wheels and the clatter of china. Right outside my room, a man was mopping the floor of the hallway. The business of the vast Oriental went on around me, although when I'd been inside my room, all seemed quiet.

As I stood there, impatient to find someone to help me, Dr. Deitch came around the corner, a nurse with him – and Uncle David. None looked happy.

I said, "Doctor, I'd like to return to my own room in the hotel."

"Later," said my uncle curtly. "Go back in, Peggy. There's someone who has asked to interview you."

Interview me?

Once I'd been pushed into the room, my uncle said, "There is a police lieutenant in Coney Island who has heard of your accident and is most insistent on speaking to you."

Dr. Deitch said, "In the past, the hotel's owner, Mr. Lancet, has been successful in preventing this particular police officer from entering the hotel. But supposedly the orders have come down from the police commissioner overseeing New York City that reported drownings and rescues from drowning must be investigated thoroughly. There has been a sharp rise because of the heat spell. Of course, your case is not like that. But this lieutenant is not an easy person to convince of anything."

This could only be referring to one person. No, Lieutenant Pellegrino was not easy to convince. I knew that firsthand.

CHAPTER TWENTY-FIVE

Unsure what to make of my silence, Uncle David said, "If you cannot face this, I'm sure I can deal with it. I'll say you're not well enough, you're resting, and then have one of our lawyers reach out to his superior office, go as high as we need to in order to make him disappear."

"That won't be necessary," I said. "I'll speak to this police officer." I sat on the edge of the bed, fastening the top button of my robe.

In the time it took for them to bring in Lieutenant Pellegrino, I sorted through my feelings. Why didn't I accept my uncle's offer to make this police officer go away? It would be risky to see him here, in front of family, in case he revealed that I had gone to him not a week earlier. But in my own way, I was trying to protect Stefan. I worried that antagonizing Lieutenant Pellegrino would have an unpleasant effect, even intensify the suspicion. But if I were honest with myself, I was also excited at the thought of discussing Stefan with the lieutenant. I longed for any scrap of news, even from his persecutor.

This was how, incongruous as it would have seemed even an hour ago, Lieutenant Pellegrino came to me in the Oriental Hotel. I'd expected him to look out of place. But he strode in with confidence, his eyes sweeping the small room before settling on me with a stony blankness.

"I understand that you had a serious mishap yesterday, Miss Batternberg. I'd like to hear about it. My name is Lieutenant Pellegrino."

Encouraged by his subterfuge, I said, "Well, Lieutenant, what happened was that I went to the hotel's private beach yesterday after lunch for swimming, as I usually do. I didn't feel well, but I thought the water would revive me. Unfortunately, once I was out there, I took something of a turn for the worse. I felt very sick and... I passed out."

"It sounds like you were at serious risk."

"My son saw Peggy was in difficulty and rescued her," said Uncle David with pride.

"That was fortunate," said Lieutenant Pellegrino. Yet he did not seem satisfied. "What is the nature of the illness?" he asked, turning to Dr. Deitch.

"Possibly a touch of influenza, or a bit of food gone bad," said the doctor.

"If there is food poisoning at this hotel, we should be told about it," Lieutenant Pellegrino said sharply.

"I ate the same lunch as others at my table: lobster salad," I said. "I don't think it was the food." The minute the words were out of my mouth, I knew I shouldn't be volunteering anything.

"Oh? Then what made you so ill that you passed out in the ocean, Miss Batternberg? It was just twenty-four hours ago, but you don't look sick now."

Dr. Deitch went over the possibilities, from a fleeting virus to a case of sunstroke, while the lieutenant listened. I wondered what would happen if I announced, "It's possible someone put chloral hydrate in my Coca-Cola." Within the hour, more police could charge into the hotel, there would be interviews, and then accusations. And if my Aunt Helen were right and someone had drugged me, *shouldn't* I seek the help of the police? Yet I knew I would never tell Lieutenant Pellegrino.

The family bond, the instinct of the Batternbergs to defend one another against outsiders, was so strong.

"I'd like to speak to Miss Batternberg alone," said Lieutenant Pellegrino.

That was met with strenuous objections from my uncle, but Lieutenant Pellegrino was adamant. I tried my best to hide my nervousness while they argued. I feared that he suspected something criminal about my near-drowning. I did not want to have to lie to the police.

The lieutenant had his way, and the doctor and my uncle left through the side door leading to a second room in the medical suite. Once we were alone, Lieutenant Pellegrino said, "When one of our sources in the hotel passed your name along, I had to make sure this collapse in the water had nothing to do with certain parties."

My relief over learning his motivation to talk to me in private was swiftly replaced with incredulity.

"Do you think Stefan made his way onto the beach of the Oriental Hotel in order to drown me?" I said.

Lieutenant Pellegrino radiated disappointment. "So you've not had any more contact with Mr. Chalakoski, but you're just as eager to defend him."

"As I would any innocent man," I said. "I'm certain that you haven't found a shred of evidence against him."

"I can't discuss an ongoing police investigation," he said coldly. I interpreted that as meaning no, he hadn't found evidence implicating Stefan, and after all, how could he? It didn't exist.

He continued, "But I did come across some interesting background on Mr. Chalakoski. And it's due to something you said."

Apprehensive, I watched him pull something from his uniform jacket. It was a magazine, its cover as colorful as the ones I'd bought during my shopping spree, but the writing was not in English. Among the words I saw: "Italia." This must be an Italian publication.

Thumbing the pages, Lieutenant Pellegrino said, "You told me Stefan Chalakoski is an artist, and we got out of him that before he came to New York he lived in Italy for a few years. I made it my business to take a look at his art for sale. He calls himself 'The Futurist.'" The police officer found what he sought and spread open the magazine on the bed before me. "They call themselves the same. It is what you types of people like to call a 'movement': futurism. I found this long article about it."

I bent down to examine the pages spread open before me. Photos of the paintings revealed a style that was similar to Stefan's: Bright colors, abstract figures, all of it caught in dazzling action, thrusts of movement. "It's not a peaceful future they have in mind, these artists," said Lieutenant Pellegrino. "They want to forget the past, they actually say museums and libraries should be destroyed." His fingers jabbed at the images. "Look at this: cannons firing. And this other painting: Men crouched in a trench. Miss Batternberg, their leader wrote a manifesto, I'll quote from parts of it here, you'll have to accept my translation: *We intend to sing the love of danger, the habit of energy and fearlessness… Courage, audacity, and revolt will be essential elements of our poetry… We will glorify war – the world's only hygiene – militarism, patriotism, the destructive gesture of freedom-bringers, beautiful ideas worth dying for, and scorn for woman.*"

At the last phrase, he looked at me with special meaning.

"But these aren't his paintings, and Stefan didn't write any of this," I said. "He's lived in America for almost two years."

Undeterred, the lieutenant said, "I'll ask you to pay close attention to a photograph of one more painting." He turned a page and pointed, saying, "This one is called 'The Funeral of the Anarchist Galli.' The man being buried was part of a workers' strike, and in all the chaos, he was stabbed to death by security guards for the factory. This painting shows the riot when the police in Milan tried to bring order to Galli's funeral. You see how extreme violence is shown as a good thing here."

I did study the photograph of the painting, and all I could feel was an awed excitement.

It must have been obvious to Lieutenant Pellegrino that I wasn't reacting the way he hoped. His voice rising, he said, "You were full of scorn for the idea that Stefan Chalakoski could be involved in anarchist activities. I've laid out for you here how the art, his ideas for the art, lead to just that type of violence. Now, I must ask you again, is there anything else that Chalakoski said or did that would assist my investigation?"

I closed the magazine on the bed and said, "No."

He snatched it up. "Fine, Miss Batternberg. All I can say is, I hope your close call in the Atlantic was just an accident. Because there's a very dangerous man out here on Coney Island."

I looked away from his angry face, toward the door. Underneath the door, in that small gap between the bottom of it and the floor, I saw a dark shadow glide, like a person who had been standing outside now moved away. My heart dropped – was Uncle David or Dr. Deitch listening? A few seconds later, Lieutenant Pellegrino strode over to the side door, yanking it open to reveal the two men seated, talking, in the middle of the next room: my uncle and doctor. So no, it couldn't have been either of them in the hallway.

All three men left together, my Uncle David asking in his most imperious manner why Lieutenant Pellegrino felt it necessary to subject me to such prolonged questioning in my weakened state. I peered out at the hallway from my door. There was one person visible: the nurse, at the end, crouched before a cabinet. I moved to return to my room when something caught my attention on the floor, right by my right foot. It was a small, loose pile of gray ashes. I was certain I hadn't seen it before Lieutenant Pellegrino's disturbing visit. I'd watched a worker mop the floor clean right before he came. Sometime during my conversation with the police officer, someone had stood here long enough to tap a cigarette, not once or even twice but perhaps three times.

CHAPTER TWENTY-SIX

"I want to go again, Mother," shouted the little boy riding the wooden horse. "Again and again!"

A woman with a face flushed red and shiny beneath the brim of her hat groaned and said, "No, Theodore. Enough."

The boy, perhaps seven years old, slammed the side of the horse's neck so hard it shook. "Again!" he cried. His mother assented; perhaps she hadn't the strength, in this heat, to oppose him.

I watched their struggle at the Central Park Carousel from under the neighboring oak tree. I frequently mopped my face with a handkerchief. This was the fifteenth day of the unbroken hot spell. Even in the Oriental Hotel, not an especially God-fearing place, there were whispers of this heat being the Lord's Will, or more specifically, the Lord's Punishment.

But I wasn't on Coney Island, I was standing in the center of a much larger island: Manhattan, the city of my birth. There wasn't a sea breeze offering relief here. Drab leaden clouds blocked all sun – and yet the temperature must have been well above ninety degrees. There was a stickiness to the air, as if we staggered through taffy. But none of that mattered to me. I was waiting for Stefan. At long last, the day had come. I'd once again arranged with my sister Lydia to tell the others

I'd be spending a quiet day in my room. She was happy to help, saying I deserved to have some fun, and promised to square things with Alice again. The train shot in so fast, I was in Central Park before I knew it.

Lydia had no idea that my escort for the day was not a journalist named Merton Desher, but an immigrant suspected of murder by a stubborn police lieutenant. And yet, as bad as that sounded, Stefan, in my opinion, was a better prospect than Henry Taul. I had come close to showing Lydia the *Town Topics* item a few times, but I just couldn't. I wasn't absolutely sure it referred to him, just as I wasn't certain that I believed Aunt Helen's theory that I'd been drugged at lunch and sent into the ocean to collapse. I lived in a fraught world of doubt and continual, grinding tension.

The carousel was located in the southern part of the park, on what would have been Sixty-Fifth Street, had it run through the flat meadows and hilly woods. I kept looking down the walkways. Each time I detected the figure of a slender young man walking in my direction, my heart thumped frantically until he came close enough for me to be sure it wasn't Stefan. In the back of my mind lurked the sad possibility he would not come. It felt like another lifetime in which we'd planned to meet on this day at one in the afternoon.

For the tenth time, I strained to see up the walkways. A new possibility emerged: a man closing in on the carousel from the west, wearing a summer suit and hat like every other male in the park. But the way he walked, the fluid gait and perfect posture… I suddenly clapped my hands. It was Stefan. I bolted from beneath the tree, my feet flying.

"Peggy, you here," he said, a delighted smile lighting up his angular features. "I didn't know."

"*You* didn't know?" I laughed.

He put out his hand for me to shake. I wanted to throw myself into his arms, feel his lips press mine, but this was Manhattan, not Coney Island, and we were in public. As I gripped his hand, I studied his face. There was a yellow bruise still visible around his eye and a mark on his chin.

"What do you like to do?" he asked. "I can take you to lunch, or picture show."

"For now, what I'd most like is a stroll," I said, taking his arm. I was too excited to eat, and I wanted to talk to Stefan, not sit next to him in a theatre, watching one of D.W. Griffith's spectacles. I'd had enough epics and disasters on Coney Island.

"A stroll?" His accent darted in and out of the word. "Let's hope sky permits." Stefan pointed at a dark bank of clouds roiling on the horizon.

"It threatens, but the rain never comes," I scoffed.

And so we strolled, among families looking for a picnic spot and people riding horses on trails. I told him a few stories I knew about Frederick Olmsted creating Central Park fifty years ago, and he listened appreciatively. I adored this – we could be any other courting couple – but nonetheless, I had to broach a subject more serious. "Have the police been bothering you?"

"They follow here and there, but no one asks me questions," he said. "Don't worry, Peggy. No one follow me today. I think now they look in other directions."

Just five days ago, Lieutenant Pellegrino had been looking very much in Stefan's direction. There was no ambiguity about the lieutenant's opinion, and Stefan deserved to know as much – and today. I was mulling over how to begin when Stefan touched his cheek, wonderingly.

"What is it?" I asked, just as a large drop of warm water splashed my shoulder. I looked up. In minutes, the sky had turned darkest gray with an ominous undertone of yellow.

The raindrops plopping, faster and bigger, made us quicken our pace.

I could make out the brownstones lining Central Park West, but that was at least a five-minute walk. A light flashed, and the sky rumbled. I reached for Stefan's hand. I feared we were seconds from being caught in a violent thunderstorm with no shelter but trees. Even I, a hopeless city girl, knew trees weren't safe to stand beneath when lightning forked the sky. Stefan pointed not toward Central Park West but a large stone archway that served as an overpass.

"Can you run?" he asked, looking down at my shoes.

"Yes – let's go!" I shouted, and, holding his hand tight, we sprinted for the archway.

The rain spattered harder, but now the drops were deliciously cold. It felt fantastic. We veered off the walkway and onto the dirt path that led right under the arch, about ten feet high at its center.

We let go of each other's hands as we laughed and gasped for breath. Staggering, I took off my hat and laid my forehead against the curved stone wall for balance, but then I pushed away. I must look such a wreck from the running and the rain, I didn't want to top it off with a dirty face. A musty, peaty smell permeated the tunnel. Although the rain began a short time ago, I could feel the temperature dropping.

"Here – Peggy, see this," said Stefan, reaching out. The rain had transformed into white and silver sheets of water, furiously pounding the ground inches from the mouth of our tunnel. Through the sheets, puddles bubbled where moments before it had been hard, parched dirt. Lightning flashed, and thunder shattered the air some five seconds later. But this tunnel, like everything else about Central Park, was built to last. We were safe.

I gazed at Stefan's profile, his high cheekbones and proud, slightly beaked nose. His tie was loosened; the top two buttons of his shirt were undone. That shirt rose and fell from breathing as I watched, spellbound. Almost without being aware of it, I placed my hand on his shirt. "I want to feel your heart," I whispered.

Stefan turned and took my hand, guiding it under his unbuttoned shirt. Feeling his bare, smooth flesh made me fall forward, as his arms closed around me, my lips seeking his. As in Hell Gate, my touching him set off an immediate passionate response in him. But I needed him more than I did before. My tongue searched his mouth with a new urgency. I tore loose my blouse from the waistband of my skirt. Seconds later his hand had snaked underneath, his fingers exploring my bare flesh, seeking out my breasts under the prim undergarments. He groaned, frustrated at that barrier. His groan was like a match struck. If I could, I would have taken a knife, scissors, anything, and snipped every string, destroyed every hook, shredded all my clothes, torn them right off my body.

His hands shaking, he stepped away. "No – we stop. We stop now."

"I don't want to stop."

"Not in dirt, Peggy," Stefan said. "I can't do that to you."

"I want you to," I begged, devoid of all pride and restraint. "I love you, I do, Stefan. I've never… felt like this."

Stefan muttered something in another language.

"We can go somewhere today," I raced on. "I have money, we can pay for a room somewhere, we can be alone."

He shook his head, his forehead creased, and I began to cry, the pain of his refusing me was so intense. My shoulders heaved. Stefan embraced me, but differently than he had a moment before. He held me with exquisite tenderness, stroking my hair and saying, "Hush, Peggy, hush." I tried to stop crying, but to my horror I couldn't. It didn't make him recoil. He comforted me, saying softly, "I know, I know," as if my desperate desire for him followed by this breakdown were completely natural.

I stopped crying, and he cupped my face in his hands. "Peggy, I love you too." With that, we kissed again. We kissed for a long time, every single second of it precious to me.

"Ah, Peggy," he said. "You are my darling."

I laid my head on his shoulder and touched his chin, his cheek. Gusts of cooler air encircled us as the rain slackened. But I was on fire with exaltation. He loved me too. Stefan loved me. *This is the turning point*, I thought. In a rainstorm, in this peaty tunnel, my entire life changed and moved in its new direction. My future would be fuller and happier than my past.

To my amusement, Stefan took pride in restoring me to propriety. He tucked in my blouse and with his handkerchief wiped my face. He smoothed my hair, brushed the dirt off my hat. I tried to do the same for him, of course. When the rain slackened, we prepared to step out and meet the rest of the world. First he cupped my chin and gave me one last tender kiss.

The rain stopped. New York City had had a few short bursts of rain in the last fifteen days – it hadn't been a drought – but each time the heat and humidity quickly returned. Today was different. The temperature dropped significantly, and that oppressive thickness in the air was gone too. As Stefan and I resumed our stroll, we were surrounded by ecstatic parkgoers. The heat spell seemed as if it had truly lifted.

"The quality of the air is different," I said. "It's like new."

"Not new to me – old," he said with a smile. "This feel like home."

"You mean Serbia?" I asked shyly.

Perhaps because we'd found this new intimacy, Stefan opened up to me about his past as we walked the paths of Central Park. I listened so closely I nearly stumbled into puddles twice. He was the youngest of three boys, living in the town of Čačak. His father died when Stefan was seven. An uncle helped his two older brothers enroll in a military school in Belgrade, but Stefan remained in Čačak with his mother; she enrolled him in school. A kind teacher gave Stefan two books on art that he pored over every night. When his beloved mother died of tuberculosis, his brothers, now junior officers, sent for him to attend their former school. It was a disaster, as Stefan showed no aptitude for army life. The only subjects he cared about were philosophy and literature – and art. When he was seventeen, his brothers intervened. Instead of reacting with anger, they pooled the small amounts of money they'd managed to save and paid for his travel to Budapest to study. From there he ventured farther from his homeland, traveling to Italy.

"You couldn't have become an artist in Belgrade?" I asked.

"In our own country, it's impossible for most Serbians to achieve," he said bitterly. "First the Turks rule with savagery, now Austrians oppress. The only way to go forward for family like ours is join army, but you risk much. You may become executioner of own people. My brothers, they can only... wait. And hope."

"You miss them," I said softly.

His lips tightened, and that faraway look in his eyes returned, one I now recognized as his yearning for the company of his brothers and his complicated feeling for his homeland.

"What about this park reminds you of Serbia?" I asked, beckoning to the vast lawn spread before us, its grass sparking with today's rain."

He snorted. "Nothing! No, it's just feeling of air: nice and dry. To make nature in center of city could never be real to me. I do not crave meadow."

I laughed a little, taking in the latest declaration of the man who endlessly fascinated me. "What in Manhattan *is* most real to you?" I asked.

"Want me to show you?"

The last time he offered to show me something, it was the spectral city of Dreamland, alive with a million lights. I eagerly slipped my hand into the crook of his arm. Less than an hour later, using Stefan's knowledge of streetcar and subway, an aptitude I, to my embarrassment, lacked, we stood on the corner of Madison Avenue and Twenty-Third Street, looking up, up, up, at the Metropolitan Life Insurance Building, a narrow square building that thrust skyward, its pointed tower gleaming in the faraway.

"The tallest building in whole world – 560 feet high," Stefan said reverently. "Engineers finish it weeks before my boat arrive in New York. I wish I was here in time to see it go up."

I felt a twinge of remorse over never making my way to the corner to witness that construction. It simply wasn't what anyone in my circle had been interested in doing. When my brother Lawrence begged to go several years ago, my mother refused, saying the site would be too dirty. Our family's priority was the same as the other privileged families of New York: to live in quiet, elegant luxury, imitating the languid landed aristocrats of England with whom we had no real link. Our own city's growth was… vulgar.

Stefan said, mesmerized, "We stand in second biggest metropolis in world, with tallest building, biggest stadium for baseball, biggest museum, biggest port, biggest amusement park with Coney Island. Richest man: Rockefeller. Greatest showman: Ziegfeld. Streetcars, subways go zip, zip, zip. This is city that breaks the record – everything biggest. New York is fastest growing city in world. I *had* to be here, to see it myself."

I wanted to soak up his enthusiasm as much as if he were the Coca-Cola I drank so thirstily. "Tell me about your days as an artist in Italy," I urged.

It was then that I learned how Stefan found like-minded people in Rome and Milan, those enraptured by inventions, engineering feats, anything that fueled their vision of the future: cars, airplanes, the rise of the machine. The artists inspired one another. But when the Italian artists and poets praised the glory and necessity of war, Stefan pulled away. "To them, war is cleansing," he said, shaking his head. He decided to move to the place he believed embodied his vision of a perfect future: New York City.

"That is tallest building, but I must pay court to most stupendous building in city," Stefan said, taking me by the hand as we darted through the madness of motor cars, streetcars, horse-drawn carts and buggies, and zigzagging pedestrians to the Flatiron Building, built like a twenty-two-story triangular slice of cake off Fifth Avenue. The traffic and the skyscrapers seemed to imbue him with energy, not fatigue, as they might have other people. Stefan wasn't like other people.

"I'm hungry, and you must be too," Stefan announced, and he led me to a restaurant in the basement of the Siegel-Cooper Company on Eighteenth Street. He devoured a sturgeon sandwich while I happily ate a roast beef sandwich, each costing a dime.

"Stefan, I have to tell you something," I said as soon as I finished my meal. I timidly reached for his hand across the linoleum table.

"You can tell me anything," he said, with a warmth that made my stomach flutter.

I began with the story of my near-drowning, which made his eyes widen in alarm. I reassured him of my complete recovery, but then had to break the news of Lieutenant Pellegrino coming to see me with his Italian magazine.

"Another artist paint anarchist funeral, so now I'm murderer," he said scornfully. "Police same all over world. They break heads of those who care about lives of working man." Stefan proceeded to inform me that in Italy he joined the Socialist Party – "One-quarter of Europe joins!" – and was beaten by the police when he supported a strike in Milan, the same kind that led to the death of Galli.

"I no longer support socialists and I was never communist," he said. "But I get punched by police in America anyway."

"How have you recovered from what they did last week?"

"Not too bad," Stefan said, pressing his chin in the place a bandage once covered. "Many good friends helped me."

I pictured the voluptuous Louise and wondered unhappily about her style of helpfulness.

"Peggy?" Stefan's level gaze met mine. "You should not fret about Louise. She is my friend. She is my good friend. We are not lovers."

At his use of the word *lover*, said openly in a basement restaurant, I felt a flush move up my neck to warm my cheeks. "I see," I said. "She is… quite good looking."

He ran his hands through his hair, seeming to weigh various pros and cons. Finally, he said, "Louise, she prefers women."

"Prefers they do what?"

He gazed upward as if hoping for some sort of rescue from above. Such rescue didn't materialize. He said in a low voice, "She loves women more than men."

"Oh." I moved the sugar dispenser from one side of the table to the other. This was unexpected. I said slowly, "I thought she was jealous of you, that's why she disliked me so much."

"She is woman of… complication," he said. "Louise is loyal to her friends, and she always protects them. She acts as if she has light heart, but it is not so. She is sad. Her life, her childhood, very bad. Harsh. Men took advantage of her. Now she takes advantage of them. Who can blame her?" He sighed. "She finds much happiness with Ruth."

"Ruth?" I said blankly.

"You saw her, that afternoon. She came with Louise."

So the lovely dark-haired woman brought happiness to Louise, who had seemed to me obsessed with Stefan – and yet viewed him purely as a friend. My ideas and perceptions shifted. "Thank you for telling me the truth," I said.

Now it was Stefan's turn to fidget with a spoon. "I tell you whole truth. I slept with Louise last year. But she met Ruth at Henderson's, and she's happiest with Ruth. We are all of us friends."

I stiffened in my chair. I couldn't be hurt that Stefan made love to a woman long before he met me, but I was. I couldn't help it. These interlocking relationships made little sense to me. Louise preferred women but she slept with men too. Or at least with Stefan. If she were to make an exception for anyone, it would have to be him.

"Peggy," he said softly. "You must know how I care for you. You are future."

I gathered a smile. "The future of the Futurist is no small matter."

Walking to the train station that would take us back to Coney Island, Stefan and I made some plans. Seeing that Lieutenant Pellegrino still had a grudge against him, we decided to wait two more weeks, until the beginning of August, to try to meet. Stefan explained that at the end of the summer Coney Island shut down, and he planned to find a job of some kind in Manhattan. Since I intended to return to the bookshop, we'd be in the same borough again, with no one to prevent us from seeing each other. What I didn't tell him was that my twenty-first birthday in October would bring even greater independence – the first part of my inheritance. These things couldn't be discussed on a city street. But my thoughts were busy.

"I have ideas of how to approach galleries to display your work," I told him.

"You have ideas?" He smiled.

"I can be quite persuasive."

"What is your plan? You walk into gallery and say, 'I am Peggy Batternberg, you will show these paintings at once'?" He laughed, but without a trace of mockery.

"Something along those lines."

*

It was a far different type of train that took us to the heart of Coney Island. Crowded, far from clean – and, to me, infinitely preferable to the train Lawrence and I took to the Oriental Hotel. No one could possibly know me in this train, and I felt emboldened to hold his hand and lean into Stefan as he put his arm around me. *We could be a married couple*, I thought. Indeed, no one gave us a second look, not even when he kissed me fleetingly on the lips a half dozen times. The feelings he aroused in me each time were exquisitely painful. I wanted to press my entire body against him, but instead I willed myself to be content with the pleasure of his lips grazing mine. Everyone in the train car seemed in a good mood because the heat spell had broken, but no one could possibly feel more happiness than me.

We pulled into the station at six o'clock. We'd agreed that I would quickly separate from Stefan, hiring a car or horse buggy to take me to the Oriental. But on the platform, Stefan and I risked everything, unwilling to part, to let go of each other's hand. He squeezed my arm, harder than at any time since the tunnel, and whispered in my ear, "I love you."

"Stefan!" It was a girl's voice.

We turned in the direction of the cry. It was Marta, waving frantically. Stefan practically leaped off the platform. I scrambled after him.

"It's Louise, something bad happen – I've been looking everywhere for you," Marta said, her eyes red, her mouth quivering. "They found her inside Hell Gate."

"What do you mean?" he asked. "Who says this? She was 'found'?"

"I don't know," Marta howled.

Stefan turned to me, "You can't come with me to Dreamland. Go back to your hotel."

"No," I insisted. "I want to stay with you."

We hurried across the road, past Luna Park, pushing past the heedless crowds waiting in lines and massing outside the attractions. All the time I tried to understand how a woman could be "found" in Hell Gate – and I couldn't. Ahead of us on Surf Avenue rose the entrance to Dreamland, and the half-naked Creation Angel. Soon we'd get the answers.

"Stop! Stop now!"

Who said that, a father shouting to his misbehaving children?

"Stefan Chalakoski, stop!"

Everything happened so fast. A woman screamed to my side: "He has a gun!" *A madman's loose in the park,* I thought, terrified. But the man I next saw was Detective Sean Devlin, standing no more than ten feet in front of us, with a gun drawn and pointed at Stefan's head.

Two police officers tackled Stefan, throwing him roughly to the ground. Other hands seized me by my arms as I screamed, "Stefan! No!"

"Take her to Pellegrino," barked Devlin. Both my arms pinned behind my back, a policeman marched me through the entrance to Dreamland, past the gaping park attendants collecting coins. My mind went blank as the police officer pushed me toward Hell Gate, the enormous demon leering down. There were no couples waiting in line now. A yellow rope sealed off the entrance.

The policeman shoved me through the side door of Hell Gate. It was not dark inside. There were electrical lights, strewn haphazardly on ladder steps, to brighten this cavernous room. One third of it was taken up by a pool of dark, filthy-looking water. A table had been shoved next to the pool. A woman was laid out on the table, a sheet over her face and body. Long strands and clumps of damp red hair hung down the table's end, reflecting in the harsh electrical light like the achingly beautiful color of a new copper penny. Louise's hair.

A man walked slowly around the table. It was Lieutenant Pellegrino, his eyes blazing.

"Now you see what you've done," he said.

CHAPTER TWENTY-SEVEN

I don't know what time it was when I finally asked for Ben. The police interrogation hammered me with questions: What time did I meet Stefan and where? What did we do? What time did we return to Coney Island? Did he tell me his plan for our next meeting? Did he ask me for money?

As upset as I was, and as terrified for Stefan, I tried to stay calm. What happened to Louise was horrific – I kept picturing those strands of red hair – but I was determined to make the police see, once and for all, they were wrong about Stefan. I told Lieutenant Pellegrino, Detective Devlin, and anyone else who came near me that he was a gentle person who had never hurt me or could *ever* hurt me. My description of our day together left them in disbelief over its banality: Meeting in Central Park for a walk, going to see the tallest building in the world on Madison Avenue, eating sandwiches, and taking the train to Coney Island.

I kept back two things: Our passionate kisses in the archway tunnel, and Stefan's telling me Louise loved women. The first was too precious to be soiled by police jeers. As for the second, I wanted to shield her private life. But it soon became apparent that Stefan was telling them things in the other room. I didn't know exactly what. Different police officers would come in and take the questions in a new direction.

"We know you talked about Louise Turner in the restaurant!" Detective Devlin shouted, slamming the table with his fist. He'd abandoned all pretense of friendly harmlessness.

"Stefan said she was a good friend," I answered, focusing on a groove in the wooden table that wasn't there the last time they questioned me. *Keep your head*, I told myself. *Keep your head.*

"A friend?" His boyish face stretched into a sneer. "She used to be much more, everyone at Henderson's knew about their affair. She was jealous of you – that's why he killed her. To get her out of the way, so she couldn't spoil things for him."

"That's simply not the way it was," I said. "Spoil what? We planned to see each other in two weeks' time. Stefan hasn't taken money from me, not a penny."

Devlin and the second police officer rolled their eyes at each other.

I said slowly, putting emphasis into each phrase, "Are you honestly saying that you believe Stefan took Louise to Hell Gate before dawn, murdered her, weighted her down and hid her in the water in Hell Gate – a place where a body is certain to be found before too long – and then met me for a stroll in Central Park?"

"Yes," said Detective Devlin. "That's what we're saying. And you'd better be telling us all you know, Miss Batternberg, or you're gonna be charged as an accomplice. Yes, you're gonna be fried to a crisp right alongside your anarchist boyfriend. I'll be waving bye-bye to you through the glass, right before they hit the switch on the electric chair."

The vicious threat dissolved my control of my temper. "No, Detective Devlin, I'm going to be waving at *you* after you've been thrown off the police force. Because when my family's lawyers are through with you, you'll be selling pencils on the street."

The second police officer, standing by the side of his table, stared at me with astonishment. But the man himself, Detective Sean Devlin, turned brick red. It was obvious that no woman had ever spoken to him, or perhaps to any police officer, in such a way within these walls.

His teeth bared like a terrier's, Detective Devlin said, "How about we trot your family in here, show the Batternbergs what a fine young lady you are?"

I knew this would come up, sooner or later. I was prepared. "Do so. Send for Benjamin Batternberg, Room 505 in the Manhattan Beach Hotel. In fact, I won't say another word until he's here." With that, I turned away from Devlin in my chair, refusing to look at him.

In the time it took for Ben to arrive, I had ample opportunity in which to contemplate how bad this was likely to get. The answer was: very bad. For getting mixed up in such a crime case, I'd be chastised, condemned, perhaps shunned forever. I honestly didn't care about that. What I must hold onto was that neither I nor Stefan had done anything wrong. It was in the family's interests to help Stefan along with me. Once a roomful of Batternberg-retained Manhattan lawyers had descended on Coney Island, the charges against Stefan would surely be dropped.

When the door to my interrogation room finally opened, my heart leaped at the sight of Ben but sank at the next person to be escorted in by Lieutenant Pellegrino: Uncle David.

"Thank God she's alive and safe," my uncle said. "Thank you, Lieutenant."

"Yes, she's been bubbling with gratitude ever since," said Lieutenant Pellegrino dryly.

"Uncle David, I was never in any danger," I said. "This is all a terrible mistake. Stefan hasn't committed any crimes, certainly not murder."

Uncle David shook his head, looking upset.

"I'm sorry – but I did warn you it would be like this," said the Lieutenant. "I've seen a lot of con men in my day. Coney Island is famous for them. Chalakoski has got them all beat. She has deep, deep loyalty to him. I don't know how he did it. I have to say, it's a miracle he brought her back to Coney Island alive and" – he hesitated – "unviolated."

"Oh, please," I muttered. I peered at Ben, who had not said a word. If anything, he looked preoccupied. The Ben Batternberg brain was clicking away.

"Peggy, this is a terrible situation for you, but it's not what I'd call ideal for the rest of the family," Uncle David said. "We are doing everything in our power to keep your name out of the newspapers. There are reporters standing outside the precinct now."

"We're not charging her; you can take her to the hotel," said Lieutenant Pellegrino. "We have another way out, through a connecting tunnel to the courthouse and then beyond that. It's the jurors' tunnel, for when they are scared about a 'guilty' verdict and need protection. I can have it opened for you and—"

I interrupted, "The most important thing is for you to listen to me, Uncle David." I turned to my cousin. "And you, Ben. Stefan didn't kill anyone. And he is not a con man. He didn't lure me out of the hotel. I met him that first night in Coney Island – and I've seen him on two occasions since then. He is not trying to get money or anything except… my company. He's an honorable person. He needs our family's help."

My uncle collapsed into the chair where Detective Devlin had sat, took out a handkerchief, and mopped his face. "I didn't control her," he said, plaintively. "I'm going to be blamed for this because I didn't pay enough attention."

Ben put a consoling hand on his father's quaking shoulder. I could tell what they were most worried about now was the opinion of Bernard and the other Batternberg brothers.

"This is ridiculous!" I cried. "Why won't you believe a word I say?

Stefan is not a criminal. Why, I even offered to pay for a room for the two of us, so we could be alone for an afternoon, and he said no. What kind of a nefarious kidnapper is that?"

The room fell into an appalled silence, broken by Ben, smiling as he said, "My, what a wicked, wicked girl."

Lieutenant Pellegrino said, "I'll be back in fifteen minutes to lead you to that tunnel."

He closed the door quietly behind him. The silence ground on while my uncle sat in the chair, but before my eyes, he transformed. He put away his handkerchief. He pulled himself out of his slouch, rolling his shoulders, cracking his neck, as if preparing for battle. Only then did he turn on me. "We'll be leaving this police precinct shortly, Margaret. Once we are back in the hotel, you will say nothing to your mother or brother about this. Not a word. Not a syllable. How much does your sister know?"

I shrugged, unwilling to drag in Lydia.

"How much does she know?" he roared.

I had never heard such a voice come out of my uncle.

I said, "She knew I met someone, but I told her it was a journalist with no money. I didn't tell her the truth about Stefan."

My uncle said, "There isn't going to be any further explanation. I don't want to hear that man's name from your lips, not to her, to me, to Ben, anyone. You're going back to the hotel, and you will behave as if this sordid disaster never took place while our lawyers work around the clock to conceal your existence from the public record."

With all the courage I could summon, I said, "And if I don't?"

He spat out the words. "I will have a doctor here within the hour. The doctor will attest to your unsoundness of mind. You'll be taken by automobile straight to a private hospital in upstate New York, where you can rave all you like about anarchist Serb lovers, and no one will listen, no one at all."

My hands, sitting in my lap, began to shake. Because of the instability that stalked the women of my mother's family, I had a special fear of sanitariums.

"You can't do that," I said. "I won't let anyone take me away. I'll – I'll scream to those reporters when you take me outside."

"You won't be screaming if you're unconscious. The doctor could give you an injection here in this very room while I hold you down, and then we will carry you out through the tunnel and put you into the motor car."

"Ben," I cried, horrified. "You won't let him do that, will you? Ben?"

My cousin looked away. Ben wouldn't go against his father for me. I was alone and powerless, within this room, this city, this world.

I walked like a ventriloquist's dummy, a creature with no mind of its own, Uncle David's hand gripping my arm through the dim, dank, cobweb-lined tunnel leading out of the police precinct. When we emerged onto the street, an engine sputtered to life. It was my uncle's Franklin Model D Phaeton. The last time his driver opened the door for me it was at Moonrise Bookstore, when Uncle David whisked me to the dinner where my family pressured me to go to Coney Island. Tears wobbled in my eyes – I dashed them away. I sat silently between my uncle and cousin during the brief drive to the Oriental Hotel, and I hated them both.

It looked to be midnight when we returned; there were two buggy drivers still idling in the lot, hoping to be hired. A couple stood on the edge of the veranda, looking at the moon. In the seconds it took for his driver to come around and open the door, my uncle said, "You are your father's daughter."

I flinched; Ben made a strange noise on my other side, a groan mixed with a sigh.

My uncle stalked to the bar that was off the lobby; perhaps he needed a whiskey before descending on his mistress. Ben accompanied me to the elevator. I said nothing in the lobby, nor in the elevator, nor in the silent hallway leading to my room. But when we reached my door, I seized him and pulled him in with me. That muffled noise he'd made in the automobile gave me hope.

"Peggy, no, no," he said, although he didn't pull away. "Don't say it."

"I am begging you to help me, Ben. You're the only one who can."

"I *am* helping you," he said with a ferocity reminiscent of his father's. "I don't want anything bad to happen to you. My God, how could I? I will look out for your interests, and I'll intervene on your behalf."

My heart leaped in joyful relief.

"As long as your interests don't conflict with the family's interests."

I dropped his hands.

"Can't you understand, Peggy? I've never thought you a fool. If this becomes a sensation in the newspapers, and it comes out you're connected to a murder, you had an affair with a murderer, that could be damaging for all of us. Not just Lydia's marriage, but to our business. The muckrakers will have us for breakfast, lunch, and dinner. The Batternbergs could all be ruined."

I wanted to throw something large and pointed at his head. Instead I tried, one last time, to make him understand. "Stefan's not after the money," I said. "He thought I was a shop girl when we met. He's an artist, a true artist." Seeing no change in Ben, I asked, "Is it that you can't conceive that someone would love me for myself, that it could *only* be a fortune hunter or a criminal?"

Ben groaned, as frustrated with me as I was with him. "Oh, Peggy. You think this is love, what you have with him? A man like him?"

"Get out," I said, turning away.

A moment later, the door quietly opened and shut.

Curled up in an armchair by the window, brimming with misery, I didn't sleep that entire night. But when the first rays lightened the sky, my eyes felt so heavy, I shut them. The next thing I knew, there was a knock on the door. Alice had brought a morning tray.

"My sweet Lord in heaven, you look awful," she exclaimed.

"I feel awful."

"Did you sleep in your clothes and in the chair?" she said, aghast. This was the worst thing she could ever imagine happening to me.

After I declined to answer, she ran a bath and selected fresh clothes, frowning with puzzled disapproval. She brushed out my hair with her usual thoroughness. I sat there, limp and dazed. It began to seem that I was detached from yesterday's crisis, from absolutely everything. It was a nightmare, the sort that Susannah Campion might be eager to analyze.

Fresh knocks at the door brought in my mother and my Uncle David. My mother was wringing her hands, and my nerves roared to life. My name must be in the newspaper; all New York City was reading lies about Stefan and me.

"Margaret, Henry's mother wants to meet us, and it has to be soon," she said.

I was relieved – and yet annoyed. "After waiting weeks, we've been given short notice to come running?" I asked.

"Cooperate, please," Mother said. "We will be taken to her room in an hour. I know you haven't been feeling your best, but I get the distinct impression this won't take long."

"Oh?"

"Margaret, I'm asking you – don't be like this today," my mother burst out shrilly. "It's important to Lydia."

This was the only possible argument that could work. I looked at my uncle for the first time, saw with bitter satisfaction that he looked tired and rather ill himself. But he wasn't so worn out that he couldn't glare warningly.

"I'll be there," I said shortly.

I ate no food but drank black coffee to prepare for the ordeal. Alice laid sliced cucumbers under my eyes, and then hurriedly whipped a light cream into my complexion before smearing my lips with an apricot-colored stick. It was to match the dress she picked for me, a palest apricot dress I hadn't worn yet this summer. She tried to string a necklace around my throat, but I said, "Jewels before one o'clock? I can't do it, not even for Mrs. Taul."

"I must help Miss Lydia finish, you're all right with your hair down, aren't you?" Alice asked. She blinked with surprise. "Oh, my, look at you, Miss Peggy. That color suits brunettes. And you're right, no jewels needed. Simplicity is best with you."

She steered me toward the full-length mirror. There stood a tall woman with glowing skin and huge haunted eyes, the Batternberg black eyebrows making their emphatic statement, and coils of thick black hair tumbling down. It felt like a rank betrayal to dress up, primp, and put on a show, when Stefan was trapped in the Coney Island jail, among his tormentors.

I silently went to my mother's room, where she nodded in approval, then turned her attention back to my sister. She had not chosen simplicity. Her white dress was a frenzy of ruffles and fine embroidery, her hair was massed into a burst of blonde ringlets interlaced with ribbons. But it was Lydia's face that I focused on: violet shadows under her eyes, her mouth pinched. She'd had a terrible night too. I whispered, "What's wrong?" when mother's attention was diverted. "Not now," she mouthed back.

Before I could puzzle it out, Henry Taul appeared to take us to his mother. I'd expected him to be as nervous as everyone else, but he appeared extraordinarily relaxed. He could almost be ready for bed, with eyes half open like this. They did flicker to life when he looked my way; then he turned his full attention on Lydia.

"You're lovely, Sweetheart," he said, with evident pride. "The most beautiful girl in New York."

"Thank you, Henry." Her voice was brittle, graceless. My mother was mystified by her tone, as was I.

Neither my Uncle David nor my brother or male cousins came along. This was to be for the women alone.

CHAPTER TWENTY-EIGHT

Mrs. Taul resided in a top-floor suite at the diagonally opposite end of the Oriental Hotel, down the hall from her son. Henry pushed open his mother's door without knocking, and we entered the largest room I'd seen yet on the premises. Vases of freshly cut lilies stood everywhere. Framed photographs of Henry at various ages crammed the tables and main fireplace mantle. Books of archaeology were strewn across the table; most had the word "Troy" on them. Perhaps they were Henry's, or his mother shared his historical interests. The curtains parted wide to yield views of the emerald lawn leading to the sea in one direction and the vast gardens of the Manhattan Beach Hotel in the other. But the only human to be seen was a maid, dusting. She wore the same initials on her black-and-white uniform as the men who worked for Henry: HT.

Singing out, "Hello, Mama," Henry led us through a doorway off the suite. Here, his mother ruled: obese, propped up in bed, wearing a pale blue robe. She wore a bizarre Turkish-style turban. Another maid hovered by Mrs. Taul's bed, standing over the tray pressed to the side of the vast bed. On it was a plate piled with cookies and pastries, open wrappers littering the tray.

"I'm so sorry I haven't been able to receive you until now, my health hasn't been good," she said in a flat, deep voice. "Lydia, it's delightful to see you again. Come near me, have a seat. I'm so very happy to have a daughter at last. Henry, make the other introductions."

"Mama, this is Mrs. Jonathan Batternberg, my future mother-in-law," he said, leading Mother forward by the hand.

"Pleased to make your acquaintance at last," said Mrs. Taul, nodding. She gestured for my mother to have a seat next to Lydia, and then squinted to see the third female in the room. "Henry, this is the other one?"

"Yes," I said dryly. "I'm the other one." Without waiting for Henry to lead me, I walked to a place near the foot of her bed, between the bed posts.

"Her name is Peggy," said Henry, standing behind me.

Mrs. Taul groped for something on her messy side table. "Where are my spectacles, Victoria? Where did you put them, you simpleton?"

The maid did not flinch at the insult. Mother took out her fan even though it wasn't hot in this room and opened it.

The spectacles were found in less than a minute. Mrs. Taul took a long, hard look at me through thick lenses. "Well you're a fine-looking girl," she said, faintly surprised, as if she'd been informed otherwise. Her gaze swiveled to Lydia. "You're so much more fragile than Peggy. You must eat more, take exercise. You've been chosen by my son, Lydia, and you'll need to be strong enough to bear children. As it is, your sister looks like a better candidate for childbearing. You don't want that, do you?"

"Mama, please," said Henry. He didn't sound angry, though God knows he should have been. It was more of a whine. As for Lydia and Mother, they were aghast.

"I speak my mind, I speak my mind," announced Mrs. Taul. "Whether it's Connecticut or Colorado, everyone knows I speak my mind. I'm on the board of four charities, and I won't be a silent source of cash. If they want my millions, they must listen!"

"Mrs. Taul, what kind of treats do you have there?" asked my mother faintly. "They look so pretty."

"Bon-bons, Mrs. Batternberg. Bon-bons sent in the post from Paris. I had them brought out of the box for you to sample today."

But you couldn't wait for us to arrive before stuffing a few in your mouth, I thought with disgust.

Mrs. Taul ordered her maid to bring the bon-bons around, and then commanded her son to leave so she could speak to the women more frankly. She'd already been overly frank, in my opinion. For the first time this year, I was sorry to see Henry leave a room.

"I want there to be no misunderstanding," said Mrs. Taul. "I'm fully reconciled to this marriage, but I was not happy in the beginning. Mr. Hezekiah Taul gave the union his blessing, and I do not contradict my husband's wishes, ever. He felt it would be providential for our Henry to wed a daughter of Israel. He believes it's a fulfillment of prophecy."

How offensive. I couldn't bring myself to look at Lydia or my mother. I could only stare at the thick carpet and try to think of some excuse – attack of illness? – to get me out of this room. "Bon-bons, Miss?" asked the maid, her voice just above a whisper. "No, thank you," I said distractedly, but then thought I might as well eat one to distract myself and I tapped the maid on the wrist to swing back. I didn't intend it, but I pulled on her white sleeve, and a dark blue and purple mottled bruise appeared just above her wrist.

I gasped. The maid shook her head, her eyes a terrified appeal, as she pulled down her sleeve. She hurriedly placed two bon-bons on my plate before making her way to my mother and sister.

That kind of bruise was caused by a nasty wrench from someone possessing strength. I stole a glance at Mrs. Taul, who was gesticulating with beefy ringed hands. A wave of outraged repulsion rippled through me.

"The most important reason I needed to see you today was that I know you are fond of this hotel, and I've found the salt-water-wrap treatments beneficial for my circulation, but we must consider leaving the Oriental after I read the newspaper this morning. Victoria, hand me the paper." Seconds later, Mrs. Taul thrust the front page before us: "*Immigrant Arrested in Dancer's Murder.*"

"A Serb! Can you believe this – there are Serbs on the same island as us. Do you know what Serbia is? The Powder keg of Europe. That's what they call it! A country bogged down in century upon century of strife. As if it weren't bad enough with all the Russians and the Italians and the Poles, the dregs of Europe …" I closed my mind to her, using all my concentration, my methods refined from years of shutting out Batternberg conversation.

I *had* to help Stefan, had to make someone believe that he could never have murdered Louise or any other woman. How could I do that, though, if by campaigning for his defense and release within my family I'd be condemning myself to a terrifying exile, a hospital for the insane?

By finding the real murderer.

Yes. It was the only possible way to clear his name. Why did someone murder Louise? To me, it seemed like an attempt to throw suspicion on Stefan. She was his former lover, and Stefan was already a suspect for the police. But why choose Hell Gate, somewhere so public, as the place to leave the body? It seemed to contain some strange meaning, just like choosing that specific place on the beach to murder that other girl, Katherine O'Malley. There was something incredibly disturbing about this, a link between the two deaths that had been nagging at me from the start.

Sitting in the room of Mrs. Henry Taul, it came to me, like a messenger riding toward me, emerging from the darkest forest. Stefan and I were the link. In both places we'd kissed, and in both places a woman was found dead afterward, spiking Lieutenant Pellegrino's suspicion of Stefan. It could be a coincidence. But my instincts told me it wasn't. To kill Louise seemed to me an attempt to point a finger at Stefan... and at me, too. I thought of what Aunt Helen had said when she talked about why someone would drug me: "To punish or to prevent."

With a shudder of horror, I realized that if this were true, and someone wished to punish me through these murders, the killer could only be someone I knew well. Stefan thought a man followed us that first night. Was someone also following us during our ride through Hell Gate? I felt deeply uneasy at the thought of someone observing our kisses.

Mrs. Taul's voice had become so loud that she broke through my reverie. "The girls encourage everything they get in Coney Island. Those rides they go on are shameless. They dress like tarts."

I said, "So you've seen the girls in Coney Island, Mrs. Taul?"

She rounded on me. "Can't you see my health prevents me from venturing there – not that I would wish to be among them. My son tells me what he sees – and my servants. They are my eyes and ears. I know all about these girls leading men astray. Shameless. Why, I would bet that a fair number of them think that, even though they are stupid sluts, they deserve the right to vote, and yet—"

"I support the suffrage movement," Lydia said, interrupting her. "I believe that women are entitled to vote."

The time between Lydia's declaration and my finding myself back in my room was not long. Mrs. Taul was dumbfounded. "I must rest – I need rest," she sputtered. We took it as our cue to leave.

On our walk back to our room, escorted by Henry, who did not know what Lydia said to his mother, I managed to squeeze my sister's arm in support. I never knew she had political feelings for the suffrage movement – or anything else.

In no time, Lydia had gotten away from Henry and our mother and was in my doorway, alone. "While you were gone yesterday, I spent some time here reading to make it look to others as if I were visiting you." She stormed past me, headed for a table by my armchair. She picked up *Town Topics*, leafing through it frantically until she found the page she sought: "Saunterings."

"Oh, Lydia," I said.

"You knew?" she demanded. "You read that item and didn't think to tell me?"

"I couldn't. I wasn't completely sure."

"Well, I am sure," she snapped. "It's Henry." Tears glittered, and her mouth trembled. I went to comfort her, but she waved me off.

"Are you going to cancel the wedding?" I asked.

She was silent for a moment. "I haven't decided what to do, but when I do, it will be final and irrevocable."

At that moment no Batternberg had ever sounded tougher than my sister.

"What about you?" she asked. "Something's wrong. You're acting funny and so is Uncle David."

I walked to the window. It was a brilliant sunny day, with waves merrily crashing and people walking on the promenade. A ferry steamed into the dock. It was quite possibly the most beautiful day since we came to the Oriental Hotel.

"Uncle David was specific that if I talked to you about it, I'd suffer a fate worse than death, and I'm not being melodramatic."

Lydia shook her head impatiently. "Tell me. No one will know you did. I swear to you."

And so I told her about meeting Stefan in Dreamland and the woman murdered on the beach, and our going to the police, and seeing Stefan yesterday, and, finally, Louise's killing. Watching her carefully, I told her that I was determined to clear Stefan by identifying the real murderer.

She absorbed everything I said without a single question. A breeze wafted in the window, stirring the blonde ringlets cascading down the back of her frilly white dress.

Lydia said calmly, "If the killer is someone else – and I agree with you that Stefan is innocent – it's a person you know. Like Henry."

She took the most direct path to understanding the problem, like the way she slammed a croquet mallet with the utmost efficiency. If it were Henry Taul, her life would be turned inside-out. The whole country would be agog. In New York City, her reputation would be shattered beyond repair.

I took a deep breath. "No matter what, Lydia, I have to find out who it is."

"Yes, you do," said my sister. "We do."

My mouth fell open.

"That's right, Peggy. I'm going to help you."

CHAPTER TWENTY-NINE

"Lydia," I said, "if I agree to let you become involved, you need to know that, yes, I think the real killer could be someone I know here, but might not necessarily be Henry."

She stared at me, uncomprehendingly.

I decided to also share with Lydia our Aunt Helen's fear that someone put chloral hydrate in my Coca-Cola. "How horrible," she said, truly shaken. When I added that Aunt Helen believed Ben was behind it, in order to rescue me and thus restore my trust in him, she protested. "But that's madness."

"Yes, a form of it."

She grabbed my arm. "But if it could be him, could it be Paul?"

"I fear that anything is possible, any of the men could be capable," I said. "Our brother is the only one I'm sure is innocent."

"Oh, this is our family," she whispered. Yes, we'd known them and lived among them, depended on them, all our lives, and yes, family meant everything. But not if a person was a killer.

It is true that hours after my suspicions crystallized, I felt the same urge to deny this. Whenever I pictured any one of the men we knew best closing his hands around the throat of a helpless woman, my mind went blank. It didn't seem possible in my heart. But in my head, I knew it was possible.

My determination to clear Stefan drove me forward – but what drove Lydia? After a long time, she said, "If it's one of them, then he must pay for it."

Ever since Lydia was a child, she had seen the world in black and white and insisted on adherence to rules. To her, rule breakers, no matter who, must be punished.

We put our minds to this and worked it out that any of them – Henry, Uncle David, Ben, or Paul – had the opportunity to commit these crimes on the days or nights in question. None reported their whereabouts to us or to anyone; they were wealthy men on holiday, free to go wherever they pleased at any time. While we women *were* accountable: watched, even followed. This wasn't going to be at all easy.

How did the murderer get hold of Louise, Katherine O'Malley, and Beatrice Stompers, the first victim? I needed to understand Coney Island better to even begin to come up with a theory. It might have something to do with the Bowery, that street of dance halls, taverns, and clubs. It had a raciness, but other than that I knew nothing. Lieutenant Pellegrino specifically asked me if Stefan mentioned it. If only I could speak to someone who knew one of the women, and hopefully more than one. It seemed to me that the best person to talk to was Marta. She was young, but Stefan had told me she had great knowledge of Coney Island, and obviously she'd known Louise Turner well. I felt I could persuade Marta to help me, if by doing so she'd help Stefan.

"Do you think we could figure out a way to sneak over to Dreamland this afternoon?" I asked.

Lydia shook her head. "They'll be expecting you to try something along those lines," she said. "You have to get them to relax their guard, make Uncle David and Ben think you're not going to make trouble." She made a face. "The trouble is, anyone who knows you realizes that that's fairly unlikely."

"Indeed."

Lydia stood up. "I should leave. I fear my being in your room for hours will create suspicion. I'll try to figure out how we can both escape scrutiny the day after tomorrow for a couple of hours."

"That's too long to wait! Stefan's future is at stake."

She said, "So is yours. We can't afford to make mistakes. And Peggy, you must be careful. It's not only that you may have been drugged. Remember the night someone turned the doorknob in your hotel room?"

Unfortunately, I did. Lydia was right. Yet I couldn't sit here doing nothing, or I'd go as mad as the women confined in that hospital. An hour after she was gone, I picked up my parasol and hat and went for a walk on the promenade along the ocean, staying close to the Oriental Hotel. The sight of the waves up close didn't frighten me, though neither was I prepared to swim again. Seagulls screamed above, couples with wicker baskets strolled by, children tossed their balls. But I could not relax. I searched the crowd for faces I knew, and every few minutes I whirled around to see if I was being followed.

I finally abandoned the walk, my nerves in tatters. That night I ate dinner alone in my room, struggling to regain my courage for the challenges to come.

Due to sheer exhaustion, I slept soundly, and I woke filled with a new determination to help Stefan. But the morning brought news that threw all our embryonic plans into disarray.

"We will check out of the Oriental Hotel in five days' time," Mother came to tell me, Lydia at her side. "I've sent word to Arthur to reopen the house."

"Five days?" I cried.

"Henry and his mother are adamant," said Mother. "He went on at great length over dinner last night about the criminal element of Coney Island, and how his mother felt endangered by immigrants." She sighed. "It was something of an ordeal." For Mother, that was quite an admission.

I'd come to Coney Island reluctantly, and I wondered now if the rest of my family had balked inwardly at a summer in Brooklyn but gone along to please Henry and his mother, both creatures driven by tyrannical whim. Now we must disperse because of their whim.

Lydia said, "We are going to have to make the most of our holiday while we're still here. That's why I'd like Peggy to come with me to hear the musical program at the Manhattan Beach Hotel. It starts at two o'clock, but we will have to go over early to get the best seats for Sousa."

"Yes, please," I said, guessing that Lydia had worked something out.

"But Peggy, you don't like Sousa," said Mother, puzzled.

"Oh, you're wrong," I said as convincingly as I could manage. "I am just mad about marching music these days."

It wasn't until Lydia and I hurried along the pathway to the Manhattan Beach Hotel that she told me her full plan. We would meet the Campions and contrive to move as far into the dense audience seating as possible. Then, far from spying eyes, we'd make our way out the side door she knew of, and hurry past the Brighton Hotel on foot over to Coney Island. Before the concert was over, we'd return to be among the hotel audience as the program broke up.

"Brilliant," I cried.

Her plan worked perfectly at first. We met the Campions, who gamely agreed to her whispered request to cover for us while we took care of some urgent secret business. The four of us made our way into the crowded music hall, one with a capacity for five hundred people. In no time, Lydia and I scurried out of the hotel. Now it was my turn to lead Lydia as we crossed from the east side to the west of the island, plunging into the heart of the amusement park.

As soon as we paid the coin of admission to Dreamland, however, the plan's weakness was exposed. Two uniformed police officers stood just inside the turnstiles. Neither was Lieutenant Pellegrino or Detective Devlin, but I turned my head and spoke gibberish to my sister as we walked briskly toward the first major attraction inside Dreamland. "Are they following us?" I asked my sister. She glanced over her shoulder and assured me they weren't.

Another obstacle lay ahead. Not two but three police officers stood outside the Art Building. Marta might very well be inside, standing guard over Stefan's paintings, but it was madness to seek her out now. Quite a few of the officers got a good look at me at me just two days ago

"Maybe they'll move on," I said to Lydia, desperately. "Let's wait and see."

The minutes ticked by; Lydia scrutinized all the nearby attractions with interest, for she'd never set foot in Dreamland or any other part of the amusement park. She laughed with delight when Little Hip the elephant lumbered past us. She was most taken with the Infant Incubator Hall, and I told her what Stefan told me, that a real physician, one named Dr. Couney, performed medical miracles by keeping prematurely born infants alive in incubators. The rescued babies were on display inside.

To my frustration, all the time that we talked, the police showed no interest in moving on. I checked the timepiece I'd brought. The one-hour mark was approaching, half the time that we could safely be away from the Manhattan Beach Hotel. We'd accomplished nothing.

Giving up on the Art Building, I said, "There's one other place I might find Marta—we have to try it." I led Lydia to the steel pier where Stefan had once taken me. My heart leaped when I saw the blonde girl I sought—Marta—along with her brother, Wiktor, stacking boxes of buns.

"I'm so glad to find you," I said to the siblings, out of breath. "I need your help."

Wiktor looked from me to Lydia, shaking his head. "*You* need help?" he said. "I say Stefan is one who needs help."

"Yes, I agree," I said. "I'm trying to find out who really killed Louise, and the others. But in order to do so, I need to obtain some information. I must ask you some questions."

Wiktor waved me off with a flurry of hands. "The police talk to us for hours and hours last night. Some questions about you. If not for you, none of this ever happen, I think."

Feeling hurt by his dislike and blame, I glanced at Marta. Her light blue eyes, set within that narrow face, gave none of her feelings away.

Wiktor put on a hat, pulled down the sleeves of his jacket. "I go to jail now, request to see Stefan as visitor," he said. "These first days, I fear what other men in jail may do to him."

"What do you mean?" I asked, panicked. "Isn't he safe from other men in a jail?"

Wiktor shook his head again, disgusted, and left, walking back toward the center of Coney Island. If I could, I would have gone with him, demanded and pleaded with Lieutenant Pellegrino to ensure that Stefan was well protected. But I could not go anywhere near the jail.

My sister put one arm around me for a quick hug, then said to Marta, "My name is Lydia Batternberg. Will you help us?"

Marta looked at the disappearing back of her brother as she asked, "How?"

I said, "I believe the only way to free Stefan is to discover who really killed Louise and the others. But I don't know how the murderer could have met the victims, how their lives intersected."

She looked at me, baffled.

Pressing on, I said, "Do you know how the Bowery might fit in?"

Marta answered, "Louise a dancer on the Bowery, at Henderson's. But Katherine O'Malley was waitress at place not on Bowery. And other girl, Beatrice, I hear she work at Steeplechase and at stationery store on Surf Avenue."

"She did both?" Lydia asked.

"In season, we do many jobs," Marta said.

This was enlightening, but not particularly helpful. "What about Mabel Morgan's?" I asked. "Do you know what it is?"

Marta pressed her lips. "Police ask me and my brother about that. I tell them, 'Never!' Stefan never go to such a place. I know him. He would not. Stefan a gentleman."

A tingling of excitement raced through me. I sensed we were about to learn something crucial. "But what is it?"

Reluctantly, Marta said, "Mabel Morgan's a brothel."

Lydia said, "But were the women – the victims – prostitutes?"

Marta said vehemently, "Louise never do that. She was dancer in best club, had lot of money. She hate men who go to whores. The other two, I don't know them. How would my brother or I know?"

For me, things were beginning to make sense. If the first two women worked at Mabel Morgan's, that might have been where the murderer met them and lured them out of the place and to their deaths. As for whether the men I knew visited brothels, certainly Henry Taul and Ben did, and most likely Uncle David and Paul. Brothels were a fact of life in New York City. "Can you take me to Mabel Morgan's?" I asked Marta.

"I know where it is," she admitted. "But Mabel doesn't know me. I can't vouch."

"I don't need you to vouch for me, Marta," I said patiently. "Just give me the address."

My sister and Marta spoke at the same time, each imploring me not to attempt it. "Give the information to the police," said Lydia. "You can't set foot in there."

"The police already know about Mabel Morgan's – Lieutenant Pellegrino was the one who told me about it. But he was only looking for one man who might have been there: Stefan. I have some others to ask about." I thought for a moment. "If necessary, I'll pretend that I'm seeking a position there as an excuse to get in the door. I need the madame to tell me a few things – whether the first two girls indeed worked there, who their customers were. Then I will go to Lieutenant Pellegrino."

Marta exclaimed, "You crazy woman! You can't go there, a stranger, push way in, do pretend games, ask Mabel Morgan about her girls and her customers."

Lydia agreed that it couldn't possibly work, that I'd be shown the door.

"Show the door?" Marta said scornfully. "You will be hurt, she may have you raped."

Lydia gasped. I too was shocked at a teenage girl's being aware of such ugliness. No question, this possible reception to my asking questions was a deterrent. I asked Marta if there were anyone else who could "vouch" for me, so that I could ask questions without risk of harm.

Marta thought it over. "There's one person: Countess Isabelle. Everyone on Coney Island respect her. She might help. She knows who you are."

"I think I would have remembered meeting a countess."

"She saw you with Stefan," Marta insisted. When I still drew a blank, Marta stretched out her hand to a distance maybe four feet above the ground. She must mean the small woman wearing the Victorian dress who walked through Dreamland with the giant. So, she called herself a countess. Fine – I'd take help from someone who called himself the Holy Roman Emperor. "Can you take me to her now?" I asked. But Marta said this was the time of day for the Countess Isabelle's afternoon show. I'd have to wait until four o'clock.

Lydia said, "That's impossible. Peggy, we need to leave in a few minutes if we're going to make it back to the hotel in time."

Marta scowled. "Impossible? But you say you want to help Stefan."

How could I possibly explain to her how hemmed in I was, the restrictions on my movements? In an agony of frustration, I said, "What about late tonight? I can get away after eleven. Everyone will assume I'm asleep."

"Peggy, that's madness," my sister said.

Over Lydia's protests, I fixed it with Marta to send word to me if Countess Isabelle would meet with me later and, if so, exactly where. I told her that the message needed to be sent to me at the Oriental Hotel. "You know someone who can send me a note?" I asked.

"On Coney Island, you can always find someone to do anything," Marta said.

CHAPTER THIRTY

In the time it took Lydia and I to rush back to the Manhattan Beach Hotel, she informed me in no uncertain terms that my sneaking away to Coney Island late at night was a terrible plan. I'd be exposed to huge risks. But with four days left until our forced departure, I had to act quickly.

"This is such a wild idea, for me to be running around Coney Island at night, that no one will expect it," I added. "Its audacity will work in my favor."

"You can't be serious."

"Lydia, I have to obtain this 'vouch.' It's the only way."

We covered ground as fast as two ladies could while wearing long skirts. As we neared the sprawling hotel, the sound of tuba and trombone rolled down the lawn. The minute that Lydia led me in through the side door, those instruments' sounds died, and applause exploded. We managed to reach the enormous hall while the audience still cheered. It was difficult to find Jason and Susannah among hundreds of exalted Sousa celebrants, but eventually we succeeded, and made a point of talking to brother and sister for a while.

As we were saying goodbye, Jason edged closer to Lydia and bent down, his face nearing hers. He seemed about to kiss her, right in front of his sister and hers. I admit I was startled. But then he slipped a folded sheet of paper into her hand and merely smiled. She smiled back at him, as if enjoying a private joke.

As soon as we left the Manhattan Beach Hotel, Lydia opened the paper right in front of me and read it as she walked – and then handed it over. "Are you sure you want me to read it?" I sputtered.

"Jason wrote down the names of the songs the band played in order," she said. "You should memorize them, too, just in case one of Henry's henchmen saw us leave and we're questioned."

"Is that what they are – 'henchmen'?" I asked.

"What would be a better word?" she asked. "'Procurers'? Where would Henry be without his?" She began to laugh, a hard, bitter laugh. What he did in Paris hurt her deeply. She may not have told me yet that she was canceling the engagement. But Lydia would not marry Henry, I was certain of it. She hated him.

But something else had occurred to me, a new fear.

"Be careful with Henry," I said. "I don't know what you've decided on the engagement, but as long as we're in the hotel, and you're thrown together with him, you should be careful."

"Now why do you say that?" she asked.

I was on the verge of finally telling her of Henry's jealous, demanding questions three years ago, of his locking me in the room in Saratoga Springs, when my mother and Aunt Helen appeared on the veranda to ask if we enjoyed the concert.

Lydia played the part to perfection, praising songs she hadn't heard with such passion that my chiming in wasn't necessary. She was a valuable partner indeed.

Between tea and dinner, a hotel employee came up to my room with a sealed envelope, bearing the words "Miss Batternberg" in elegant

Spencerian script. I tipped him and opened it eagerly. The paper was of the thickest cream-colored stock. It bore one sentence, without salutation, date, or signature:

We shall meet with you at the hour of midnight in Lilliput to decide if your request warrants our assistance.

I ran my finger across the formal sentence, feeling the tiny bubbles of raised ink for the letters "i." This could not be coming from Marta, whom I had seen leafing through comics. The Spencerian style of script, looping and feathery, had largely been replaced by the Palmer method – that was the only handwriting anyone had used at Moonrise. The person who wrote this note was of an earlier, more elegant age. I suspected it was the woman who called herself Countess Isabelle. Wasn't Lilliput her domain? I wondered if she used the word "we" in the royal sense, or if she was including Marta in the decision.

I decided it was prudent to join my family for dinner. I needed to be as visible as possible during the early evening. With the heat spell thankfully a thing of the past, we took our dinner in the main room. It was not even half full. I would have thought with weather turned more palatable, the hotel would fill up, not empty. But it turned out we were all wrong about the financial soundness of the hotels of the east end. Ben brought news that, even with my preoccupation with secret plans, I found startling. After forty years of prominence, the Manhattan Beach Hotel was set to close at the end of the 1911 season, which meant this September.

"Shall it reopen with a new owner?" asked Lydia.

"No," said Ben, spearing a slice of duck with his silver fork. "I believe it's to be torn down. Probably the Oriental will follow within the next few years. The time for the grand old hotels is passing. It's the amusement park that's breaking attendance records."

"You got it wrong," said Henry. "The hotel won't close. You shouldn't listen to housemaids' gossip."

Ben finished chewing his duck, then wiped his mouth. I could tell he was offended by Henry's words and was delaying a response through these deliberate movements until he was completely calm. "I didn't hear it from a housemaid," he said finally. "It's true."

"But that's terrible – it's wrong, wrong, wrong," exclaimed Henry, so agitated that he knocked over a water glass with his right hand. Lydia, sitting next to him, flinched but said nothing. Water poured in a stream headed for Lawrence's plate, who watched the approach with interest. Waiters flocked to our table, to repair the damage while acting as if no one at the table had done anything wrong.

After dinner, I offered to organize a euchre game for the foursome of myself, Mother, Lydia, and Aunt Helen. We played in silence. For all of us, the game was a useful distraction from difficult thoughts. The men had broken away, as usual, to wander off for brandy, cigars… or something else. If only there were a way to have any of *them* followed.

Lydia pulled me to the side of Mother's suite at the end of the game. "I should go with you," she whispered.

"Definitely not," I said. "Don't worry, I know my way around Dreamland."

Lydia said, "And when you return without an escort well after midnight? You don't think the hotel staff will notice, or the Pinkertons?"

"I'll manage them," I said, although I didn't know how at that moment.

Lydia gave me a stern look, then made me promise that, when I returned, I'd knock loudly three times on her door before going to my room – "I won't sleep a wink until you do."

For my night's mission, I chose my most inconspicuous clothes, the skirt and blouse I'd worn the last day that I worked at Moonrise Bookstore. It felt exhilarating to put them on again. I pinned up all my hair under a plain hat. I took two emerald earrings from my jewelry box and slipped them in the side compartment of my handbag.

Peeking out, I saw no one in the hallway. I didn't want the elevator operator to see me going down alone after eleven, so I took the stairs to the lobby. Whether the door to the stairs would be unlocked when I returned, I didn't know. I couldn't worry about that now. That was something I hadn't anticipated. I hoped I hadn't neglected to anticipate anything else.

My biggest problem was always going to be the lobby. Henry could very well be on the loose. But I didn't see or hear him or anyone else I knew as I crossed it, walking briskly, the eyes of framed Teddy Roosevelt upon me. I made my way to the automobiles and horse-and-buggies lingering in the lot. I couldn't help but smile when, by the light of the street lamp, I spotted the same bristly handlebar mustache of the buggy driver who took me over to Dreamland.

"Remember me?" I asked. He grunted in reply.

Once he helped me into the buggy, I showed him the earrings. "I need you to take me to Surf Avenue, find a place for your horse as close to Dreamland as you can get, and then wait for me to return to you, no matter how late it gets," I said. "I'll give you one earring once you find a place to wait, the other when I return. You *must* wait for me if you want both earrings."

"Yes, Miss, I'll be glad to, Miss," he said, gloating under the moustache.

He no doubt thought I was a fool to part with this expensive gem for an hour to two of waiting. I didn't care. After my meeting was finished, I couldn't stumble around alone in the dark looking for a way back to the hotel. This was well worth the earrings – I had many, many more.

Once we reached Surf Avenue, he shook the reins to direct his horse to an open place. "I'll look for you here," I said emphatically. He leaned back, pulling his cap low on his head, as if it were time for a nap.

People were pouring out of Dreamland. It must be approaching closing time, and I had to be insistent with the girl working the entrance before she would take my dime. "Don't come back and complain that everything's shut down," she said sullenly.

I approached Lilliput, one of the largest attractions on the west promenade, with a burst of confidence. I should be able to persuade the Countess Isabelle to make the necessary introductions to this madame called Mabel Morgan.

The first hour I ever spent in Dreamland, when I wandered unhappily in the thickest of crowds after arguing with Ben, I'd glimpsed the long building called Lilliput, or, as defined by a second sign posted out front, "Midget Village." I got a fuller view of it tonight. It rose on the park promenade like a thirteenth-century German castle, with circular towers and steep sloping roofs and a hint of a battlement, though who would fire weapons? I felt like I was stepping onto a page from *Grimms' Fairy Tales*. Peering down, I saw the castle front interlocked with other types of architecture: a half-timbered Tudor manor, followed by a nineteenth-century-era plaza. A dozen people filtered out through the main doors, the last show having obviously ended. I was the only one who would be seeking entrance. I girded myself for another struggle with the person in charge of admissions.

"This way, Miss," called a man standing just inside the front doors, beckoning to me. As I drew closer, I realized that with a height reaching less than four feet, he was part of the Lilliput community.

"Miss Batternberg?" he asked courteously.

I was surprised and grateful to be expected – and impressed by the Countess' influence.

He was not a young man. His rather large forehead was creased with wrinkles, and gray strands showed in the hair pushed behind his ears. He wore a checkered shirt and suspenders and trousers, all of which fit perfectly. I wondered if they employed their own tailor and seamstress here.

"My name is Peter," he said, extending a hand to shake.

I followed him through another set of doors into an enormous hall. On one side were rows of seats for the audience. On the other, the European village thrived, displaying a similar castle to the one seen outside, but here, part of the castle was opened up so the audience could see what happened within: a dining chamber and a parlor, a kitchen quarters. Outside the castle a fair was erected with black-smith and grocer and apothecary stalls. Every wall, every stall, every table and chair were constructed to a certain size. It was all scaled to the convenient use of the residents of Lilliput. None of them were acting out anything right now; I spotted only a few workmen cleaning and sweeping.

Peter beckoned to follow him through to the next hall. Now I passed more conventional spheres of entertainment: a theatre, followed by an opera house, followed by a fire department.

"This is so elaborate," I said admiringly.

Peter said, "Mr. Samuel Gompertz scoured the four corners of the Earth to find the best of the best. He went to every World's Fair, every successful burlesque show, every traveling circus of repute, to find us, all three hundred of us, and bring us to Coney Island. We are the preeminent Lilliputians."

"Three hundred?" I exclaimed.

He nodded gravely and said, "Each one of us well paid, too." He was leading me to what looked like the last structure to be displayed in Lilliput. What was left to see? I wondered. My excitement dimmed as the words "Court House" stared back. In its brick walls and double doors and narrow windows, it looked eerily like the Coney Island Court House adjoining the police precinct, only smaller.

My guide stood next to its doors, his hand on the right doorknob, waiting to usher me inside. I could hear voices – definitely more than one, and male – on the other side. I tensed, studying Peter's expression. Could his courtesy, his proud tour of Lilliput, be a ruse? He was, after all, a performer.

I pushed down my fears. Why would anyone lure me here for unpleasant purposes? That made no sense. If there were still a chance of finding a way to clear Stefan of suspicion, I had to take it. I stepped forward with a nod, and Peter pulled open the door.

I expected a facsimile of a courtroom, such as the castle rooms I'd seen in the beginning, but there was no jury box or judge's platform. Despite all the careful effort that went into creating a perfectly reproduced courthouse front, behind the wall, out of view of the audience, was only a dirty floor covered by a few benches, boxes, and some chairs.

And people. Perhaps ten people. Large, small. Men, women. As I surveyed them, I spotted several familiar faces. Marta and her brother Wiktor sat side by side on a bench to the left. I smiled at Marta, but she did not smile or indicate that she'd ever spoken to me, much less helped arrange this. The very tall man who had walked with the countess and greeted Stefan that day sat on a large box. I gave a start when I recognized Ruth, the woman who came with Louise to help Stefan and was, he told me, her lover. Grief obliterated her beauty. Her face was chalky white. It was otherwise with the blonde woman sitting next to her: She wore heavy dark-beige makeup and bright rouge on her cheeks; her hair braided as if she were a milkmaid. On the other side of Ruth sat a floridly handsome young man with wavy black hair whose face was darkened with cosmetics, something I'd never seen before on a male face. He wore a crimson shirt and black trousers. Sitting in chairs to the side of them were two less dramatic-looking people: a black man who looked to be my age and a humbly dressed woman perhaps ten years older.

"Good evening, Miss Batternberg."

Countess Isabelle approached me with a smile, spreading her hands in welcome, as gracious as any hostess at a grand social occasion. I'd not heard her voice until now. She spoke in a sweet southern drawl and was dressed in a bustled silk gown like a New Orleans belle.

"Good evening, Countess," I said politely.

"As the murder of Louise Turner and the false arrest of Stefan Chalakoski is a serious matter, I've asked those who are most affected to join me in order to hear what you have to say," she said.

"So I gather."

The woman with the blonde braids said, "She's got guts, I'll give her that."

"Guts? Are you kidding?" The handsome man in the red shirt leaped to his feet with panther-like grace. "Of course, she's cool as can be. She's a Batternberg! She's a member of the ruling class, I bet she's used to having her way at all times. It's rare to get one of them alone, and we should take advantage of it."

"How?" asked Countess Isabelle. Far from being my friend, she seemed interested in hearing his idea.

The man treated me to a slow, taunting smile. He said, "Let's hold her hostage and tell the police we won't release her until they free Stefan. That should make a few people start to take notice."

CHAPTER THIRTY-ONE

This man, smirking, looking at the others for support for his criminal plan, may have thought he frightened me, but he had no idea what sort of dinner tables of "the ruling class" I'd grown up at.

"If I thought your plan had a chance of working, I'd be only too happy to oblige," I told him. "But they'd certainly never release Stefan in exchange."

"Oh, they wouldn't?" he challenged. "How the hell do you know?"

"Their priority would be organizing a manhunt, tearing Coney Island apart, using the entire city's police force plus an army of Pinkertons."

"She's right," said Countess Isabelle. "We don't want to draw that sort of attention. Sit down, Dimitri."

Her opinion carried the most weight, and any idiotic idea of my being kidnapped and held in a ransom exchange dissolved into the air.

Wiktor spoke up. "Stefan won't want anything bad to happen to Peggy." He said it with obvious reluctance.

"You saw him?" I asked. "They let you see Stefan today? Is he all right?"

"For two minutes," answered Wiktor. "He is all right."

I was equal parts relieved and tormented at the thought of Stefan in a cell.

"Stefan loves you, and you love Stefan," said Countess Isabelle gently. "I saw it in your faces when you walked through Dreamland."

"How romantic," spat Dimitri. "But what about Louise? How do we get justice for her?"

The countess gave him a stern look. "That is why we are here." She turned back to me. "You must forgive Dimitri. He was partnered with Louise in the Henderson shows, and he was fond of her."

"Fond? How could anyone be fond of her? She was a nasty, selfish cow who wouldn't learn the damn steps until dress rehearsal." His voice broke on the word *until* and tears gleamed in his eyes. I saw Ruth, in his shadow, bow her head, and the blonde with braids put her arms around her in comfort. The three stage performers drew together in a tight ball of misery.

"I want to find out who murdered Louise," I said, trying to speak to everyone. "That person must be punished. And it's the only way to convince them that Stefan is innocent."

For the first time, the black man spoke. "Why can't your people help him?" he asked. "They must have plenty of lawyers."

Countess Isabelle introduced me to the man and older woman sitting with them. Their names were Wallace and Berenice. Stefan had been giving them art lessons – free of charge. My heart swelled to hear this. It was so like Stefan. But I was ashamed to have to tell his students the truth.

"My family hates my being involved with Stefan – more than any of you do. I've asked for their help, and they won't give it. I've tried to tell the police they're wrong, and they won't listen either." I looked directly at Ruth, the person feeling the most pain in the room. "I'm sorry."

Countess Isabelle said, "So you propose to find this murderer all alone." Dimitri snorted his skepticism.

"Not alone," I said. "With your help. I know there is a Bowery connection with the victims. Louise danced at Henderson's. But the first two women, there must be something else. I don't want to cast aspersions on Katherine O'Malley or Beatrice Stompers, but I believe they might have worked at Mabel Morgan's and—"

Countess Isabelle said, "They did. They came and went; not regular girls, but on any given night there's a chance one of them would have been there."

"What fools," said the blonde with pigtails.

"If they had regular, normal jobs, why would they step inside a brothel?" I wondered aloud, and with that I felt the glare of ten people upon me.

"For the money," snarled Dimitri. "Why else?"

Countess Isabelle said, "A girl with an ordinary job stands to earn ten dollars a week for full time hours of hard labor, while a prostitute can easily earn seventy-five dollars a week."

I could feel everyone in the room silently condemn me for my ignorance of such realities.

It was Dimitri who moved the conversation along. "You think some client of Mabel Morgan's scooped them up at the brothel and talked them into a walk along the water, strangled them. But who? You can't think Mabel keeps nice, neat lists, and even if she did and she gave them to you, which she wouldn't, we're talking about hundreds of men!"

This was something else I hadn't anticipated, and I really should have. How to explain why I thought I could succeed at finding the killer without sharing too much.

"You have an idea who the man might be," said Countess Isabelle, the most perceptive person in the room.

"It's possible," I admitted. "But I can't tell you who. I can't share my suspicions with you at this stage. If it means you won't vouch for me, then I understand. But I hope you will."

Countess Isabelle inclined her head. "I'll give you a letter of introduction. It will mean Mabel Morgan will speak to you, and no harm will come to you. But I can't promise she'll be of help. That's her decision."

"Louise was never at Mabel Morgan's."

It was the first time Ruth spoke, and she was vehement.

The pig-tailed blonde quietly reassured her that no one was saying otherwise, but that didn't calm her. "She didn't meet this man at any damn whorehouse," she said loudly. "I don't know where Louise met him, how this bastard got to her. Maybe she *didn't* meet him – he came up behind her and grabbed her."

A painful silence settled over the group. But it was broken by Dimitri. "Ruth,' he said. "This does no good."

"No," she said.

'Say the word."

"No," she said, nearly shouting.

"Then I'll say it," said Dimitri. But he didn't, not for a minute. He seemed afraid to say it, making me wonder – an arrogant, impetuous, possibly reckless man such as this one, what would make him hesitate?

"Kschessinska," he said, his brash Brooklyn voice suddenly sounding very subdued – and very Russian.

A spasm of regret passed across Countess Isabelle's serene face.

"I told her not to go there anymore," said Ruth, wiping tears from her face. "We didn't need the money, no matter how much they would pay her."

"What is it?" I asked.

"You mean *who* is it," said Countess Isabelle, with a deep sigh. "Mathilde Kschessinska is a prima ballerina of the Imperial Ballet in St Petersburg. She was the mistress of Nicholas, Czar of all the Russias, until he married. Then she moved on to having affairs with the grand dukes in the House of Romanov."

I couldn't help but laugh. "You're saying this woman has come to Coney Island?"

"No, of course not," said the countess. "The real prima ballerina is in St Petersburg and has, I believe, married. But a Russian woman opened a private establishment here seven years ago, who has taken her name and identity, and you'd be best not to give her any indication that you don't accept that she *is* Kschessinska."

"So this is another brothel?" I asked.

"That's a word that could never be said in her presence, Miss Batternberg. Neither can you say 'prostitute' or 'madame.' Gentlemen are invited to be members of her club, where she serves as hostess, in order to have private conversations with women, the most beautiful in New York City. Such conversations could last an hour, two hours, maybe more."

"I see," I said, glancing at Ruth, wracked with grief and fury.

"She opened her club in Coney Island because the racetracks and athletic clubs brought the richest men of the East Coast out here. Now that the racetracks are closed, some of us thought that she might be moving on. But she hasn't, not yet. And the rich men still find their way to her door."

Rich men seeking the most beautiful women in the whole city. That made a knot of dread form deep inside me. Aloud, I said, "I wonder why Lieutenant Pellegrino didn't mention this place, only Mabel Morgan's."

Dimitri said, "Word on the street is she pays off the police in a big way. Politicians come to 'visit,' even senators, you know. No one in uniform ever gives Kschessinska a bad time. If she has to use any muscle with ordinary guys, rich drunks, or just plain jerks, she always has her Cossacks."

"Don't tell me the Cossacks are real," I said.

Dimitri shrugged. "Everything is real on Coney Island – and nothing is real."

Countess Isabelle said that tomorrow she would send over to the Oriental Hotel a letter of introduction vouching for me to Mabel Morgan. She'd also write a letter for me to present to Madame Kschessinska, although she said it might not make too much difference. The Russian woman held herself aloof from people of the amusement park, although she'd made her living just blocks away from them for years.

"If she doesn't care for your letter, is she going to call for the Cossacks?" I asked. The countess shook her head at my bad joke. "I doubt she would behave in such a crude fashion, Miss Batternberg, but you would be wise to treat her with caution. When are you going to be paying your calls?"

"Tomorrow night, same time, I suppose," I said.

For the first time, the giant spoke. "I will escort Peggy," he said solemnly.

Countess Isabelle said, "Ah, my dearest friend, your nobility is your greatest gift to us all. But I wonder if your presence would draw more attention than is wise to her mission."

Dimitri said, "Hell, I'll do it. I'll see her to the door of Mabel Morgan's and wait outside."

"Please don't trouble yourself on my behalf," I said coldly, not wishing to spend additional time with the man who suggested holding me hostage.

But my response made him retort, "This isn't for you, Your Ladyship. I'm doing it to help Stefan and to find Louise's killer."

I bade farewell to the group of people who cared most about Stefan and Louise. Regretting that I hadn't gotten to know Stefan's students, I lingered by their side. I knew nothing about them except that they had jobs on Coney Island and wanted to create art. Now it was rather late to ask questions, but I hoped I might gain some inkling. The woman, Berenice, who had not spoken, who looked uncomfortable and sad the entire time, still avoided looking me in the eye. I thought it best not to force her away from her shyness, so I merely extended my hand to shake hers.

Her hand stayed by her side. Instead she looked at me and said, "The Batternbergs own mines all over the Americas, don't they?"

Startled, I nodded, and she said, "Have you ever gone underground and talked to one of the miners?"

"No, I haven't."

"Don't you think that you should?" she asked.

I had no idea what to say. Countess Isabelle tactfully drew me away. She shook my hand before advising me to wear "something of the latest fashion" the following night. "Madame Kschessinska in particular will appreciate that."

Marta and her brother Wiktor walked me out of Lilliput and Dreamland, and all the way to my buggy driver on Surf Avenue, who had not budged, his palms itching for my other emerald earring. "Good luck tomorrow," Marta said, while Wiktor nodded stiffly. I'd not gained an inch from him. With all of them, even Marta and the Countess, I sensed a lingering suspicion. To varying degrees, they all disapproved of me, resented me.

"See you at this spot tomorrow night," Dimitri sang out from the sidewalk as the driver helped me in. I hadn't realized he followed too. I raised a hand in reluctant acknowledgement.

I was swiftly returned to the Oriental Hotel, where I dropped the second earring into the driver's palm and proposed hiring him to perform the same task at the same time the following night for more earrings. He agreed at once.

Now came my greatest challenge: a young woman, unescorted, walking into the hotel well after midnight. It must have been one o'clock in the morning. Thank God there were still people around. Men and women drifted across the lawn and sat on the veranda. After all, none of them had to report to a factory floor early the next morning. But would every one of them shrug off seeing me now? Even if they did, a Pinkerton guard or hotel staff member could notice me. As I lingered near the horse and buggy, undecided, a motor car rumbled to a space close by. I watched two young couples step out of the vehicle, laughing and moving unsteadily, for they had clearly all been drinking. As they made their way toward the walkway, I fell in behind them, so that I just might be mistaken for one of their group. I followed the quartet into the lobby, reaching the door leading to the stairwell and edging toward it. The door was not locked. After trudging up the stairs, I made it to the corridor of the Batternbergs, and I knocked on Lydia's door twice, as we agreed, along the way to my room.

It was a relief to have made it through the night without things going awry. But I knew that the next night could be a far greater ordeal.

CHAPTER THIRTY-TWO

The next day, a messenger arrived by noon with a large envelope for me and, within it, three smaller sealed notecards. They were all sealed with wax. The smaller one for me contained the two addresses and the Countess's best wishes. The second envelope was addressed to "Mrs. Morgan" and the third to "Madame Kschessinska." I had no idea what Countess Isabelle wrote in her letters to the brothel keepers. I could only hope that she was persuasive.

Lydia frowned at the sight of these envelopes. "This all seems real to me now," she said somberly. I'd already told her everything that was said last night. Like me, she flinched at the question over whether I had ever talked to a miner working for the Batternbergs. We'd been protected from such questions all our lives. Last night I stepped outside of the protection. I had a feeling that before this all was done, I stood a good chance of stepping farther outside of it.

Lydia said, "It does seem possible that at least one of the men in our family visited these brothels since we came to Coney Island."

"Well, I know Ben has in the past," I said. "He had a little book listing the best ones in New York City called *The Gentleman's Directory*. He used a special name when he visited – Mr. Franklin. Of course that was a few years ago and—"

"Oh, Peggy!" Lydia grabbed my arm, dismayed. A second later, I realized why. The men probably hadn't used their real names! My visits to the brothels, which I'd gone to such trouble to arrange, could be a waste of time. But how else could I begin to find the true murderer, and in the three days left to me?

"You couldn't describe them, they look too much like a lot of other people. Even Henry is hard to describe in a way that expresses how different he is than other men," Lydia said. "Only photographs would convey it. And even if we persuaded them to be photographed, those photographs wouldn't be ready by tonight."

Elated, I said, "Photographs exist! They're in Ben's room. Paul took them." This presented our next problem to solve. My visiting Ben in his room and somehow absconding with the pictures was unrealistic. Not with the present state of our relationship: mutual wariness.

Lydia said, "I'm sure I could talk a hotel maid into letting me into his room."

"Yes, but Ben might be in his room at this very moment," I pointed out. "We have no idea what he's up to this afternoon, just that we're all meeting for dinner at seven. He's brought some work with him on this holiday, believe it or not. Family business."

After a few minutes Lydia said, "We know he will be out of the room at dinner time. Why don't we eat at the Manhattan Beach Hotel tonight? I'll excuse myself to seek out the powder room, and that's when I'll go upstairs, talk my way into Ben's room, and get those photographs."

"That sounds risky to me," I said.

"Riskier than you knocking on brothel doors at midnight?" she demanded.

She had a point. Lydia and I turned our attention to how to best go about changing our habitual place of dinner. It was difficult to think of a reason that would be persuasive. We both agreed the request should come from her, not me. She enjoyed higher standing among the family. But still, it was unlike either of us, for any of the Batternberg women, to suggest such a thing. Raising her chin, Lydia said, "Are our lives so insubstantial, so frivolous, that we cannot even take a role in changing the place the family eats dinner?" Her question pitched me into gloom, for the answer was yes.

"I'll ask Henry to suggest to everyone that we move dinner to the Manhattan Beach Hotel as a favor to me," she said.

"I don't like you asking him for favors. Not under these circumstances."

"It's the least he could do for me," she said intently, though what her precise meaning was, I didn't know. I very much wondered what Lydia intended to do about marrying Henry, but I knew my sister well enough that I didn't pose the question. When she was ready, she'd tell me.

Lydia hurried off, and word soon drifted back to my room via Lawrence that Henry Taul had moved our dinner to the Manhattan Beach Hotel. It was a bittersweet moment, to realize yet again how the only way that women in this family could get what we wanted was through whispering in the ear of men.

I expected Lawrence to return to collect me for our walk over, but to my surprise my cousin Ben knocked on the door, asking for the privilege of escorting me.

"You look very pretty," he said, his guardedness a thing of the past. "Quite the New Woman this evening, eh?"

I'd decided that, for this dinner, I would wear the only dress that had intrigued me when we were being fitted for our summer clothes that rushed week in Manhattan. It was a silk dress in the Chinese fashion, suggesting a kimono, its pattern a deep violet with light pink blossoms. The neckline was high and only a bit of ankle showed below, yet it was daring in its tight fit.

As Ben and I stepped out of the Oriental Hotel, the late-day sun bathed the beach in a yellowish orange glow, and the salty mist of the Atlantic hung in the air. It was as if the long heat spell that blanketed the city with suffering, madness, and even death, never happened. We took the longer way to the other hotel, swinging close to the water. Nannies frantically called to their charges to forsake the beach, for they needed to bathe and dress the children to be presented to their parents before dinner. But the boys and girls leaping in the damp sand defied them. An elderly couple I vaguely recognized from the hotel passed us; they were coming up as we were going down. They looked deeply content, their soft, wrinkled hands tightly interlaced, and the woman's eyes flicked over me and Ben before she smiled at us, as if acknowledging a fellow couple in love.

Ben laughed dryly. I wondered if my cousin were inclined to walk this route not to soak in its golden pleasure, or even to suck on his cigarette, but to tell me something significant I should hear before dinner.

"Look at these crowds," he marveled. "And to think, sixty years ago, Walt Whitman could swim naked here with no one seeing him and then shout Shakespearean verse to the seagulls."

"I do think," I said, "you may have some news that occurred more recently to tell me."

"Yes. Well. As a matter of fact, a solution of sorts might have been found for Mr. Chalakoski." His bringing to me a solution should be welcome, but I noted the waft of disdain with which he framed Stefan's name, and my stomach fluttered with nerves.

"The newspapers have taken up this murder, Peggy. It's not the crime of the year – no one ever heard of this redhaired dancer outside of one dance hall in Coney Island – but still, the sort of light shines on it that makes it difficult for our lawyers to freely maneuver. We have limited influence on the city prosecutor's office. But we have great standing in the Department of State because of our business interests overseas. The diplomats have been making telephone calls, and one informed me two hours ago that there's hope of getting Chalakoski deported to Serbia."

The misty, sunny day turned as dark as if thunderstorm clouds gathered.

"Deported means sent out of the United States, doesn't it?" I asked.

"It does."

"But he left Serbia years and years ago – and he chose the United States very deliberately. It's been his home for two years."

"I think, presented with the option of a trial followed by, most likely, the electric chair or a life sentence, Mr. Chalakoski would prefer the Old World charms of Belgrade."

Put like that, it seemed the lesser of two evils. I pressed Ben, saying, "But he wouldn't be put in prison in Serbia – you're sure of that?"

"Our sources tell us that he has two brothers in the officer class of the Serbian army, the elder having some significant connections. They might be able to exert influence."

We'd reached the border of the gardens of the Manhattan Beach Hotel. I cried, "Might? Might? But if they can't? You forget that Stefan has done nothing wrong, committed no crime at all. If the lawyers would back him, defend him properly here in the city—"

"Ah, but if this case were to enter the criminal courts in New York, and he pleaded 'not guilty,' there is no way that your name wouldn't come out," said Ben. "Say he was cleared of the murder, but only after a long public trial. Even if he won, our family would have lost. And that's the question that matters."

How very cold he was, my beloved cousin. Peering at him, I wondered, not for the first time, if he were jealous of Stefan. All at once, a new reason for his hostility occurred to me.

"You hate him because of that hotdog cart, don't you?" I asked. "You can't bear the thought of the mighty Batternbergs being associated with an immigrant like Stefan. But our grandfather pushed a cart when he came here, don't forget that, Ben. We're not so different."

He shook his head. "Oh, if you're going to put us back behind the pushcart, why stop there? How about we all share the same room growing up on the Lower East Side, our parents stitching garments a few feet away?" Ben ground his cigarette into the freshly trimmed emerald grass bordering the Manhattan Beach Hotel with disdain. "God, you can be such an idiot, Peggy."

Stefan silenced and exiled, the actual murderer still at liberty. How could this be a sane solution? But perhaps that was what Ben really wanted. Walking past the fragrant rose bushes, I took stock of my cousin, trying to quiet all my warring feelings where he was concerned and determine his true objective. In significant ways, he fit the profile of the killer, especially if the man were to turn out to be a connoisseur of brothels. He had not shown me a physically violent side. Yet I knew there were depths to him I'd never fully grasped. Tonight, if Lydia succeeded in getting me those photos, I'd come closer to the truth.

But first I had to endure this family dinner. Once we took our seats, unpleasantness ensued. No one seemed to enjoy the meal but Paul and Lawrence. My mother, ill at ease, found fault with everything, from the temperature of the baked clams to the freshness of the peonies in the table vases. My Uncle David toyed with his food, speaking little, his eyes reflexively roaming the room. I wondered if he feared his secret mistress would materialize between courses. But my occasional surveying of the vast room yielded no sight of the delectable Thelma. Taking in Aunt Helen's stony serenity, I wondered if Thelma were really a secret to anyone.

Sitting on the opposite end of the table, I didn't hear the argument between Henry and Lydia until it reached full boil. "So I am informed enough to run several households and raise sons but not enough to cast a vote in an election?" asked Lydia, anger enunciating every syllable.

"That is the woman's sphere – the home," Henry retorted. "My mother is right. The man's sphere is the world, and to use his calm and his reason to vote for the best candidates. Women are too ruled by whim and sentiment."

My sister said, "And you honestly believe that I am more ruled by whim and sentiment than you are?"

I don't think she had ever criticized Henry before, in private or in public. And she did so with the jeweled pendant hanging from her throat, his gift presented in the parlor of our Manhattan home. He sat there, a fork hanging loosely from stunned fingers, as he absorbed what had just happened.

"I think it time for the powder room," said Lydia, rising from the table. When Mother said she would accompany her, my sister insisted she enjoy her meal, her gaze settling on me. I immediately said I would accompany her.

I realized that Lydia had allowed the quarrel to happen, perhaps even instigated it, to give her an excuse for a prolonged absence from the table. If she had told me beforehand, I'd have advised her not to use this dangerous ploy.

My more immediate worry was how we'd talk our way into Ben's locked room. Again, I had underestimated my younger sister. Batting her eyelashes and affecting helplessness, she was easily able to coax a maid into letting us into Room 505.

Inside the room, I pointed out the line of photos on Ben's mantle. However, their scarcity presented a problem. I feared that to snatch up these few would draw Ben's attention when he returned.

"Isn't Paul's room next to this one, adjoining it?" Lydia asked, pointing out a side door. She was right again. But inside Paul's room we found something as upsetting as anything that had happened during my time in Coney Island. There were reams of family photos. Paul wouldn't miss us taking a few from this pile. I selected one of Ben and Paul posing with their proudly smiling father, and one of Henry and Lydia, taken that first day at the hotel, Henry's driver carrying bags behind them. I hated to expose Lydia's face to brothel madams, but there were no photos of Henry alone. He was always with my sister.

What disturbed us both was a folder to the side, containing more photographs. Still looking for one of Henry without Lydia, I leafed through it, and saw three photos of an unknown woman. She wore nothing but a black corset, the kind I'd never seen before, and had her wrists tied together with rope. She held up those bound wrists toward the camera – which I must assume Paul wielded at that moment – a sneer on her young face.

My hand recoiled from the folder as if I'd touched a poisonous snake. "I have what I need – I have what I need," I said hurriedly, tucking the two of Henry and the Batternberg men into my handbag.

"How dreadful," Lydia whispered about the other photographs. As much as we adopted sophisticated airs, we were both of us virgins, sheltered from the realities of vice.

We hurried down the hall and rang the button for the elevator.

"Lydia," I said. "What do you feel for Jason Campion?"

"He's my friend, and just my friend," she said. "I'm not in love with him, if that's what you think. But it's fun and it's – comfortable. I don't think I've ever felt comfortable with Henry. Not really."

It had been in the back of my mind that Lydia would shift from Henry to Jason, that she would become engaged to him even in the face of our mother's undoubted fury over losing one of America's richest men for a doctor son-in-law. But I'd been selling Lydia short. It was hard to believe this was the tense sister who pleaded with me to come to the Oriental Hotel to help her impress Henry and his mother. What happened to that girl?

We went back to the dining room, taking our places. It was difficult to even look in Paul's direction while I forced down dessert. I most worried we'd return to an explosive Henry, but he seemed to have moved on from it. He was solely focused on insisting that after dinner we join him for the famed firework show on the lawn of the Manhattan Beach Hotel. I needed to find something to do for the next couple of hours, so I agreed.

The crowd on the darkening lawn was massive. I lost track of Henry and Lydia shortly after he recognized some friends of his from town, and they mingled with the new group while I stayed with my mother and Aunt Helen. I saw my sister just once more, and it was when a red shooting star exploded in the sky, shining light on us all for a few seconds. They were a distance away, Henry's arm lightly around her waist, Lydia pointing to the sky.

The fireworks turned out to be a consuming event for the east end of the island, ending later than I expected. I hoped the crowds milling everywhere would give me welcome cover for my own discreet departure. After saying goodnight to my family and letting Alice know I'd get ready for bed myself, I didn't have time to change my dress myself and safely make the rendezvous time for the horse and buggy and Dimitri. This dress was fashionable, if conspicuous. To conceal it, I threw a wrap around my shoulders and slid out of my room, making my way to the stairs.

If there were any hope of vindicating Stefan, I'd have to come back with something real.

CHAPTER THIRTY-THREE

My mercenary buggy driver awaited me, helping me into his buggy with a gap-toothed smile, happy to receive a second pair of expensive earrings. Part of me hoped that Dimitri wouldn't be waiting for me on that corner of Surf Avenue, although he undeniably offered some protection with his presence. I had the addresses and was capable of locating the two brothels on my own.

Sadly, the man was present and accounted for. Who could miss him? His face was scrubbed of pancake makeup; still, he was dark with olive complexion, black eyes, and blackest hair. He wore a jacket for the occasion, but under it radiated a shirt of a shade of blue I'd never seen on a man before – or a woman, either.

"Good evening, Miss Batternberg," he said with a mocking twirl of his hat, his gaze traveling from the top of my head to the tips of my shoes. "May I say you're looking fetching tonight?"

"Good evening," I said coldly. "That's quite a color you have on."

"Isn't it smart, though?" he said, missing the sarcasm. "My favorite turquoise."

As Dimitri confidently led me through the still-crowded streets of Coney Island toward the Bowery, he kept up a steady patter of conversation as if he'd found a new friend. He told me of coming to the United States as a boy, of his passion for dance that led to traveling the country with troupes, giving lessons, and, unfortunately, having to earn his bread as a "taxi dancer," paid to tango with wealthy women. It seemed his ambitions lay not on the dance floor or in theaters but in the burgeoning motion-picture industry. He was certain that his brand of handsomeness was what women longed to see rendered huge on a flickering screen, and it was only a matter of time before D.W. Griffith or some other director recognized his potential for fame.

Once we reached the Bowery itself, the noise on the streets ratcheted up to a fierce din. Warring orchestra pits mingled with the sounds of hundreds of men out for the night, most of them laughing and nearly all of them drunk.

"Hello, my beauty," slurred one man, his face shining with cheap whiskey as he stumbled across our path. I took a step closer to Dimitri, who laughingly linked his arm with mine.

"Now you're mighty glad I offered to come," he said, only too willing to rub this fact in my face. I ached to step on his foot with the heel of my shoe, but instead I nodded tightly. He was a necessary evil.

Mabel Morgan's house, unsurprisingly, was not on the main Bowery street. It stood on the next street, one which echoed with raucous noise but was not nearly as populated. I don't know what I was expecting of the brothel, but it wasn't this: a three-story wooden clapboard house with six windows fronting the street, the shades all drawn but candle-light glowing behind each. In the puddle of yellow thrown down by the streetlamp, I spotted two rows of pink and white petunias flourishing in a tiny plot of soil in front of the house. The flowers showed evidence of careful watering and pruning. Piano music tinkled within, along with the deep boom of a man laughing.

"Scared?" Dimitri asked.

"No," I lied, and he banged on the front door. A tall, hard-faced man wearing a bowtie opened the door. I extended the envelope to him, which didn't provoke a welcome. He took it as if it bore a new strain of cholera and shut the door in our faces.

The minutes crawled by. The only thing that would be worse than listening to Dimitri go on about the motion-picture industry was to have to listen to my own thoughts without the distraction of his rambling. I was plagued by doubts as I stood on this front step, staring down at the vigorous petunias. A series of assumptions led me here, beginning with Marta's assurance that Countess Isabelle held sway everywhere on the island and concluding with my own belief that what was written on the paper now in the hands of a brothel madame would make me welcome inside. How could I be so sure of this?

When the door opened the next time, we were both beckoned inside. Dimitri had said he would wait outside, but now he appeared more than willing to cross the threshold of Mabel Morgan's. We stood in a tiny foyer, a large empty umbrella stand at our feet and a chandelier glittering above our heads. The bow-tied man indicated we should wait here a while longer. He slipped through a door to the right, closing it quickly behind him. On the left an archway opened to a larger room where the hum of male and female conversation filled the air, but all I could see was the back of a man sitting at a piano bench. A few bars of music began to sound pretty familiar.

With a horrified jolt, I recognized it as the Scott Joplin song "Wall Street Rag," Ben's favorite tune. Was my cousin sitting just inside this room, making requests of the piano player?

The door to the right opened, and the bow-tied man beckoned for me alone. Trying my best to look unafraid, I walked toward him, preparing for the umpteenth time the words I would use with Mabel Morgan. Glancing behind me the second before I stepped inside, I noted Dimitri edging toward the sound of the piano.

The woman who awaited me within this comfortably furnished parlor was not the burlesque creature of any schoolgirl's imaginings but a respectable-looking woman well into her forties. She might have sprung from the same mold as one of my mother's most relied-upon dressmakers: smartly dressed herself and exuding the calm, shrewd air of someone accustomed to dealing with difficult requests and unreasonable demands. Fair-haired, she had large hazel eyes and thin lips, her throat softening with age under her chin.

"Please sit down, Miss Batternberg," she said, her voice flatter and rougher than her appearance. "I can give you five minutes. Countess Isabelle said it would 'behoove me' to answer your questions about the deaths of the women in Coney Island, though I'm not sure why I should, since they have the murderer in custody."

"Stefan Chalakoski is an innocent man," I said, sitting in the upholstered chair facing hers.

"Well, I know he's innocent of meeting either Beatrice or Katherine under my roof, but whether he came across them elsewhere is anyone's guess," she said sharply. "The police have been here four times – it's a miracle I could stay open. I had to grease a lot of palms! There is no possibility of a Serbian artist being welcome at Mabel Morgan's. I admit no immigrants, no Russians or Italians, and I definitely wouldn't want a dirty bomb-throwing Serb in the same room as one of my girls."

I froze in angry dislike.

"If you think I'm going to give you the names of any of my customers, you're mistaken," she continued with a toss of her head. "I'm simply not sure what the point of this is."

"I have some photographs to show you of men who may have been here," I said. "One of these men may be the real murderer. You don't have to say his name. You can nod or point."

She pursed her lips, skeptically.

"You knew those two girls," I pressed her. "Don't you want to make sure the real killer is brought to justice?"

"Not if it's going to shut me down," she said. My face must have shown how appalled I was, for she thrust out a hand and said, impatiently, "Show me the photographs."

My fingers trembled slightly as I took out the photograph of Uncle David with Ben and Paul. I was putting before her images of a wealthy womanizer of many years' standing, with an older son who enjoyed prostitutes and a younger son given to perversion. Would one of this trio set off a start of recognition? I studied Mabel Morgan's face as she looked at the photograph and saw… no reaction at all. Either she was a superb actress, or she genuinely had never seen any of them at her establishment. I felt both disappointed and relieved.

"Next," she said.

I handed her the second photograph.

"What a pretty girl," said Mabel Morgan. Then her eyes shifted to the other side of the photograph, and I detected the slightest of movements, a tensing of her shoulders and a flicker in her hazel eyes.

"You know him," I said, surging forward in my chair. "You know Henry Taul."

"That is Henry Taul? Ah, of course."

I knew my mistake at once. Henry was a famous name on the Eastern seaboard. She could say that she was merely reacting to a face familiar from newspapers and magazines. Which is what she proceeded to do.

"Mr. Henry Taul has never been here," she said in conclusion. "I wish he had. I'm certain he'd leave a satisfied client." She allowed herself the sort of laugh that no seamstress would ever utter, before saying, "And now I'd like to ask *you* some questions, such as why this is your business and what you have against these men, but out of respect to Countess Isabelle, I will refrain. Good evening."

She rang a bell on her side table, and the bow-tied man appeared to steer me out of the room. Dimitri awaited me by the front door; he hadn't found his way into the piano parlor after all.

"No luck?" he asked after we'd been more or less pushed out the front door.

Revolted by Mabel Morgan, I shook my head without speaking. She definitely didn't know the members of my family as seen in those photographs. If she knew who they were – Batternbergs – then she wouldn't have been so puzzled as to why I was involved. As for Henry Taul, I sensed something there. But I couldn't force her to tell me the truth – if that were the truth. It was possible she honestly recognized him only because he was a well-known playboy.

I'd learned nothing in this brothel that would help Stefan. I said, "Now take me to Kschessinska."

Dimitri winced. "I thought you'd given up on that," he said.

"Louise never worked a day in this place." I jerked a thumb at the clapboard house behind us. "If you really want me to find the man who killed her, then I have to get inside Kschessinska."

The formerly garrulous Dimitri walked me four blocks deeper into Coney Island's west side in brooding silence.

Once he stopped, the building I found myself staring up at was a three-story brownstone, austere and unwelcoming. No geraniums stirred in any plot out front; no ragtime tune wafted from an open window.

Dimitri accompanied me up the five steps leading to the front door.

I was the one to reach out and tap the large brass knocker. No one answered. I began to wonder if the woman I sought had moved on, as Countess Isabelle said she might after the state's religious leaders successfully shut down the racetracks.

After a full minute, the door eased open. A tall, thin man wearing the coat and tails of a butler stared at Dimitri and me with brown eyes set deep in his skull.

"I'd very much like to speak to Madame Kschessinska," I said. "I don't have an appointment, but I do have a letter of introduction." I handed him the Countess's envelope.

The butler did not make us wait on the street but opened the door wide. "If you please," he said. Dimitri followed me in this time, looking as if he were arriving at a place to have his teeth pulled. Once we were both over the threshold, the butler extended a gloved hand, and I handed him the envelope. We stood in a high-ceilinged foyer, dominated by a wide staircase, the bannister polished to a chestnut sheen.

"A moment," said the butler, walking up the staircase.

"This is not good – not good," muttered Dimitri, shifting from one foot to the other, his insolent grace gone.

This fearfulness was the last thing I needed. "Hush up," I hissed. "Can't you pretend this is a D.W. Griffith movie and you're the star?"

He shook his head as if this were the most idiotic thing he'd heard. But at least he didn't say another word – not until we heard a creak at the top of the stairs. A man stood looking down at us, but it wasn't the butler this time. This man was young, with a beard and mustache, wearing a tall, round fur hat and an army uniform, belted, his trousers tucked into high leather boots.

"Mary, Mother of Jesus," said Dimitri, making the sign of the cross as the man – who I concluded was dressed like a Russian Cossack – strode down the stairs. Once he was a few feet away, I realized he had a long pistol shoved in his belt, inches away from a long sword.

"Peggy Batternberg?" the Russian asked at the bottom of the stairs, and when I nodded, he said, "Madame says come now." He was well over six feet tall.

Dimitri babbled, "Let's go, forget it, we can't stay here."

But the way this man said my name – "Peggy" – reminded me of Stefan's pronunciation, and although Dimitri obviously thought I was putting myself in harm's way, I disagreed. This Cossack uniform was meant to intimidate, but my instinct told me it was more costume than soldier's kit.

"Go if you wish," I told Dimitri. "I'm staying."

"You fool—" he began, but the Cossack roared, "You want to go, go, little man! Leave her with Madame."

Dimitri did exactly that. He turned and bolted out the front door. It hung open behind him, as the sound of his frantic footsteps echoed inside the house.

CHAPTER THIRTY-FOUR

I straightened my shoulders, turned and started up the stairs, ready for what awaited me at the top. The house was completely silent – I found it hard to believe there was illicit activity of any sort being transacted here.

The room the Cossack led me to was of startling opulence: gilded mirrors, tapestries on the wall, and plush furniture. Medieval-era Russian icons covered the walls. There were only two images of more modern human beings. One was a portrait of the Russian czar, Nicholas II, a mildly handsome man who wore centuries of Romanov autocracy on his slight shoulders. The other was a full-length photograph of a woman in a ballerina costume, her arms lifted gracefully above her head. Her figure was exquisite and her face attractive, though she was not a classic beauty: dark hair, a heart-shaped face, large eyes, a long nose, and full lips.

"Hello, Miss Batternberg," said the woman sitting in the middle of the room, in accented English. She did bear something of a resemblance to the prima ballerina in the photograph, though she was at least ten years older. She too had a heart-shaped face and full lips. Her black dress, with a low square neckline, revealed her beautiful shoulders and bust.

Countess Isabelle had made no bones about it – this woman was not the ballerina who lived with Nicholas when he was Tsarevitch of

All Russia. This room's décor, her presenting herself in the shadow of the photograph on the wall, the Cossack, it all added up to a determination to present herself as Mathilde Kschessinska. What did Dimitri say? "In Coney Island everything is real and nothing is real." I must try my best not to offend her, while believing this charade strange and rather pathetic.

Madame Kschessinska rose to shake my hand and then offered to take my wrap. Uncertainly, I handed it to her, but instead of finding a place for it, she stood a few inches away, the wrap flung over her arm, her gaze traveling up and down my face and dress. This was more than just an interest in fashion. She studied my face as if she were searching for something lost.

"I don't believe I've ever met Countess Isabelle in person, but I'm sure she's a commendable person," said Madame Kschessinska. "Please tell me why you are here, and I'll do everything in my power to help you."

I took a chair and then gave my hostess an explanation for my presence similar to what I'd offered up at Mabel Morgan: The man arrested for a series of murders, most recently Louise Turner's, was innocent. I believed the real killer might have met Louise here, under this roof – I dared not use the word brothel – and I wanted to show her photographs.

"You know this man, this Stefan Chalakoski?" she asked. "You champion him?"

How swiftly she came to the correct conclusion. I nodded.

She took out a long brown cigarette, put it in a handler, and struck a match with a ferocious blue puff. After lighting it and inhaling deeply, she said, "Why?"

Although she was a madame in a brothel, someone who profited from crime, Madame Kschessinska had shown me nothing but hospitality and courtesy. I decided to tell her the truth.

"I'm in love with Stefan," I said. "My family is staying at the Oriental Hotel this summer and I met him in Coney Island. Stefan would never hurt anyone – this arrest is a mistake. I don't know who the actual murderer is, but I have some suspicions. I have no intention of sitting back and letting them put him on trial, throw him in prison, or ... worse. My family doesn't want me to do anything to help Stefan. Obviously, if they knew I was here, it would go very badly for me."

Her reaction was completely unexpected. She broke into a delighted smile. "Ah, you are like him," she said softly.

"Like who?" I said, confused.

Madame Kschessinska took another puff of her cigarette. "I appreciate frankness, and while I wish to repay you the favor, there are considerations. I've enjoyed your company so far, and I would like to think you have enjoyed mine. This may change after you hear what I have to tell you."

"I assure you, I am ready for anything," I insisted.

She tilted her head, a gesture faintly reminiscent of Stefan, and said, "When I first opened this house, it was at considerable risk, financially and in other ways too. I was a woman attempting something alone – I'd never permit a man to control my business. There were certain people in the first year whose support and affection meant a great deal to me and helped me make this a success. There was one man in particular, who died too young but whose memory I cherish to this day." She met my gaze directly. "I'm speaking of your father."

For a few seconds it seemed as if time had stopped, as if I were no longer in this room but elsewhere – on the sand, under the waves, in the stars, anywhere. This was such a shock, coming years after the last time I thought my father could shock me.

Finding my voice, I said, "Now I understand why you were willing to see me. You recognized my name."

She said, "I knew the names of Jonathan's children."

With that sentence, I was plunged unwillingly into the truth of their intimacy. She was not just a plaything, intriguing him with her theatrical idea for a brothel. He talked to her, confided in her. She was important to him. For all I knew, when I shattered our father-daughter relationship, asking him if he was going to see his mistress, he might have been coming here.

I said, "My father was in this house? In this room?"

"That's correct."

I felt the old jealousy for the rivals for my father's attention, the surge of confused loyalty for my mother. But the brunt of the shock passed. I gathered myself and said, "You will help me?"

"Yes, I will help you and this man you love. Though I would do anything, within reason, to see justice done to the murderer of Louise Turner as well. She was not an easy woman to employ, but I liked her. I'm sorry she came to a terrible end."

The sound of a woman laughing penetrated the wall of the parlor. So there was business being done elsewhere in the house. It made me feel uneasy, but not so much that I'd decline to continue. I handed her the photograph of Uncle David, Ben, and Paul. She looked the men over carefully and said, "None of these gentlemen have ever been my guests."

I was not as crushed as I'd been at Mabel Morgan's, for I was certain that it was the next photograph that would yield answers if any were to be found. My throat dry, I presented the former mistress of my father with the second purloined photograph.

She didn't comment on Lydia, and I wanted to, if at all possible, avoid telling her that the beautiful young woman was my sister. She pointed at Henry's smiling face and said, "He has never been to this house."

I felt my body sag in the embroidered chair.

"However," she said, moving her finger a couple of inches to the face of Henry's flat-nosed young driver, "this man has come three times in the last month."

"You mean Jim?" I asked, stunned.

"Jim? He told me his name was Andrew O'Connell, and he worked at a bank, although from your face, I assume this is not true."

"His name is Jim and he works for this other person . He is his driver," I said.

"I see," she said. "How odd." She thought for a moment. "I do think that he spent time with Louise when he was here."

Did this mean Jim was the murderer of women? I knew little of the man except that he was Henry's devoted employee, at his beck and call. He was a uniformed driver and he was a spy but yes, he was even more than that. Lydia had said, "Where would Henry be without his procurers?"

At that moment, sitting in the upstairs parlor of a brothel, my mind curled around a possibility, a dark and terrifying possibility. Henry Taul, with his face in the newspapers and his actions the subject of gossip columns, did not dare set foot in brothels with his fiancée close by. But with the money he gave Jim, his trusted servant, *that* man could cross such thresholds, and, after sampling the charms of the women, doubtless make arrangements that brought them to Henry, wherever he awaited them. With the huge sums offered, the women might be willing to go anywhere.

If Henry Taul was the murderer, he must be brought to justice, I felt no hesitation. But before I summoned the police, I had to prepare Lydia, and soon. Tonight. I'd need to wake her and start this terrible conversation.

Seeing me in a sea of distress, Madame Kschessinska said, "I must ask you how you are planning to return to the Oriental Hotel and rejoin your family party at past two in the morning, unless your plan is to stay out another four hours or so and return discreetly after dawn."

I explained to her how I'd managed it last night. She shook her head. "You are lucky that such a foolhardy tactic worked last night, but it's unlikely to again. And after two, I have reason to believe the Pinkertons are in full control of the hotel lobbies on the east end, and no doubt they've locked that staircase. I think it best you stay here until six in the morning, and then I'll have you taken to the hotel. I believe some people are up quite early there, to see the gardens and observe the birds. You could mingle among them before going upstairs."

I had to admit that her plan was superior to mine. I told her about the buggy driver who awaited me – and my earring – on Surf Avenue, and after thinking it over, Madame Kschessinska said she would send an emissary to the driver with my payment and direction to cease waiting. At the sight of the earring, her eyes widened. "But this is valuable," she said and then smiled, shaking her head, allowing herself some private comparison.

She offered me a room with a bed to sleep in, but I recoiled at that; I couldn't help it, though such a gesture was rude payment for her thoughtfulness. She did not seem offended. Ever the solver of problems, she offered me the couch in this room, her parlor, while she saw to business elsewhere. That offer I did accept, and shortly after I was provided with a tall glass of water, a blanket, and a couch to lie down on. She then tactfully withdrew.

I threw the blanket across my lap but did not lie down. As my mind raced to explain various possibilities now presented by this evening's discovery, I kept coming back to Lydia. I was poised to ruin her life with this revelation. She'd taken up this challenge like one of her sporting games, with courage and determination, seemingly on the point of breaking the engagement. But when Henry was arrested and his name no longer shielded in blind items but trumpeted, how could she cope?

There was a deeper torment. Of the first woman killed, I knew nothing. But the second, Katherine O'Malley, to murder her in the spot where I sat with Stefan? And the third, Louise Turner, to leave her body in Hell Gate – and to select Stefan's former lover – it must mean that Henry in some bizarre fashion sought to punish *me*. How would Lydia react to all of this?

Dawn finally arrived, and with it Madame Kschessinska, bearing a long white dress and a straw hat in her arms. "You can't show up at the hotel in an evening dress," she pointed out, quite correctly. "I think I have your size right."

As I changed from my kimono-style dress to the surprisingly maidenish white dress, I thought about how this revelation would not only embarrass and pain the Batternberg family but also cause upheaval to Madame Kschessinska. I'd not be able to take these findings to Lieutenant Pellegrino without telling him that Louise entertained Jim, Henry's driver, under this roof.

My hostess had already reached similar conclusions. As she walked me down the staircase she said, "Do not worry about these revelations' effect on my business. We Russians believe in omens, signs, and portents. Your coming here confirms what I've known for several months. It's time for me to move on."

Although her speech was flavored with an accent hinting of Russia, her sentences were constructed perfectly. A teacher of English composition would labor in her shadow. I wondered anew what her true origins were, while knowing there was no chance whatsoever of learning them.

The butler, now wearing a summer suit and hat, stood ready to drive me back. I turned to shake her hand and caught a wistfulness in Madame's eyes before she resumed her sophisticated stance. "I hope we shall meet again," she said, but guardedly, as if prepared for a rebuff.

"I hope so too," I said, and meant it. I had the fleeting thought that in her intelligence, her sophistication, and her sexual rebelliousness, she was a more fit companion for my father than my mother ever could be. What would have happened if he hadn't died in Long Island Sound?

The butler helped me into the large motor car that would convey me back to the Oriental, my evening dress in a light borrowed satchel. After a sleepless night I felt faintly ill, and the belching fumes of the automobile quickly soured my stomach. At this early hour, workers shuffled about with brooms and buckets and carts to clean the Coney Island streets of the litter, their faces grim. What a Herculean task – empty liquor bottles and food wrappers and plenty of other trash formed mountains on the borders of the amusement park.

It couldn't have been more different at the Oriental Hotel. As I walked up the path, morning dew glistened on the manicured lawn. Smiling people ventured out on the veranda, and impatient children raced for the beach and boardwalk. With a smile pasted on my face, I made my way into the parlor lobby, feeling safe to use the elevator. No one stirred on our hallway – none of us woke before eight in the morning – and I let myself in my room. Before I faced Lydia, I needed to bathe. This would be a long, difficult day. I must gird myself.

I ran my own bath and slipped into the warm water. Although I could not condemn Madame Kschessinska, I had spent the night in a brothel, and was now consumed with desire to clean myself. Afterward, I rested my head on the back of the tub. *Just a few minutes of rest, and then I'll prepare to talk to Lydia,* I thought as I slipped into a doze.

A loud banging on the door made my eyes fly open. I didn't know how long I'd slept. In thick-headed confusion, I staggered out of the soapy bath and flung on my robe. It must be Lydia, impatient to hear what I'd learned. But the banging grew ever more fierce, louder than I thought her capable of.

It was not my younger sister at the door but David Batternberg, and in a rare state.

"Something terrible has happened, Peggy," my uncle said. "Lydia is missing, and there's a note in her room. A ransom note. We fear she was kidnapped."

CHAPTER THIRTY-FIVE

Within the hour, there were so many people in my mother's room that I found it difficult to count them. Mother herself was not present. She was under sedation in the hotel's medical suite, Aunt Helen and Lawrence by her side. It had been suggested, more than once, that I join them. But I needed to be here, listening and watching. The more officious the men who crowded the room and the wilder their theories, the more determined I was to figure out what really happened to my sister.

Lydia was gone – how could I not accept this fact? However, I didn't believe she'd been kidnapped. I was not positive about what happened to my sister, but my eyes rarely left Henry Taul, pacing the room, ranting to all who came near him, berating the police for not doing more.

Mother's room was chosen for all to convene in because the note Alice found on Lydia's bureau said a phone call listing the kidnapper's demands would be put through to "Mrs. Jonathan Batternberg." Hearing Father's name hours after it was spoken at Madame Kschessinska's was disconcerting, but far from the strangest thing I faced right now.

The phone to Mother's room never rang that long day, nor did any other notes materialize.

It seemed the last person to see Lydia from our party was Alice, in

353

the hallway at just after eleven o'clock. Henry kept saying he brought Lydia back to the hotel following the fireworks. They said goodnight in the lobby. She took the elevator up to the Batternberg corridor, stopping Alice outside her room to say she didn't need any help in getting ready for bed.

By my calculations, Lydia had walked out of the elevator and toward her room a few moments after I had made it to the door to the stairs on that same floor and disappeared down it, on my way out of the Oriental Hotel. Of course, I couldn't tell the police that. I said the same as Mother and Lawrence had, as well as Uncle David and Aunt Helen: No unusual sights or sounds last night.

Most of the police officers and other city officials crowded in Mother's room talked about which criminal gang had abducted my sister. I heard the phrase "Black Hand" dozens of times. It seemed to be an Italian crime group with a presence in New York. How they managed to break into Lydia's room and whisk her out of the hotel was attributed to their nefarious boldness.

"If one of them touches Lydia, I swear to God…" Henry Taul's voice was hoarse.

Mr. Lancet assured him no one would dare. He looked as terrible as my uncle, and with good reason. A guest being abducted from his hotel could deal his business a fatal blow.

Henry shook off the hotel owner and announced, "My mother has need of me, she is quite upset," before stomping out of the room. Mr. Lancet watched him leave, his eyes brimming with terror.

It was Lieutenant Pellegrino, up to now one of the room's quieter presences, who said, "I'm wondering why she didn't ask for her maid's help, why she made a point of saying she didn't need it."

Uncle David, who overheard him, said, "They don't need a maid for everything, the girls are not completely helpless."

"But our inventory of the things in her room showed she didn't change out of her dress and into her nightclothes," said the Lieutenant. "So either she was kidnapped as soon as she stepped in her room or she sat up for a period of time, fully dressed, or she may have decided to go out again."

"Go out? Alone and after midnight? A Batternberg girl?" With each question, Mr. Lancet's voice turned shriller, attracting the attention of everyone on this side of the room. "Keep your tawdry opinion to yourself – and concentrate on finding out which of your Italian countrymen are holding Lydia Batternberg hostage."

Lieutenant Pellegrino did not flare in anger, merely turned away from the hotel owner, but not before I felt his speculative glance rest on me. He knew well that a Batternberg girl was capable of a great deal of independent movement.

Ben returned to the room and made his way to my side. "I saw Henry down the hallway, I thought he was going to throttle me or anyone else in his path." He lowered his voice. "If I were him, I would not use narcotics in front of half of New York City's police brass."

"Narcotics?" I whispered. "What do you mean?"

Ben said, "I've thought for a while now that Henry's moods, his periods of strangeness, might have to do with illicit drugs. I can't be positive, but in the last few days I've felt sure he is taking cocaine, either inhaling it or injecting it."

I knew nothing of illicit drugs. But it was another piece to the puzzle. And with that, I decided to speak up. Henry had something to do with Lydia's absence. Their relationship had been under increasing strain over the last few days, and last night he either lured her out of her room or she decided to talk to him again after returning to her room. Perhaps she tried to break off the engagement last night.

I warned Lydia to be careful of Henry, but I hadn't told her how he once locked me in a room and scared the hell out of me. *Why* didn't I tell her that?

"Ben, there are things I have to tell you about Henry," I said.

"About him and Lydia and all not being well?" he asked, quickly taking my point. His mind could be running on the same track.

"Yes – and other things about Henry," I said, thinking of the two brothels and his servant Jim. "I've learned something very disturbing."

I forgot, however, that Ben wasn't the only Batternberg in the room. A hand closed around my upper arm. Uncle David said, "Peggy, no one wants to hear your wild thoughts at this particular juncture. Do you realize you are the only woman in this room? Your place is with your mother." He turned to Ben. "Bernard and the others will be here any minute."

The entire Batternberg clan was descending on the Oriental Hotel, but if I knew one thing for certain, it was that not one of them would listen to me – and I was the only person possessing the truth: this wasn't the work of a criminal gang but could only be Lydia's fiancé.

I turned and left, but not to report to the medical suite. No one would listen to me without some sort of proof; I knew I was too discredited to expect otherwise. I'd obtain evidence of Henry's involvement, one way or another. I would start with confronting Henry himself. What could he do to me with his mother present, and servants besides?

I made my way to the Taul rooms on the other side of the Oriental. I knocked on the door for a long time before an older maid, one I didn't recognize, opened the door.

"I need to speak to Mr. Taul. My name is Peggy Batternberg."

"Mr. Taul is not here," she said.

"When did he leave?"

The maid hesitated, and at that instant I knew. He'd lied about intending to see his mother, and it was a lie he'd used many times before. I pushed open the heavy door. "I must speak to Mrs. Taul immediately."

In the darkened bedroom, Henry's mother sat, propped up in her bed, in the same spot I'd last seen her. But she didn't exude arrogance today. Her eyes tracked me, behind those spectacles, her lips working as if she were preparing words. Why was she afraid? There could only be one reason.

"You know about Henry, don't you?" I said. "You've always known everything about him."

She said in a rush, "Your sister is fine, I know she is fine. It's all a mistake. There's a doctor coming from Connecticut, we've used him before in times of crisis, he's very discreet. He'll take the situation in hand with Henry and reason with him, help him get rest. His name is Dr. Schepard. It will all be made right."

"This is past time for doctors!" I shouted. "The hotel is crawling with police. Where is my sister? Where's he hiding her?"

"It will all be made right," she babbled. "The doctor is very discreet. He will know how to handle Henry and the police too."

"Where is Henry right now?" I demanded, gripping her bedpost. She shook her head.

"Do you have any idea where Lydia could be?" I repeated.

She clamped her mouth shut, sticking out her lower lip like a child in defiance. It could be she was as mad as her son.

I heard a rustling of skirts in the doorway. It was the other maid, Victoria, the one who'd passed out bon-bons with a badly bruised wrist. I looked at her, my face a plea.

"He's at the stables," the maid told me.

"Shut your mouth!" screamed Mrs. Taul. "Disloyal bitch. I dismiss you. I'll have you whipped for this!"

I turned and picked up my skirts to run out of this room. I had to make it to Ben. If I told him what I'd just learned, on top of everything else, I knew he'd believe me. He was forming his suspicions already; he was no idiot. But I couldn't see Ben or Uncle David in Mother's suite. As I stood in the doorway, searching frantically, it was Lieutenant Pellegrino who walked over to me. "They went to be with other members of your family. Your uncles, some lawyers and some bankers too, to discuss the expected ransom."

"There isn't going to be a ransom," I said flatly.

Something flickered in Lieutenant Pellegrino's eyes. But he didn't say anything. The police officer who always had a quick retort, a plan of action, waited.

"I have to talk to someone, and it seems that person is you," I said. "Please come to my room at the end of the hall in five minutes."

I told Lieutenant Pellegrino the entire story, beginning with meeting Countess Isabelle and the others in Lilliput, continuing to Mabel Morgan's and Madame Kschessinska's, and her identifying Henry's driver, Jim, as a client. I finished with my forcing my way into Mrs. Taul's suite and her insisting that this doctor from Connecticut could fix the disaster, as, it was implied, he had others before. The lieutenant no longer scoffed about my being a deluded victim of a murderous anarchist. His expression turned grimmer. Suspicions had apparently grown within him while he heard the speculations in the hotel suite. Now he knew that Henry might have not only abducted my sister and staged the scene as a kidnapping, but he could be involved in the murders of three women.

"Taul's at the stable now, the one where he keeps his horses?" asked Lieutenant Pellegrino.

"Yes, though I've never been there," I said.

"I don't need you to take me there," he said. "I just need to know which racetrack. There are three of them."

"It's Sheepshead Bay Race Track, but I am going with you," I said. "I'm ready to leave now. No one will miss me. I'm just an annoyance to everyone here."

"I'm not worried about being annoyed," he said, in a tone of voice that sounded extremely annoyed. "I'm worried about your safety, if this man is all worked up and crazy. It's best that I go in alone, tell him there's a development and he needs to be briefed. Once I have him in a room, I should be able to crack him if his brain is scrambled with narcotics."

He turned to leave, but I jumped in his path. "I know who the servants are by sight: Jim and Francois. You don't. I can point them out to you."

He gave a heavy sigh. "And you'll remain in the motor car at all times?"

I promised I would, and minutes later, Lieutenant Pellegrino and I had left the Oriental Hotel in search of Henry Taul.

CHAPTER THIRTY-SIX

Lieutenant Pellegrino had a look on his face I'd not seen before: deep worry. I was certain that he alone had disbelieved the note, the story of a kidnapping, from the beginning. "People up in that room should be listening to you," I said. "Doesn't their bigotry concern you?"

He shot me a sideways glance. "Doesn't the bigotry at the Oriental Hotel concern *you?* The first owner, Austin Corbin, used to have a rule, and he advertised it: no Jewish guests allowed. Corbin died fifteen years ago, and Lancet changed the rule, but still, this was a well-known anti-Semitic hotel for years."

What an ugly, ugly revelation. So this is why we heard odd comments about staying there at the beginning: "It's so big of you to stay here." Just another awful thing my family was subjected to, at the instigation of Henry and his mother. But it wouldn't have happened if the Batternbergs weren't so eager for the marriage to Lydia.

Lieutenant Pellegrino drove his motor car with more speed than I was used to. I had to grip the door handle tightly to avoid being flung up and down on the upholstered seat. He gunned the engine as he headed off the island, taking a bridge over the creek. He banged on his horn impatiently when a small car puttered in front of us.

Within minutes, I spotted the weathered sign "Sheepshead Bay Race Track." Closest to us was the clubhouse, beyond it the huge grandstand overlooking the long oval track, with the stables on the far side of the track.

The afternoon had shifted to evening as Lieutenant Pellegrino downshifted the gears of the motor car. A grove of thick-branched trees as well as the clubhouse itself cast long shadows across the patchy grass and drive. The lieutenant gripped the steering wheel as he drove past the clubhouse, looking this way and that. The sound of the gravel under the slow-moving wheels was like the rat-a-tat of a gun.

There was no sign of life in the clubhouse. The doors were shut and padlocked; windows were not boarded up but streaked with dirt and grime. Frayed beige shades were drawn to the bottom of each window from within. I couldn't believe this was the club for the praised racetrack that not only Henry but others at the hotel talked about. The place exuded a sad defeat, a shame that was perhaps inevitable when a closing was pushed through as a supposed vortex of vice.

Lieutenant Pellegrino turned the motor car around to get a closer look at the track. Here, too, I saw signs of desertion: crabgrass everywhere, and broken wooden rails. The grandstand was absolutely enormous, like everything in Coney Island. It had been constructed for thousands. Now it was as empty as the Colosseum of Rome.

The police lieutenant stopped the car, peering across the track and toward the stables. The wheels still, I could hear the hum of the amusement park a few miles away: band music and the screams of those on the rides. A snatch of piano even drifted on the evening breeze from the ocean, and I remembered the jaunty ragtime tune in Mabel Morgan's parlor.

"What's that?" said Lieutenant Pellegrino, scowling at the stables. "Something moved in a second-floor window." My pulse racing, I studied each of the five windows, but saw nothing.

He drove carefully on the narrow dirt road that connected the front of the track to the stables. I spotted something red gleam on the other side of a row of bushes and trees. "That's Henry's motor car," I said. "Why park it there?"

Lieutenant Pellegrino drove to a spot near the bushes and turned off the motor car engine. He patted the pocket of his police uniform coat. I realized with a start that he was checking for his pistol.

About twenty feet from Henry's car yawned the mouth of the stables, straw on the floor. As we sat there, Lieutenant Pellegrino preparing to get out, a man appeared, walking toward Henry's motor car. He didn't see us, but I recognized his weasel face.

"That's the other servant of Henry's," I whispered. "Not Jim. Francois. He lived in France."

Lieutenant Pellegrino pushed open his car door and got out. "Hello, Sir," he boomed. "I'm Lieutenant Pellegrino with the Brooklyn police. Can you take me to Henry Taul?"

Francois stood stock still, his mouth falling open. He took one step toward us, and then whipped around and ran, not back into the stable but streaking to the side of it, a path plunging deeper into Brooklyn.

"Stay in the motor car," Lieutenant Pellegrino shouted, and then took off after Francois. Within seconds, they'd both darted beyond a building and disappeared. The entire area returned to silence, except for the faraway fluctuating roar of the park, of Dreamland and Luna Park and Steeplechase.

I pushed down on the handle and stepped out of the police motor car. I couldn't sit here while the possibility existed of Lydia being kept inside. Time could be running out. Henry's mother said that this Doctor Schepard would "fix" everything. But how could her faked kidnapping be explained away by any doctor? I feared that in a panic, Henry would hurt my sister more than he already had. Lieutenant Pellegrino had seen movement in an upstairs window. I had to search for her.

I stepped into the stable, my heart beating so fast it sang in my ears. "Lydia?" I called out.

There was no answer.

Halfway down the length of the stable, I was at first comforted by the sight, smells, and sounds of thoroughbred horses in their stalls, three of them. These must be Henry's. At least that part was real. But where were the trainers, the jockey, the help I knew he brought with him? They had apparently all left. I found that as ominous as anything.

I spotted stairs at the end of the row of stalls and toward the left, leading to those upstairs rooms. It wasn't dark, thanks to the widows in the main part of the stable down here – I could see everything in every stall so far. I made it to the last one: flattened straw was all that remained of some long-ago equine champion.

The stairs frightened me. I stood at the bottom, working up my courage. Was Henry up there with Lydia, preventing her from answering me? A long stick lay in the straw; picking it up, I spotted rusty nails sticking out. This would have to serve as my weapon.

I put one foot on the stairs, then another.

Lydia needs me. Another step.

I should have warned her, better protected her. Another step.

If you've hurt her, Henry... I tightened the grip on my stick.

At the top of the stairs an open doorway yawned, darkness beyond it. Not as many windows up there affording light. But the lieutenant said he saw movement. I had to keep going. I pushed myself to the second-to-top step – and a hand grabbed me by the arm and dragged me to the top, slamming me onto the floor, flat on my back.

I lashed out with my stick, but it was knocked out of my hand, and a shoe pressed onto my right wrist. It hurt, badly.

I stared up at the face of Jim, Henry's other servant.

"Hello, Peggy," he said, pointing a pistol at me head. "I don't want to hear a single scream."

"Miss Batternberg to you," I hissed.

"Ah, no, I don't think so. I'm the one who's been watching you whore yourself all over Coney Island."

He was the spy not just of Lydia but of me too. Jim must have been the one who followed me and Stefan that first night.

"You're a sneaky slut too," he said. "You gave us the slip and made it to Manhattan."

"Where's my sister?"

"My question first. I thought I heard a car. Who drove you?"

"Lieutenant Pellegrino of the Brooklyn police."

He made a face and swore. "Where the hell is he? Why would he send you up here alone?"

"He's chasing Francois. But he'll be back any minute. Where is my sister? If you've hurt her…"

I heard something move behind Jim, far behind him. I peered in that direction, but it was dim, and from a position flat on my back, I couldn't see.

"You're the one who's hurt Lydia," said the voice of Henry Taul. "It's your fault."

"Henry, what have you done?" I shouted.

Jim pressed harder on my wrist; the pain was terrible. "I said no screaming," he said, and smiled. His eyes shone. Hurting me was pleasurable.

"Henry, you're… a coward," I managed to force out through waves of pain. "You don't have… the…. guts to face me?"

Jim said to Henry, "We have to get out of here before that cop comes back. We'll take both the girls." The way he spoke to him; they were more like partners than employer and servant.

"Let her up," Henry said.

"Henry, we don't have time."

"Is he the boss, Henry?" I shouted. "Does he tell you what to do?"

Through my back, I could feel the wooden planks bend on the floor as Henry walked toward me. I tried to fight down my terror over the coming confrontation with a tall, muscular athlete who had lost his mind, almost certainly killed more than one woman – and who hated me. Jim finally took his foot off my wrist and backed away. Using my other hand, I pushed myself up, so I was at least sitting up.

Henry did not look good. His round face was wet with perspiration, dampness circled his armpits. His mouth twitched in both corners. He had crossed some sort of line while here, and it left wreckage where there had once been the confident Henry Taul. He was a confused, sick boy, not a man.

"Oh, God, what have you done, Henry?" My voice broke, and in response his eyes glittered.

"*You* did it," he said. "You turned her against me."

"Take me to Lydia, please," I begged. He reached down and took me by the left hand, pulled me to my feet as easily as he did when I'd fallen on the beach. And then he led me down the hall. I was so filled with dread – and the pain from my wrist – that I began to weep.

Lydia lay on a cot in a small room, lit by a single white candle on the floor. She wore the dress I last saw her in, with her blonde hair spread over her shoulders, so long it had pooled on the dirty floor. Her eyes were closed, her lips parted. It was horrible, like she'd been laid out for her coffin.

"No, no, no," I sobbed.

"She's alive," Henry said behind me. "We just gave her a shot."

"Why did you do this? Is it because she broke off the engagement?"

Henry came around to my side, staring at me. His confusion and weakness were not as apparent now. "She loved me before – she did. She worshipped me. You told her bad things."

"I never told her about Saratoga."

"I don't believe you," he said, his voice growing stronger.

"She read that blind item in the magazine all by herself, and she knew it was you in Paris, Henry. Don't blame me."

He began to tremble, and I wondered if Henry would disintegrate completely before me. Then I'd only have Jim to worry about.

"I figured it out," he said, rallying again. His moods fluctuated minute by minute. He pointed at me accusingly. "It was your cousin Ben who spoiled you. You're degenerates, your family. Only Lydia was pure."

"I am a degenerate? How many people have *you* killed?"

"But that's your fault, Peggy. All yours! When Francois listened outside the door of that medical room, he heard you talking to the cop who was investigating the murder on the beach, looking into things. We had to steer him toward the man he conveniently already suspected: your lover, that Serb. We had to set him up for the crimes."

I was so horrified I found it hard to speak. "Henry, why?" I forced out. "My God, why did you even want me here this summer? You were the one who insisted on it, not your mother, right? She barely knew who I was."

"I wanted to correct you. No one else has. No one else could."

I covered my face with my hands. "Were your men following me all the time?" I whispered.

"Of course. Jim saw you have dinner and dance with the Serb, and then, on the beach, you were disgusting, *disgusting*, just like you were with me once. I had to scare you, punish you, try to correct you, but you wouldn't learn, ever. You kept seeing him, letting him touch you, walking around half naked in front of every man… I had to make you stop."

Henry stepped closer to me, his hands clenching and unclenching. He didn't look weak now. The women had been strangled. Was I moments away from being strangled by Henry Taul? I should have tried to calm him, but instead I asked, for I had to know, "Did you have chloral hydrate put in my drink that day?"

He nodded and took a step even closer. I saw his hands rise.

Jim said from the doorway, "Henry, I'm telling you, we have to get out of here. I'll take this one down to the motor car first, gag her and tie her up. You carry Lydia."

Henry nodded, mutely.

Jim grabbed my arm, making me cry out with pain, and dragged me out of the room. The pistol was shoved in his belt, I saw. But at the top of the stairs he took out the pistol and cocked it. "You first," he said.

I made my way down the stairs. It was drawing closer to sunset, so the stalls were bathed in dark shadows. But it wasn't so dark that I couldn't see Lieutenant Pellegrino crouched in the straw, off to the side. He put his finger to his lips. Two steps behind me Jim was coming down.

I walked the rest of the way down to the main stable floor without reacting or saying a word.

"Freeze!" shouted Lieutenant Pellegrino, his feet wide apart, both hands on his pistol. "Drop your weapon."

I dove to the side, rolling in the straw.

Two gunshots exploded in my ears, and a cloud of white smoke blinded me. When it cleared, Jim lay crumpled in the straw, a spreading wet circle in his chest. Lieutenant Pellegrino remained where he was, unharmed.

A second later, the shattering of glass above made me jump. "Lydia!"

I screamed. The lieutenant and I ran up the stairs. Lydia lay, still unconscious, on the cot. But the window was pierced with a huge hole, broken glass everywhere.

Henry had escaped out the window.

Lieutenant Pellegrino stuck his head out. When he pulled it back in, he looked at me and said, "Taul's gone."

The lieutenant did not give chase after Henry Taul. He organized the summoning of help. Francois was already handcuffed to Lieutenant Pellegrino's motor car. A fleet of police cars and one long white vehicle appeared at the racetrack. Two nurses and a doctor jumped out. As the police officers fanned out, beginning the search for Henry, the medical workers carried Lydia down with great care and put her on a stretcher. "We will examine her here briefly and then take her to the hospital," the doctor said.

"Not the hotel, right?" I asked. "I don't want a hotel medical suite, I want a real hospital for her."

"We're taking her to a real hospital," the doctor reassured me. "Just one year old – we have everything there she will need."

Suddenly a new police motor car came careening down the drive. Two officers burst out the doors and ran to Lieutenant Pellegrino. I heard the word "fire."

After consulting with them, the lieutenant hurried over to me. "The search for Taul is gonna get tougher. There's a major fire at the amusement park. Every fireman in Brooklyn is gonna end up there, and they need police too. I was going to take you to the hotel, tell your family the situation, but…"

"Go," I said. "I'm staying with Lydia. I'll use the telephone at the hospital."

He nodded but did not go at once. The lieutenant stared at me.

"I'm sorry I didn't stay in the motor car," I said. "I couldn't."

"It would have been tough to take both of them, armed," he said. "If it hadn't been your coming down the stairs like that, keeping your head, I don't know how this would have played out."

Once we were in the hospital I held off the doctors' efforts to treat my wrist. I telephoned the Oriental Hotel, asking for Ben Batternberg. I told him enough that my entire family, including three of my uncles, and several of our lawyers rushed over to Coney Island Hospital. When Lydia was revived, in deep disorientation, I was sitting by her bed with Mother and Lawrence. She remembered nothing that happened to her since the fireworks.

Only then did I allow a doctor to examine my wrist and treat the swelling with ice bags and aspirin. The wrist was not broken, and their treatments dulled the pain. I only wished I could erase the memory of Jim grinning sadistically as he ground his foot into me.

It was late when I agreed to stay in the hospital overnight. I heard the word "shock" murmured by someone in the family who thought I wasn't listening.

"I'm not in shock," I announced. "I'm only agreeing to this to be near Lydia in case she needs me."

The hospital was nine stories high. The nurse who led me into the room I'd been assigned, on one of the higher floors, fussed with the electrical light by the bed. But it wasn't necessary, for it was not dark in there. Orange light flickered in the room, many hours after sunset. I walked to the window and drew a loud gasp. It was the fire in the distance, the flames soaring skyward. It wasn't a couple of buildings. It was a dozen of them. More. Acres and acres of land, all incinerating.

I put on the hospital gown the nurse gave me, but I didn't get into bed. I sat curled up in a chair by the window and watched and listened.

There were screams in the night, but not of excitement or the fear of someone who knows the experience isn't real. It was all real.

When Ben came by he said, "We heard from the police that they can't put out the fire, there is not enough water pressure. When the fire started in one park, the other competing parks, the businesses in Coney Island, all tapped into the water. So they couldn't get enough water to put out the fire in the first park – and now it's burning right down to the ground."

"Which park?" I asked.

"Dreamland."

I nodded.

"They say it started in Hell Gate," he said. "Some electrical problem."

Ben pulled up a chair next to me and we watched the fire in horror. All of those attractions, the buildings and rides and audacious curiosities, were disappearing. The screams wailed on, and the endless sirens of fire trucks and police vehicles. The smell of smoke filtered into the room, but I wouldn't let my cousin close the window completely.

"Peggy, we should have listened to you earlier," said Ben. "About a lot of things. We were wrong. Stefan Chalakoski will be released – I'll see to it myself. I'll help him. I'll help you both."

I didn't say anything; my eyes were fixed on the fire.

"They haven't caught Henry yet," he said. "But the hospital is on alert. We'll protect you and Lydia."

"Henry won't come here; he's in there," I said, pointing. "He's in Dreamland. I feel it."

He had always been drawn to Coney Island; it must have been Henry's idea, not his mother's, to stay at the most luxurious hotel of them all because he knew how close it would be to the streets and the people who called to him. At night, he could slip out and roam those streets. Henry's voiced disgust of "Sodom by the Sea" was what he wished polite society to think he felt. It was the vice of the Bowery, the lure of the brothels, that Henry could not resist. But such is the case with many rich men of New York. I believe what led to his disintegration was the disappearing boundary between the classes and the sexes – he desperately needed to feel that the workers could never challenge the wealthy, and the women could never dare to defy the men. The unforgiving heat, his use of drugs, the strain of being so close to me and to Lydia, he had lost himself. Now, tonight, with his worship of spectacle, of disaster, he'd also be drawn to the epic fire that raged. Would he try to put out the fire or immolate himself? That I did not know.

Ben returned to silence, and a while later I heard his breathing change. He'd fallen asleep in the chair. But I couldn't sleep. I watched the flames move up and devour the 275-foot Italian tower, the tallest in Dreamland. It slowly turned red and orange and white, flames licking.

Finally, at three in the morning, the Dreamland tower collapsed, plunging onto the park grounds with a sound louder than the crack of ten thunderbolts.

Only then did I crawl into the bed and pull the sheet over my head, willing myself to oblivion.

CHAPTER THIRTY-SEVEN

They discovered Henry Taul's body in the smoldering rubble of Dreamland the following day. No other people died in the fire, which all the newspapers called a miracle. There *were* deaths: some of the animals of the circus. The workers managed to herd many of Joseph Ferrari's lions, pumas, bears, wolves, and leopards into cages, or put blindfolds on them and lead the animals to safety. But Little Hip, the elephant I adored, refused to budge without his trainer and could not be dragged out in time. In the end, Ferrari himself was among the weeping workers who tried to shoot the large, panicking animals as the flames closed in on them. In other parts of the park, Dr. Couney and his nurses wrapped the premature babies in blankets and evacuated them, and all three hundred inhabitants of Lilliput made it out alive.

But within two days of the fire, the news spread that the financially challenged owners of Dreamland hadn't paid for insurance, and there was not enough money – or will – to re-create it. The year 1911 was the last one that the world experienced Dreamland. For those who witnessed the fire, it was something they could never forget. Many, many people saw it: even the ocean liners moving through the dark, cold Atlantic Ocean saw the flaming tower from miles away. The Brooklyn firemen could not put it out, and when they were needed in the real world, the play-acting firemen of the Dreamland nightly attraction were of no use. The fire didn't stop until it burned itself out.

Henry Taul was given a lavish funeral attended by New York society. He was not written about in the newspapers as a murderer or a drug addict or an insane person. The Taul and Batternberg lawyers were busy. Hours after Henry's body was found, the story was released that Henry's driver, James Twilton, had been a suspect in the murders of three women, and he was shot when he refused to surrender to a lone Coney Island police lieutenant, an officer to be rewarded for bravery. Henry himself had rushed to Dreamland to help in the rescue efforts, the newspapers insisted. Henry's other servant, Francois Sacron, gave lengthy statements to the police supporting the story of James Twilton's depravity and violence.

As soon as Lydia was physically able, we left Coney Island Hospital and drove to Manhattan. We never set foot in the Oriental Hotel again; our belongings were removed without any of us being there. Once we returned to Manhattan, both my mother and Lydia required rest and quiet. Even with me, Lydia said next to nothing about her ordeal with Henry. I never learned the terrible truth of what happened when she said she didn't want to marry him. One day, staring up at the ceiling, she said, "They would have soon killed us both." And that was all.

"We did it for Lydia," they all said about the cover-up of Henry Taul's heinous crimes. But to their frustration, Lydia refused to attend Henry's funeral, and the story had to be put out that she was too devastated to leave our house. Only my brother Lawrence represented us, along with Uncle David and his family. Another story that was whispered in society parlors at the end of the summer was that Mrs. Taul settled a large financial amount on the Batternbergs because, she said, it was what her beloved son, Henry, would have wanted. She left the city and Connecticut too, retreating all the way back to Colorado.

Ben told me what they'd really discovered. Jim and Francois, both hired two years ago, had gradually changed from being servants to something else. Francois obtained drugs for Henry and for himself. Jim's needs and desires were even darker, dovetailing with Henry's sickness; his alternating need to debase and to worship women. Jim obtained women for Henry, sometimes sleeping with them first, in Europe. By the time Henry came to Coney Island, in his drug-fueled state, he had reached a line governing human behavior – and then he crossed it. Beatrice was the first woman killed. Francois said that with her long black hair, she'd reminded Henry of me. That made me ill, as I remembered the sight of her dark tresses wrapped around her head in the water. The other two deaths were also connected to Henry's fixation with me. Yet posterity would record only Jim as the murderer. In return for his warped statements, Francois was allowed his freedom. I would never be able to think of that without anger.

It was four days after Henry's funeral that Ben brought Stefan to see me. He'd been quietly released from jail. With the Dreamland fire, Henry's death, and Jim's being blamed for multiple murders, the redemption of an obscure immigrant artist drew little interest from journalists.

Ben rang me on the telephone to say that Stefan would be coming to the house. I did not know what else to do but see him in the parlor. I waited there, unable to even drink a glass of water.

Finally Arthur opened the door and announced, "Stefan Chalakoski." Not Ben. My cousin discreetly held back.

When Stefan walked into our parlor, it felt as if my heart stirred within me for the first time since Dreamland died.

"Hello, Peggy," he said.

How I'd missed his voice. His eyes met mine as steadily as that first afternoon when we spoke to each other next to his paintings of the future.

"I'm so very glad to see you," I said.

He smiled, but it was a tentative one. He bore no marks of violence, but Stefan was thinner than before, his cheekbones more pronounced. I noticed his hair was newly cut and he wore a suit I'd not seen before, a formal one that didn't fit well.

He looked down at the carpet with the head of the bear and at the oil paintings, the tapestries, and it was obvious how uncomfortable this home made him.

"We can take a walk in Central Park, it's across the street," I said idiotically.

"No, I don't have time for walk," he said.

A bad feeling growing inside, I said, "Why are you short on time?"

"My boat sails late this afternoon. I'm returning to Europe."

I leaped toward him, exclaiming, "No, no, that can't still be the case. You are not being deported. It's a mistake."

Stefan took my hand, squeezed it, and led me to the couch to sit together.

"Is not deportation," he said gently. "Is regular passage."

A flash of understanding came. "This is Ben's doing. So this is how he helps me!" Rage smoldered; how could I have allowed myself to think Ben would work toward keeping Stefan at my side?

Again, Stefan squeezed my hand. "Ben helped with tickets, yes. He argued first. He offered job with Batternberg family – become mapmaker, cartographer, good salary." He paused. "Ben try hard to persuade me. He reminds me of you."

I could not take this in. "You don't have to take any position with the family, Stefan, but why would you want to leave? Your life is here."

"I don't belong here," he said. "Not just in room like this with you, but in New York, in America."

"You do," I cried. "You love this country."

"I thought I did. But I love idea of America – its future. Its present?" His face hardened. "I know truth about the man Henry Taul. He murder Louise, do it to put blame on me so police will not suspect. But to also punish you. He was – what's the word? – obsessed with you." Stefan shuddered, and then burst out, "How can I live with this? Poor Louise. She die because of me. No other reason."

"I know," I said. "It is terrible."

He was silent for another minute before saying, "Rich people play games and Louise and me get caught in it, like animals in trap." When he said, "rich people," I realized he meant not just Henry but me, while he sided with Louise. I was deeply, deeply hurt.

Stefan saw he wounded me and raised my hand to his lips. "Ah, Peggy, I care for you." He kissed my hand, tenderly. "It's truth. But I belong with my family, my brothers. I know it."

"Stefan, you're an artist. You have amazing talent."

When he pointed out that Belgrade possessed canvas and oil paint, I sputtered, "Your country is in such distress. And if war comes…?"

"More reason than ever to be there, to fight alongside them." His eyes took on that faraway look. But in this room, I realized, his eyes weren't the color of cognac. My father's bottles sat on the table ten feet away for comparison. His eyes were something else, a color I'd never be able to describe.

"People fight with more than sword, gun, bombs," Stefan said. "I can help."

"I don't understand," I said, struggling through this bad dream.

"I know that I am needed there," he said with the same strange resignation of the day we'd gone to the police. "America – New York City – it doesn't need me."

But I need you! I wanted to throw myself at his feet, beg forgiveness for dragging him into the orbit of a deranged murderer, tell him I loved him. If he must go, I would go too. Make a life in Europe. I'd follow shortly.

For the rest of my long life, I would become known not only for what I would achieve, the lives altered, the buildings raised with my name on them, but for my passionate heart. There would be husbands and lovers, night after night of intense desire, deep needs within me never wholly met but very close to it. How many stormy dissolutions and reunions there'd be, of promises made and words said that should never be said.

Yet I would always through the years cling to this memory, of losing my first love, in some ways my purest expression of love, but not losing my dignity. Somehow, I found it, a reserve of strength within, and I did not beg Stefan to change his mind and stay with me. It would be wounding without purpose, for I knew that Stefan was not only leaving America but leaving me. He had not said he loved me in this house. He loved an idea of me, perhaps, and now he was letting go of the dream.

"Goodbye," I whispered.

"Goodbye, Peggy. You're remarkable woman. You have ability – you have power – to do important things." I felt his lips on my cheek, and then he stood, regarding me with sadness.

"If Dreamland weren't gone, would you be leaving?" I asked.

He gave a little shrug, and seemed on the point of saying something more, but then Stefan turned to go. I heard the murmur of Ben's voice outside the door of the parlor, they spoke together, and other doors closed as they both departed.

When, days later, I felt able to speak about it, I went to Lydia who listened with sympathy and love and dried my tears as we sat in her bed. "He's right – you are remarkable," she said.

"That's absurd," I said. "People say it, but it's not the truth. I'm nothing, without any idea whatsoever what to do with my life." My mother wouldn't need my inheritance after all, but I had no notion of what to do with my money either.

"What about the bookstore?"

I thought of my co-workers at the store, my friends, and of the thrill I'd felt just being near important writers and thinkers. How excited I was to attract the mild interest of the pallidly wicked G.T. Samuels. But I was a different person now. To be near creative, important people for my own diversion and edification – my own entertainment – wasn't enough. There had to be a next step.

"But you will figure this out," said my sister. "You'll have lots of ideas when you're ready. Creative ideas. Audacious ideas. Don't let what happened this summer stop you, Peggy. You have to be strong. Take the good things from this and not the horror."

I looked at Lydia's pale, drawn face, and I asked her if she could do the same.

"Yes, I can," she said. "I want to go to a university and take a degree." She smiled at the shock in my face, then grew somber again. "It's the only way I can live with having Henry's money, if I put it toward learning and toward supporting rights for women. We must secure the right to vote. I don't have anything more specific planned than that, not yet."

"I'm so proud of you," I cried, throwing my arms around her.

"The world better watch out for the Batternberg women," Lydia said, with her old spirit.

"It should indeed," I said.

And I sat with my sister as, for the first time, I dared to look forward.

Author's Note

The idea for this novel came to me while I was writing a nonfiction story on the 4 July hotdog-eating contest at Coney Island. While researching, I tumbled down the rabbit hole of turn-of-the-century Brooklyn and discovered the existence of the grand hotels – the Oriental Hotel, Manhattan Beach Hotel, and Brighton Beach Hotel – that co-existed, not always happily, with the raucous amusement park on the same four-mile-long island. I was mesmerized by photographs of the hotels and reminded of a place that I loved as a child, the Hotel Del Coronado. My grandparents owned a condominium on Coronado Island in San Diego, California, and the sight of the nearby enormous wooden beach resort, built in 1888, left me awe-struck. Though it faced the Pacific, the Hotel Del Coronado had the same "Victorian splendor on the ocean" look as in the Coney Island photos I discovered, and I knew then I wanted to set a novel in the luxury hotels built in the nineteenth century, of which not a trace remains in Coney Island or Manhattan Beach.

The character of Peggy Batternberg is loosely inspired by the early life of the amazing Peggy Guggenhein. What many people may not realize is that Peggy Guggenheim, lacking direction in her life, worked without salary at the Sunrise Turn bookstore in Manhattan, an avant-garde gathering place, when she was twenty-one, before moving to Europe and carving out her trailblazing career of discovering and promoting modern artists such as Jackson Pollock. To my knowledge, Peggy Guggenheim never ventured to the hotels or attractions of Coney Island, and while her dissolute father, who died wearing full evening dress as the *Titanic* sank in 1912, also inspired Jonathan Batternberg, the characters of Lydia, Sarah, Lawrence, Benjamin, Paul, David, and Helen Batternberg are completely fictional.

The character of Henry Taul is inspired by Harry K. Thaw, the playboy heir to a fortune who married Evelyn Nesbit and in 1906 shot and killed architect Stanford White for "spoiling" his bride years earlier. He lodged an insanity defense in the "trial of the century," and was found not guilty by reason of insanity. A decade later, after he was arrested for an assault on a young man, he attempted suicide and was then confined in a mental institution. He was released, lived quietly in Virginia and then Florida, and died at the age of seventy-six. Other real-life people who inspired characters in *Dreamland* are D.H. Lawrence, Nathan Handwerker, and Rudolph Valentino. As for Stefan Chalakoski, he is completely fictional. However, during this time period, Coney Island did excite Italian artist Joseph Stella when he was influenced by the Futurism movement, as shown in his work *Battle of Lights, Coney Island*. Joseph Stella's paintings at the 1913 Armory Show, which tore New York City loose from its art conservatism roots, caused the best kind of uproar. In Stefan and some of the other characters in the book, I wish to honor the rich immigrant experience of New York City.

I was told by a woman who gives excellent walking tours of Coney Island that the place "gets under your skin," and truer words were never spoken. The hotels have left not a trace, but there are still rollercoasters and Ferris wheels, hotdog stands, carousels, funhouse mirrors, and even a "freak show," at Coney. My many visits, walking the same ground as Peggy and Stefan and breathing the Atlantic Ocean salt-tinged breeze, were essential. Coney Island is, however, much diminished from its heyday. In 1911, it was enjoying its Golden Age. Each of the self-enclosed parks was fantastical, but for me the most beautiful was Dreamland. I took some creative license in moving its destruction by fire from May 1911 to July 1911. Other than that, I tried in my months of research to re-create its manic magic with as much accuracy as possible.

I received valued help from the New York Public Library. Special thanks in tracking down photographs and archive material must go to Paul Friedman of the General Research Division. Visits to the New York Historical Society, the Museum of the City of New York, the Tenement Museum, the Brooklyn Historical Society, and of course the Coney Island Museum (special thanks to curator Lisa Mangels-Schaefer), as well as trips to the Modern Museum of Art, the Metropolitan Museum of Art, and the Solomon R. Guggenheim Museum. Interestingly, several years ago, the Guggenheim put on the best exhibit ever assembled on Futurism in New York City: "Italian Futurism, 1909–1944: Reconstructing the Universe."

Acknowledgements

This novel would not have been possible without the support of certain wonderful people. I'm grateful to publisher Alice Rees for her enthusiasm for *Dreamland* and her careful editing of the novel. Her comments and questions brought it to a higher level. I have enjoyed working with Hannah Groves, Imogen Streater, James Faktor, Cate Bickmore, Rufus Cuthbert and the rest of the team at Endeavour Quill.

Whenever my spirits flagged as I worked on the book, I was heartened by encouragement and insightful feedback from my friend and fellow novelist Emilya Naymark. The book also benefited enormously from the notes given by Michele Koop, Elizabeth K. Mahon, Harriet Sharrard, and Sanya Popovic. Whether it was comments on a character's motivation, a college, a sunburn, a fashion choice, or convincing dialogue, they were extraordinarily helpful.

When it comes to friends and colleagues, I am particularly fortunate in my Queens writers' group: Laura Joh Rowland, Mariah Fredericks, Triss Stein, Jen Kitses, and Shizuka Otake. I'd be lost without our monthly dinners. I've benefited greatly from my participation in two writers' organizations: Mystery Writers of America and Historical Novel Society. Within those two fantastic entities, my special thanks to Laura K. Curtis, Jeffrey Markowitz, V.S. Kemanis, Erica Obey, Charles Salzberg, Annamaria Alfieri, Dru Ann Love, Margery Flax, Richard Lee, Sarah

Johnson, E.M. Powell, Rosanne Lortz Spears, and Faith Justice. My salutations to colleagues at the Center on Media, Crime and Justice and John Jay College: Stephen Handelman, Ricardo Martinez, and Richard Relkin.

A huge thank you to my friends: Kris Waldherr, Sophie Perinot, Dawn Ius, Judith Starkston, Radha Vatsal, Pam and Mary Kramer, Mark Alpert, Christie LeBlanc, Dick Belsky, Donna Bulseco, Ellen Levine, Max Adams, Timothy Miller, C.W. Gortner, Barbara Claypole White, Beth von Staats, Joshua Todd James, Bruce Fretts, Bret Watson, Aleksandra Andonovska, Elizabeth Angell, Sue Trowbridge, Russell Rowland, Natasha Wolff, Adam Rathe, Theresa Defino, Victoria McKenzie, Sandra and Brec Morgan, Rhonda Riche, Delia Blackler Perretta, Evelyn Nunlee, Elaine Devlin Beigelman, and all the friends I cherish from our crazy youth in Livonia, Michigan.

I thank Max Epstein for his legal work on the contract for the book and for agenting it so well.

Without my family, I couldn't function, much less write books. My love to my husband and children, my sister Amy, my mother, and all my cousins.